Contagi̇ous Minds.

by Steve Wallin

With alphabetical order thanks to

Adam, Elaine, Heather, Jan, John,

and Wikipedia.

Copeland. Friday 26th August, 2016.

How many terrorists mess up making their dirty bomb and take themselves off to the nearest hospital for help? The question had occurred more than once in the mind of Larry Copeland during the last twenty four hours and he always arrived at the same answer: none.

The hospital administrator put a hand over the phone. 'This shouldn't take long, Inspector,' she said with a weak smile.

Copeland smiled just as weakly back. He had shown his badge and said, 'Detective Inspector Copeland, Metropolitan Police,' only three times to get into the Chief Administrator's office. He always said Metropolitan Police and not S.O.15 because all that got was quizzical looks and then he would scare people when he used words like 'anti-terror unit'.

While he waited for the hospital lawyers to tell the Administrator patient confidentiality was indeed trumped by anti-terror law, Copeland reflected with satisfaction on the quality of the full English breakfast in the hotel. The breakfast had been as good as the wholesome game pie at dinner the night before. The apple crumble and cheeseboard were pretty good too. When he had ordered the second bottle of Merlot his conscience had said, *'You used to have such good intentions, Copeland,'* but he had stopped listening to his conscience when it had started referring to him by his last name.

He looked at his watch. If Adams and the lawyers did not get a move on he would not have time to do anything before it was time for lunch. Bored, he gazed around the office. On the Administrator's desk was a white hospital promotional folder with the phrase 'The start of your amazing journey...' in red and blue italics across the top. Underneath was a clinical photograph of something that might be the inside of a stomach, or a throat, or possibly a rectum. Apparently, 'your amazing journey' took you places you would rather not go. It even made Copeland stop thinking about lunch. He looked out of the window and mentally revised his plan for the day.

'Very well,' said Chief Administrator Adams eventually as she put the phone down. 'I will inform the ward and the relevant departments of your arrival and the need to grant you full access to the patient, the patient's files and all test results. What's this all about, Inspector?'

'I can't tell you that, Ma'am. National security,' replied Copeland, knowing that always saved the time to explain things, and explaining things usually resulted in a late lunch.

He followed the signs to the ward where the suspected, incompetent terrorist Jakab Popov was. Under his arm, Copeland carried a small, black faux-leather conference folder, sold to him as an 'executive portfolio'. It had a built-in clipboard ready for case notes. He knew he did not need it any longer, because the voice recorder he was supposed to have in his pocket could do all the work now, but he still liked pen and paper and he always felt the leather folder made him look more official. For the same reason, he wore a dark blue suit and a dark blue tie to add extra gravitas. Old habits die hard.

As he approached the ward he instinctively finger-combed his silver-grey hair back and gave the back of his jacket a tug in case it was ruffled. He stopped and thought: reading a patient file, interviewing staff and interrogating Popov himself – all that could take some time. On reflection, he thought it might be a good idea to go outside for a smoke. He checked his watch thoughtfully: better get a coffee too, and maybe a Danish pastry to keep the energy levels up.

Dr. Beth Spencer. Friday, August 26th.

Dr. Beth Spencer knew the meeting had not gone well on many levels. Besides being drafted in from Lincoln to take over the case, which had caused some resentment, Senior Nurse Jones had banged on about lacking proper protective clothing, Dr. Canning from pathology had found nothing and wanted more samples and Dr. Denning from dermatology had said he had seen nothing like it. He doubted it could be a caustic substance, as they had first thought, because it continued to advance, so believed it must be some new sort of aggressive pathogen that was eating Mr. Popov's arm. At this, the diminutive and balding Junior Administrator, Tom Benson, had finally stopped staring at Beth as if he was moon-struck, become horror-struck instead and cried, 'Zombies!' followed by anxiously asking if Popov had bitten anyone yet.

Beth frowned, ignored Benson and summed up. At least they had decided new samples and a MRI was needed, along with getting Mr. Popov into a hospital with an airtight isolation unit in case this was indeed a virulent new pathogen.

'Are we all agreed?' asked Beth. They all nodded at exactly the same time as her pager buzzed. 'Good,' she said ignoring the buzzing. 'So let's get moving. Time is not on our side.'

'The only reason for time is so that everything doesn't happen at once,' said Benson, stressing his point with a raised finger.

Beth stared at him. 'Have you really gone from *has he bitten anyone?* to quoting Einstein, Mr. Benson?' she said, frowning. She turned back to Nurse Jones. 'Nurse, please wait while I find out what this page is for, then we'll get as much protection on as we can and go and get new samples while our colleagues get back to their busy jobs.'

Beth phoned The St. James Hospital switchboard and was put through to the Senior Administrator. She listened for a few moments and said, 'Thanks for letting me know. We are on our way there now.' She slipped the phone back into her jacket pocket and pulled her jacket on.

She looked at Nurse Jones. 'It seems the Metropolitan Police have taken an interest in our Mr. Popov. One Inspector Copeland has just left the Senior Administrator and is on his way to see him now. Let's get some speed on, Nurse.'

They arrived at a police free ward, stopped just through the security door and peered into the private room where Popov was lying motionless in bed and quite alone. A ward nurse scurried up to them. Beth Spencer thought it best to let Senior Nurse Jones take charge; the wards were her domain. Beth turned to Nurse Jones, who had fallen more than a few paces behind going down the final corridor, and Beth saw she was going to be unable to say much at all for several minutes. Her face was red and perspiration was dripping down her forehead. Her breathing was sharp and shallow. Beth resisted the temptation to shake her head. The panting Nurse Jones feebly waved a finger from side to side which Beth took as a sign that she should deal with the ward nurse.

'Has a police Inspector been to see Mr. Popov?' she asked the nurse.

'No, not yet. We did get a call from the Administrator's office that he was on his way, but no one has shown up yet.'

'Good. Let's get all Popov's patient files together and I will see if there are any pages we need to lose for an hour. Nurse Jones, perhaps you could stay here and intercept him if he comes and tries to go straight in to see Popov while I am at the nurses' workstation?'

Nurse Jones nodded, glad she did not have to walk anywhere at all just yet.

Nurse Jones had long since got her breath back and had time to go out of the ward and look up and down the corridor several times by the time Copeland eventually arrived at the ward. He flashed his badge to her through the round ward door window and she pressed the green button to open the door.

'Inspector Copeland from the Met,' he said. 'I believe you have a Mr. Jakab Popov here. I need to speak with him.'

'Use the sanitizer on the wall over there,' Nurse Jones pointed and Copeland did as he was told. 'Good. Now, follow me, Inspector,' instructed Nurse Jones, leading him down the ward to the nurses' workstation where Copeland saw a seated nurse typing and a rather striking woman with short blonde hair reading a file standing behind her.

'This is Dr. Spencer, Inspector,' said Nurse Jones. 'She is the lead for the HPT regarding Mr. Popov.'

Whatever a HPT was this young woman looked the part of the lead, thought Copeland. The well cut black jacket and skirt and white blouse said 'official person in charge'.

She emerged from the workstation and held out her hand. 'Pleased to meet you, Inspector. What can we do for you?' she said with a firm handshake.

Copeland resisted the urge to wince. 'What's a HPT?' he asked.

'Health Protection Team. One is set up if there is something deemed to be potentially dangerous to public health or, as in this case, for something that is unusual and needs an interdisciplinary team to investigate. The hospital contacted Lincoln, told them about Mr. Popov's unusual symptoms and they sent me. My specialism is currently epidemiology, with a background in pathology. Enough about me, now tell me all about you.'

If he cared, Copeland may have felt he was on the point of being railroaded by a woman young enough to be his daughter. He chose to answer her question with his own. 'So you think Popov has something that threatens public health, then? He's contagious?'

'Probably not,' answered Dr. Spencer.

'But he **might** be,' added Nurse Jones over Dr. Spencer's shoulder, helpfully.

'Thank you, nurse, for your input,' said Dr. Spencer brusquely. 'I'll just take the Inspector into the office and he and I will continue there.' She looked over her shoulder at the nurse. 'Alone,' she added.

The office was empty and Beth shut the door behind them. There was no desk or table, the office was only large enough for six red plastic chairs. A small window was on the far, narrowest wall, with a stack of plastic chairs in front of it. A coffee vending machine and a waste bin filled with plastic cups and crisp packets sat between two chairs on the right wall, and the left wall had four more chairs below an old notice board. The 'office' was clearly a common room, and a rather run down one at that.

'Please have a seat Inspector and tell me why you are here,' she said.

'Doctor, er, Spencer, is it?' asked Copeland, still standing. 'I really do not have the time to have a discussion with you. I need to speak to Popov and read his file.'

'Believe it or not, Inspector Copeland, I am a busy person too and I've wasted the last twenty minutes waiting for you. So I'm not sorry to tell you that you will not be able to speak to Mr. Popov. He went into shock and we have had to sedate him quite heavily. You may have noticed him when you came into the ward. He's the one you passed in the private room near the ward door. The symptoms that first presented themselves on his hand now seem to be spreading up his entire arm. Mr. Popov apparently became quite upset and began shouting in Bulgarian before they sedated him. Mild sedation was not enough, he quietened down but started shaking and staring at the empty wall, so they sedated him more heavily. He also has a saline drip and a catheter. Anyway, besides the sedation, the Bulgarian interpreter is refusing to go anywhere near him again. Now, as I said, I am pushed for time myself. Nurse Jones and I have to get more samples to send over to the labs and we have to work out how to keep him in some sort of isolation and get him down for an MRI at the same time.'

Copeland had registered the word 'Bulgarian'. It confirmed all his suspicions about why he was really there.

She handed Copeland a file. 'You can read his file if you like, but you are not going to speak to him. Not today anyway. So do sit down and read the file. I'll be back within the hour to answer any questions you have then,' she said and abruptly left him alone.

Placing his executive folder case down on a chair, Copeland sighed and took out his packet of Marlboro. He flipped it open. Enough there to last the rest of the day but he would have to get a new pack in the morning. He closed the pack and returned it to his jacket pocket. He flicked remnants of Danish pastry off his tie. He apathetically opened the file and counted how many pages there were. Not many, but someone had shown enough sense to take photos. He closed the file, placed it on the chair next to him and put on his reading glasses: anything less than arm length was a bit blurry these days. He picked up his executive folder, unzipped it and folded the cover back to expose the A4 notepad clipped onto the thin plywood inside the cover of the case. He slipped a biro out of the pen holder at the spine of the case and, with pen poised over the notepad, leaned over and opened the patient file with his other hand.

He scanned down the A & E admission sheet. He jotted down the address the interpreter had obtained from Popov. There was not a place of birth except for 'Bulgaria', religion was recorded as 'none', and there was no national insurance number, health card number or passport number recorded, but at least there was a date of birth so checking should be easier. He knew even if Jakab Popov was a real Bulgarian born on that date it did not mean this man was the actual, real Jakab Popov. He needed to see his personal effects. It would take a good fake passport to fool Copeland. He had seen quite a few. The patient file had nothing of particular interest on the first page except he noticed the reason for admission was recorded as 'burn', then, with a different pen, the words 'suspected caustic' had been written above it. He wrote: *Initial diagnosis – burned hand.*

He turned the page over. Date stamped at 2 p.m. on the 23 rd. was a photograph of Popov's hand. Copeland rolled his eyes. He had seen burns before. OK, this was a bad burn and Popov's palm was not only blistered and looked as if someone had also taken a cleaver to it, but Copeland thought if people forget to use oven gloves then they should at least let go of the oven tray before it sears their skin off. He sighed and turned to the next photo.

His eyes did not roll. His mouth fell open. He checked the date stamp on the previous photo before looking back at the second. This was twenty four hours later? Half the damn hand had almost disappeared and the fingers and wrist had all the purple and black blisters the palm had shown the previous day, along with the deep canyons of the accompanying cleaver, while the palm now looked like a combination of a rare steak and the Black Death, served on pink spaghetti.

There was no photo since. No wonder Popov had gone into shock. His hand was dissolving before his eyes.

Copeland put the photographs down and wrote on his pad:

'Chemical weapon? Was Popov making a dirty bomb? Was he priming one he had been given and something went wrong?'

He stopped himself and crossed everything else out except 'chemical weapon?' It did no good to get ahead of yourself in this game. Let's stick to the facts, Larry, he said to himself, just turn the page and look at the test results. He turned the photos face down and picked up three stapled pages of test results. He put his pen down and turned the pages. He was unsure what almost all the medical words down the left side meant, but he understood they had done a whole battery of tests. There were sections of results headed blood, skin, urine and even hair, and next to some scientific name for something or other was the same word over and over again: 'negative'. He took out his phone and photographed each page in the file.

He slid his phone back into his pocket, considered for a moment and wrote: *Popov dissolving from cause or causes unknown.* He had hesitated to use the word 'dissolving' but could not think of anything more appropriate. OK, it was not exactly a medical term, but it was pretty descriptive. He had seen the term 'rapid necrotizing fasciitis?' scrawled at the top of the test results page, but still thought using 'dissolving' was more descriptive so kept it.

He leaned back into his chair and shook his head. 'Great,' he said out loud. 'They don't have a bloody clue what this is.'

He flipped over the test results and there were the pages he really wanted: notes from the Bulgarian interpreter. The notes were as illuminating as the medical tests hadn't been. Except for information that Popov claimed he did various occasional work for something called 'The European Agency', there was nothing helpful there either, decided Copeland. He stood up and put his folder on the chair. He sucked on his pen. It was a poor substitute for a cigarette. His mind was dodging the nicotine cravings and the warning signs from his stomach that lunch would be needed soon. His eyes wandered from the window to the staff notice board. Small posters with colourful warnings told him how he needed to wash his hands every time he entered or left the ward or MRSA would kill him along with everyone he met, some told him how smoking killed him, and other posters told him he needed to exercise moderately every day (he patted his round stomach and nodded) and how he should eat 'five a day' of all the sorts of foods he tried his best to avoid. The poster informing him of the recommended alcohol maximum, with glasses of beer, wine and spirits filled up to appropriate heights seemed about right until he realised that was supposed to be weekly, not daily. It was the final straw. He took photographs of each page in Popov's patient file, tapped all the sheets back into place and closed the cardboard folder. Let them do the medical stuff – his job was to investigate what it was if it wasn't medical, or if it was medical whether it was man-made, or more precisely, terrorist made. He needed more information. He removed his spectacles, rammed his pen into his inside pocket, picked up his folder and the patient file and walked out of the office.

As he approached the nurse's workstation the middle aged nurse, who was half bent over and shuffling papers, looked up. Copeland placed the patient file down on the counter

He took a breath and as calmly as he could said, 'If you could provide me with a gown, some gloves and a mask, I think I will go and see Mr. Popov now.'

As she scuttled off, head down, he turned and leisurely walked towards the ward entrance door. Beyond the three beds occupied by newspaper reading patients on his left was the side room where Popov had been recently moved. He looked in through the window. The room was standard four metre square with the outside windows along the wall opposite the ward. The left wall had a door which Copeland guessed was an en suite. Beside that door was a TV mounted on the wall with a metal, wheeled cabinet underneath it. The bed was against the wall to his right, with a monitor and drip attached to Popov's healthy, nearer arm. Nurse Jones and Dr. Spencer were still in there, wearing surgical gloves, masks and green surgical gowns for added protection. Nurse Jones had her back to him and her large frame obscured his view of Popov's head. Dr. Spencer was on the far side of the bed, leaning over her patient and doing something to his withering arm. Nurse Jones moved to one side to pick up something from a tray and Copeland could see Dr. Spencer had a scalpel and was cutting samples out of the arm. It looked like she was digging pretty deep.

As she leaned forward to drop the newly mined specimen into a dish held out by Nurse Jones, she glanced up, saw him and gave a slight nod. He heard a laugh. Clearly, Dr. Spencer had made some comment and Nurse Jones obviously had a laugh loud enough to be heard at a rock concert. Dr. Spencer lifted the tongs to show him the specimen, waving it a little for effect. Nurse Jones looked over her shoulder. She laughed again as she saw Copeland turn away. He had seen plenty of grisly sights in his line of work, many of which he had bricked up in dark corners of his memory, but seeing someone digging chunks out of a living arm was too much, especially this close to lunch. He had to maintain his priorities.

The scuttling nurse returned and handed him gloves, mask and a white coat she had found from somewhere. Without eye contact, half bent, she scuttled off again. Copeland wriggled his arms into the tight fitting white coat, knowing it would never fasten over his generous stomach. He shrugged, pulled on the gloves and tied the mask across his mouth and nose. Deciding that would have to do, he turned to go through the door into Popov's room.

Nurse Jones was on the other side, with one hand on the glass door panel and the other raised with the palm at his face. She shooed him back. 'Wait!' she shouted through her mask and the glass.

Reluctant to attempt to match her volume, he pointed to his watch and held it out towards the glass.

She held up a finger. 'One minute! Nearly done. Wait there.' He heard her clearly, nodded and took a step back to show his agreement, though he suspected this might be a very long minute. She stared at him for a moment, judged he was going to do as he was told and went back to assist Dr. Spencer.

Dr. Spencer drew blood from both of Popov's arms into four small, labelled vials. Nurse Jones pressed cotton wool onto the punctures then taped it over. Dr. Spencer passed the vials across the bed to Nurse Jones who placed them alongside the other Popov samples on the stainless steel trolley. Nurse Jones wheeled the trolley to the door. She waited there for Dr. Spencer who put her hand on the door and stopped. Her head bobbed three times as she counted, then she pulled the door open wide, Nurse Jones accelerated through with the trolley and Dr. Spencer was on her heels through the door before quickly closing it.

The haste was not lost on Copeland. 'You   think   he's infectious, don't you?' he said.

'No sense taking chances,' replied Beth. 'Nurse Jones, if you would kindly get the samples to pathology and remind Dr. Canning he agreed to get working on them straight away.

Before we dress the patient's arm, we must let the inspector see what we are dealing with.'

Must you? thought Copeland. *Another photo would do. You can use my phone...*

'Yes, Doctor,' said Nurse Jones and wheeled the trolley toward the ward door. Copeland noticed she was keeping her protective clothing on.

Beth remained, blocking the way into Popov's room. She pulled her mask down below her chin. Copeland had two conflicting reactions. One was a wish that he was at least twenty years younger. The other was a fear she was going to engage him in conversation when the clock in his stomach was already gearing itself up to chime for lunch. A pint or two might be welcome too, and maybe a whiskey to calm his nerves after seeing those photographs.

Beth glanced at her watch. 'He's got an MRI booked for this afternoon,' she said, nodding toward Popov's room. 'So, now I have more time, Inspector, tell me why the Metropolitan Police has an interest in my patient.'

You haven't got time for this, Copeland, said his inner voice.

He evaded. 'I can't really discuss the case, Doctor,' he said as he started to try to go round her.

'No?' she said, holding out her arm to block him. 'But I do think I am within my rights to ask you to show me your warrant card. And please don't tell me you have already shown it to the hospital's administrator. I would like to see it.'

He shrugged, lifted it from his pocket, flicked it open, held it out and flicked it closed.

'Oh, no,' she said. 'That was flashing it, not showing it.'

He flicked it open again but held it steady this time.

'S.O.15?' she queried.

He hoped he would not have to explain. He closed the card and slipped it back into his inside pocket. He went to move past her again.

'Not so fast, Inspector,' she said. 'Is my patient suspected of terrorism? Do you have any evidence? Or is this just the way things are now for any Eastern European or Muslim who comes on the radar? I am investigating this man's illness on behalf of the Health Trust and I need to know, right now, if there is any terrorism link.'

He looked at her. He knew he could refuse to tell her anything and blame it on the need for national security. She did have a point though, and he got the distinct impression she was not the sort of person likely to be pacified easily, or move from the doorway unless he satisfied her curiosity.

'My D.C.I. has sent me because the Commander thinks the guy in that room may have connections to...' he said but slowed to a halt. He paused, looked down, looked up to meet her eyes again.

'Of course he's not a terrorist,' he said. 'The truth is I am an old, washed up embarrassment to SO15 and they think it's easier if they can get me to quit than it would be to take me through incompetency procedures and transfer me to community policing or something worse. They've sent me here to piss me off so I put in for retirement. GCHQ flagged Popov up when the hospital's A & E put him on the system and my crazy Commander has it in his head that our man Popov *might* not be who he says he is and *might* really be a Chechen terrorist, or so I've been told, but he sees terrorists everywhere. This is a Commander who was so happy when they passed The Investigatory Powers Act he bought everyone in the office a cream cake. He thinks the bloody snoopers' charter is a good idea – that's not policing! And he won't really be happy until everyone in England has their phone tapped!'

He saw her frown and fold her arms.

'Yes, so, the thing is,' he continued, 'I was told the Commander had this theory that Popov could be some sort of Chechen terrorist and has got hold of something toxic, but instead of wiping out half of London, he has somehow accidentally dissolved his own hand instead. But it's all nonsense.' Copeland was becoming animated and talking faster. 'And if he's some master terrorist with some unknown, secret chemical cocktail, then he's not very good at his job, is he? And have you ever heard of a terrorist reporting to his local A & E when things went sideways? It's just a wild goose chase and my D.C.I. knows that, just like he knows that shipping me off to a shitty little town in the middle of nowhere is going to push me one step closer to quitting. And if this doesn't work and I don't get the message, he'll send me somewhere worse next time. Maybe even Wales! Is that honest enough for you?'

Her frown had deepened and her folded arms had clenched. He thought she did not look convinced.

'You know, Inspector,' she said, 'besides the fact that this is a nice town and my parents are Welsh, for someone in your line of work you are a terrible liar. I have never heard such a lot of garbage. I can read between the lines here. You can't tell me what you know so you feed me a load of nonsense. You need to tell me everything you know so we can treat him!'

Copeland was lost for words. He had risked sharing the truth with her and she didn't believe it anyway. This was unfamiliar territory and he needed a way out.

'I understand, Doctor,' he said, calming down. 'I will inform you of any developments as soon as I discover anything. You have my word.'

My God, Copeland, you had better hope the old clichés work! his inner voice shouted.

She nodded resignedly and moved aside, but grabbed his shoulder as he went to open the door into Popov's room. 'Wait,' she said pulling her mask back up over her mouth. 'This may be nature at work here or it may not be and it pains me to say it but it may be for the best that you are, as you might say, checking him out. Just remember, we have run all the usual tests and have no idea what is causing his symptoms. So be very, very careful in there, Inspector. Even with gloves and mask on, I would strongly urge you not to touch him or get close enough for him to breathe on you directly.'

He stared at her, nodded and made sure his mask was on very, very securely. He continued to stare at her very, very hard. Even with his police training and years of experience he could not tell if her hair was dyed. Then he realised she had kept her hand on his shoulder longer than was necessary before she had dropped it. His vanity brought a brief smile to his face before two logical truths kicked in: one was that she was just stressing her point; the other was that he had just opened the door to a room with an inexplicably decaying man lying on the bed in front of him. He suddenly hated his job.

Standing beside the bed near Popov's feet, he studied the man's face. He looked older than his date of birth on the admission form suggested, but perhaps that was because he had four days of stubble growing around his broad lips and heavy jaw. A sheet and a blanket covered him up to the waist, but his arms were above the sheets, the right one lying on sterile film.

Copeland steered his eyes from Popov's face to the hand. A tingle went down his spine.

Behind his shoulder, Beth's voice whispered, 'He arrived in emergency on Monday morning. The triage nurse saw him and deduced he had a very nasty burn on his palm, along with what appeared to be a gash. She would have treated it herself but fortunately discovered he had no pain – none at all, even when she prodded it. A doctor saw him a few hours later and kept him in for observation. By the time he was seen in a ward the next afternoon his palm was disintegrating as if it was melting and his fingers were showing the same signs. They had the sense to try to isolate him in here. Now you can see it has spread almost to his elbow. The inflammation is the first sign. His hand has almost gone after only four days.'

'I can see some of his bones,' observed Copeland.

'And the pink strands are what's left of the muscles in his hand,' Beth informed him. 'It's not just a skin eating disease. Nothing is working, not even intravenous broad spectrum antibiotics. This is either a whole new pathogen, which cleverly hides from microscopes... or it's something else, Inspector.'

Copeland looked over his shoulder at her. She sighed, shrugged and said, 'I'm going for some water before we wrap it in sterile film again. Take your photos or whatever.'

Copeland watched her leave, took out his phone and took three photographs of Popov's face, the last one by holding the phone out over the bed and directly in front of Popov as he lay there in his sedative induced sleep. He would send these back for the tech department to run face recognition and Sergeant Brandon would send them to GCHQ too, as long as he wasn't trying to sweet-talk Holly at the coffee machine again.

He aimed the phone at Popov's arm. *His arm looks like a pack of rats has feasted on it, Copeland. What the hell could do this in just a few days?* asked the voice in his head. He clicked, checked the photo and left it at just the one close-up.

For a moment he considered whether he should handcuff Popov to the bed but dismissed this idea because, firstly, it was clear Popov was too sedated to even stand and, secondly, because the handcuffs were still back in his room at The Red Lion Hotel.

Going over to the locker underneath the window, he took out Popov's belongings. There were the clothes he had arrived at the hospital in: a cheap brown and blue check shirt, faded jeans, unbranded trainers and dirty white sport socks. The most desperate charity shop would take none of these. The pockets were empty so Copeland put the clothes back in the bottom of the locker without bothering to fold them. He doubted Popov would ever need them again. The key had been left in the top part of the locker so he unlocked it and reached inside. He had been hoping to find a passport or a phone but found only a few coins and a creased ten pound note and – aha! – a door key.

It was annoying that there was no phone or passport, but the key had made it a fruitful five minute search. He could use the key, find the passport and confirm Popov was, after all, an immigrant worker who had got some disease or other. That was a NHS and not a SO15 problem. He could still get the last train back to London and be on the golf course tomorrow.

'Inspector Copeland,' he said, pleased enough with himself to rub his latex gloved hands together and grin, 'your work here is done. Time for a spot of lunch then an afternoon visiting the home of Mr. Popov.' He patted the key in his breast pocket.

Jakab Popov struggled to keep his flickering eyelids the slightest fraction open, but he saw enough for a warning to feebly start sounding somewhere deep inside his sedated brain.

A tall, dark haired man makes a phone call...

Less than twenty miles south of Copeland, a tall, dark haired man made a phone call.

'Scorpion? It's me.

(Pause.)

'No, nothing's wrong. Just checking in to say all the others are here. We've checked all the equipment and we've started the initial tests on the product ready for the release.

(Pause.)

'Yes, it's safe. We're keeping the containers in the fridge to be sure.

(Pause.)

'Everything is going better than expected. Early indications are the stuff will be even more potent than we thought.

(Longer pause.)

'I'm not sure when it will be ready for full scale use. We only have six rabbits as guinea pigs to test it on.

(Short pause.)

'Of course. I won't call them that again.

(Very long pause.)

'Well, we could try to speed things up but it may mean using most of one of the six canisters.

'Very well, Scorpion, if you say so. I'll keep you informed.'

He ended the call. He knew he should have said something about what happened the evening he brought the canisters to the secret location, but that could wait: The Scorpion would not want to hear about stupid accidents.

Copeland was sure the taxi from the hospital was taking him around the whole town before driving to the centre. Suburbia ended and shops, warehouses, commercial units and garages lined both sides of the dual carriageway. He was soon passing the first sign saying 'THE BEST TASTES OF EUROPE' in unapologetic capitals.

The taxi delivered him to the corner of Dragon Street. He gave the driver a twenty pound note and held out his hand for all the correct change. The UK government does not give tips. Copeland folded another receipt into his wallet and hauled himself out of the taxi, emitting a soft groan with the effort.

He looked around and soon worked out Popov's bedsit must be above one of the shops, most likely Fenney's Kitchens right here on the corner. He tapped the key in his breast pocket and decided searching the flat could wait. His attention was drawn to the other side of East Street where two men, barely beyond their teens, stood smoking under the sign of 'The Happy Jack'. A flag with the cross of St. George hung limply in the window of the pub. It was clear to see where the loyalties of this landlord lay and what sort of clientele he preferred to serve. Without hesitation, Copeland crossed the road, nodded to the two smoking skin-heads and went inside to get his much needed lunch, and maybe that glass or two to satisfy his thirst. He had, after all, earned it.

While Dr. Beth Spencer watched Jakab Popov being wheeled into an MRI scanner with his arm encased in extra layers of low adhesive cling film used for burn victims to prevent contagion, and while the pathology department dripped Jakab Popov's blood onto slides and added different reactive agents one after another, Inspector Larry Copeland was standing outside The Happy Jack lighting a cigarette, finishing off his second pint of Boston Best and enjoying the mid afternoon sunshine. He felt content after his salty gammon, oven chips and tinned peas. It was just like home cooking. His home cooking, anyway. He had enjoyed the partially frozen apple pie and milky cream, and had enjoyed his chat with the patrons of the bar who had all declared themselves to be patriotic and 'could not wait for the foreigners to be thrown out so we could take back our country again', and the barman had joined in with some particularly novel suggestions concerning just how they should be thrown out, including one method involving a very large catapult. Copeland had nodded a lot and internally disagreed with every word.

Blissfully inhaling, he gazed up and down the street and could not help overhearing passers-by who spoke in several languages, including the occasional English. He swallowed the final mouthful of his beer, thinking that there would be a lot of empty shops if all these shoppers were sent home. Lowering his glass, he realised there would not be many of the shops left either. He left his empty glass on the window ledge and crossed the street to find Popov's home.

He finally found the door to the flat after circling round the back of Fenney's Kitchens. Lifting a wooden gate over broken stone paving, dodging the brambles in a narrow back alley, he climbed a metal fire escape which swayed as if someone had stolen a majority of the bolts holding it together. He got to the door, took the key from his pocket and slid it into the door. It turned easily and he pushed the door slowly open.

'Hello? Anyone home? It's the police,' he shouted. When no reply came he removed the key and replaced it in his pocket, walked inside and closed the door softly behind him.

He mentally recapped his priorities. Find Popov's passport to check if it is forged. Find any evidence linking Popov to bomb making, weapons, any terrorist organisation or any of their affiliates. Or better still, to *not* find any evidence linking Popov to anything at all and find a perfectly legal passport, then check out of the hotel and get the next train home.

But what the hell was that?

Rotting food in an unsealed black bin liner had been happily decomposing during the hottest week of the year. He dropped his executive notepad case. He hastily pulled out the mask and gloves he had kept from the hospital, but threw them on the floor as he rushed over to open the wooden window. It needed a couple of thumps with the flat of his hand before it opened. He pushed his head out of the window and took a few deep breaths before going to pick up the mask and gloves.

As he stood upright again his head swam for a moment. He wondered whether there were toxic fumes in the room, perhaps masked by the rotting food? Perhaps leaking from a terrorist poison gas canister? Or could it be the second pint after the double whiskey having an adverse influence on his balance? He took another deep breath and, feeling glad it had made him feel better rather than kill him, he put on the gloves and mask and surveyed the room.

This was what they called a bed-sit, but this one had no bed and nowhere to sit. Had someone got here before him and ransacked the place or did it normally look like this? Besides a pile of clothes half in and half out of a large black Nike sports bag, an old, flat pillow and a dark green sleeping bag lying on a single mattress on the floor, it seemed Popov had no possessions. The room itself was about ten feet square with the narrow window overlooking the street. Thin, dirty brown carpet covered the floor and the walls had been painted to match. Against the wall on Copeland's left was the mattress with the sports bag and an empty vodka bottle next to it, and against the wall on Copeland's right was a cooker, a full sink, a small worktop with a small cupboard above it and a small fridge below. Another door was in the corner, dented from where it had been repeatedly opened against the worktop. There were no clothes drawers, no wardrobes, no shelves, and no sources of heating. This would not take long to search.

After a brief rummage through the rotting rubbish and not finding a single receipt, he tied a knot in the top of the bag and turned to the sports bag and the clothes. Popov had seemingly made no distinction between washed and unwashed. Copeland was glad he had kept the surgical gloves, especially when handling the stained underwear and odious socks. There was a pair of jeans and a waterproof jacket in the bottom of the bag but all the pockets were empty, as was the zipped pocket down the side of the bag itself. He felt under the cardboard base of the bag, shook out the sleeping bag, turned the mattress over and felt inside the pillow.

Next he tried the oven. That too was empty except for black grease and a base littered with burnt pizza toppings. He checked through the unwashed mug, plate and saucepan in the sink. The cupboard under the sink was empty except for a frying pan and a sieve, both of which looked clean and fairly new. The cupboard above the worktop had two glasses, one more large plate and a mug housing a single set of cutlery. On the worktop there was half a loaf of white bread, three cans of soup and a half empty jar of cheap coffee. He opened the bread and flicked through the hard slices, but there was only bread. The inside of the fridge was equally fruitless, with an almost empty carton of rancid milk, a plastic tub of margarine and a jar of green mould jam. Nothing terrorist related, but there was enough bacteria and fungus to decimate a city. He opened the small freezer compartment and saw it was empty. He closed the fridge and glanced around the room again.

He tied his mask tighter and went through the door into a narrow, windowless bathroom. He thought it was more like a corridor going behind the kitchen units, then realised that at one time it probably was. The owners had seen the commercial advantage of converting one two storey flat above a shop into several one bedroom flats and had squeezed in bathrooms to push up the rents. It had a sink, a toilet and a shower unit, all in the smallest sizes possible. There were no cleaning materials in sight and the odour of stale urine reminded him of his old school toilets. He had to stand on his toes and take small, sideways steps to get his stomach over and round the sink before inspecting inside the cabinet above it, then feeling the rim of the cabinet mirror in case it had been loosened. He lifted the lid of the toilet cistern and checked inside and pressed each mould-rimmed shower tile to see if any were loose. Without consciously realising it, he had gone from searching the obvious to searching the unlikely. He ran his hand along the underside of the sink and the underside of the toilet. He checked the cabinet did not have a false back.

Returning to the main room, he looked around again. The curtains were too thin to be hiding anything but he gave them a shake anyway. He ran his hand around the entire edge of the mattress to feel for any slits where something could have been slipped inside. With the knife from the mug in kitchen cupboard and on his knees, he began levering back the carpet from the edges of the wall. He found money. Five piles of twenty pound notes, each one with five notes, were under the carpet where the mattress had covered it. He checked under the last few feet of carpet but there was no more.

With the five hundred pounds in one hand and the cutlery knife in the other he knelt on the floor and mentally ticked off each part of the room one last time. He ticked them off very quickly so he could escape from the stench seeping from the black bin-liner. No, there was nowhere else to hide a passport or a bomb or a gun or anything else. Nothing here suggested terrorist activity. The money was suspicious, but it was just money.

He stood and went to return the knife to its mug in the cupboard. He tossed the money onto the work surface, lifted the mug down from the cupboard and was replacing the knife when he saw something in the bottom of the mug. He tipped the mug's contents out onto the work surface. There was a silver key. He picked it up and examined it. It was not quite big enough to be a door key and had the word 'Snauzer' imprinted on it. He turned it between his finger and thumb then pushed it into his top pocket with the door key. He put the cutlery back in the mug and replaced it in the cabinet.

He wished he had found the passport and wished he had not found the money or the key. Now he would have to find out why Popov had so much money, find out what the key was for and still track down his passport. He would have to continue investigating and there would be no train back to his own bed tonight, and probably not tomorrow night for that matter. He knew his persistence had once been a virtue but now it had turned into a fault. He should have checked the obvious places and left it at that, filed a report that pacified the Commander's paranoia, and left Popov to suffer in peace. He waved the money up and down. He knew he had no warrant so should not be in the bedsit, so he should put the money back. Popov was not likely to be coming back soon though, if he ever came back at all. He could take the money to the hospital and lock it in Popov's bedside locker for safe keeping, or he could keep it safe for him until he got out of hospital, or he could find a travel agent and treat himself on a nice holiday somewhere. Or he could find out how an immigrant casual worker like Popov had managed to get this much money, and whether it was payment for something he had done or finances to bankroll him for something he had been hired for.

The need to pee came on quickly and with the intense severity known only to the over sixties, especially after two pints. Copeland rushed for the toilet and was soon exhaling his relief.

'Right, Larry, you stupid fart,' he said to himself as he stood there waiting an age for the stream to end. 'The question is how does your average migrant worker who has probably been here a few months manage to stash five hundred quid? What the hell has he got a key hidden in a mug for? And where is the damn passport? Popov's got some secret locked away somewhere and like it or not you have to find out what it is. You've prodded and poked every inch of this place and there's no sign of human dissolving terror weapons!'

The stream was subsiding. Copeland peered over his stomach.

Er, Copeland, do you know what you've done? asked the voice in his head.

'Shit!' he screamed, throwing his hands out wide. 'Oh, shit!'

He stared at his gloved hands. Yes, he had poked every inch of the place and his hand might have gone exactly where Popov had been making or storing his dissolving terror weapon. He had poked around Popov's hospital room and through his clothes there. These gloves had touched everywhere, and now they had been touching the skin of a very delicate part of his anatomy... Popov's hand was dissolving... so... *Bloody dissolving, Copeland! You moron!*

He felt beads of sweat pour down his cheeks. Keeping his hands out wide, he looked down again. In response to the renewed attention, his bladder gave one last effort and stained his trouser leg. Motionless, he stood crucifix-like with arms outstretched. But Christ was rarely depicted wearing purple latex gloves, or with pee down his leg, or with his todger hanging out.

Copeland burst into action. He tore a glove off his one hand, thrust it in his pocket, rinsed that hand under the tap then used it to splash water between his legs, aiming at the most delicate part of his anatomy, then tuck himself back inside and zip up. He rushed back into the main room, slammed the window shut, grabbed the money and stuffed it as deep as he could into his inside pocket, picked up his executive folder and shut the door behind him.

Doctor Beth Spencer.

While Popov was being pushed back to his room after his MRI scan, Dr. Spencer had stayed to speak to the radiologist.

'I might be able to give you some preliminary results in about an hour, Doctor, but it will take me up to twenty four hours to do a thorough analysis of the data,' the radiologist told her.

'You do realise how urgent this is? We need to know everything in case he's contagious,' she said waving a finger at him.

'I am aware. Junior Administrator Benson was more than clear when he spoke to me about this, but I can only do what I can and an hour is the best I can do, especially since I don't even know what I'm looking for. If I get lucky and pick something up I may be able to give you more before twenty four hours, but I can't promise. It's Saturday tomorrow and although I have agreed to come in, the rest of the department will be on a skeleton staff. I'm not going to get much help.'

'OK, do your best,' she said with a sympathetic nod. 'I'll see you in an hour. Now I think I have a phone call I should make.'

She found her way back to the small office the Administrator had found for her in the administration block and searched through her phone contacts to find the number for The Ministry of Health. She used the hospital phone on the desk and pressed the numbers for Richmond House.

After twenty minutes of ringing, choosing options that often circled her back to where she had started, and being told to hold and subjected to music clearly made by a five year old hitting a xylophone, there was an actual person on the other end of the phone.'Department of Health, Richmond House,' said a voice.

Twenty minutes of waiting seemed to have earned Beth Spencer the right to speak to someone who sounded like he was young enough to be an intern.

'My name is Doctor Elizabeth Spencer. I am calling from The St. James Hospital in Boston where I am the lead professional on a HPT. The case needs upgrading to have an OCT and the patient needs to be placed in strict quarantine conditions at The Royal Free.' She thought that covered it.

'OK. Just getting that down... Dr. Spencer... Boston... HPT,' came back a hesitant voice on the other end of the phone.

Beth Spencer sighed and rubbed her brow with her free hand. It was too hot for this sort of crap, she thought.

'It's Friday afternoon,' he said.

'What?'

'I said it's Friday afternoon,' he said.

'I know that,' she replied calmly.

'There's no one here,' he said.

'I need to speak to the Under Secretary of State responsible for public health,' she said. 'It is very important and very urgent.'

The young male voice was silent. 'There's no one here,' he eventually repeated.

'Well, you're there. There must be someone else. Perhaps your head of department? Your boss?' she said.

'Just left. You know what commuting is like on Fridays. Just about to leave myself when I picked up the phone.'

'Fine, right,' said Beth Spencer, now gripping the edge of the desk. 'Just give me the mobile or home number of the Under Secretary.'

'Can't do that,' he said. 'Not allowed to. Sorry.'

'What's your name?'

'Er, Giles.'

'Listen, Giles. We have a serious situation here. We need to set up an Outbreak Control Team and get a patient properly isolated. I need to speak to someone with the authority to get those things done,' she said, hoping she had finally impressed the need for action on him.

'Right, ok, just hang on a minute,' he said.

Finally, she thought. Let's get things moving!

Her optimism plummeted as soon as the xylophone playing infant came back on the line. She resisted the urge to hit her head against the desk. When the music stopped and the same voice came back on she could not resist tugging her short hair.

'So,' he said, 'I need you to answer some questions first.'

'Go on,' she said, already sensing this was not going to go well.

'Has the outbreak been reported in the local or national press?' he asked. She guessed he was reading from something.

'What's that got to do with it?' was her reply.

'You need to answer the questions before we can go any further,' he said.

She took the phone from her ear, closed her eyes and counted out three steady breaths. 'No,' she said. 'There has been no press coverage.'

'Right,' he said. There was a silence as he wrote this down. 'And how many patients have been infected?'

'One so far, but there may be more we are not yet aware of,' she said.

'I'm going to put one, then,' he said. 'Let's see... hmmm. The rest of the questions are not relevant in light of the first two answers. Sorry, Doctor, your case does not meet the criteria for setting up an Outbreak Control Team. Have a nice weekend.'

She sat in silence until another voice came on the phone. It was a woman's voice saying, 'The other person has cleared. The other person has cleared. The other person...' She put the receiver down.

She drank most of the bottle of water and ate the banana she had left in the office earlier. So much for that, she thought. When there were people dissolving in the High Street and The Daily Mail had banner headlines, she would phone Richmond House again and see if they thought an OCT and quarantine might be a good idea then. 'Damn,' she said as she tossed the banana skin into the basket, but she knew young Giles was right, at least to some extent. There was no evidence there was anything contagious here. There was still only one patient, only Jakab Popov. Until there were more cases there was no evidence of an outbreak and without an outbreak there could not be an Outbreak Control Team, but it had been worth a shot, and would have been a good precaution to try to get ahead of whatever this was. But there *was* only Popov. Only one victim so far.

Except for the one in the mortuary she did not yet know about.

Copeland, Friday August 26th.

Copeland walked briskly back to the hotel, holding the end of his jacket in front of him in the vain hope of covering his pee-stained trousers. He had thrown the mask and gloves in the first litter container he had passed, not caring it said recycling only. He hurried past the closed and closing shops. He needed a very long shower. He was hoping to spot a clothes shop. He would need a new suit, at least one new shirt and probably more socks now it looked like he would be spending the weekend here. There were takeaways in abundance, along with money exchanges, Polish food shops, betting offices, cafes and the ever-near Pizza Hut, but no clothes shops.

As he neared the hotel, the adrenalin started to subside and he had relaxed further when he saw the heat had dried out the wet patch. For medicinal reasons, he told himself, he picked up a bottle of red and a single malt at a shop that sportingly had a range of small flags alongside the Union Flag in the window – a sound marketing tactic clearly approving of intoxication for anyone of any nationality as long as they had the money to pay for it. As a sign of solidarity he had thrown the end of his cigarette into the gutter outside before entering.

Back in his hotel room, he had a large glass of Scotch, threw his clothes off and showered vigorously, washing one part of his anatomy particularly thoroughly. He discovered he had clean clothes for one more day, including a pair of grey trousers he had forgotten he had packed. Clean, dry and clothed, he collapsed onto the armchair and poured himself a glass of Merlot.

After ten minutes of steady breathing, and a lot of sipping, he poured a second glass and opened his laptop to write his report.

•Subject currently isolated in a single occupancy side room off a main ward.

•Subject's symptoms spreading rapidly. Cause unknown. More tests underway. Still resembles aggressive form of necrotising fasciitis. (Photos attached – Google it, Sergeant Brandon!)

•Subject has deteriorating health and in shock. Subject is heavily sedated and unable to communicate.

•A Dr. Spencer has been sent down from Lincoln Hospital to head a Health Protection Team (HPT). More information on her is required.

•Subject's belongings have been searched at his current location and his residence. No passport found. No phone found.

Copeland's fingers hovered over the keyboard. He had another gulp of the Merlot and folded his arms. He blew out his cheeks, clapped his hands together and typed:

•Subject had £500 hidden under carpet and a key hidden in a mug.

•Next step: track down the people he says he works for called 'The European Agency' and subject's other contacts, if any; find out where he got the money and what key is for; locate subject's passport.

•Conclusion: case ongoing. No proven radical links at this time.

He read it through, satisfied he was as concise as ever. Not quite right, though, was it, he told himself as he swallowed a mouthful of wine. He changed the last line to 'No proven or unproven radical links at this time'. He scrolled up and deleted the reference to Dr. Spencer and Lincoln Hospital. He was going to have to use the hotel's internet connection and any names would have to be left out, just in case. The other side were always watching.

Then, also on the grounds of just in case, but mainly because he wanted to annoy his immediate boss, D.C.I. Ross, for sending him on a wild-goose chase in the first place, he deleted the whole report, leaving only:

Case ongoing. No proven or unproven radical links at this time.

He downloaded the photos from his phone. He omitted the photo of Popov's hospital admission form with the address on it, and the photos of the interpreters notes and the photos of the test results because Popov's name appeared, and chose only the most recent photo of the withering hand and the least blurred one he had taken of Popov's face. He logged in to the department's secure server and e-mailed his report and the photographs to the D.C.I. No doubt it would end up on the desk of Sergeant Brandon first and he wished he could see the

D.C.I.'s face when Brandon handed him a report consisting of just one line and two photos.

He had another half glass of Merlot and went down to dinner, unaware two Russian Secret Service agents were on their way.

Lunch had been satisfying but had only been just a single course and, after all, he had had a full day. (Copeland did not count the dessert as it had been less than a full bowl.) Then there was that Friday night feeling. It was the start of the weekend and he was here giving it up for work. Warm Camembert seemed a good starter, followed by the eight ounce sirloin steak. The waitress had been particularly helpful by giving him excellent directions to Marks and Spencer's, where he intended to buy extra clothes for his extended stay. (He would include the clothes receipts with the other receipts and see what happened.) To celebrate the waitress being so helpful he ordered a Châteauneuf-du-Pape. What else was there to have with steak? Sod the D.C.I. and his 'don't order the most expensive wine' crap.

He was just enjoying the hand cut chips that accompanied his steak when his mobile rang. He guessed it was D.C.I. Ross timing a call to interrupt his meal, but the display said 'unknown number'.

'Hello,' he said, not giving his name because he fully anticipated he was about to be told he could get his PPI back or claim whiplash for an accident he did not have in the last two years.

'Inspector Copeland?' said a female voice.

'Yes, this is Copeland,' he said.

'This is Dr. Spencer. I got your number from the Administrator and wanted to give you a call to update you,' she said.

Copeland looked at his steak and his chips and his mushrooms and his onion rings. The tomatoes looked healthy and did not receive the same amount of attention. He put his fork down and lifted his wine. You just couldn't beat a Châteauneuf-du-Pape – not when the tax payer picked up the bill anyway.

'Good of you to call', he said and took a swig.

'We have some preliminary results from the MRI. We still don't know what it is but almost all of the skin from his hand and the outer layers of his fore-arm have now gone. The hand's muscles and tendons are under fifty percent. We still can't work out why he is not bleeding profusely or why whatever it is does not seem to be being transported to other parts of his body in the blood stream. We think there is no pain because the nerves seem to be being attacked first.'

'I see,' said Copeland, looking at his steak, remembering the chunks taken from Popov's arm and wishing this conversation was not taking place while he was eating.

'The extra tests in pathology have shed no more light on the illness either. They think it could still be viral or even bacterial, but if so it must be very small and we would need very specialised microscopes to get to that sort of level.'

There was a pause as if she was waiting for him to say something. 'I see,' he said again.

'So, er, is there anything you can do? You know, pull a few strings or something?' she asked.

'Well, Dr. Spencer, I could, but this seems to be more of a medical need than a policing one, so there is probably not much I can do,' he said, not wanting to make waves or more work for himself.

'Oh, right,' she said, unconvinced. 'I have also tried to get in touch with the Ministry of Health to try to talk to the Under Secretary for public health, but have had no luck there. I think we need to get Popov to The Royal Free where they have the best isolation facilities. Could you help there?'

He swallowed another mouthful of wine. He knew her persistence was going to ruin his meal if he didn't try a different tack.

'I will speak to my superiors about moving him and about access to high level microscopes,' he said, hoping that would suffice and she would hang up.

'We probably need university ones. They usually have the best. NHS can't afford all the latest stuff anymore,' she said. 'Students don't get ripped off for nothing.'

'Right, of course not,' he said, not rising to her sarcasm.

Another long silence.

'So that's it,' she said eventually. 'We still have no idea what's going on, but I thought I would let you know. We will get a better MRI analysis sometime tomorrow. Shall I call you then?'

'Please do. Thank you for calling. Have a good evening,' he said and pressed 'end call'.

Copeland started to think ahead. He knew what needed to be done. He caught the attention of the waitress. 'Another bottle of the same, please. And a little French mustard, if you don't mind,' he said.

With the looming disaster of an empty glass averted, his detective brain started deducing: so, she phones me out of hours and tells me they have found nothing new. Perhaps there was more to the phone call than meets the eye. She had obviously been trying to get information out of him. Perhaps she thought London had fed him something new on Popov, or something on the substance eating into him. Or something else – something like she had been back into Popov's room to see if he had taken anything. Yes, she had known Popov's door key was there and now she knew it was no longer there. She had phoned him hoping he would tell her what he had found in the bedsit. He finished his first bottle and smiled to himself. Genius hotshot doctor she may be, but her interrogation skills were all nursery school. She would have to get up early in the morning to catch Copeland of S.O.15 out, he thought. He reflected on the reality that he rarely got up early, but decided the 'early bird' analogy would have to stand because he had a steak going cold.

Doctor Beth Spencer had taken a moment to realise Copeland had ended the call. She looked at the blank screen on her phone, but spoke to it anyway. 'Right, you tubby bastard! Don't tell me if you found anything at his place! I've tried being nice and got nothing. If you are not going to play give and take then you'd better get yourself a search warrant the next time! And you'd better bring that door key back before I tell the press about illegal police searches!'
She threw her phone at the sofa.

Dr. Beth Spencer, Saturday, 27th August, 2016.

Beth Spencer had not slept well even after her anger had subsided. She had laid awake going through all Popov's symptoms and possible causes yet still felt there was something missing, or that she was missing something. After a few hours alternating between sleep and wakefulness she had finally given up trying and went for her swim even earlier than usual.

The day staff had just started their shift when she arrived on the ward. She sat at the nurses' work station going through Popov's notes and checking the record of his vitals over the last twenty four hours. Blood pressure and heart rate were above normal but nothing to cause alarm, and the amount of fluid in and out balanced as expected. She was about to close the folder and go and see Popov when two of the nurses came to the workstation.

'Hello, Dr. Spencer. You're bright 'n' early today,' said one of them as she unlocked a metal cabinet and started passing the patients' medicines to the other who was placing them on a small trolley.

Beth Spencer looked up from the notes and recognised a nurse she had seen the day before. 'Good morning, nurse,' she said.

The nurse stopped taking out the medicines and leaned on the desk beside Beth Spencer. It creaked. 'Is that bloke Popov gonna die?' she asked.

Beth looked up at her and noticed she was still a student nurse, decided to cut her some slack, despite the excessive make-up, nose ring and purple hair, so smiled and shook her head. 'He's not dead yet, but please don't ask me what's wrong with him,' she said.

'Nah. We all knows no one can figure out what he's dyin' of. Lot of it goin' round', she said tapping the side of her nose.

Beth was not used to nurses being quite so familiar with senior doctors but was intrigued. 'Come again?' she said, leaning forward and placing her hands together on the desk.

'Well, I were tellin' my boyfriend Kev about Mr. P and about his 'and thingy and how nobody knew what he 'ad got and the big bosses 'ad even sent a doctor down from Lincoln and she 'ad no idea either – no offence – and he was tellin' me they 'ad a bloke in a body bag and 'e only 'ad one 'and no one knew 'ow he died either. Said there ain't a mark on 'im , 'cept for the missing 'and of course, and they would 'ave to do one of them auti-opsies to find out.'

'An autopsy? A post-mortem?'

'That's right, Doc, an autopsy. That's what I said he said,' said the nurse, confident she was repeating herself and wiping her nose on the back of her hand.

'They have someone in the mortuary with a missing hand? When did they get him in?' asked Beth anxiously.

'Kev didn't say. Just said a Doc had given the poor chap the once over, said they would have to do a... autopsy, then zipped 'im up and shoved 'im in a drawer. That's all I know. You 'ave a nice day now!' She sprang from the desk and was gossiping down the ward with the other nurse and the medicine trolley before Beth could say another word.

Beth had wanted to ask one more question along the lines of, *'How the hell did you become a student nurse?'*

Beth looked at her watch. The mortuary was one place that never closed. It was always open for business. She had once heard another doctor say it was the one department that never slept, but another had corrected him and pointed out that there was quite a lot of sleeping in there. Yes, she could get down there first, then see Popov and then check in with the radiologist to see if the MRI analysis had proven more fruitful than the initial results.

She grabbed a pair of gloves and a mask from the drawer and threw on the white coat she had brought down from her temporary office.

She strode down the hall, clipping her ID badge onto her top pocket as she went. She glanced into Popov's room as she neared the ward door. He looked the same, but she knew she could only see his good, left side. He looked like he was having a better night's sleep than she had managed.

She remembered the question she should have asked and turned round. She soon caught up with the nurses and the medicine trolley.

'There you go, Mr. Wilson,' the student nurse was saying to an aging, half propped up, bleary eyed patient. 'Them should shrink your prostate in no time. But don't you worry. Them doctors can soon get up there and cut it down to size if them pills don't work.' She laughed. The patient did not, but swallowed the pills with gusto.

'Nurse!' said Beth through clenched teeth. 'Come here!'

The nurse put down a bottle of pills and went over to Beth. 'Something else, Doc?' she said.

Beth grabbed her by her chubby elbow, steered her across the ward to an empty bed and thrust the curtains shut.

'That 'urt my elbow! You can't grab nurses like that just 'cos you'm a doctor, you know,' she said, sounding on the edge of tears.

Beth was unmoved. 'If you do not change your attitude and show more professionalism with patients then this will be your last week here. Am I clear *student nurse*?'

The student lost the crocodile tears and became defiant. 'You ain't my boss. You don't even work here really. You can't tell me what to do.'

'Do you really want a consultant to recommend a disciplinary hearing?' threatened Beth.

The student remained stubborn. 'You ain't even a consultant. You'z much too young!' She pointed her finger inches from Beth's nose.

Ignoring the finger, Beth locked eyes with the student. 'Google me,' she said, 'then get a better attitude.' She waited for the finger to lower and the doubt to start showing. 'Now,' said Beth, 'have you been in to see Mr. Popov today?'

Beth watched the student nurse's eyes lower and her shoulders sag.

'No, Doctor Spencer,' she said. 'I were told to tell everyone not to go into his room.'

'Instructions from whom, nurse? The ward sister?'

'Nah, she's been off sick for ages. Senior Nurse Jones it was what said it', said the nurse.

Beth lifted the nurse's ID with one finger and said, 'I see. Thank you Student Nurse Zora Smith. Now you have a nice day, and make sure the patients do too!'

'Yes, Doctor. Thank you Doctor,' she said and disappeared though the curtain.

Zora? What sort of a name was that, thought Beth. She slapped herself on the thigh, mildly annoyed that she had judged what could quite conceivably be a name of foreign origin, or, judging by the accent, even Wolverhampton, and she usually considered this sort of judgmental thought to be bordering on racism. Carry on like this, Beth Spencer, she said to herself, and you'll be joining Copeland in SO15 soon.

Her mouth still shaped the word 'Zora' with a huge question mark after it as she went through the curtain. She really wanted to go in and see Popov, but a suspicious death raised new questions. And a corpse without a hand? If there was any link to Popov then this was a whole new scenario, and not a good one. She would have a little chat with Senior Nurse Jones later, though she feared Nurse Jones' instructions may have been, after all, prudent, and she knew it was time to enlist more help.

She walked briskly down the ward, glancing over her shoulder at Zora a couple of times as she went. In the corridor she rang the hospital switchboard, hoping to be put through to the Administrator then the pathology department. She had walked to the administration offices and still there was no answer. She tapped 'end call' and pocketed her phone. She opened every door and looked inside every office. The whole department was empty. She checked her watch. It was just after seven. She went to a nearby window and looked down at the sparsely populated staff car park.

The pathology department, she found, was as empty as the administration department and the door to the lab was still locked. Passing an occasional nurse, an occasional cleaner, and several breakfast trolleys making their way to the wards, Beth made her way to the mortuary which was, as it was in just about every hospital she had ever been in, the furthest place in the hospital. If a hospital had a basement, the mortuary was always there, if not, it was pushed to an extremity, but never near a visitors' car park, as if hospitals were denying death happened at all. This one was tucked away next to the hospital boiler room.

At least someone was there. The department that never sleeps, she reflected, as she went through the swinging door and was hit by the stench of greasy bacon. Her stomach turned. This was not the way a vegetarian wants to start the day it told her. She grimaced, screwed her eyes and willed her stomach back down, then approached the tall, thin attendant as he ate his bacon sandwich. He looked up from the tabloid that was spread across a metal table.

'Good morning,' she said holding out her hand.

He switched hands with his sandwich, wiped his hand on his unwashed lab coat and shook her hand. His mouth was full of sandwich and Beth was not impressed by the sight of half masticated bread and bacon pieces in ketchup when he said, 'Good morning,' back.

She let go of his hand and hoped he did not see her wipe her palm down the side of her white coat. 'I am Dr. Elizabeth Spencer.' She lifted her badge slightly. 'I am heading up a HPT and I have heard you have a body that requires a post-mortem, or, as you seem to call it here, an autopsy. I would like to see it please.'

The mortuary attendant swallowed and put the remains of the sandwich down on the newspaper. 'We don't get many people down here,' he said. 'Not alive.'

Beth had deduced that fact already from the state of his uncombed hair. Her lack of sleep was making her more intolerant than usual, and that was pretty intolerant on a good day.

'The body?' she said.

'We have a few at the moment. Young guy in a crash. Seems the driver was texting and went into a tree at full pelt. Then there's a few from the old folks wards, then there's...'

'No. Not one of those,' she interrupted. 'Not an accident or old. Probably not from a ward. As I understand it, this is a male who was seen by a doctor who said the body needed an autopsy. I've heard he only had one hand. Ring any bells?'

He folded his arms and rocked slightly as he thought. 'The vagrant guy?' he asked.

'He had one hand?'

'I'm sure he's the one. Ambulance crew brought him straight here. I remember now. They said someone had called it in. Thought they were going to a heart attack but when they got there this guy was dead with blood all around him. Had to tie his arm off and put it in one of those plastic thingies to stop the blood draining everywhere. They found him in that little park down by the docks. Must have put the kids on the adventure playground right off, eh?' he laughed.

Beth did not share the morgue humour. 'When was this?' she asked.

He rocked again, looking up and clearly counting. 'Let's see,' he said. 'Night shift last night. That was Friday night, wasn't it? Must have been Wednesday or Thursday when I was still on day shift. Thursday, yeah. Afternoon. Or maybe Wednesday afternoon.'

'And you told your girlfriend, nurse Zora, about the Doctor and the autopsy yesterday evening?' she said, trying to work the timings out.

'Zora? From Wolverhampton? My girlfriend? Give me a break!' he said and Beth thought maybe he was not as stupid as he looked. 'She's Kev's girlfriend. Must have been Kev what told her. I told him all about it. He likes to impress the young nurses, Kev does.'

Beth was thrown for a second. Who in their right mind would want to impress Student Nurse Zora?

'OK, right. So tell me about the doctor then we'll have a look at the paperwork to see which day it was,' she said.

'Well, he showed up after the ambulance crew had left. He came in and wanted to see the body the ambulance had brought in. Suppose someone must have told him. Anyway, the guy was there on the table and the Doc checked him over. He got me to roll the guy on his side while he checked his back.' He leaned towards her. 'I think the Doc was checking for stab wounds. Then he tells me there would have to be a post-mortem and he would sort that out.'

'Which doctor was it, er..?'

'Oh, I'm Stalker,' he said with pride.

'Your name is Stalker?' asked Beth hesitantly.

'That's what my friends call me. Short for Deathstalker 'cos I work down here. You know, Assassin's Guild? Warcraft? My *actual* name is Ronnie, but *you* can call me Stalker, little lady.'

'So, *Ronnie*,' said Beth, who regarded herself as neither a lady nor little, but still unable to fathom what the hell he was talking about, 'which doctor was it?'

He shrugged. 'Don't know and don't care. Black guy. They never tell me their names and I don't ask. Just call 'em doctor. But you, well, you I'll call Liz.'

Beth rolled her eyes. 'Right. Great. OK. So, can I see the body? Which drawer is he in?' She began moving towards the rows of metal doors along the wall.

'Oh, he's gone,' said Ronnie The Stalker, sounding surprised she would think the body was still there.

'They took it for the autopsy?' she asked.

'Yeah, that's right, Liz. To Nottingham.'

'Nottingham?' said Beth, amazed. 'Nottingham?'

'Outsourcing,' he said shaking his head. 'Been going on for a few years. They say it's cheaper than doing it here. We only have a body for maybe a day now and it's either off to a funeral home or to Nottingham. We zip them up and they get collected and off they go.'

Beth needed coffee. She leaned against the metal table, her hand just missing the bacon sandwich remnants. She recoiled. 'Great. Just great,' she said with her eyes closed. 'OK. So show me the paperwork.'

He went to a clipboard hanging next to the door and brought it over to her, tracing his greasy finger down the top sheet as he came.

'They took him yesterday afternoon,' he said as he handed her the clipboard.

She found herself looking at a sheet with handwritten names in the left column, a date and time in the middle column, and a scrawled signature in the final, right hand column.

She held the clipboard up and looked up at Stalker the attendant. 'What's this?'

'It's the log sheet,' he replied with a '*don't you KNOW?*' clearly implied behind the statement.

'A log for...?'

'The bodies, the corpses, the cadavers.'

She waited.

He shook his head, moved alongside her and pointed to the sheet. 'Look, Liz,' he said. 'Their names are in this column, this column says what time they were collected, and this end column says who collected them and where they were from. You know, which funeral home or whatever.'

'Where's all the other paperwork? The admissions, preliminary cause of death, next of kin? All that sort of stuff?'

'That goes when the body goes. We just give it to whoever collects the body. Don't know what happens to it after that. Never bothered to ask. We just wheel 'em in, shove 'em in a locker for a while, then wheel 'em out.'

She held up the clipboard. 'But these are just unreadable signatures. Where does it say where whoever collected the body was from?'

He looked at her as if she was mad. 'Kev and I have been doing this for years,' he said. 'We know 'em all.'

She raised her eyebrows. 'Oh, right,' she said. 'So which is the one I'm looking for?'

'Well, gorgeous, that would be our friend right there,' he pointed at the sheet as he moved closer to Beth. 'Picked up by our friends from GSMS, Nottingham. Don't know what GSMS stands for. Sorry... Liz.'

She felt their hips touch, adding to her 'gorgeous' indignation. She literally and metaphorically bit her tongue as she took the clipboard and looked to see where he was pointing.

The body of Usman Fayad had been collected at 2 p.m. on Friday 26th.

Beth had made sure she handed the clipboard back forcefully enough to bruise at least one rib and pointedly said nothing else to the mortuary attendant when she left. As soon as she was through the swinging doors and in the corridor she took her notepad out and wrote *Fayad, Usman* in large letters. One mystery illness and one unexplained death within a week in a small town was giving her a bad feeling. It was time to see if the Administrator had got to work yet.

Larry Copeland, Saturday, August 27th

Copeland had made an early start too; early for him, at least. He had scrutinized his nether regions and made his decision before getting into bed: he would get up early and sort the case out so he would be home for his usual golf club Sunday roast. He had left almost a half bottle of the second Châteauneuf, so believed he was sober enough to make such decisions. Brushing his teeth before bed had proven a greater challenge: he had been thankful that the sink was handy to grab onto and prevent him from tottering over.

Worry about his possible genital contamination had built up and was putting him off eating, at least without a few alcoholic beverages to calm his nerves first. He could only manage just one slice of toast after his full English breakfast, and now that his health was at risk he had chosen muesli to start the day. He didn't like it.

He was in Marks and Spencer by nine and leaving with a full bag of shirts, underwear and socks by ten. He had taken the opportunity to buy a new dark blue suit that matched his other one so closely it was too good an opportunity to miss. It was all on expenses, so why not? And what if the jacket would not fasten across his stomach? The only time he needed to fasten it was to cover his holster when he was armed, and he had not been armed since... since he had been unable to fasten his jacket.

That had reminded him, and back in room 105 he checked his Glock 17 pistol and his holster were still untouched on top of the wardrobe before a quick change of clothes and another self-examination 'downstairs'. As he left his room he met his new neighbours leaving room 103. He nodded and wished them 'good morning'. The taller of the two nodded back politely, the other did not turn and kept his back to Copeland. They had obviously seen the weather forecast and knew a cloudburst was due and were prepared for it with full length black raincoats and even blacker fedoras nestling above their ears. He thought about going back into his room to get his raincoat, but decided he would risk it. It was too hot to carry anything, even his executive case.

The instructions the waitress had given him were excellent. She had been right to tell him it was only a short walk round the back of the hotel and along the river and the taxi he took arrived outside the very new, three story redbrick and reflective window police station in no time.

He was equally impressed by the interior of grey slate floors, stainless steel and large plants. The waiting area was more upmarket than a four star hotel. A smartly dressed civilian woman with grey hair was sorting mail behind a glass panelled enquiries counter. She slid the glass panel to one side when he held up his warrant card.

'I would like to see whoever is in charge, thank you,' he said, recalling that course where they told them 'thank you' was assertive and carried the expectancy of compliance but 'please' just sounded like you were pleading. He had decided to be assertive today. Being assertive would be the only way he could get the 6.30 back to London.

'Of course, Detective Inspector. Please take a seat and I will see who might be available, though all the officers do seem very busy today so I can't promise anything.' She said and slammed the glass panel shut.

That assertiveness worked well, thought Copeland. Glad I didn't pay for that course myself. He sat and waited. At least the seats were very comfortable and there were a few daily papers on the coffee table.

He had only just finished the back page of a tabloid, which seemed to know what was going on inside every major football club, when he heard his name. He looked up to see the outstretched hand of a grey suited detective. He stood up and shook it.

'D.S. Hesterman. Welcome to our humble little nick, Sir' said the man as he shook Copeland's hand.

'Not so humble or little by the look of it,' smiled Copeland.

'You're right there, Inspector. All spanking new, this is,' Hesterman smiled back. 'If you would follow me, Sir. D.I.

Bell is running the shop today, Bank Holiday week-end and all.'

He swiped his card and led Copeland through the security door and up a flight of stairs. Half way along a corridor he knocked on a door and opened it before there was a reply.

'After you Sir,' said Hesterman.

After the customary handshake and offer of tea, Copeland sat alongside Hesterman, facing D.I. Bell across his desk. He looked young to Copeland, but not as young as Hesterman. Copeland realised they were probably in their thirties, but Copeland was at the age where all police looked like they were too young to have left school.

'So, Inspector,' said Bell, 'we received an email on Thursday evening from a Sergeant Brandon with instructions from your D.C.I. to give you every possible assistance and, quite frankly, we expected you sooner. What's going on that's got SO15, no less, so interested.'

Copeland felt the urge to tell them there was not actually anything interesting going on at all, just a guy with some unknown flesh-eating disease melting away in a hospital, but telling them that his D.C.I. and his Commander were putting him out to pasture did not seem the wisest move. There were still a few loose ends to tie up, number one of which was finding Popov's passport, and he needed their committed support.

'I'm afraid I can't tell you any specifics, Inspector,' Copeland nodded to his side, 'Sergeant. All I can say is that I do need your help tracking down a passport to find out if it is genuine. The passport is in the name of Jakab Popov and he is, allegedly, a Bulgarian. His English is almost non-existent but I have managed to find out he often worked for an outfit calling themselves 'The European Agency'. We need to know where and when he worked over the last few weeks.'

Inspector Bell exchanged an undisguised smile with Detective Sergeant Hesterman. He picked up a pen from the desk and started twirling it between fingers and thumbs of both hands.

'I think we may be of some assistance, Inspector,' Bell nodded, 'but I think we deserve a bit more than that. If SO15 is here, then there is a possible terrorist threat, here, in our town. I assure you that apart from a verbal report to my D.C.I., any information you care to share will not leave this room.'

Copeland wanted to shed his jacket and roll his sleeves up like his two local colleagues. It was even hotter than yesterday, and there was no sign of rain. Not a single cloud in a pure blue sky. He was aware of something gnawing at the back of his brain; something he should have noticed that was not right; something to do with the weather... something to do with raincoats... some*one* he should have recognised...

'Aha!' exclaimed Copeland. 'Biscuits!'

The door had been hesitantly opened by a young uniformed constable carrying a tray. 'Your tea, Sir,' he said, laying the tray down on the Inspector's desk.

'Thank you, Constable,' said Inspector Bell.

Nice, thought Copeland. Tea in an actual tea pot, and actual cups and actual saucers. Milk in a little matching flowery jug. Sugar in a little flowery bowl. And one spoon each. All very civilised. But no bloody biscuits. Bloody cutbacks!

Inspector Bell poured the tea and handed him a cup. 'Well?' he said.

For a moment, Copeland thought he was asking for his opinion of the tea so took a sip and decided he would not make a fuss about the lack of biscuits, then remembered the conversation before he had been bothered by the heat and something to do with the weather.

'Very well,' he said. He took another sip of tea and placed the cup and saucer down on the desk in front of him.

'Here's the short version. This Popov guy, if that's his real name, may be a Chechen terrorist and has possibly been involved in making a terrorist device. That was just a theory the Commander had that got passed down to me. Since I have been here I have found something else – I can't tell you how – and getting on with this has just become rather more urgent.' He couldn't tell them he had been in Popov's place and searched it without a warrant and he couldn't tell them it had become more urgent because he wanted to get to the golf club for Sunday lunch.

Copeland took out his handkerchief and wiped his forehead, then reached into his breast pocket and pulled out a key. He checked the key was the right one and dramatically placed it on the desk in front of him.

Inspector Bell leaned forward, picked it up and examined it. 'Snauzer?' he said reading the side of the key. He shook his head and handed it to Sergeant Hesterman.

'Looks too small to be a door key,' said Hesterman. 'Bigger than a normal padlock key, but might be for a heavy duty padlock.'

'Correct, Sergeant.' Copeland clapped his hands. 'I googled it yesterday evening.'

Inspector Bell wrote the word 'Snauzer' on his pad. 'I'll get a message out to all uniform officers to check any lock ups and garages to see if they can spot any with a heavy duty Snauzer padlock on them.'

'Thank you, Inspector,' said Copeland. He held out his hand to Sergeant Hesterman and Hesterman dropped the key onto his palm. Copeland put it back into his pocket. 'Let me know if the uniforms find anything. From what I have learned it should be pretty conspicuous, but it's supposed to be drill-proof and saw-proof and we will need the key to open it. Besides, I would rather it be me who sees what might be inside first. You understand, of course.'

'Right, yes, of course. Understood,' said Inspector Bell with an inappropriate exaggerated wink.

Telling them enough to get their help seemed the best course at the moment, and keeping the five hundred pounds and chemical weapons in the mysterious category should increase their motivation. Five hundred pounds was – well – five hundred pounds. It wasn't quite the same as finding a bomb making manual, and he expected any lock up to be full of stolen TVs rather than chemical weapons, but it didn't hurt to leave something to their imaginations.

Inspector Bell took a few sips from his cup. 'Three questions occur to me, Inspector Copeland. Is there an imminent threat here, in Boston? Second, do you know where this Popov character is now? And do you want us to start a search?'

Copeland picked up his tea, waiting for the third question. Wasn't that last question just two parts to the same question? He sipped his tea then gave up waiting.

'I don't think you need worry about an incident here, Inspector Bell,' said Copeland. 'And I know where he is and he's not going anywhere.' He felt suddenly relieved the hospital had sedated Popov unconscious. He would sort this first, but he thought it might be wise to visit Popov with his handcuffs soon, just in case.

'Glad to hear our town is safe,' said Bell, not sounding convinced. 'I suppose we have to trust you on that. I won't ask any more questions about his location either. I think I would prefer not to know. I don't want a reporter coming up to me in six months time to ask me if I knew this chap was being tortured.'

Copeland wanted to object to the implication but thought that might just lead to him into having to give more information. He remained emotionless and said nothing. He sensed the sergeant shuffling in his seat.

'So, Sergeant,' said Bell, 'please educate Inspector Copeland of the famous SO15 about passports and The European Agency. Hesterman is our resident expert for all things going down on the street, as they say.'

Hesterman cleared his throat and turned to Copeland. 'Well, Inspector, there's good news and bad news. If and when we find your suspect's passport it will probably be real. It's easier to fake the documents these people need to use to get a real passport than it is to fake the passport itself – a fake birth certificate, a fake residency, all that sort of thing. These countries don't have sophisticated data bases to check, especially when an official is slipped a few hundred dollars and is told the passport is needed urgently.'

'Surprised you lot at SO15 didn't know that,' interrupted Bell.

Was he smirking? Blank faced, Copeland turned back to Hesterman. 'We are, of course, aware of that,' he said, completely ignorant of what SO15 did or didn't know: he never read memos. 'Is that the good news or the bad?'

'That's the bad news. The good news is that I can take you to the boss of this so-called Agency right now, and if your man has worked for them, I'll bet you a pound to a penny we will find his passport there.'

'Good,' said Copeland.

'Not so good,' said Bell, and addressing Hesterman: 'Are you sure that's such a good idea? It may be better for you to go alone, Sergeant. Alexei is not known for his hospitality to strangers.'

'I need to go,' said Copeland, standing up.

Hesterman shrugged and stood up too. 'Good job you're not armed or you wouldn't get out alive,' he said, but Copeland noticed him wink at Bell. 'May we go, Sir?'

'Go, then. I don't think Inspector Copeland is going to share any more information with us, and we have been ordered to assist in any and all ways possible. Look after him, Danny,' said Bell, shaking his head and waving them away.

Dr. Beth Spencer, Saturday, August 27th.

From the table where she sat to drink her black coffee, Beth could see into the A & E. It was already filling up with patients, most of whom, Beth guessed, should be seeing their GPs but could not get an appointment. She had not seen anyone who looked like they needed A & E until someone came in with blood dripping from his thumb. People will use electric saws and have a conversation at the same time, thought Beth.

Once she had found the administration offices still deserted, Beth had decided coffee was the best option. She had asked for a double shot and had got a blank look, so had settled for two large polystyrene cups instead. Hadn't they heard of recycling or non-biodegradable?

She tapped her watch, sure it was going slower. She checked the time on her phone. She waited and sipped the insipid coffee. She thought about phoning Copeland, but it was only a passing thought. What would she tell him? She had nothing to link Usman Fayad to Popov. It was just an unusual death. If Copeland was even out of bed, she was sure he would be unhelpful, or worse still leap to all the wrong conclusions when he heard the deceased's name. Best to stick to Plan A and collar the Administrator. She looked at her watch again. It was time.

Neither the Administrator nor any of the secretaries were in the offices, but Junior Administrator Benson was. Through his glass panelled door, she could see his Friar Tuck head and black rimmed glasses intently staring at a screen while his little legs dangled above the floor. He typed a few words and stroked his beard before typing a few more. Now there was finally someone to speak to, Beth realised she had not worked out what approach she should take. Should she plead or demand? Be nice or be tough? She knew what she wanted but had not worked out how to get it.

She knocked softly on the glass. Not turning to look, Benson held up one hand, telling her to wait, while he typed with the other. When he looked up and saw her he leaped instantly from his chair and rushed to open the door.

'Beth, er, Dr. Spencer! Nice to see you. Please come in. Have a seat,' he said, ushering her in, bowing as if she was royalty.

She knew she had decided to play this the right way. She gave him her best '*I'm so happy to see you*' smile.

'Thank you for seeing me, Mr. Benson,' she said, sitting down on the chair at the side of the desk. 'I know you must be a very busy man.' She leaned forward, causing him to step back into his desk, adding, 'But I really need your help.'

Still facing her, he slid around his desk and sat in his faux-leather chair. 'Not at all,' he grinned. 'Here to help, after all.'

'But your work must be *so* important for you to come in Saturday morning, all alone with no-one else here.' She waved her hand in the direction of the empty offices beyond the glass.

'To be honest', he said earnestly, 'I have to catch up on all this paper work I should have done yesterday when I was in your meeting and juggling patients around to get Mr. Popov that MRI. How is he, by the way?'

'Not so good. But you did a brilliant job sorting that MRI so quickly. I am really in your debt, Mr. Benson. And I always repay my debts.' Her head was tilted to one side as she flashed her eyes wide at him.

'Please, do call me Tom,' Benson said, gulping.

'I'd *love* that. And please call me Beth. No need for formalities, is there, *Tom?*' said Beth, huskily.

His face was flushed. 'No. Er, quite, er, no formalities. Of course', he said as a bead of perspiration trickled in front of his ear.

One last card, she thought. 'What surprises me, Tom, is why you are in this office. I mean to say, the way you conducted the meeting yesterday and got things sorted so well – you were so commanding... so *dominant* – I would have thought you would have had another office, like the bigger office down the hall.'

He wheeled his chair to her side of the desk and whispered confidentially, even though the whole department was empty. 'I'm glad you think so too. It's wonderful to be appreciated for once. I did go to Oxford, you know.'

She reached forward and stroked his beard with the back of her hand. He sat rigid, probably all over. She continued stroking. 'I think it's the beard, Tom. I'm sure you would appear more like senior management if you lost it. It makes you look too boyish. I like to see them noble and strong... I like to see them firm... chins, I mean.'

Tom Benson wanted to nod but feared the beard stroking would end. He cleared his throat. It was clear she was persuading him to get a substantial raise. He bit the bullet.

'You're right, Beth. The beard has been holding me back. My career re-launches tomorrow!' He punched a weak fist into the air, just missing her ear. 'Oh, no, it's Sunday tomorrow. And Monday is Bank Holiday. So...' another limp air punch, '... Tuesday is the day! Hurrah!'

She had forgotten the Bank Holiday. That would make things even harder and, damn! There was that half marathon up north tomorrow. The rest of the personal development advice she could give him would have to wait. There was also a problem with where she would start. Lose the plastic black rim spectacles and get some modern ones? Grow six inches to be nearer a normal height? Work some weights before a breeze blows him over? Get a toupee?

She let her hand drop and sat back. 'So thank you for your help yesterday. The MRI data is still being analysed by the way. Now, I do need your help with two urgent matters.'

He glanced at his computer screen. 'Beth, you know I would love to help, but, the thing is, I do have a lot to do. I was supposed to clear ten percent of patients from every ward yesterday because, well, you know, the weekend staff is a bit thin on the ground, as they say. With the Bank Holiday on Monday – you know how it is. And then there are all these admission forms to be entered on the system. We just haven't got the admin staff to keep up anymore. Cut the admin staff they keep saying. Who needs pen pushers anyway, they keep saying. Well this is what happens when they cut admin staff – everything grinds to a halt!'

'I know, Tom,' she said, taking hold of his wrists, which were resting on his thighs. 'There's only you to save the day for the whole damn hospital.' She slid his wrists nearer his waist, her hands brushing the tops of his legs. 'But I need you, Tom,' she said softly in a tone that could advertise dark chocolate. She could feel him shaking.

He spoke painfully slowly. 'What do you want me to do?'

She moved his wrists together, into the middle of his lap. 'I just need two things, Tom. First, I need to see the paramedics' reports for their calls on Wednesday and Thursday and any copies of paperwork from the mortuary.'

Looking down at where his hands were with her hands on top, he nodded.

'Thank you, dear Tom. Second, since you seem to be in charge today, I need you to order Nurse Jones to make her staff do their jobs and get in there and treat Popov like any other patient. His fluid bags all need replacing and he needs a bed bath and a bed pan too.'

She felt him tense as soon as she said 'Nurse Jones'. He pushed her hands aside, sat upright and kicked his chair back. The wheels took him to the other end of his desk.

'No way! That's the Director of Nursing's job. You know that. And I haven't got time to sort out all the emergency calls reports for two whole days and then the mortuary reports. And what the ..?' He calmed down a little. 'And what the heck do you need all those for anyway?'

Annoyed with herself, Beth slapped herself on her leg. *I should have just done it the nasty way and not wasted my time*, she thought. She stood up and took out her phone.

'Back in a jiffy, Tom,' she said.

He watched her through the glass. She made her call, waited, smiled, gave him a finger-wave, then turned her back.

A minute later she was sitting back in the armchair staring at a worried looking Tom Benson. 'Who did you call?' he asked.

She put one finger to her lips, raised her eyebrows and pointed at the phone on his desk. She folded her arms and sat back in the chair, smiling. She could see his mind racing but finding no solution to the maze it was in.

When the phone rang he jumped and grabbed the receiver.

He said: 'Yes... but... and what... yes... yes... but... yes... understood, Administrator.'

He put the receiver down and looked at it as he murmured, 'You phoned my boss.'

'Yes,' she said. 'At home. She was having a lie in. I told her there was a certain junior administrator blocking the work of the Health Protection Team and that I had phoned the Under Secretary of State responsible for public health.' Beth was confident this was the truth. She had phoned the Under Secretary. The fact that she hadn't actually spoken to her was just a detail.

'Senior Administrator Adams did not sound pleased,' said Tom Benson. 'I don't think I have heard her shout or swear before. I've been told I work for you until this case is finished and, because I have caused such a storm, I have to work tomorrow and the Bank Holiday too.' He put his head in his hands.

Beth thought he might cry. She began to feel guilty. She rubbed her forehead. She blamed her lack of sleep. 'Never mind, Tom. I'm sure you will find the time to catch up from somewhere.'

'She's sending in a secretary to sort the ward beds out. I thought I was the only one who could do that. Oxford degree, you know,' he said, his head still down. He sniffed.

She felt even guiltier. She went over and stood behind him. She placed her hands on his shoulders and said, 'Tell you what, Tom. I'll sort the nursing out. I'll talk to Nurse Jones. We're a team, aren't we?'

It was if she had injected him with a stimulant. He sat up, tilted his head back, looked into her eyes and placed one hand on top of hers. 'Really? You'll see Nurse Jones? Thank you so much.'

'No problem. You can just find me *all* the exact files I'm looking for. The name of the deceased is Usman Fayad,' Beth informed him, trying to move on from the guilt of her sexual harassment.

'Of course, Beth,' he said. 'Can I still call you Beth? Thanks. But first, now we're a team – like Mulder and Scully – there's something really big I have to show you. You might like this.'

Copeland and D.S. Hesterman.

'Nice car,' commented Copeland sarcastically as DS Hesterman pulled out of the station car park. 'What happened? All the money get spent on the new building and none left for new vehicles?'

Hesterman smiled at him. 'Nothing wrong with a Ford. Even a five year old one. When the cuts came the boys in traffic got new ones but that was the budget gone. We have a couple of these left over for us plain clothes to run around in.'

Copeland liked Hesterman. He looked like he had been round the block a few times, and his broken nose looked like he had run into it once or twice too. His short brown hair accentuated his sharp features and revealed a scar on the side of his forehead.

'Can I call you Danny, Sergeant?' asked Copeland.

'Yes, Sir, that would be fine,' replied Hesterman, formally.

'Been a long time since I had a partner, Danny. You can call me Larry.'

Sergeant Hesterman glanced across. 'If you say so, Sir. Larry it is.'

'So how did you get that scar, Danny? I'm guessing it was breaking up a knife fight outside a pub,' said Copeland, half out of curiosity and half making conversation.

Danny Hesterman laughed. 'Strangely enough, that's what I usually tell people. Helps to be known as a hard man on the streets, especially these days. Truth is, I got my head too close to someone's boot when I used to play scrum half.'

'Nice one,' said Copeland. He could see it now. Danny Hesterman was that stocky scrum half who could take, and give, a good hit. This was Copeland's sort of copper. 'What do you mean, though, Danny? Why especially these days?'

The car slowed and stopped behind a line of cars at a traffic island, allowing Hesterman to turn to Copeland. 'How long have you been here, Sir? Two or three days? You must have seen how many immigrants there are. That brings in organised criminals like Alexei – you're going to love him, by the way. Then there's the other side. A few are Nazis in all but name. Since the Brexit vote they think they can do what the hell they like. A lot of the immigrants won't go out after dark any more, and even the few Pakistanis we have who have lived here for years are being targeted. Pretty nasty stuff.'

The cars in front crawled forwards.

'So what about you?' said Hesterman. 'You must have seen a few things in S.O.15 – all that spooks stuff.'

'Not so much, really,' said Copeland, but Danny Hesterman noticed he was looking out of the side window.

'How long have you been with them?' asked Hesterman, giving it a second try.

'Since it was set up in 2006. S.O.12 before that,' said Copeland reluctantly.

'Special Branch? Were you ever just a regular copper?'

'I suppose I was, once. That was a few lives ago.' Copeland paused. 'Can we change the subject, Sergeant?'

Hesterman had collared enough criminals to read when questions were getting too close to the truth. He drove in silence for a few minutes while Copeland still stared out of the window.

'Sir,' he finally said, 'were you in Ireland?'

Turning his head, Copeland stared at Hesterman for a few moments. He was keeping his eyes on the road, shifting gears, turning, accelerating, not the slightest glance toward Copeland.

'Sealed files, Danny, so not a word. Not even to your boss or your wife,' said Copeland nodding at Hesterman's ring. Hesterman nodded his agreement, but did not speak in case he ruined the moment.

Copeland sighed and turned his attention to the side window again. 'OK,' he said. 'Two years undercover in a loyalist paramilitary. My marriage had gone and the ex wouldn't let me see my daughter, so, like an idiot, I volunteered. I have a drawer full of medals and commendations for what they're worth.'

That was it. He wasn't going to share any more. The engine and the tyres seemed to sense the sound vacuum and grow louder.

'Shall I put some music on?' said Hesterman as they approached a bridge across the river.

Copeland gave him a friendly punch on his arm. 'Don't worry, Sergeant Danny. I left the past behind a long time ago and took up my favourite hobby – golf. Well, golf and eating.' He laughed. 'And drinking.'

Hesterman still felt guilty he had pushed the subject. First names seemed not quite so appropriate now. 'Nearly there, Inspector,' he said.

'Good. What can you tell me about this Alexei, Danny?'

'They are from the east. You'll soon see, Sir. His brother Ivan will probably be there too,' said Hesterman as he pulled the car into a scrap yard on the edge of an industrial estate and parked next to two old minibuses.

Copeland swung his legs out of the car and heard himself grunt as he hauled himself out. He grabbed his jacket from the back seat and looked around as he pulled it on. It was a typical scrap yard, filled mostly with rusting cars, but with a few old washing machines and tumble driers near the barbed wire topped fence next to the minibuses.

At the far end of the scrap yard, with cars precariously piled three high on either side, was an old tourer caravan.

'Come on, Inspector,' said Hesterman setting off towards the caravan which, Copeland guessed, doubled as the site office.

As Copeland caught him up, Hesterman said, 'By the way, their surname is Karamazov.'

'Thank you, Sergeant,' said Copeland. It was going to be interesting to meet the brothers Alexei and Ivan Karamazov, thought Copeland just before the penny dropped.

Two men came out of the caravan as they approached, but Copeland's attention was fixed on the dog one of them trailed on a thick leash. It was a jet black Rottweiler and they were close enough for Copeland to see the saliva dripping between huge yellow teeth. The dog sat, still too close for comfort, and Copeland managed to steer his eyes away and consider the two men.

Both men wore black vests, jeans and heavy work boots. Both had blue swirling tattoos down their muscled arms. One was big. The one holding the dog was bigger. The dog and the mountain man stayed in front of the caravan, the other strode towards them.

'Hello, Alexei,' said Hesterman.

Alexei grabbed Hesterman's shoulders and shook him. Copeland tensed.

'Danny, my boy! Iz good to see youz, yes? Vy you no come wisit Alexei more often?' said Alexei with a huge grin. Copeland relaxed. He tried to place the accent. Something eastern he guessed, but could not seem to narrow it down further.

Alexei had finished his shaking, but had grabbed Hesterman's hand and was vigorously shaking it while simultaneously slapping him on the shoulder with his other hand. Given the size of Alexei's biceps, Copeland was impressed that Hesterman was standing his ground and not being knocked sideways.

'Good to see you too, Alexei. This is my fellow officer, Detective Inspector Copeland,' said Hesterman still gripped in the handshake.

Alexei looked at Copeland, then back again to Hesterman. He dropped his hand but gave him one final slap on the shoulder.

'Iz good you bring friend. Ve celebrate, yes?' He turned to the man mountain and the slavering dog. 'Ivan, go fetch vodka and three glasses!'

He approached Copeland, who had remained a strategic few paces back. Copeland stretched out his arm to its full extent, hoping a long range handshake would avoid the shoulder thumping. His plan was half successful. Alexei moved inside Copeland's arm and threw his arms around Copeland to give him a less than tender bear-hug. As the air erupted from his lungs, Copeland could not help be impressed by the strength of the man, and also by the way he had managed to extend his arms around Copeland's not inconsiderable girth. His feet lifted slightly from the floor, he dropped his just-lit cigarette and he heard Alexei shout, 'Hello, my friend Danny's friend! Hello!' right into his ear.

Copeland was beginning to understand why he could not place the accent when Alexei shook his hand like a water pump, shouting, 'You drink vith Alexei, Danny's new friend, yes?' This was an accent learned from Hollywood films. The real one, lurking below the surface, was East End. Copeland wondered if the brothers Karamazov had named their dog Dostoyevsky.

Copeland decided to play along. 'It's good to meet you too, Alexei. I've heard so many good things. I am on duty though.' He waited for Alexei to feign his disappointment before adding, 'So only one glass. And if it's just one, I suppose it better be a large one!' He slapped Alexei's shoulder.

A confused look shot across Alexei's face, then he regained his persona. 'Good, good. Ve drink best Russian wodka, yes?' he said and reciprocated the shoulder slap.

Danny Hesterman was now alongside Copeland. 'We need your help, Alexei,' he said.

Ivan had emerged from the caravan with a half bottle of cheap vodka and three unwashed tumblers, minus the hellhound. Hesterman held up his hand to stop him and whispered in Alexei's ear.

'We need a passport, Alexei. His name is Jakab Popov. Probably Bulgarian,' he whispered.

Alexei pulled away. 'Passport of somevon Alexei has never heard of. Vy vud Alexei have man's passport?' he protested, arms open wide. 'And vy you are whispering?'

'We also need your records of when and where Popov worked over the last two weeks, or three if you can find them,' said Danny Hesterman, louder.

'Danny, my good friend. Vy you think Alexei vud know zeese things? You hurt me here, in my heart, Danny, my friend.' Alexei thumped himself in the middle of his broad chest.

It was Hesterman's turn to grab Alexei by the shoulders, his face close enough their noses almost touched as Hesterman pulled Alexei down nearer to his own height. Copeland noticed Ivan slip back into the caravan, no doubt to replace the vodka with the dog.

'Listen, Alexei,' Hesterman was saying, 'we both know what those minibuses are for. You collect the Easterns every morning and take them to jobs. You get paid in cash and you give some to them, minus the rent you charge them for staying in the squalid little bedsits you own all over town. You know I know this, and you know we leave you alone because it's live and let live these days, right? If the Inland Revenue want their share they can do their own legwork. I also know you keep the passports until they have paid you back for whatever else they owe you, like helping them with their travel over here or the extortionate bills they get for heating and cooking. You make money, local business gets cheap labour and the Easterns get enough to get by and even send some home from time to time. So, unless you want some genuine police harassment, then give us what we came for.'

Copeland was impressed. Alexei had not said a word and had taken it all, fixed by Hesterman's unflinching stare. A dog growled and Copeland saw Ivan had emerged, as expected, with the Rottweiler. It was giving a strong signal through bared teeth. It did not like one of its masters being manhandled.

'Keep him back, Ivan,' shouted Hesterman but kept his stare fixed on Alexei. 'No need for any unpleasantness, surely Alexei?'

Alexei broke the stare and took Hesterman's elbows in his hands. 'No, no, Sergeant Danny. Ve are all good friends here.'

Ivan pushed the dog on his hind quarter and the dog sat, its tongue lolling to one side.

Alexei stepped back and threw his arms wide. 'But ve cannot share vot ve do not 'ave, Sergeant Danny.'

'Right!' said Danny Hesterman. 'Get your brother to come over here. But tie that bloody hound up first. Inspector Copeland, would you come closer, please?'

Copeland took the few steps forward and stood shoulder to shoulder with Hesterman. Ivan looped the dog's lead around a metal ring in front of the caravan and stood shoulder to shoulder with his brother. Copeland was beginning to think a contest of fisticuffs was not such a great idea with men who had biceps thicker than his leg. He coughed nervously but stood his ground.

'Detective Inspector,' said Hesterman, 'please show the brothers Karamazov your warrant card.'

Copeland was beginning to see the plan. He took out his warrant card, flicked it open and held it in front of the brothers' faces.

'Zo? I have zeen police varrant card before. I knew you vos police anyvays,' said Alexei with a shrug.

It was time for Copeland to take the lead in the police duo. 'Look harder. See it says S.O.15? I am from the specialist Metropolitan Police anti-terrorist unit.'

Alexei and Ivan were backing away. 'We ain't no terrorists, guv!' exclaimed Ivan.

Alexei punched him in the shoulder. 'Ivan! You... voo... you mean, 'Ve are not terrorists'!'

Hesterman gave Copeland a nudge with his elbow. 'Alexei, Ivan, my dear *Russian* friends. Please not to vorry!' he said. He put a hand one each of their shoulders, turned them round and walked them over to the side of the caravan, but well away from the dog.

Copeland kept a stern face, put his card back inside his jacket and stood with his hands behind his back. He resisted the temptation to bend his legs up and down three times or he would have been forced to also say 'Hello, hello, hello – what's all this then?' He felt his shoulders start to move up and down uncontrollably and the corners of his mouth begin to twitch. To save himself from the erupting laughter, he looked at the dog and coughed into his fist.

D.S. Hesterman finished his private collaboration and started walking back over to Copeland. The Karamazov brothers were waving and sticking their thumbs up.

'OK, Sergeant Danny,' Alexei was shouting. 'Ve zee you in an hour.'

'Let's get in the car,' said Hesterman as he walked past Copeland.

Copeland and Hesterman threw their jackets into the back again and shut the car doors. Hesterman started the engine, turned the air conditioning to full and reversed out of the scrap yard.

'You could have warned me,' laughed Copeland. 'They were no more Russian than a pint of Fuller's. You said they were from the east. I take it you meant the East End?'

Hesterman looked at him and laughed. 'Clever buggers in S.O.15, aren't you Larry?'

'I'm guessing you told them I could bang them up without trial on anti terror charges without even a hope of seeing a lawyer.'

'Quite right, Detective Inspector S.O.15,' said Danny Hesterman. 'They like to keep up the appearance of being Russian. Keeps the workers a bit scared. Some of them even believe the Karamazov's used to be KGB despite the fact they are way too young. As an added incentive, I also told them if they got funny you would get an armed response team there within the hour.'

'Do you have an armed response team in Boston?' asked Copeland, still smiling.

'Course we do. There's an officer up in Lincoln, I think. We could have got him to come down!'

'OK, Danny. We have an hour to kill. Time for lunch?' said Larry Copeland, looking at his watch and noticing they were heading further out of the town.

'Still a bit early for lunch, isn't it inspector? Thought we could go to Ashburton while we were this side of town. We had a report of an explosion there. Thought you might be interested?'

Copeland's head jerked round. An explosion? And no-one had thought to mention this to him before? 'An explosion?' he blurted.

Danny Hesterman laughed and turned to his passenger. 'Thought that would get your attention,' he said. 'Don't get too excited. It was probably someone with a shotgun out poaching a pheasant for supper. Still want to come? Should take about an hour and then we can visit Alexei and Ivan again, get your stuff off them, then maybe go to lunch?'

Copeland thought for a moment. His stomach was being unusually quiet. Probably subdued by the stress of a possibly dissolving penis, he thought. He started to feel sick. 'Fine. Let's go,' he said. 'Lunch can wait.' He couldn't remember the last time he had used *that* phrase.

Dr. Beth Spencer.

By late morning, Beth Spencer was in Jakab Popov's room with two nurses. Thankfully, Zora was not one of them. Nurse Kacharski and Nurse Hussein had changed all Popov's tubes and his arm's cling-film with expert precision, and had performed a very professional bed bath.

Senior Nurse Jones had been a breeze.

'I did not say not go in Popov's room,' she had told Beth. 'I told them not to go into the room *without the protective clothing*. It was that student nurse with the funny name wasn't it? Play Chinese whispers with my words would she? Well, she'll soon find out she was playing with fire!'

Beth wondered if Nurse Jones was being literal – she was a bit of a dragon.

Beth had become Nurse Jones' new best friend when Beth had handed her four fully protective yellow anti-viral suits, complete with built in face masks. Tom Benson had taken a bunch of keys from his drawer and taken her to the pathology lab, where he had proceeded to unlock a metal cabinet and reveal the suits. He had been under orders not to tell her about them at their HPT meeting because, apparently, they were expensive, and it would cripple the pathology department's budget if they had to replace them, but now the Administrator had decided she would be able to find the money from somewhere, or just not replace them at all since they were bought during the Ebola scare and there had never been a need for them. Beth did not like to mention the suits were at quite reasonable prices if you got them online instead of of one of the so-called 'specialist' hospital suppliers who undoubtedly got them from the Internet anyway, then quadrupled the price. Probably something to do with financial auditors not liking 'dodgy' online sellers or hospitals not having anything as modern as a credit card, she thought.

Armed with the suits and her new Senior Nurse Jones ally, it had been easy to convince the ward nurses not having the suits earlier had all been a big misunderstanding. Of course, Nurse Jones had stressed, someone would have to pay for such an 'inexcusable mistake' of not tending to Popov and left the nurses with no doubt who that would be by tilting her head towards and glaring at a certain student nurse.

When Beth came out of Popov's room, Tom Benson was waiting for her. She was surprised to see him. He was waving a piece of paper at her and had evidently found someone to lend him an electric razor – as Beth had suggested, his beard had disappeared. He looked ten years younger.

'Give me a moment, Mr. Benson,' she said as she took off the suit's hood. 'And stay well back while we bag the suits.'

He took three steps back, considered why she had told him to step back and took two more. He watched them slowly peel the suits off and put them into black bags.

'First class job in there,' said Beth to the nurses. 'You can both put that on your c.v. when you apply for a promotion. Now, could you take these and give them a good wash down in a shower, but be really careful how you open the bags and don't wave the suits around. Put fresh gloves and surgical masks on first to be on the safe side.'

The nurses looked at each other, worried.

'It's OK,' Beth reassured them. 'Just basic precautions. If he was contagious we would have more cases by now,' she said, praying the information Tom Benson was about to give her did not make her a liar.

Hesitantly, the nurses picked up the bags and went off down the ward. Beth shushed Tom Benson before he could speak.

'Let's go into the common room, Tom,' she said, leading the way.

As soon as he had shut the door behind them he gave her the sheet of paper. 'I found everything I could about Fayad and summarised it all onto one sheet for you. How's Mr. Popov?' he said.

She held the paper in front of her but looked at him. 'Not good. He seems to have come out of shock so we are going to ease off on his sedatives, but his upper arm is showing all the same signs. I think we will have to amputate to stop it spreading.'

Tom Benson looked appalled. 'His whole arm?'

'At least. But we may be able to save the shoulder. Depends on the MRI analysis,' she said. She waved the paper. 'This is brilliant work Tom. Oxford education, eh?'

He grinned.

'You didn't tell me which college. Trinity? Baliol? Magdalen?'

'Brookes,' he said proudly.

She let that pass. 'Much better without the beard,' she said, trying to sound convincing. 'Now everyone can see that smile.'

Seeing Popov's arm was one thing, but having to watch Benson's freshly shaven face crack into a grin would be too much so she turned her attention to the paper and began reading.

'There's more, er, Beth' he said after giving her a few moments. 'I have been in touch with pathology and the radiologist. Pathology thinks they have found something and the radiologist wants to see you. He's finished his analysis of the MRI.'

'About time we had some good news,' she said as she scanned the rest of the sheet before folding it and putting it into her pocket, 'because there's none here. I see the hospital have referred Fayad's body to the coroner to oversee the post-mortem. I'll go to pathology and see the MRI radiologist in a while. First, I need to speak to the doctor who referred Fayad, this Dr. Masilela, and to someone from the ambulance team that brought the body in. But it's been hours since I had breakfast and I need an early lunch. Let's grab a sandwich and make some calls and crack this case.'

'Like Holmes and Watson,' said Tom Benson, holding the door open for her.

Beth could not stop the thought that popped in her head. *Only if one of them had a striking resemblance to a chubby version of Woody Allen,* she thought, looking at him, and her feelings of guilt came back with a vengeance.

Beth Spencer was unusually quiet walking to the restaurant to get their sandwiches.

'Everything alright, Beth?' asked Tom, eventually.

She went to speak, glanced at the others in the queue around them and remained silent.

'Whatever is bothering you, Beth, just remember – honesty is the first chapter in the book of wisdom,' he said, an index finger pointing up.

She thought about this while paying for her egg and cress on wholemeal seeded. She waited for him to pay for his tuna and sweetcorn on white and catch her up.

'Thomas Jefferson?' she guessed.

'I thought you studied medicine!' he joked. 'How do you know that one?'

They walked. She stopped halfway along a deserted corridor. The guilt was too much. She knew she had used blatant sexual harassment to get him to investigate Fayad and sort Nurse Jones. What else could you call stroking his beard, being suggestive and holding his hands on his thighs? Beth refused to blame tiredness or the stress of the Popov case for behaviour she would have appalled in others and was considering handing in her resignation.

Tom had carried on a few paces down the empty corridor before realising she had stopped. He turned and came back, looking quizzical.

'Tom, I am so sorry about what I did earlier,' she said, bowing her head (which she had to do to look down at him).

Tom nodded. 'Apology accepted,' he said, smiling. 'Phoning my boss wasn't very nice, but I'm always in trouble anyway so...'

Beth cut-in with, 'Not that. The beard stroking and...'

'Great advice, Beth! Thanks!'

'And the hand holding...'

'You reminded me of my Grandma. She used to take my hands like that and tell me I was bound to get bullied at school because I looked like a garden gnome with glasses so I should learn to run fast,' he said as he pointed to his face.

His Grandma? thought Beth. *Is it sexual harassment when you behave like a grandma?*

He looked up over his thick frames at her. He gave her an exaggerated wink and pointed to the ceiling again. 'The only way to have a friend is to be one,' he said with meaning. 'Emerson,' he added. 'There's nothing to feel guilty about, Beth. You're forgiven.'

Beth understood, nodded and smiled at him. 'And I think I'm glad to have made a new friend,' said Beth. 'I promise to make it up to you.'

He smiled back and broke into his stride again. 'Come on then. Let's keep this team going, like Han Solo and Chewbacca!'

Beth stopped and called after him. 'And which one of us is Chewbacca?'

In the quiet of his office, Beth phoned Dr. Masilela and Tom phoned the ambulance crew. They ate their sandwiches and compared notes. He told her, out of respect for her vegetarianism, he had chosen a meat free sandwich. She told him a fish was not a vegetable. They had both laughed nervously.

From the phone conversations and from Benson's scoring of the files, they managed to piece together the story of Usman Fayad, deceased.

The ambulance had been sent on a call from a member of the public at 12.10 p.m. Thursday. A mother had taken her toddler to the park after collecting him from morning nursery and had seen the stricken man. The ambulance had arrived just before twelve thirty and found the body of Usman Fayad. His arm was still bleeding onto the grass. The paramedics in the ambulance thought it looked like the hand had been cut off just above the wrist and, judging by the cut's straightness, it had been cut off intentionally. This view was supported by Dr. Masilela. The ambulance crew had contacted the police, but had not got past the switchboard operator. They had found some ID on the body – a biometric residence permit – so were able to give Fayad's name and tell the police switchboard operator he appeared to be a vagrant. The ambulance crew had been told no-one would be available until the following day, at least. The paramedics were clear in their belief that the operator had decided a dead foreign vagrant who had probably had an accident was not a police priority. They had decided they could not leave a dead body in a pool of blood next to a children's playground on the off-chance the police would want to examine the scene at some stage, so had tied a tourniquet around the forearm and improvised with a sandwich bag and rubber bands around the stump, and had put the body in the ambulance and taken it to the mortuary. They had reported all this to the ambulance controller and had put in a full report (and Benson had thanked them for their thoroughness).

Dr. Masilela had remembered the body well. He had been paged and told to go to the mortuary to complete a death certificate, but when he got there he had been shocked. He had not expected the missing hand and an arm still dripping blood, and had not expected the corpse of such a young man. He had confirmed the hand appeared to have been intentionally removed, but it had not been by a single clean blow. Perhaps three, perhaps four attempts had been made before the bones had been severed. Because of the missing hand and because of the apparent youthfulness of the body, he had suspected Fayad had been murdered and the hand had been cut off as part of some ritualistic or revenge killing. Consequently, he had examined the rest of the body for anything resembling an attack, but had found no other wounds or bruising. He had even checked under the hair. Unable to determine if Fayad had died from lack of blood or some other reason, Dr. Masilela had decided the only course of action was a post-mortem so had ordered one to be done. He had referred it to the coroner for a post-mortem, rather than a hospital post-mortem, because of the circumstances of the death and where the body was found and because of the deceased's ethnicity. He had been unaware the hospital pathology department no longer carried out the post-mortems and was unaware Fayad's personal effects would be transported with the body. He did remember seeing the biometric ID though and could confirm Fayad had been a twenty two year old Afghan.

Tom Benson and Beth Spencer finished comparing notes and looked at each other. Each knew they were both thinking the same thing.

'Didn't you say you thought you would have to amputate Jakab Popov's arm to stop the disease spreading?' said Benson, finally breaking the uncomfortable silence. 'Maybe Fayad...'

Beth stood up and tossed her sandwich wrapper and empty water bottle into Benson's waste basket. Her hands were on her hips.

'You phone the people who have the body in Nottingham, Tom. Warn them he might be contagious. Then get on to your interpreter and find out the Bulgarian for 'we need to cut your arm off or you will die'. I'm off to MRI and pathology to see if we have a possible epidemic on our hands,' she said.

'I'm on it,' he said. 'I'll find you in pathology later.'

'And don't tell me which team we're like,' she called back as she left.

He was going to use Kirk and Spock, but since his job seemed to be making phone calls he felt more like Communications Officer Lieutenant Uhura.

Copeland and D.S. Hesterman.

Hesterman pulled the car up outside the end house of the village and Copeland opened the door and stamped on the remnants of the cigarette Hesterman had allowed him to smoke as long as long as he blew the smoke out of the window.

'Nice place,' commented Copeland, appraising the nice detached house and nice orderly garden surrounded by nice golden wheat fields. It was all very nice.

The door was opened by an elderly man with thinning grey hair and a white Scottish terrier straining to get through his legs. Hesterman showed his warrant card and introduced Copeland and they were greeted with 'about bloody time!' and the offer of tea. The dog was bundled into the kitchen and they were shown into a 1960s retro sitting room, complete with red leather sofa, lace coasters, net curtains and ducks on the wall. A gold clock under a plastic dome ticked loudly on the wooden mantelpiece. The burgundy swirl pattern carpet reminded Copeland of a cheap curry restaurant he once frequented. It smelt of stale dog.

Copeland excused himself to go to the avocado green bathroom to perform another examination on his 'extremity'. He was still clear. Like every sixty year old he seized the opportunity while he could and used the bathroom's amenities. He returned to the sitting room to find a tray of Earl Grey and digestives, and a woman with a grey hair bun and a smiling face. She poured. Copeland hated Earl Grey but politely took the cup and smiled.

'Now, Mr. Sawyer,' Hesterman was saying.

'It's Professor Sawyer,' said the elderly man. 'Retired.'

'Sorry, Professor. My mistake,' said Hesterman. 'So, Professor, what can you tell me about this alleged explosion?'

'Nothing alleged about it,' said the woman. 'We both clearly heard it.'

'Are you sure it wasn't a gunshot, Mrs. Sawyer?' asked Hesterman.

'Professor,' she said. 'I'm a Professor as well. Retired.'

Copeland had taken a sip of tea to be sociable and almost choked on it. An interview with two people with the same name was going to get confusing. He wondered if Hesterman would revert to calling them Mr. Professor and Mrs. Professor.

'Are you alright, Inspector?' said the male Professor. 'Go down the wrong way? Have a biscuit. That always helps.'

Copeland did not need the offer to be made twice.

'We have lived here since we retired twenty years ago, Sergeant,' said female Professor, 'and we know what a shotgun sounds like. What we heard was not a shotgun.'

Hesterman took a small notebook from his jacket pocket. 'And where did this explosion come from?' he asked, dubious but diplomatic.

'Up the lane, on the edge of Horseshoe Farm,' said male Professor.

'We think it was Ronaldo,' said female Professor.

Hesterman stopped writing and looked at her. 'Ronaldo? The footballer?'

'Yes, that's the one,' she nodded.

Copeland was glad he had just swallowed the biscuit.

'We know it's not *the* Ronaldo, we're not senile yet,' said male Professor. 'He just looks like him.'

Well, that saves getting a sketch artist out here, thought Copeland. Looks like Ronaldo, eh? Lucky bastard.

'And why would you think this, er, Ronaldo caused an explosion?' said Hesterman, flashing a pleading look at Copeland.

'Shady fellow. He's been up and down here all the time for months,' said female Professor. 'Well, when I say all the time, I mean once a week. Or sometimes once every couple of weeks.'

'Normally at week-ends,' said male Professor. 'He shoots past here in his bloody Mercedes, hurtling up the lane like there's no tomorrow.'

'Tell them about last week, Philip,' said female Professor.

'Just give me a minute, Emily. I was coming to that,' snapped male Professor.

Copeland guessed they had retired to this peace and tranquillity and soon realised being married and having a career was not the same as being alone in a house in the country with only a dog as conversation. But at least they had other names now.

Professor Philip turned back to Sergeant Hesterman. 'So, if I can finish without my wife constantly interrupting...'

'Please go on,' said Hesterman, pencil poised.

'Well,' said Prof. Philip, putting his tea down and clasping his hands together.

'Oh, my God,' said Prof. Emily. 'Just give them the short version, Philip, not one of your interminable monologues.'

'I was going to, Emily! Just give me a bloody chance!' growled Prof. Philip, glaring at her.

She sat back and waved the back of her hand at him.

'This chap, Ronaldo, comes down most weekends and has done for months now. We always know when it's him because hardly anyone else comes up this road and when they do they slow down. It becomes a single track road after our house, you know. So we see him and his black Mercedes shoot past quite a lot. About a week ago – yes, it was a week ago because it would be Saturday morning because that's when that awful radio programme is on Radio 4 so I get out of the house well before it starts and I take Benjy, our dog...'

'My dog,' cut in Professor Emily.

Professor Philip shot another glare at her. 'I was walking **the** dog and I saw him get out of his car to open the gate that leads onto Horseshoe Farm. That's when I got a good look at his face. Spitting image of Ronaldo! He didn't like me looking, though. As soon as he saw me, he sort of crouched down as if he was trying to hide his face behind the car. Very dodgy, I thought. So we call him Ronaldo now, instead of Maniac Mercedes Man.'

'So he was going up to the farm?' asked Hesterman.

'No, that's just the thing,' said Professor Emily, unable to sit back and listen anymore. 'That gate is only for a track that leads to one of the farm's furthest fields. It's just for tractors really. So where is he going up a farm track in a Mercedes? Only to the field where the explosion came from, that's where!' she said, answering her own question, folding her arms and looking pleased with herself.

'For once,' said Prof. Philip, 'I have to agree with my wife. The explosion came from exactly there.'

'And how far away would you say this track was, Ma'am, Sir?' said Hesterman.

Prof. Emily grabbed Hesterman's notebook and pencil with the speed of a striking viper and said, 'I'll draw you a map. All distances will be in metres,' and scribbled furiously.

'Emily!' said Prof. Philip, whom Copeland was beginning to sympathise with.

'Nearly done,' said Prof. Emily, having just started.

'So, Professor,' said Hesterman, 'we have had no reports of an explosion from anyone besides your good selves. Have you spoken to anyone else who may have heard it?'

'To be honest, Sergeant, it wasn't exactly what you might call a loud explosion. If I hadn't just turned Radio 4 off, we may not have heard it. It happened just after sunset and I daresay everyone was in watching some mindless Saturday night TV garbage and had probably closed their windows to keep out the gnats. It gets awful around here at sunset in the summer you know, when I was walking Benjy last week...'

'Oh, do shut up Philip. You'll get put inside for murdering police officers with boredom, and as usual you have left out the most important thing,' said Prof. Emily. She raised her eyebrows to her husband.

'No, dear, I can't think what you mean. What have I left out?' he said, blankly.

Prof. Emily huffed. 'You *went* there!'

'Oh, yes, silly of me!' A sudden realisation had struck Prof. Philip. 'Yes. Took Benjy for a walk the next day and *checked it out* as they seem to say these days. The old shed – cowshed or machinery shed or something – was demolished. Like it had been blown up!'

'Don't get yourself excited again, Philip. You know it gives you indigestion,' said Mrs. Professor and handed the notepad back to Hesterman. 'Up the lane passing the wheat field on your left, then pass the rape field – you know, yellow flowers – then through the gate at the end of that field. That takes you on a track alongside that field and into the next one, also rape, I believe. The shed is at the end of that.'

'Not anymore!' said Prof. Philip and laughed at his own joke. 'No rape either,' he put his hand to his mouth like a schoolboy saying a naughty word. 'They've harvested it.'

Hesterman was pretending to admire the detail of Prof. Emily's map. 'Thank you, Professor Sawyer,' he said.

'I'm not a Sawyer,' she said. 'I kept my maiden name. Wasn't taking *his*. I'm Emily Churchill.'

Copeland stood up and shook the professors' hands. 'Thank you both,' he said. 'We'll look into it and let you know.'

'But you haven't drunk your tea yet, Inspector,' said Professor Emily.

'Another time, perhaps,' smiled Copeland, praying another time would never come.

Mr. and Mrs. Professor stayed on their doorstep waving them off until they had thrown their jackets on the back seats,

Copeland had lit another cigarette and Hesterman had started driving down the lane.

'You smoke a lot, Larry,' remarked Hesterman.

Copeland laughed. 'After meeting them I do! Where are we going? Don't tell me you believe them? The shed probably fell down weeks ago. And he probably hasn't got a clue what Ronaldo looks like!'

'Come on, Inspector. It's only just up the road and the car was already pointing in the right direction. Only take a few minutes, then I can phone them later to tell them we didn't find anything and it's one more case closed.'

'OK,' nodded Copeland, blowing smoke out of the window. 'But let's be quick. It's definitely not too early for lunch now.' His stomach had awakened since his last all-clear genital inspection, and one digestive biscuit was not keeping it happy.

Ronaldo Makes a Call.

The tall, dark man they called Ronaldo had locked the door before leaving to make the phone call.

'Scorpion? All the initial testing has gone very well. It's incredibly potent, Sir.'

(Pause)

'Most of the six flasks are left. We only used about a quarter of one flask for the tests so far.'

(Pause again.)

'No, you should definitely not come, Sir. It's best if you are not directly linked to any of this, just in case...'

(Big pause.)

'No, no-one has been around here. Nothing suspicious at all. If there was a parked car within a mile I would have seen it. I'm sure this location is safe.'

(Short pause...)

'Yes, Sir. I am absolutely sure I was not followed from the farm.

'Well, yes. The car might have been seen by the old people in the end house. And I suppose I should have told you before but... but there was a... slight accident.

'No, no, Sir. Not in the car. The shed sort of blew up when I burnt it.

'Yes, Sir, I did indeed realise I should have expected it when I was on my backside after it had blown me over and the doors had flown over my head and I had dodged the side of the shed falling on me.

'Well, possibly. The old couple might have heard it. Their house is the nearest, Sir.

'Do you think that's really necessary, Sir?

'If you insist, Sir.

'I suppose you're right, Sir. They might tell their neighbours and we're too close now to arouse the wrong sort of interest.

'Yes, we're agreed. Do you want me to take care of them personally, Sir, or shall I send one of the others?

'Yes. One of them has seen me. The old man knows what I look like.

'OK. I'll send one of the others. Someone who will make sure it gets done properly.   .

'I know, I know, Sir. No names on the phone, Scorpion.

'No, Sir. I think everything should stay as it is. If we take care of the old couple then our secret remains safe.

'Don't worry. We can handle all the tests here. No-one will suspect anything out of the ordinary.

'Of course we will take all the necessary precautions. I know what this stuff can do!

'Yes, that's right. A few more days should still be fine for the rest of the tests, Sir. After that, we are ready for our first, er... *demonstration.* It could be as soon as the end of next week. But you haven't told me where yet.

'Really? That's an excellent place, Scorpion Sir. It's that sort of thinking that has got us this far.

'Ha, yes. Quite right. The money helped too.

'OK. I'll call with an update after we do the first major tests on it.

'Yes, Sir, and when the old folks have been taken care of.'

Inspector Copeland, Saturday 27 th. August.

Hesterman had driven the car off the lane, along a rutted farm track bordering the side of a field of yellow rape, then on a bumpier dirt track the length of the hedgerow on their right and the harvested field on their left until they reached their destination at the far end. The journey from the professors' house had taken less time than it had for Copeland to finish his Marlboro.

They sat in the car and looked at the shed.

'Mission complete,' said Copeland. 'One fallen down shed. Can we go now? I need some lunch.'

Hesterman was getting out of the car. 'Just a quick look,' he said.

Copeland climbed out of his side. 'Hmmph,' he said as he hauled himself out. 'I'm going for a pee.'

'Again, Inspector?'

'Yes, Danny. Again. When you get to sixty you will be making humph noises when you get out of cars and need to pee after every cup of tea,' said Copeland and made his way to the bushes behind the collapsed shed, then along the hedge a short way for a little decency.

Hesterman walked round the collapsed shed. He kicked one of the rusty side pieces and it crumbled. He thought about lifting it up but knew it would just snap. The rust had eaten through it too badly. The roof was in better condition than the sides and had buckled on top of some blackened farm machinery. He looked around? Where were the doors? They must have rotted long ago, he thought, and been taken away as scrap.

'Hey, Danny! What's this stuff?' shouted Copeland pointing into the bushes.

Hesterman skirted the fallen shed and joined Copeland. He looked where Copeland was looking. There were three waist high mounds of black shards resembling broken pieces of dark slate. A wheelbarrow lay, upturned, next to the furthest mound.

'Not sure,' said Hesterman. 'Maybe some sort of waste from whatever is grown here? Can't think what else it could be. Then again, I'm a copper, not a farmer.'

'Just curious,' shrugged Copeland and started walking back to the car.

Hesterman considered collecting some of the black shards but thought better of it. What would he do with them? Send them off to forensics with a note saying 'Found on a farm and unrelated to any current enquiries?' He followed Copeland.

'And for my second discovery,' said Copeland, pointing at the hedge, 'I give you shed doors.'

Hesterman's mouth fell open. The doors were impaled into the hedgerow, ten yards further back down the track than where the car was parked. 'How the hell did they get there?' he said.

'Simple, Sergeant! Explosion,' said Copeland, slapping Danny Hesterman on the back. His good humour was short lived when realised what he had deduced. A dissolving man, five hundred inexplicable pounds, a hidden key, and now an explosion. He went back to the car and flopped onto the seat, his legs still out of the car. He bent his head as far to his knees as his stomach would allow and clasped his hands behind his neck.

Hesterman put a hand on his shoulder. 'Larry? Sir? Are you alright? Feeling sick or something?' he asked.

'Shit, shit, shit,' said Copeland. He sat up and leaned the side of his head against the head rest. He opened his eyes and looked at Hesterman. 'You know, Danny,' he said, 'my D.C.I. sent me here because he thought it was a waste of time and he could piss me off. I didn't mind that, as long as I got back for my usual Sunday golf. Now we have an explosion to add to the key and the five hundred pounds. It looks like an actual case.'

'What five hundred pounds?' said Sergeant Danny Hesterman.

'I'll tell you later. First, let's go and have a look at those shed doors and see if we can see signs of an explosion. They may have just been taken off and dumped there,' said Copeland, knowing if someone was going to dump corrugated iron doors then they would dump them as close as possible and not haul them fifteen yards first.

His suspicions were correct. One side of the doors were blackened and the bolts that had held the door on its hinges had been sheered clean. 'Better radio in and get a forensic team down here,' said Copeland, glumly.

'Yes, Inspector. I'll also get a uniform sent out to take a full statement from the old professors and to track down the farmer and get a statement from him too. Maybe he was storing petrol in here and it blew up somehow? Who knows? But it might take some time for forensics to confirm anything. It's Bank Holiday weekend for one thing. And, to be honest, forensics hasn't been quite so reliable since it was outsourced.'

It was a less than jovial Copeland on the journey back to town. He did not engage Hesterman in conversation of any kind. Copeland only emerged from his silence to moan about the bloody hot weather (Is it always this bloody hot here? Has nobody up north heard of air conditioning?) , the bloody insects (Been bloody bitten again! Look at the size of that bugger I just killed sucking my wrist!), the bloody pollen (Three bloody handkerchiefs I've got through! My nose has been bloody streaming since we left town!), bloody Earl Grey tea (Who would drink that bloody stuff? Do they put dead bloody rats in it?) and complain how bloody starving he was – more than once. Hesterman drove in silence and did not raise the matter of the five hundred pounds and hoped revisiting the Brothers Karamazov would cheer Copeland up.

When flat green fields surrendered to a new housing estate and they passed the brown sign saying 'Boston historic market town', Copeland slapped his hand on the dashboard.

'Right! That's it!' he said angrily. 'Sergeant, we are going to lunch. Now! That's an order! I know just the place. And when we get there you can contact your Inspector and tell him S.O.15 will require your services for the rest of the day. The bloody Karamazov's can wait. I need a pint.'

'Right you are, Sir. Town centre is it?' said Hesterman, wise enough not to protest and glad Copeland hadn't told him it was his round.

Inspector Copeland and Sergeant Hesterman go to the pub.

The Happy Jack was exactly as Copeland had remembered it. Twenty four hours had not changed it at all. He instantly cheered as he went through the door and saw the unwelcoming plastic green seating, reminiscent of a synthetic church pew, stretching the complete length of the pub down the long wall to his left. There were the same square wooden tables he remembered so fondly, in a neat row between the green plastic and the bare wooden seats.

The large screen TV on the narrow far wall was still on and still silent, and devoid from the clutter of subtitles. The slate grey flooring looked modern and may have been out of place were it not for the stains, some of which Copeland suspected might be blood.

A pool table half blocked the entrance and they had to wait until some sort of crucial shot had been made and the white ball thudded against two side cushions before edging its way into a pocket.

'Jolly good shot, old chap,' said Copeland as he steered his stomach around the table.

The bar itself was equally welcoming with a mock oak front and damp bar towels haphazardly strewn on top. The bar towels added to the ambience by emitting stale beer odours. There was a good array of beers, though, and that was enough for Copeland.

Besides the two young pool players dressed in tee shirts which revealed swastika tattoos on their biceps, there was only a quartet of bald fifty-somethings playing dominoes on the table beneath the TV. They had stopped and stared when the two police officers had entered, then wordlessly returned to their game. The occasional click of dominoes and chunk of a pool ball being struck resonated in the silence. Conversation was not on these men's agendas.

The barman was wiping pint glasses with a stained tea towel. He was as tall as Copeland, but leaner and with a gaunt, angular face and a long nose. His sharp looks were heightened by the way he parted his short black hair down the middle. His thick ear rings helped give him his less than endearing look.

He looked up from the pint glass and into Sergeant Danny Hesterman's eyes. 'Hello, Danny,' he said, monotone.

'Hello, Bill,' said Danny.

'You're not welcome here,' said barman Bill.

Copeland had wondered why Hesterman had protested once they had parked and headed for the Happy Jack. He had even resorted to tugging the back of Copeland's jacket just before they had entered. This pub and the police were not friends. Maybe there had been too many customers done for drunk and disorderly, or maybe a bar fight had been broken up with unusual police aggression?

'The Inspector and I just want a bite to eat and a drink,' said Danny.

'Find somewhere else, then,' growled barman Bill and returned his gaze to the glass.

Copeland had to intervene. 'You have no lawful reason to refuse sustenance to two members of Her Majesty's Constabulary,' he said.

Bill pointed to a sign above his head which said the establishment had the right to refuse service to anyone it deemed. He glared at Copeland.

'Hang on,' he said, abandoning the growl and returning to his monotone. 'You were in here yesterday, weren't you?'

'Correct. I had the gammon and a very nice chat with some of your patrons,' said Copeland with a hint of pride.

'I remember. You're alright, you are. I'll serve you. Maybe you can talk some sense into this young bleeding heart commie bastard,' said Bill, pointing the pint glass at Danny.

Copeland nodded. 'I will endeavour to do my best. He is a sergeant and, as you heard, I am an inspector. I can always pull rank on him,' he said with a theatrical laugh. 'Ha, haa!'

Barman Bill put the glass down and leaned on the bar. 'So what can I get you,' he said. 'All our ales are good English ales here! No foreign muck!'

Copeland was spoilt for choice... Guinness? Carlsberg? Stella? San Miguel? Which of these good English ales would he choose?

'Two pints of Boston Best please, my good man. And the menu for luncheon, if you would be so kind,' said Copeland.

Pints poured and money for them paid, they sat as far away from the bar as they could, which was not very far and risked them being hit with the back stroke of a pool cue. Copeland sat on the green plastic bench seat facing the door, throwing his jacket on the seat alongside him. He scraped the majority of the generous head off his pint, swallowed half the glass in one go and leaned over the table. Hesterman met him halfway.

'What the hell was that about? How come you are so unwelcome here? Most places make a fuss of the fuzz!' said Copeland, barely audibly.

'He's my father-in-law,' said Hesterman.

Copeland did not how to respond. He opened his mouth twice and nothing came out, then managed, 'And why doesn't he like you?'

'It's my name,' said Hesterman. 'He thinks it sounds German.'

'And he doesn't like the Germans? Because of the war? That's a long time ago.'

'No, not the war. Because of the EU. He probably likes the Germans most. He really hates the French.'

'Oh, I see,' said Copeland. 'Like that is it? Still, you can't blame him about the French, though'. He picked up the menu and settled back in his seat.

Copeland had just given their order to Bill and returned to his seat with his second pint when there were new arrivals. How nice, thought Copeland, it's my two new neighbours from the hotel. And they are still wearing those raincoats and hats and it hasn't rained after all! What a coincidence they should come in the same pub. After all, he had only found this unique watering hole because he had been on his way to search Popov's bedsit.

'Shit! Don't turn round!' he whispered to Hesterman.

Hesterman immediately turned round. What else can you do when you are specifically told not to?

Hesterman spun back to Copeland. 'What?' he said.

One of the pool players was lining up his cue to take a shot. The butt of the cue blocked the entrance. The taller of the two newcomers grabbed it and pushed it out of the way so the smaller man could pass. The taller man followed, only letting the cue from his grasp when he too had rounded the inconveniently situated pool table.

'What the..?' protested the pool player, standing up and revolving to look at the two new arrivals, who were casually sauntering to the bar.

Hesterman had leaned across the table and was about to speak, but Copeland raised a finger, widened his eyes and gave a subtle shake of his head. Hesterman looked over his shoulder at the two men at the bar. The pool player, backed up by his playing partner, had walked behind them. He had flipped the pool cue and was holding the end like a cosh. The two raincoat men at the bar seemed oblivious to the approaching pool players.

'Two pints of Guinness, please,' said the shorter raincoat man with perfect elocution, taking his fedora off his head and slowly placing it on the bar.

The cue wielding pool player poked a finger into the shoulder blade of the taller raincoat man, who unhurriedly revolved to face his poking antagonist. Confronted by the front of tall raincoat man, the finger began jabbing him in his raincoat chest.

The cue wielding thug's friend was behind his shoulder with half clenched fists raised above his waist and heard his finger poking friend say, 'You can't aaargh...' as the raincoat man grabbed the poking finger with one hand and hit his arm across the elbow with the other. The former pool cue wielder was now on his knees with his hand behind his ear. His other hand had dropped the pool cue and was clawing the air.

His fist-ready friend darted forward and was greeted by three of raincoat man's fingers thrust straight into his throat. He collapsed gasping.

Bill the barman put the pint glass he was polishing down on the bar and signalled to the domino players to sit back down. They retired to their seats but continued to stare. They had subconsciously picked up their dominoes.

Barman Bill peered over the bar at his two regulars on the floor. 'You lads get yourself back to your game and let me deal with my new customers,' he said.

Tall raincoat man looked at smaller raincoat man, who nodded, and let go of the contorted pool player's hand. Still on his knees he picked the pool cue up, hesitated, then helped his friend up. They staggered back to a table near the entrance and gulped down their flat beers.

Barman Bill was leaning on the bar. He spoke to smaller raincoat man. 'You fellows live local?' he asked.

Smaller raincoat man replied with the refined Queen's English of a 1950s BBC continuity presenter. 'Sorry to say, Mr. Barman, we do not hail from these parts. I am from Moscow and my friend here is from...'

'Crimea,' said taller raincoat man, who had taken his hat off once more and was holding it across his chest, 'which is now part of The Motherland again. As it should be.'

'Russians, eh?' said Barman Bill.

'You are clearly a student of world geography,' said shorter raincoat man with a small head bow.

'And I know Russia isn't part of England, so you can find a drink elsewhere,' said Bill, leaning further over the bar. He gave a not so subtle 'get up' signal to the domino players. Chairs scraped as they stood.

Tall raincoat man calmly replaced his fedora on his head and, from the corner of his eye, watched the domino players stand.

Smaller raincoat man said, 'We are with them,' and pointed at Hesterman and Copeland. He half turned, gave a little wave and a big smile and called, 'How are you, Larry. Nice to be here having a drink together, isn't it? Just like old times!'

Copeland half heartedly returned the wave. 'Hello, Vasily,' he said, smiling falsely.

'You know him?' asked barman Bill, holding up a hand to stop the advancing domino players. His curiosity and 'nationalism' struggled. Curiosity won. He gestured for the domino quartet to return to their game and said, 'Two pints of Guinness coming up.'

Taller raincoat man took his hat off again and smoothed down his blonde hair.

Copeland swigged his Boston Best, leaned across the table and dragged Hesterman's ears close. 'He's ordered Guinness!' whispered Copeland.

'Er, yes, so I heard. You *know* him?' whispered Hesterman.

'Guinness takes time to pour .We have a bit of time to work this out. Get our stories straight, that sort of thing...'

'He's a Russian and you're on first name terms? They're KGB aren't they? No, no, it's FSB now isn't it?' whispered Hesterman, hurriedly.

'Neither. He's SVR. Russian intelligence service.'

'But..?'

'I know, Danny. They are FSB on TV, but FSB is the internal security, like our MI5. He's an overseas operative, like our MI6, and he's SVR.'

Still confused, Danny Hesterman nodded.

'Now listen, Danny. Careful what you say. Not a word about Popov, the key, the five hundred pounds or the farm.'

'What five hundred pounds? You said you...'

Copeland grabbed his wrist. 'Danny, I need you to be your normal self. Be a curious detective asking about why these guys are on your patch. You can dig in places I can't. On everything else agree with me and run with it, OK?'

'Understood, Larry,' hissed Copeland.

'And call me Inspector,' said Copeland.

Vasily was approaching their table, pint in one hand, fedora in the other, and no free hand to wipe the Guinness cream from his upper lip. He tossed the hat onto the seat so it landed on top of Copeland's jacket and stretched out his hand.

Copeland's inner voice was shouting. He had not heard it do more than mutter its disapproval for fifteen years, but then again, there was its use of his last name thing.

Look, Copeland! He's thrown his hat on top of your jacket so he can rifle through it when he picks it up later!

Copeland was about to think back that he knew that, but thought it unnecessary to have a conversation with his own brain.

'Detective Inspector Larry Copeland,' said Vasily, shaking his hand. 'Or is it Chief Inspector, or perhaps Commander by now?'

Sarcastic bastard! He knows very well you're still an inspector, Copeland.

'Major Vasily Goraya! So nice to bump into you. Please sit. Join us,' said Copeland, standing.

'I am a colonel now, but I am still Vasily to old friends like you, Larry,' said Vasily, removing the rain coat and, seemingly without looking, managed to toss that on top of Copeland's jacket too.

The bastard's a colonel now!

'And who is your friend, Larry?' asked Vasily.

'My apologies, Vasily. This is Detective Sergeant Hesterman of the local constabulary. He is my chauffeur for the day.'

Vasily shook Hesterman's hand. 'And where have you been chauffeuring my friend Larry to today, Sergeant?'

And so the games begin!

'Just here and there,' said Hesterman releasing Vasily's hand.

Vasily placed his Guinness on the table and sat. Copeland slid into his seat. They looked at each other. *Why do they always do this stare-you-out sparring first?*

'I have come to see you, Larry,' said Vasily.

How the hell did he know I was here? And if he knew I was here he must know why I am here. And it's no coincidence here's in the pub right across the street from Popov's bedsit! Don't rise to the bait Copeland – play this out.

'I saw you this morning, Vasily. Your friend spoke but you did not turn round. You are staying in the same hotel. In the next room. What are the odds?' said Copeland.

Vasily smiled.

Slimy Russian snake!

'I did not know it was you, Larry, or I would have greeted you with the utmost warmth, old chap,' Vasily said, adding a hollow laugh. 'But let me introduce my more gregarious friend. Gentlemen, this is Nikolay Ivchenko. He is my... chauffer.'

Introductions and handshakes all round were made and Vasily raised his glass and said, 'Zazdarovye!' and they all swallowed a mouthful of beer.

'I thought you Russians said 'nostrovia' for 'cheers', Vasily,' said Hesterman.

Good! That's the sort of stupid comment that will convince them he's just a local cop and they might let their guard down. Well done Hesterman.

'Ha, ha, Sergeant Hesterman,' said Vasily, 'you watch too much Hollywood. We say nostrovia when we are thanking someone at the end of a meal, or perhaps when they have bought us a drink. You may guess, but Larry has never heard me say it! Ha! I suppose, Sergeant, you also think Russians go around slapping people on the shoulder and giving them big Russian bear hugs?'

Hesterman laughed. It was a real laugh. 'To be honest, Vasily, I did. Just like...'

Oh, shit, Copeland! Danny's not used to drinking at lunch time! He's going to tell them about Alexei and Ivan!

'...TV,' finished Hesterman.

Phew!

Hesterman became serious and lowered his voice, knowing the pool players would hear every word and, behind him, his father-in-law, Barman Bill, would have moved as far as he could to their end of the bar. 'So you are here looking for the Inspector?' said Hesterman. 'And why is that?'

Yes, why is that?

'Larry and I go back a long way. Back when I was still KGB,' said Vasily and paused to read any reaction from Hesterman. There was only a nod of encouragement to continue. 'We had our differences in the past,' continued Vasily, obligingly, 'but that is all water under the bridge and off the back of a duck. We can't get the good old days back when we Soviets were trying to bring equality to all the world's downtrodden workers.'

Or the good old days when we at Special Branch stopped the KGB from taking over organised crime!

'Come on, Vasily,' said Copeland. 'We may have had a few drinks together once upon a time, but we were never bosom pals. What the hell is the SVR doing here?'

Shut up, Copeland! His inner voice hit volume eleven on a ten point scale.

'Having a drink,' replied Vasily, turning to him. He took another sip from his Guinness. Taller, blonde raincoat SVR man nudged him. He wiped the cream from his lip.

'We are here as your friends,' said Vasily. 'Yes, we had... some minor differences in the past, and I know there are... tensions between my country and the west, but you and I have always been... 'straight', as you say. We may not always have been completely open with each other, but you and I have never lied to each other, Larry.'

The brain volume went to a four. *That's true. You may have deceived me and I certainly deceived you on more than one occasion, but we never actually lied. And there were times when you helped us and we helped you – like when...* His brain searched and found nothing to complete the thought. It went on silent mode.

'We need to speak privately,' said Vasily. He spoke in Russian to taller raincoat man, Nikolay. Then he spoke to Hesterman. 'You can stay Sergeant Chauffeur,' he said.

SVR agent Nikolay went to the bar where Bill was watching. Nikolay produced a wad of notes from his raincoat pocket, pulled four from the restraining elastic band and placed them on the bar. He said something to Bill which Copeland could not hear. Bill replied. Nikolay removed one more note and put it on the bar. Bill picked the notes up and put them in his pocket, then gave a thumbs-up sign to the domino players before disappearing through the door behind the bar. The domino men were watching Nikolay walking towards them. He methodically placed a note on the table in front of each of the men. He said something to them. They put their dominos on the table, face down, picked up the notes, put them in their pockets and left the pub without another word.

Nikolay was now walking the length of the bar to where the pool players sat, still nursing their injuries. As he neared them, they both held out a hand ready for the money.

Nikolay leaned over their table and stared at them.

They looked at each other and rushed out the door.

'Good,' said Vasily once Nikolay had returned to his seat across the table from him. 'Now we can talk.'

Copeland's brain woke up as if it had drunk a quadruple espresso.

The guy with the coat – Nikolay – he must be armed! That's why he's kept his coat on when it's sweltering. If you don't tell them what they want then you'll be out the back with a bullet in your brain! In me!

'Just shut up!' snapped Copeland.

'Larry?' said Vasily.

Copeland hesitated. Where the hell was his brain when he needed it. 'Sorry, Vasily. I was talking to the Sergeant. I thought he was going to interrupt. Again!'

Saved you there, Copeland! You owe me one. Now about the gun...

'You are here regarding a man name Jakab Popov,' said Vasily as if it was common knowledge, and Copeland's brain went very, very quiet. 'Please do not even attempt to deny it,' continued Vasily. 'We know he is claiming to be Bulgarian but he is really a Chechen terrorist. We Russians have a special interest in Chechen terrorists, as you know. We also know he attended the hospital here and they treated him for burns from a caustic substance. You were sent here on Thursday. No doubt you used yesterday to search Popov's accommodation, which is just over the road from here.'

How do they know all this? But listen carefully Copeland. They said something not quite right there. What was it?

'And no doubt you have spent today tracking down his associates and where he might be now. We know he must be on the run. The question is: has he got the Nosoi with him or is it somewhere else?'

That was it! They did not know he was in the hospital!

But Copeland had so many questions he could not even begin to count how many. The one that came out was: 'Nosoi?'

'That is what we called it. Do you know the story of Pandora's box? The story says when she opened the box, all the terrible things which affect our world came out. The Nosoi were the worst. Terrible demons that brought plague, disease and suffering. They were demons of pestilence, Larry. The Soviet Union made new Nosoi. We made it thirty kilometres south of Grozny.'

Colonel Vasily Goraya, SVR, stopped. He waited for the revelation to sink in.

Copeland and his brain were back on the same page. *Why is he telling you this, Copeland?* 'Why are you telling me this?' Copeland asked.

Vasily smiled. He sat open palmed. 'I think you can guess, but one thing at a time,' he said. 'Yes. We in the Soviet Union made a chemical weapon. A terrible mistake and against all treaties and conventions, I know. But what is it you British say? We did not have the benefit of hindsight. The Warsaw Pact had been falling apart for decades. Lech Walesa was stirring the unions in Poland, and the Poles have hated the Russians for a thousand years. Czechoslovakia, as it was then, had democracy in its soul from before the last war and they were listening to that playwright Havel. Romanians hated Ceausescu, etcetera, etcetera. We knew once the Pact was over NATO would have all the cards. And what if the other countries joined NATO? We couldn't contemplate that. We thought Russia would be dead. The Americans would bomb us and roll over our borders once we had lost our allies. We had to have a new strategy. Nuclear was the last resort, but we needed something that could stop tanks without destroying our own Motherland.

'Our scientists worked on a new weapon. In its liquid state it was safe, unless you physically touched it. Once the liquid heated up, say by something as simple as an electric device or simply pouring it on a heat source such as a radiator, then it turned to gas. If you touched the liquid it would dissolve tissue. If you breathed in the gas it would dissolve tissue in the lungs. After the first tests, our scientists saw what it did. It was like a disease that ate the body until there was nothing left. So they called it The Nosoi. After a while it was just called Nosoi.

'Of course, no one conceived the USSR itself would fall apart, but once it did it happened fast. The facility and the Nosoi were, on September 6 th 1991, suddenly in another country. In the laughably named *Republic* of Chechnya! Dudayev's rebels didn't just storm the Supreme Soviet in Grozny, they took over every government building in the whole province. The scientists were ethnic Russians and ethnic Russians did not do well. We didn't tell our new president, Yeltsin, but our special forces went in to recover everything from the facility, but it had all gone and the scientists' bodies had been left where they lay. All the Nosoi that had been made already and all the scientists' notes were nowhere to be found. We in the KGB tried to find where the Nosoi had gone. I was one of them who tried, but the whole country had turned on its head. It was a madness of power-grabs, infighting and distrust. Two months later, we gave up looking.

'Then the first Chechen war came and we invaded. We managed to interrogate some of the leaders that we managed to take alive. We pieced together what had happened. Most of this terrible Nosoi weapon and the scientists' notes had been sold to an arms dealer from The Middle East in exchange for conventional arms. We thought the Chechen rebels kept some, but when we invaded they did not use it. Then we invaded the second time and they did not use it. We expected them to. Their armaments were low and the Americans had also stopped supplying them after Dagestan had been invaded by the so-called Islamic International Brigade, yet they still did not use Nosoi on our forces. History says Grozny was soon taken and the war was over in a matter of months, but you and I know it went on for years with partisans attacking our troops everywhere. Yet still they did not use the Nosoi, even when facing certain defeat, and even though all other acts of terror were not beyond them – our train stations, the theatres, even the schools.

'And do not tell me we did terrible things to them. I know. I was there. When two peoples live on hate, anything is possible. And it was. But still they did not use the Nosoi. Why not? Maybe they had sold everything to somewhere or someone in The Middle East, or maybe a leader had hidden it and then died or been captured. Who knows? No-one... not until now, Larry.'

Vasily fell silent. He gradually reached for his beer and took several small sips. His swallowing could be heard in the utter silence. A car went by outside. A radio started blasting a pop song from the kitchen.

'Oh, dear,' muttered Hesterman.

He's just told us how a bloody lethal gas has ended up here and all you can say is 'oh, dear'! I know I ordered you not to give anything away Danny Hesterman, but really?

Copeland had many concerns. How had the Russians found out he was here? How had they found out about Popov? Surely it was no coincidence they had checked into the same hotel, was it? How had they found Popov's address? Surely they had picked the lock and searched his bed-sit? How come they knew Popov had been to hospital yet did not know he was still there? And, most puzzling of all, why were they being so honest?

'I have a lot of questions, Vasily, and a lot of concerns,' he said. 'But my main concern is getting to the loo as quickly as possible. Excuse me a minute.' He shuffled out of the seat and grabbed his jacket from underneath Vasily's coat and hat. Now Vasily rifling through his pockets and finding the Snauzer key was one less problem.

Once alone, he had another quick check to make sure he had no 'symptoms'. He saw nothing unusual when he leaned to peer over his stomach. It helped cheer Copeland a little. It had been twenty four hours since a possible 'infection'; or perhaps contamination would be a better word after what he had just heard. He used the time his body took to expel the first pint of Boston Best to think and devise a plan.

He was still drying his hands on paper towels when he returned to the bar. He shoved the used paper towel into his jacket pocket; that would hinder their search if they tried. With luck, they might think he put the paper towel in that pocket on purpose to cover something and when they tried a spot of pick-pocketing, they would go for that pocket and ignore the breast pocket and the key.

'All is well, Larry,' said Vasily as Copeland sat down. He raised an eyebrow. 'You are not hot in your jacket?'

'Must have gone a bit chilly after hearing your story!' laughed Copeland. 'Have I missed anything?'

'No. Sergeant Hesterman was just helping us out and telling us where we could get some decent food in this town,' said Vasily, knowing Copeland would know he had been checking if Hesterman really was a local.

'OK, Vasily, tell me the answers to all my questions,' said Copeland, mainly because he had not been able to develop a plan other than have another pint.

A door opened and Bill's head stuck out. 'Can I bring your food now?' he called.

Hesterman had never seen his father-in-law so light on his feet. He danced across with their meals, their cutlery, their salt and pepper, and then the mustard and second pint Copeland asked for. Finally, the door behind the bar closed again.

Copeland ate his salty gammon, oven chips and tinned peas. He had enjoyed it yesterday, so why not the same again? Better still, he would not have to keep stopping to ask Vasily questions. Asking him to answer them all had turned out to be a good plan after all and, besides, Vasily had always liked to hear the sound of his own voice.

'Very well, Larry. I'll answer all your questions,' said Vasily. 'The Russian Government has authorised the sharing of this information because if this Nosoi is used in an attack it could come back on us. We also think our embassy will be Popov's target. Yes, he could use the Nosoi and wipe out everyone in a tube station or a department store, but Chechen's hate Russia with a vengeance, so we think the embassy must be his target. Needless to say, what I have told you, along with the few scientific notes we had, has all been conveyed to your Government, along with the governments of the other members of the UN security council. We are not ashamed: it was the USSR who made this abomination, not the Russian Federation!

'As for your second question – you do not have a mole. Don't waste your time looking for one when you need every resource to track down Popov and his fellow terrorists. Our knowledge comes from intercepting communications. Don't look worried Larry. You may eat in peace. It wasn't anything to do with you.

'Your next question would be about how we knew Popov went to the hospital and where he lived. Now, remember I am really a cultural attaché at the embassy and have diplomatic immunity, but I will just say that the security on the hospital's computer system is not all it should be.

'Finally, and I think this should wrap it up, as you British say, we have a better access to Bulgarian data bases than you in the Metropolitan Police, Larry. We have seen what Popov looks like, and know his height and date of birth and so on. Don't ask me how many people they had working on this at SVR and FSB headquarters, but we know his Bulgarian residency papers were fake. He is not a Bulgarian. His photograph and height match the description we have for a known Chechen terrorist – though we do not have a definitive photograph of this terrorist so the face matching software was not conclusive that he and Popov are one and the same. None-the-less, his fake identity, the Nosoi nature of his burns and the fact he has gone on the run all indicate we have 'the real McCoy' on our hands. I am getting good with these little phrases, aren't I? I like that one, especially... the real McCoy! I must find out where it came from!

'But I digress. To allay your fears, let me tell you we will not hamper your search. We are returning to London as soon as we have got our belongings from the hotel. We have found Popov's flat but we could not get in. Did you get in?'

Hesterman had been dumfounded by the whole encounter. When he walked into the pub all he had expected was an argument with his father-in-law and a quick exit. He had been turning his soggy green salad leaves over with a fork while Vasily was speaking, but now he stopped. He did not dare look at Copeland. Vasily had shot a question at him from nowhere.

Copeland finished chewing a chunk of gammon and laid his knife and fork down on his plate. He leaned on the table and meshed his fingers together.

'Complete disclosure, Vasily,' he said. 'As you said, we have never lied to each other. I found five hundred pounds in his bedsit. He had hidden it under the carpet and put the mattress on top. It is in my other suit back at the hotel. I was thinking about keeping it quiet and using it for a little holiday. I reckoned however Popov had got that money it was undoubtedly not legal, so what the hell! I also found some photos at the hospital showing his hand dissolving. He had gone to their A & E and they had coated it with iodine or something and bandaged it up. He never returned to the hospital. But he didn't go back to get his five hundred pounds either, so I reckon he just ran and went right off the grid.'

Vasily seemed to take the bait. 'That money must have been to finance him while he planned his attack. Thank you for sharing that. Naturally, we have seen the photographs of Popov's hand, and his arm, taken by the hospital. They are what confirmed he had been handling Nosoi. He is corroding in just the same way as those whose skin came into contact with the liquid when we – I mean the Soviets – were making it. I cannot believe the hospital did not admit him, but we have scoured their computers and he has no admission recorded. Now he is gone. I hope your people find him soon – before he unleashes this terrible gas and kills thousands.'

Copeland nodded reassuringly and put a thumb up for good measure before he went back to his chips. Hesterman kept his head down, turning his lettuce over.

Vasily stood, picked up his hat and coat, said, 'Until we meet again, Larry,' and left with taller raincoat man Nikolay behind him.

'How's your salad, Danny?' Copeland asked nonchalantly.

'It's shit, but I wasn't going to order anything my mother in law had actually cooked,' answered Hesterman, glancing at the door closing behind the Russians. He looked at Copeland

and hissed, 'What do you make of that? This Popov guy is a terrorist with a load of poison gas!'

Copeland spoke with a full mouth and Hesterman could barely make out what he said. He thought Copeland might have said, 'Russian SVR always talk bollocks.'

Doctor Beth Spencer.

The radiologist had taken half an hour to tell Beth what he had found. He had insisted she review all the MRI results he had taken pains to prepare: every enhanced photo and Himalayan profile graph. She had listened as he repeatedly explained how interpreting an MRI was an art, and in cases like Popov's it had taken the artistic skill of a Renoir.

The tedious explanations had finally led to the conclusion that Popov's arm was irrecoverable but the rest of his body was completely unaffected. Or as the radiologist had put it: The arm is truly knackered in a bad way but on the bright side the rest of him is tip top. Beth doubted Popov would be celebrating any time soon.

The detailed analysis had at least confirmed what she already knew. The necrosis, the dissolving, *the disintegration* of Popov's arm was continuing not only up the skin of his arm, but inside it too. The bones were resisting, but not much else was. Two new pieces of information were interesting. After penetrating the dead layers of outer skin, the nerves had been attacked first, explaining Popov's lack of pain. Nerve disintegration was ahead of other tissue, and the disease seemed to be using the nervous system as a main line for its advance. The second new finding from the MRI analysis was that Popov's blood vessels were progressively being closed, like a squeezed straw, as the necrosis moved up his arm, which explained why he was not bleeding, but did increase the risk of other complications such as gangrene.

The radiologist had kept stressing how certain he was that this was a disease related to the flesh eating disease necrotising fasciitis, and even if the pathology department had ruled out the usual bacteria then they should still be looking for something similar and something incredibly more aggressive.

When she went to the pathology department, the first thing Dr. Canning told her was that he and his team were sure this was not a bacteria and nothing to do with necrotising fasciitis. The second thing he told her was how unhappy he and his team were to find their virus protection suits had been loaned to Popov's nurses.

Canning's team had worked late and kept testing until they found something – anything –to explain what was happening to Popov and, equally importantly, to determine if it was transmissible to others.

What they had found made some sense and no sense at all. Beth was sat in front of a screen linked to a microscope. She guessed she was looking at one of the tissue samples she had taken from Popov the previous day, probably some of the muscle tissue. She watched as one cell after another started to shrink then explode, then the next ones started to shrink and explode in exactly the same way. A chain reaction of exploding cells.

Canning flicked a switch and she was looking at another sample. She recognised it as skin. She stared but nothing was happening. She waited. Still, she saw nothing. She swivelled and looked up at Canning.

'That's impossible!' she said. 'There's nothing there!'
'Exactly!' said Dr. Canning.

Ronaldo makes another call.

'Hello. It's me.

'Me, me. No names on the phone me.

'Yes, *that* me. We need you to do a job. We need an old married couple taken care of.

'Tomorrow.

'What do you mean, you're busy tomorrow?

'I know it's bank holiday Sunday. And?

'Well un-invite the family round.

'They may well be upset. I don't care. You are supposed to be committed to this.

'What do you mean, you may never see your mother again?

'Get caught? Go to prison? No-one is ending up in prison!

'No. I can't get anyone else. You are the best person for the job. I know you have done this sort of thing before and we need it done professionally.

'Yes, it does have to be tomorrow.

'Because Scorpion wants it done as soon as possible.

'Who's Scorpion? Scorpion is our leader. That's the code name he's using.

'I don't know why he's chosen that as his code name. Maybe it's because there's a lot of sand where he comes from. But he said it has to be done tomorrow.

'I don't care what you tell your mother, or your aunts or anyone else you have invited round.

'Well let them have the barbecue without you.

'I don't care who prepares the salad. Surely you are not the only person who can prepare salad. Now stop whining about this, Fatima, you are doing this job for Scorpion and you are doing it tomorrow.

'I know I said no names, Fatima, but I'm starting to lose my cool a bit here.

'No, it's not alright for you to use my name as well.

'I know you don't want to do it. I know you have a family barbecue planned. I also know that if you refuse to do it then I will have to inform Scorpion and you know what the consequences for you might be then.

'That's right Fatima. We would have to terminate you.

'Good. I'm glad I finally have your agreement.

'We need two old folks taken care of.

'Why? Because Scorpion says so, that's why.

'Yes, an elderly couple – an old woman and an old man.

'Glad you don't see a problem. Oh, and there's a dog.

'No, it's just a little dog.

'Yes. The dog as well. The dog does have to go too. It may arouse suspicion if the dog is still around after they've, you know, gone.

'What? You are ok with an old man and an old woman, but not a dog?

'I don't care how you feel about dogs, Fatima. Your instructions are to take care of the dog as well.

'Yes, that's right. Termination.

'I have everything you need to do the job here.

'What do you mean, *where's here?* The secret base, of course.

'You didn't know there was a secret base? We said we were setting up a secret base months ago!

'Yes. That secret base.

'Yes, I know you know it's a disused airfield, but we're calling it The Secret Base now!

'No, I'm not telling you where it is. It's a *secret base!*

'Well, I am there now. Well, close. Can't get a decent signal there. I have to keep going outside. Yes, the stuff is here. And it works. It's in the fridge. Can you believe it?

'Yes, I know we need a name for it.

'I know we can't keep calling it *the stuff,* but...

'No! I've told you before, we are not calling it that. Not anymore.

'Look, Fatima, for the hundredth time, we are going to think of a new name for it. A name that everyone will remember!

'Stop! It is definitely *not* a good name. Now, back to tomorrow.

'Just outside Boston.

'No, there is no airline ticket for you to get there. It's not *that* Boston. The old people live near Boston, Lincolnshire.

'To be honest, Fatima, I have no idea why they would want to live there either.

'Yes, Fatima. You will need your car.

'Yes, you'll get your petrol money.

'Diesel then. Whatever.

'Oh no! Not the barbecue again! Look, if you get here early enough you can get there, take care of the old people...

'Yes, and the dog. You can do the whole job and get back for your family get together before they even notice you're not there.

'Yes, maybe I was exaggerating and maybe they will notice there is no salad. Are you in or out, Fatima? And remember, you know what I mean when I say *out!*

'Right. Eight o'clock it is then. I'll save you some time and meet you at the A1 services just south of Peterborough. I'll be there with everything you need and I can give you the GPS co-ordinates for their house.

'Very well. I'm sure Scorpion will be pleased to hear that you won't let him down. See you tomorrow.'

Dr. Beth Spencer visits a patient.

Visiting time had started before Beth had got to the ward. Nurse Jones had said she understood why they needed to get into Popov's room, but had to consider the effect on families visiting their sick relatives and having them see a nurse and a doctor dressed for the Apocalypse might not be such a good idea. Beth had been forced to agree. The last thing the hospital needed was panicking relatives or the press banging on the doors, and seeing two people in full yellow anti-viral suits, looking like they were emerging from inside a nuclear reactor, might cause more than minor alarm.

She watched the visitors file-in, almost all of them were armed with books, newspapers, chocolate or drinks. Some were young and barely over the over twelve years old age limit, some were old and could do no more than shuffle along. They passed her and chatted about their days, TV, the inadequacy of hospital parking. Rarely did any use the hand sanitizer. Beth knew she had to get Popov moved. He was feet away from patients and the general public, separated only by a window and a flimsy door. And if he was contagious...

She shut out the voices and the distraction of passing visitors. She stared through the glass at Popov. He was sitting up in bed and had recently finished demolishing a tray of food by using a spoon with his good hand. He saw her looking and gave her a smile and a wave. From where she stood, he looked fine. Circle to the other side of his bed and unwrap that hand and arm and he did not look fine at all. She smiled and waved back.

Pathology had made some discoveries, two of which she had viewed herself. Cell destruction was not a surprise; the naked eye could see that by looking at Popov's hand. The lack of anything on the second monitor was more surprising. His arm was not being destroyed by bacteria. There were no bacteria. None at all. She knew everyone's skin is usually covered in bacteria, most of which live with us quite happily and generally aid our health by attacking other, invasive bacteria. There was no trace of any of the usual symbiotic bacteria and no trace of invasive, harmful ones either. Whatever was killing Popov's cells had killed all the usual skin bacteria too.

The pathology department had made other disturbing discoveries, mainly thanks to a new biochemist who had recently joined the department and had tried some more unusual tests. They had found traces of formic acid, ether and hydrogen peroxide. In layman's terms these were the acid that causes pain from bee stings, a substance that was once used as anaesthetic and should oxidise as soon as it made contact with the air, and an ingredient in the most common antiseptics bought from any shop. This acid and the two corrosive substances were all present in the tissue samples the pathology team had studied, and none of these three substances seemed to diminish until all the cells in the sample were destroyed. Worse still, they were in their concentrated forms, infinitely beyond the diluted forms that man or nature made, and unimaginably more acidic and corrosive.

Then there were the enzymes. Common enzymes found in everyone's stomach to break up food were seen in abundance in Popov's samples once they had been stained. Lipases, as these enzymes were called, should be inside Popov, not on his skin. Beth had pointed out to the pathology team that the common thrush infection produced a lot of lipases, but thrush is fungal and they had already checked for common fungi. The team suspected there were other enzymes, and tested for all they could think of but without luck.

One final discovery was made on Popov's old samples, taken before Beth had arrived. On skin taken from his fingers, when he still had skin on his fingers, there were traces of glycerine. Beth suspected someone in the pathology team had heard they had had a visitor from the anti-terror unit to see Popov, and that had given them the idea to conduct the test. So they had found glycerine – as in nitro-glycerine; as in explosives.

The one positive thing the pathology team came up with was a plan to slow down Popov's deterioration and she needed to get into his room right now, but the plan was being held up by these visitors. Pathology also needed more samples.

Beth mentally recapped. Popov was seeping bee sting venom, an outdated anaesthetic, common disinfectant and common thrush enzymes. The trouble was, he was producing these in such pure forms meant that his body had no chance. Any living human cell that came into contact with Popov's exploding cells would no doubt suffer the same fate, and that meant just as Popov's cells were exploding one after the other, so would anyone else's which came into direct contact with them. His infected areas could not be touched by anyone else. If their skin touched his they could suffer his symptoms, and their body's cells would start exploding, one after the other, just as Popov's were – first their skin and then their entire bodies.

And speaking of explosions, she needed to contact Copeland and tell him about the residue of glycerine found on Popov's fingers. She lifted her phone from her pocket and turned to walk to the common room. She crashed into Tom Benson.

'Where the hell did you come from?' she said.

'Been standing here a few minutes. Didn't want to disturb you. You looked deep in thought,' said Benson.

'Sorry I bumped into you. Didn't see you down there,' she said and instantly knew that she had just been far from tactful. 'I mean... Oh, I'm sorry, Tom.'

Benson's quote finger pointed up. 'It's not the size of the dog in the fight, it's the size of the fight in the dog!' he said.

'Er, Snoopy or Scooby Doo?' she asked.

'Ah, ha! Got you! Mark Twain,' he said, but Beth did not join in with his good humour. 'Anyway,' he said, 'I spoke to Nottingham and warned them, but the interpreter is not answering his phone. I've left voice messages and texted him.' He leaned forward and whispered, 'Maybe he's infected?'

Beth put a finger to her lips and shook her head at Benson. 'I need to make some phone calls,' she said. He looked quizzical and she thought she owed him a brief explanation. 'I need to phone that SO15 officer, Inspector Copeland, and I need to try again and get Popov into a proper isolation facility.'

'Oh, dear. That all sounds rather bad,' he said. 'But tell Copeland we need the police to find the hand.'

Beth Spencer took three paces and stopped. 'What hand?' she said.

Two visitors were passing on their way out. They did not sanitise their hands. Benson moved in closer to Beth and dropped his voice again. She bent down so her ear was level with his cupped mouth.

'After ringing countless times, I finally spoke to the people in Nottingham who have Fayad's body. I warned them about him possibly being infectious. They have his body, but not his hand,' Tom Benson informed her.

Copeland and Hesterman eventually leave the pub.

Every time Hesterman had begun to speak, Copeland had said, 'Shush. I'm eating.'

Hesterman had eaten nothing. Hearing about a devastating chemical gas weapon called Nosoi had diminished his appetite, and a salad of out of date vegetables prepared by his mother in law had killed it completely.

Copeland finally finished his food, laid his knife and fork on the plate, wiped his mouth with a serviette and stood up. At last, thought Hesterman. But Copeland leaned across the table and poked a finger into Hesterman's shoulder. Hesterman winced and gave Copeland a stare. Copeland was pointing at him. Then Copeland pointed to his own eyes, then to his own chest. 'You watch me,' was Danny Hesterman's interpretation of Copeland's mime, so he pointed to his himself, then his eye, then at Copeland and nodded. *Why are we doing a mime?* he thought.

Copeland took off his jacket. He removed everything from all of his jacket and trouser pockets and put the contents on the table, making a pile with his wallet, spectacles case, warrant card, phone, cigarette packet, lighter, handkerchief, several paper towels and the Snauzer key. He opened the cigarette packet and emptied it out, then took a comb from his back pocket and placed it on top of the pile. He turned each of his pockets out and gave each one a shake. Hesterman copied him. He made his own pile with his warrant card, wallet, car keys, phone, notebook, pen and a small round silver object that looked like a watch battery. Before he could speak, Copeland's finger was on his lips.

'I need a smoke, Danny,' said Copeland, matter of factly, as he picked up the device, took it to the bar and slipped it under one of the damp bar towels.

They collected their things and left. Gathered outside were the pool-playing duo and the domino quartet. They all jostled to get back into the pub as soon as the police officers were through the door. Copeland lit his Marlboro. Sergeant Danny Hesterman could not contain himself.

'Was that a bug?' he blurted.

Copeland exhaled his smoke and his stress. 'Yes, Danny. That was a listening device. That Nikolay chap wasn't just the muscle – God knows, Vasily doesn't need protecting. While he sat there looking ever so quiet and ever so stupid, our friend Nikolay was slipping a bug into your pocket. Had to check he had not slipped one into mine too, though I had been careful to keep an eye on him and my pockets covered. Did you see how his hand was in his raincoat pocket for almost the entire time? He was cloning your phone too. Any call, text or anything on that phone can be heard by them now. Mine has special protections put in by our tech department. Just be careful what you say to your wife when you call her or Vasily and everyone at the SVR will know all your intimate business and what she's wearing for you when you get home.'

'How can you joke at a time like this?' said Hesterman. 'We have Russian spies bugging us, and a group of terrorists running round with a lethal chemical gas! This Nosoi stuff! It's a good job your boys have this Popov fellow locked up and can get some information out of the bastard!'

Copeland inhaled. A small convoy of cars went past. A mother pushed a buggy along and a kid on a bike swerved to avoid hitting Hesterman.

'We don't have him,' said Copeland. 'He's in the hospital.'

Danny's eyes widened. 'What?'

Copeland flicked ash and rested his backside on the window ledge in front of the huge flag of St. George. 'He's in the hospital,' he repeated, this time adding, 'He's heavily sedated, so don't worry.'

'But, but the Russians said...' stammered Danny but came to a halt.

'I know, Danny. They seemed to know a lot. Like about me being here and why, and that I had been in Popov's place – you didn't hear that by the way. They say they didn't get in, but they've searched it too. That's where they had just been when they saw us. They have hacked into the hospital computers but don't know he's there. They think he was seen and sent home, so he clearly hasn't been entered as an admission. NHS bureaucratic inefficiency might be a good thing after all. But sooner or later, some junior administrator will do their job and Popov will appear on the hospital system and the SVR will be back if we haven't moved him first.'

Copeland threw the cigarette down and squashed it under his shoe. 'Another thing, Danny,' he said. 'Whether it's KGB or FSB or SVR, the Russians are not usually the most honest intelligence service out there. I'm taking it with a bigger pinch of salt that I just put on my chips. Let's get to the car.'

'Yeah, right you are, Inspector,' said Hesterman, fishing the car keys from his pocket, 'and thanks for lunch by the way.'

'I didn't pay. I told your father in law you would.'

Danny Hesterman rushed back into the pub with his wallet already half open.

When Hesterman returned he found Copeland sitting on the bonnet of the car, looking at his shoes and with his phone pressed to his ear. When he saw Hesterman approach he gesticulated that he needed his notepad and pen. Hesterman gave him his pen and put the notepad down on the bonnet.

'You do realise I don't understand a word of that,' said Copeland into his phone.

'Who is it?' asked Hesterman, but Copeland waved the pen and shook his head. Hesterman shuffled his feet, passed the car keys from one hand to the other and waited.

'Well, I hope that works,' Copeland was saying. 'Now give me that name again.'

He wrote something down on a fresh page of the notepad. 'Got it. Now, I need to tell you something. We have reason to believe Popov may have been exposed to an extremely toxic chemical called Nosoi. And just one more thing – and this is important, Doctor Spencer – keep his name off the hospital system there and when you get him into another facility make sure he is not, I repeat not, entered onto their computer system. I'll do what I can to help you get him moved, but it's a matter of national security that his whereabouts remain secret.'

Copeland switched off his phone, tore the page out of the notebook, folded it and put it in his shirt pocket. 'Let's go and visit the Karamazov brothers again, Danny,' he said, almost with enthusiasm.

The Brothers Karamazov. Again. Saturday, 27 th. August.

On the way to pay the second visit of the day to the brothers Karamazov, Copeland reminded Sergeant Hesterman that he had signed The Official Secrets Act and told him all he knew. He had reduced Dr. Spencer's phone call explanations of Popov's condition to 'they've found something to do with bee stings and stuff that burns stuff and residue from explosives'. Copeland was disappointed that Danny had not heard of Usman Fayad because it meant there was yet one more loose end to chase and, thus, one more step away from the golf club carvery lunch, but he was relieved Danny did not ask if he really intended to use the five hundred pounds for a holiday.

When they arrived at the Karamazov's scrap yard, Hesterman had to sound the car horn before Alexei emerged from the little caravan carrying a full plastic bag in one hand and something smaller in the other. Hesterman got out of the car to speak to him and Copeland reluctantly followed.

'Here iz pazzport you vanted,' Alexei said, handing a passport to Copeland. 'And here iz all verkers information.' He handed over the bag.

Copeland put the bag on the floor and flicked to the last pages of the passport. It was Bulgarian and it was Jakab Popov's. He put the passport in his back pocket and picked up the plastic bag.

'You owz me ten pence for bag!' laughed Alexei.

Copeland did not smile but looked in the bag. 'What's this?' he said.

've no have files. Ve have peezes of paper to tell us vhere ze vorkers go. Place calls us and ve write down when zey vant us and how many vorkers zey vant. Ve take zee vorkers. Zey pay. Ve throw paper in waste basket. I empty basket and put papers in bag and give zem to you.'

Copeland looked in the bag again. 'So these are from the waste basket?'

'Yes! From ze *vaste* basket,' said Alexei, remembering to change the consonant this time. 'Zo zorry zey are, how you zay, crumpled.'

'And when we straighten them out, these papers will tell us where Popov has worked for the last few weeks?' asked Copeland.

'Ah, not exactly,' said Alexei, arms open wide. 'Papers vill tell you vhere vorkers vorked. Not vich vorkers vent to vot place. But there is something Ivan remember about your Mr. Popov. He never vork at veekends! You believe that? Poor immigrant man not vork at veekends? Ve had to persuade him to vork last veekend. He say NO! But Ivan say, you no vork then you no have place to live and he vorked. Vas there ready to get on minibus vith other vorkers. Vos right on time too. Ivan, he remember. He drove minibus.'

Copeland's brain was seizing up through lack of a lunchtime dessert and an absence of the letter 'w'.

'Right,' he said. 'Let's get this straight. This bag of crunched up papers will tell me how many of your workers went to a place and when, but not which workers went there?'

Alexei nodded. 'There iz list of vorkers in bag. Two pages. Fifty vorkers.'

'But Ivan remembers Popov because Popov refused to work at weekends and Ivan had to threaten him and he worked?'

Alexei nodded. 'But Ivan not threaten. Just say you get no home!' he said.

'I see, Alexei,' said Copeland, understandingly. 'There were no threats. Of course not. I understand. And Ivan drove the minibus that Saturday. Is this last Saturday or one before that?'

'Ah, I zink Ivan he say last Saturday,' said Alexei.

'And where did he go in the minibus last Saturday?'

'I go ask Ivan. He having crap,' said Alexei and disappeared into the caravan.

Copeland turned to Hesterman. 'They have a toilet in there?'

Hesterman shrugged. 'Probably not. I doubt Ivan is actually house trained.'

Alexei reappeared. 'Zey go to vork on farm,' he said.

'Where?' asked Copeland.

Alexei had a pained look. 'It facking stinks in there, so this better be the last question 'cos I'm not going in to ask him anything else for at least half a bleedin' hour,' he huffed.

Copeland remained motionless until Alexei went back into the caravan. When he came out again his accent had been restored.

'Ivan he zay farm vos near place called Ashburton. He no remember farm name. It vill be on papers in bag,' he said, pointing at the plastic carrier.

From the corner of his eye, Copeland had seen Hesterman stare at him with surprise when Alexei had said where the farm was. Copeland kept his poker face. It wasn't hard to look miserable when each new fact added more work to his schedule.

'And how did you get paid?' asked Copeland.

'Oh, bloody hell, Inspector,' said Alexei with a certain resignation as he turned to head back to the caravan once again. He opened the door, went inside, then instantly reappeared. 'What the fack you been eating, Ivan?' he shouted into the caravan. He continued shouting from the doorway, but with his head partially across the threshold. The two police officers could not hear distinctly, but this conversation was more than just one question and answer.

Hesterman whispered, 'He said a farm in Ashburton!'

'Yes, he did. Look disinterested and let me do the talking,' Copeland whispered back as Alexei, once again, approached them.

'Iz OK. I ask him all possible questions so I no have to go back in there, er, zer again,' he said. 'Ve not go to that farm before. Many farms have big machines and they not need human vorkers much zees days. Ivan say it was job with money in envelope and I remember now. Ve get envelope with money and note saying where and ven and how many vorkers. It was five vorkers and it voz a Saturday, last Saturday, zo there vos much money in envelope.' Alexei grinned. 'Yes! Much money! Ivan, he say he dropped vorkers off in field but he no see anyone. He go back before dark to get vorkers and they waiting by side of road. He say they filthy dirt and looked like they vork hard. Ivan not know what work voz. Ve get paid, ve not care.'

Alexei had stopped and Hesterman waited for Copeland to ask another question. What he asked shocked Hesterman.

'Do you know an Afghan kid named Usman Fayad?' said Copeland. 'Was he on the minibus to that farm?'

Alexei was more shocked than Hesterman. His eyes widened just before he spun round and bolted into the caravan.

'What the..?' began Hesterman, but Copeland was already striding towards the caravan door. He was banging on it when Hesterman reached the caravan's steps. There was a scraping sound from inside as Alexei barricaded the door with furniture.

'Fack off copper!' Alexei shouted through the door. 'We'll set the facking dog on you! We had nothing to do with what happened to that kid! We ain't murderers!'

Copeland calmly handed Hesterman the carrier bag and put his face near the door. 'I am not accusing you of killing him, Alexei,' he shouted through the door. 'I just want to know if Ivan took him to the farm that day.'

There was silence followed by muffled voices as the Brothers Karamazov conferred.

'He wasn't one of ours,' shouted Alexei through the key hole. 'Lived rough on the streets, he did, not in one of our places. He was always hanging around here wanting work and we had a lot of jobs on that day so Ivan took him along. Paid him good and proper like, though. Twenty quid!'

'Thank you, Alexei,' shouted Copeland. 'And it's good to hear your enterprise is not being held back by the minimum wage. We'll be going now. Shouldn't need to trouble you again. Just one more thing, Alexei – up the Orient!'

An incensed Alexei screamed back. 'Fack off copper, I'm a Millwall fan!'

Danny Hesterman did not want to spoil Copeland's mood and allowed him to laugh to himself all the way back to the car. Copeland opened the boot for Danny to put the carrier bag in.

'So this Fayad is dead, then? You didn't tell me that, Inspector,' said Hesterman, closing the boot.

'Didn't I?' said Copeland. 'Seems they found him down by the docks – you have docks here? Really? – down by the docks. His hand had been cut off. His body has been sent for an autopsy... hang on! What's this here?'

Copeland tried to squat down but the size of his stomach had other ideas, so he leaned on the car boot and lowered himself down as far as he could. Danny squatted effortlessly beside him.

'It seems we have a tracking device on the car, Danny,' said Copeland. 'Now... I wonder who could have put that there?'

Danny reached to pull the magnetic device off, but Copeland put his hand on top of his, stopping him.

'Let's leave it there until we find a suitable home for it. If you see a delivery van parked somewhere, pull up behind it. We can give this little bugger a new home and let my old friend, Comrade Colonel Vasily, track all the deliveries it makes for the next week, or at least until he works out it's not us he's tracking anymore. I told you, Danny! You can't trust them pesky Russians in the SVR!'

Dr. Beth Spencer visits Jakab Popov.

The last visitor had gone and Beth Spencer had given up trying to contact anyone at the Ministry of Health. At least she had spoken to Copeland and had made sure Tom Benson kept Popov off the computerised admissions register before she had climbed into an anti viral suit and gone into Popov's room.

Popov's sedatives had worn off. He had found the TV remote and was sitting up in bed flicking through channels. When she entered he muted the TV and looked at her quizzically, dropped the remote on the bed beside him and pointed up and down at the yellow suit.

'You go...whoooshh?' he said in his thick European accent as he pushed a straight fingered hand slowly towards the ceiling.

Beth pushed the trolley she had wheeled in to the end of his bed. He repeated the gesture and pointed at the suit again.

'Oh, rocket!' she said. 'Into space! Whoosh!' She shook her head. 'No, Mr. Popov. This suit is because of your arm.' She pointed at her suit then at his film-wrapped arm.

It took a moment for him to understand. Popov's smile vanished and he nodded very slowly.

She knew he would not understand hardly anything she said, but still felt she had to talk to explain things to him. At the very least, she hoped it would soothe him while she worked. She moved round the bed to the side where his crumbling, necrotising arm was. She lifted his hand in one of her gloved hands and started unpeeling the cling film with her other hand.

'I am going to take this off, Mr. Popov. Then we will place your hand and arm in the water I have brought in this baby bath,' she said loudly through the head-mask, hoping the bath she had ordered to be sent over from the maternity wing would be big enough and deep enough to immerse all of his arm. 'I have put some isopropyl alcohol in it to keep it sterile.'

He smiled at her as she cut and unwrapped, cut and unwrapped layer after layer. She smiled back at him each time she turned to pick up the scissors. She unwrapped the final layer very slowly, very carefully. Although the film had been designed not to stick, she still did not want to take any chances or tear off any more of Popov's shedding skin.

She froze. Why hadn't they thought of this before? Popov's skin was flaking. Skin was a major constituent of dust. Popov's skin was in the dust. And once it touched their skin, that skin might turn anyone into a Popov. Anyone touched by the skin floating in the dust could start necrotising – would start, cell by cell, organ by organ, to dissolve... What if they breathed it in? If what was happening to Popov's arm started in someone's lungs..? She felt herself getting hotter inside the suit. Where had he been? The accident and emergency waiting room. In a ward. How many shops, cafes, other enclosed places had he been in before he came to the hospital? Hundreds could be infected, and they could infect hundreds more. Get a hold of yourself Beth! Finish this first, then you can panic!

'Doctor?' said Popov, still smiling at her.

She snapped out of it. 'Nearly there, Mr. Popov. Nothing to worry about,' she said, wishing: if only that were true!

The final layer of film came off cleanly. Popov stopped smiling as soon as he saw his own arm. She feared he would go back into shock.

'Shiiiit!' he quietly said, proving he had learned some useful conversational English at least.

The arm was no worse than Beth had expected, but the hand was. All of Popov's finger bones were clearly visible and the rest of his hand had lost most of the tendons and muscles. His wrist was approaching the same state, with the wrist bones already showing. The forearm had lost nearly all of the skin and raw, red muscle fibres were splaying like an unravelling woollen scarf. The arm above the elbow had started losing skin and was red raw up to the middle of his bicep.

She decided she had other priorities now and did not have time to take fresh samples from the arm. Supporting the arm just below the elbow, she pulled the trolley closer. It was heavy with the bath of water on top and she wished she had found a free nurse to help her, but this was Saturday with Bank Holiday week end on top. She gradually hauled the trolley into position and lowered Popov's arm into the water. She puffed her relief.

'There you go, Mr. Popov.' she said. 'That should help.'

It might slow the spread down, but she knew it would not really help, not in the long run. They needed that interpreter to get here and get Popov's consent to an amputation. Once this necrosis had spread to his torso he would have no chance: his lungs and heart would soon be failing and death would soon follow. The amputation was his last chance.

'Thank you, Doctor,' he said and smiled at her again.

She reached across and squeezed his good shoulder. She could not believe this man was a terrorist. Were dying terrorists always this polite? No. He was just too genuine to be other than he seemed. Or he was very good at pretending.

'We are trying to get you moved to another hospital, Mr. Popov,' she said in her best patient soothing voice. 'We will be able to look after you there.'

He lifted his good arm and tenderly grasped her elbow. 'Thank you... doctor,' he said with a tear in his eye.

As she left the room, Beth felt tears run down her cheeks too. She knew he had probably not understood a word she had said.

As soon as she was through the door she ripped the suit off and threw it on the floor. She rushed over to the nurses' station, in no mood for conversation or explanations.

'Get some gloves on and get that suit under a shower,' she snapped. 'Now! That's a direct order from me and from Nurse Jones. I'm going to go and do my damnedest to get him moved into total isolation. I'm going to phone the Royal Free direct. Sod the Ministry of Health!'

Copeland Goes Home. Saturday 27 th. August.

Hesterman drove them back to the new police station. Together, he and Copeland briefed Inspector Bell, who agreed to use every available officer to search for the hand, with the utmost caution, as well as the matching padlock to the Snauzer key. Inspector Bell said he would ensure all three constables on duty make both things their top priority. Hesterman himself offered to go to interview the farmer who owned Horseshoe Farm, near Ashburton, the following day, saying he did not care if it was Bank Holiday Sunday or not, he wanted to sort this Nosoi business out before his wife and kids were at risk.

Copeland had other ideas about working on Bank Holiday Sunday. He went to the hotel, had a quick check *down there*, smiled with relief, threw items into his case, including his pistol, told the girl on the desk he would be back Monday and not to worry because the Metropolitan Police would be paying for the two nights he was away.

Inhaling a cigarette, he returned to the police station with his case trundling behind him to find Hesterman sitting in an old Nissan, waiting as promised to give him a ride and drop him off for his train. Hesterman had kindly transferred the carrier bag donated by the Karamazov brothers into the Nissan and Copeland scrunched the bag of papers into his little case.

Any intentions Copeland had of doing his report on the train journey were soon squashed. The previous train had been cancelled and passengers were squeezing into every space on every carriage. It was stiflingly hot. Squealing toddlers, four sorts of music and banal chattering on mobile phones filled his ears. Suitcases clogged the aisles and teenagers with rucksacks jostled past. He had momentarily felt a glowing satisfaction when he thought he was actually going to get home and go for his usual golf club Sunday carvery, washed down with an excellent glass or three of fine port. A baby filled its nappy and Copeland's glow of satisfaction was severely dimmed. He had a gnawing feeling he had forgotten to tell someone something or to do something he had meant to do. His anxiety grew, then really took hold when he realised he would never get through the teeming throngs and make it to the buffet car.

Worse followed. The Commander phoned him. The Commander *never* phoned him. The Commander *never* phoned anyone. Someone else *always* phoned for him. The Commander was stressed beyond the Richter scale. Copeland found it hard to hear in the noisy train carriage, but there was something about something hitting the fan and Copeland would be somewhere without a paddle if he did not get a full – a very, very full – report in by midnight and get himself back for a priority double A meeting – whatever that was – at noon tomorrow. Copeland had been so shocked by the Commander's tirade, he had actually heard himself call the commander 'Sir'.

And it took a while for it to dawn on him that the meeting was to be at lunchtime. So much for a carvery lunch and port. He would be slaving over a report and suffering takeaway pizza tonight with no hope of a decent lunch tomorrow. There were two hours of laborious train journey in front of him and he already needed a cigarette and a large whiskey.

Doctor Beth Spencer takes a bath. Saturday August 27 th.

Beth Spencer had done all she could do. She had contacted the Royal Free Hospital in London. They had not been at all happy about accepting a patient without an Outbreak Control Team having met, but once she had spoken with the Trust Administrator in Lincoln itself and had persuaded him to lobby the Royal Free, they had agreed to send a specialised ambulance to collect Popov tomorrow. In fact, they had agreed surprisingly easily.

She had texted Copeland with the grim news of a possible epidemic of 'Popov Disease', as she had labelled it, and she suspected Copeland had made a call to someone who had made a call to The Royal Free to tell them they had to admit

Popov. So she had texted him again and thanked him for his help, unaware he had done nothing to help at all.

A lack of sleep had suddenly caught up with her and, after briefing the nursing team, she had decided to go home.

Once home, after kicking her shoes off, she had phoned her partner, Simon, and told him she was too tired to go out with friends as they had planned. He did not take it well and said she was always putting her work before his needs. She felt glad she had kept her semi-detached vacant and had moved back out of his apartment, and wondered if she would be bothered to phone him again anytime soon.

She soaked in the bath and contemplated staying in bed for the whole of Sunday. She had promised to do the half marathon and the sponsorship she had raised would not be going to the children's leukaemia charity if she pulled out. She had to do it. There was nothing she could do at the hospital: the ambulance would arrive and Popov would be gone. The Royal Free had the best facilities to do all the tests that needed to be done and Popov would be properly isolated in an air filtered room.

She made herself a quick pasta meal and drank some fresh orange juice. She was too tired to worry anymore about the spread of Popov Disease and the impending apocalypse: she had done all she could. She set her alarm and slid under a sheet. Although her views had changed, she recited The Serenity Prayer she had learned in school. She was soundly asleep before dark.

The Brothers Karamazov again again.

When Colonel Vasily Goraya, SVR and former KGB, spoke in Russian, Alexei and Ivan 'Karamazov' had looked at each other. They had collected, dropped off and minimally paid their workers and were about to lock the caravan door and head home when they saw the short man in the raincoat and fedora hat.

'What did he say?' Alexei said as he came down the steps and stood next to the Rottweiler being held by Ivan.

Ivan did not answer. Neither did the dog.

Alexei shouted to the man standing twenty yards away in the scrap yard entrance. 'Vot did you zay?'

Colonel Vasily Goraya, SVR, former KGB and Order of Lenin, shouted again in Russian.

'Vy you no speak English?' Alexei shouted back. The dog snarled and strained on his leash.

Alexei, Ivan and Dmitri the snarling dog watched as the short raincoat man began striding towards them. He was followed by a dark green car of indistinguishable make. He stopped ten feet away, stood with legs astride and hands behind his back. The car stopped a few feet behind him. It turned its headlights on. Full beam.

Alexei and Ivan winced and shielded their eyes. The dog shook its head and growled. 'What the hell, mate?' shouted Alexei.

Colonel Vasily Goraya, SVR, former KGB, Order of Lenin and Order of the Red Star spoke again in Russian.

Alexei and Ivan looked at each other and shrugged. The dog went back to snarling.

'Forgive me. I was led to believe you were Russian,' said Colonel Vasily Goraya, SVR, former KGB, Order of Lenin and Order of the Red Star, and also known as The Kamchatka

Killer in some circles. (These circles consisted of those who survived. They were very small circles.)

Alexei turned to Ivan. 'First he's spouting some foreign lingo now he talks like a bleedin' toff!' he said, pointing at Vasily. Ivan laughed.

'My name is Vasily and I am terribly sorry to trouble you at such a late hour, but my associate and I require some information,' said Vasily as a taller man in a raincoat and hat joined him from the car. The engine was still running and the headlights still glared.

Alexi laughed. Ivan joined in. The dog barked. Alexei had just had his Saturday night kicked off to the best possible start – a fight *before* going to the pub, and with a couple of nimwits in hats and raincoats. Brilliant! Ivan could take these two on together, with one hand behind his back, but Alexei was determined to have his enjoyment too. He thought, *If you put one raincoat man on the shoulders of the other, then they might, just, be Ivan's height. This is going to be fun!*

'Bugger off,' said Alexei, 'or we'll set the dog on you!'

'Wishing me to go away will not make it so. Just answer a few questions to my satisfaction and we will leave,' said Vasily Goraya, SVR, Order of Lenin, etc.

'Right, Ivan, set the dog on 'em,' shouted Alexei.

'Dmitri! Kill,' said Ivan, letting go of the leash.

A few minutes later Dmitri the dog was staggering about the scrap yard wondering why it could not close its broken jaw. Ivan was writhing on the ground, clutching three fractured fingers that pointed in three different directions. Alexei was on his knees holding his bleeding, broken nose.

'What do you wanna know?' asked Alexei, nasally.

'The police were here earlier. Don't try to deny it: we had a tracker on their car,' said Vasily, annoyed. He was annoyed his hat had come off during the brief fracas. To relieve his tension he kicked the hand-clutching Ivan in the stomach.

'Yeth. Dey wath here,' said Alexei with difficulty.

'Tell me what they wanted and tell me everything you told them,' said Vasily as he rotated Alexei's ear.

Detective Inspector Copeland. Sunday, August 28 th. 2016.

Copeland had sent his report in at 12.36 a.m. He hoped it was not too late and it was very, very full enough. He feared a failure would not just leave him up a creek without a paddle, but without a boat either, and it was not the sort of creek he had any desire to swim in. He had not mastered the art of breathing without inhaling.

Too tired to clean his teeth or have another scotch, he had fallen asleep on top of his bed in his underpants and socks.

He had woken up flat on his back, opened his eyes and panicked because he could not see his feet and for a moment his half-asleep mind thought they had been eaten by Popov Disease. When the rest of his brain woke up he saw it was just his round, hill of a stomach blocking the view. Relieved, he let his head sink back into the pillow and reached for his cigarettes. He groped the bedside table but they were not there. Inconveniently, he had to turn his head and look to check. He had left them by the laptop in the lounge. Now he had an impossible choice. Should he stay in bed or should he get up for a smoke? He debated the answer for several minutes before before his bladder cast the deciding vote. He swung his legs to the floor and padded downstairs to the lounge.

His head fell back as he took his first nicotine of the day. His eye caught his wall clock. He thought Mr. and Mrs. Professor would like that clock, it would really go with – was that the time? He went double normal speed up the stairs, threw his cigarette into the toilet bowl and climbed into the shower (where his bladder finally got the benefit of its vote). He breathed a sigh of relief and got out of the shower to take off his underwear and socks. More haste less speed, Larry, he said to himself, but still took time while he was in the shower to check he was still all clear in 'the nether regions'.

He arrived at S.O.15 with a few minutes to spare. The door to the conference room was open and he could see the Commander pacing to and fro. Before he got to his desk to pretend he had been there for hours, D.C.I. Ross poked his head out of his office and beckoned Copeland to him.

'Quick, Lawrence, come in,' he said, closing the door as soon as Copeland was through it.

They stood behind the door. Ross had almost pushed Copeland so he had his back against the closed door.

'I don't want anyone to see us if I can help it,' said Ross, keeping his voice down.

'Why's that, Sir?' asked Copeland.

'I think you and I, Lawrence, are the... Wait a minute, you called me Sir!'

'Yes, Sir. You are my superior officer, so I am required to address you accordingly,' said Copeland.

'Why?' said a bemused D.C.I. Ross. 'I mean, you never have before.'

'I've been thinking on the way here, Sir. I have a very strong sense this is my last case at S.O.15. Call it a gut feeling, Sir, and I don't want everything here to end on any sour notes. Hell, I've even decided to be nice to Sergeant Brandon.'

'Jesus, Lawrence. This is a turn up for the books. I've been waiting for you to call me 'sir' for the last three years, and hearing you use it now just makes me feel, well, just uncomfortable. I would be quite happy for you to call me by my first name, but that's not the done thing is it?'

Copeland knew he would find it hard to call D.C.I. Ross by his first name too. He had forgotten what it was.

'Tell you what, Lawrence, you can call me 'Chief'. How's that?' said Ross.

'Fine with me, Chief, as long as you stop calling me Lawrence and call me Larry. No-one has called me Lawrence since... well, not for a very long time. So why are we in your office, Chief?'

'Ah, yes,' said DCI Ross. 'The Commander was summoned to a meeting late yesterday afternoon. You'll find out why in a few minutes, but you are not going to like what's going to happen. The Commander doesn't like it and I don't like it. But we all have to keep our cool in this meeting, like it or not.'

'What's going on, er, Chief?' said Copeland.

'No time. Also wanted you to know there might be things we might agree on. Something rotten in the state of Denmark, and all that.'

Er, Copeland...When did the Danish get involved? said Copeland's inner voice.

'Just keep your cool – they're here,' said Ross and he dragged Copeland away from the door so he could open it. 'Come on!'

Three figures were striding down the office. SO15 officers stood to attention as they passed because the lead figure was Sir Richard Grey, Chair of the Joint Intelligence Committee and their ultimate boss. He was also the ultimate boss over MI5, MI6, GCHQ, Defence Intelligence and Armed Services Intelligence.

Ross followed the trio and Copeland followed Ross, and they all finished their journey in the windowless, oak panelled briefing room. A highly polished oval table was in the middle of the room, with pitchers of water and glasses strategically arranged. Twelve red velvet chairs were around the table.

Circling the room was another twenty four similar chairs, arranged against the oak panel walls where large portraits of the greats looked down on them – Churchill, Wellington, Marlborough, Peel and two others Copeland had never been bothered to identify. It was a large room, probably modelled on the meeting room of an exclusive men's Mayfair club.

Sir Richard moved to the head of the table to the left and stood behind the chair there. The man and woman who had arrived with him passed behind him. The woman stood behind the chair immediately to Sir Richard's left, the man stood in front of one of the chairs against the wall, immediately behind her.

The woman was strikingly tall, strikingly thin and looked strikingly rich. She wore a black, soft leather jacket, a black blouse with the strikingly wide collar outside the jacket, and black trousers on her strikingly long legs. Her shining black hair was bob-cut and stopped two inches short of her strikingly broad shoulders as it fell down the sides of her strikingly smooth-skin face. She wore Dior sunglasses with jet black frames. They were strikingly reflective.

The man was built like a professional wrestler. Even if he was not wearing the full dress uniform of a US marine master gunnery sergeant and carrying his white brimmed hat under his arm, his close cut hair and set-square chin would have given him away. He, too, was wearing reflective sunglasses. Standard issue, not Dior.

The inner voice in Copeland's brain stirred. Following a full analysis of the situation it said: *Oh, CRAP! Not Danes! Yanks!*

The Commander stood behind the seat to Sir Richard's right and the DCI stood behind the one in front of them by the door, so Copeland made his way to the right and passed around the end of the table, young Sergeant Brandon and, on the end of the table an OHP.

Brandon appeared to be in a state of shock: a rabbit in the headlights, and Copeland had to squeeze between him and the table while simultaneously avoiding knocking the OHP machine off the end. These contortions had caused him to almost walk into a chair occupied by, what appeared to be for all intents and purposes, a bag lady. She looked twenty years older than Copeland. She was a small, frail woman, wearing a baggy grey cardigan that was fraying at the sleeves and had a hole in one shoulder. Her dry grey hair was pulled back from her wrinkled face and forced into a pony tail. A pair of cheap spectacles hung on a piece of fraying string around her neck. Copeland resisted the urge to scan the room for her shopping trolley.

'Ooops. Sorry,' said Copeland, stopping himself from walking into the previously unseen old woman by putting his hand on the back of her chair. She smiled warmly and for an instant Copeland thought she seemed vaguely familiar, but he got that feeling a lot at his age and most 'vaguely familiar' people he saw crossed his path again in Tesco. He rounded her chair and stood behind the one next to her.

I suppose she's sitting down because she's too old to stand up.

He heard a mid-west accent from the black haired woman at the other end of the table, saying, 'What the heck is that?' and looked to see her pointing at the OHP.

Sir Richard answered her in a hushed voice, as if it were top secret. 'It's an OHP,' he said. 'An overhead projector.'

'What does it do?' she whispered back.

'It projects, um, overhead,' whispered Sir Richard.

She nodded, unconvinced.

Sir Richard looked around the room, making eye contact with everyone present except the seated bag lady.

'Gentlemen,' he said, clapping his hands together, 'and, um, lady,' he added looking over the head of the bag lady. He extended his left hand towards the black haired, black clothed, Dior wearing woman on his left. 'I would like to introduce the Acting Head of CIA Operations in the UK, Chief Special Agent Liza Clinton.'

She smiled and momentarily lowered her sunglasses and said, 'No relation.'

'And behind her,' continued Sir Richard, 'is Master Gunnery Sergeant Brett Gregg.'

Brett Gregg took off his sunglasses and nodded. He put his sunglasses back on.

Bloody hell, Copeland! What sort of a name is 'Brett'?

'Agent Clinton, let me introduce the room to you,' said Sir Richard and proceeded to go round the table in a clockwise direction. 'The Commander of SO15 you already know. This is Detective Chief Inspector Ross. At the end of the table we have Detective Sergeant Brandon, and this is Inspector Copeland.'

'I thought he would look much younger,' said Agent Clinton.

*Well that's nice! We are **not** going to like her, are we Copeland? And how come he missed bag-lady out? Is she one of the cleaners and everyone's too polite to kick her out?*

'Please be seated everyone,' said Sir Richard and they obeyed the Big Boss. Sir Richard poured himself a glass of water. He offered one to Agent Clinton. She declined because she had not brought her sterilising tablets. 'Sergeant Brandon,' said Sir Richard, 'please begin.'

Sergeant Brandon nodded and pulled a string cord dangling down the wall behind him. A large screen came down. He picked up the plug of the overhead projector and plugged it in.

'Please remind me to unplug this when we finish. I would hate anyone tripping over the wire. We don't seem to have the yellow tape required by Health and Safety,' he said.

Behind her glasses, Agent Clinton rolled her eyes. Master Gunnery Sergeant Brett Gregg may not have even seen the screen. He was at attention even when sitting down and, as far as anyone could tell, he was staring at DCI Ross.

'Get on with it Brandon,' said the Commander discouragingly.

Brandon nodded, placed a sheet of acetate on the OHP and switched the machine on.

It's a technological miracle of the 1980s! Look, Copeland, something has magically been projected onto the screen.

Copeland sighed loudly. Was he going to have an internal running commentary again? He sighed louder.

The old bag lady leaned over to him and whispered, 'Still having trouble with that inner voice, Lawrence?'

That's a bit personal! Who the hell IS she?

Copeland finally forced himself to care enough to look at the screen. He quickly looked away again and disguised his laugh with a minor coughing fit. Brandon had, apparently, been busy. He had found lots of coloured markers and surpassed himself by importing photographs. The result was a big screen version of a murder investigation board, with red lines and arrows linking suspects, evidence and crime scenes.

Copeland looked at the others. Was Agent Clinton smirking behind those glasses? Was Gunnery Sergeant Gregg asleep behind his? He saw DCI Ross glaring at him, mouthing the word 'watch' and pointing discretely to the screen. The bag lady elbowed Copeland in the ribs.

'Ow,' said Copeland. They all (except the bag lady) looked at him. 'Er, 'ow did you get all that on one screen, Sergeant Brandon? Good work!'

Brandon glowed. He had heard rumours about Copeland and could not believe one man had saved the country so many times. 'Thank you, Inspector Copeland, Sir. I'm glad you like it. It took me all night after we received your excellent and detailed report.'

'Brandon!' snapped the Commander.

'Yes, Sir. Of course, Sir,' said Brandon and promptly disappeared under the table. He emerged with an arm-length piece of wood that looked suspiciously like half a snooker cue with the blue tip still on it.

Utilizing his new pointer, Brandon started at the right of the screen and went into an obviously well rehearsed presentation. 'The former Soviet Union. The province of Chechnya, capital Grozny. It was near here that...'

'Shut up and move out of the way Sergeant,' said Sir Richard, shooing Brandon to one side with the back of a sweeping hand. 'We can all see what it is so just sit down and let us study it for a moment. We'll let you know if we can't read your handwriting.'

Head bowed, Brandon silently slunk to a chair in the corner and laid his snooker stick pointer across his lap.

That was a bit harsh. Poor lad had worked hard on that and was doing his best. And it's not handwritten either, it's all word processor.

'Just what I was thinking,' whispered the bag lady.

Is she bloody psychic?

She whispered again. 'No. And mind the language, Lawrence.'

Not daring to think, Copeland stared at the screen. In the middle of the screen was the word BOSTON accompanied by a picture of the town's market square. An arrow from the right pointed to the town picture. There was the picture of Popov with his eyes closed that Copeland had taken in the hospital. Underneath the picture it said POPOV in capital letters. Above his picture was a picture of Sofia and above it the words SOFIA, BULGARIA. So far so good, Popov had travelled from Sofia to Boston. But an arrow came into the picture of Popov from the right. At the other end of this arrow was a photo of a bombed out Grozny and the words GROZNY, CHECHNYA underneath it. More disturbingly, next to the picture of Grozny was a picture with the word NOSOI on it. The picture was of a milk churn.

Nice bit of computer skill there, Brandon. Must have taken ages to import that word onto a milk churn.

The top right corner of the screen had a photo of a desert with mountains in the distance. Above it were the words USMAN FAYAD. AFGHANISTAN. A huge arrow went from these words halfway across the screen into the picture of Boston town square, through it and out the other side to a photograph of a statue of Robin Hood. The word NOTTINGHAM was written above the photo.

I'm sure the Yanks will at least get THAT connection!

And, rather distastefully, below Robin Hood shooting an arrow, there was a picture of a corpse, and under the corpse was a photo of a disembodied, floating hand with a huge **?** next to it.

Above the Boston photo was an arrow leading to the top of the screen and a picture of the St. James Hospital, which had clearly been lifted from its publicity website because the red and blue motto 'Your Journey Begins Here...' was visible at the bottom. Next to the hospital photo, Brandon had put the words HOSPITAL PATHOLOGY REPORT.

Underneath the Boston photo, with no arrow to or from it, was the picture of a run down, corrugated iron shed with the words HORSESHOE FARM under it.

Now that IS a good likeness of what the shed looked like – before it blew up.

And next to the shed photo was a picture of a key. It had the word KEY next to it.

Finally, in the bottom left hand corner, taking up almost a quarter of the screen was the word RONALDO and the largest picture on the screen. There was the footballer Ronaldo celebrating a goal and sliding towards a corner flag in his Portugal shirt.

Well, looks like we're taking on the FIFA international terror brigade next. I hope not – they'd be too bloody well financed.

Sir Richard Grey stood up and pulled his jacket straight. His was not a suit one bought from Marks and Sparks. His pedigree was Eton, Oxford, Foreign Office, various embassies around the globe and Chair of the Joint Intelligence Committee. His family history dated back to before the Wars of the Roses, where they had ended up on the winning side, and counted a Queen of England as an ancestor, despite Lady Jane's reign lasting a mere nine days. Sir Richard Grey was one of the most powerful and most wealthy men in the country, and he looked the part.

He stood erect with his hands clasped together in front of him. 'Two months ago, the Russian secret service informed all Western intelligence services that they had captured several Chechen terrorists. Under interrogation these terrorists informed our Russian counterparts that other Chechen's had fled the country and intended to carry out attacks in Western Europe and the USA to publicise their cause. At that time they informed us there might be some sort of chemical weapon in play, but gave us no further details. Consequently, all monitoring and border agencies were put on alert for anything suspicious relating to Eastern Europeans who had recently entered the country.

'There have been several false alarms so when GCHQ intercepted the St. James Hospital's communication requesting help from Lincoln for a Bulgarian with unusual chemical burns it did not seem a high priority. Fortunately, the Commander saw the connection as being more significant and had one of our... um, one of our most experienced officers sent to investigate.'

He means old, Copeland.

'Early yesterday morning the Russians summoned the ambassadors of all the U.N. Security Council countries and Germany to the Kremlin. The ambassadors were informed that further interrogation of the captured Chechen terrorists had yielded more information. The Russians had managed to extract the word Nosoi from one of the captured Chechen's before he, um, expired. The ambassadors were fully briefed on how The Nosoi – an unimaginable chemical weapon – had been produced in the bad old days before the fall of the Soviet Union. The Russian Federation also shared the documentation they had on Nosoi – a few handwritten notes and some chemical formulas. We all have our best scientists working on these notes to try to work out what this Nosoi actually is, how it might be made and, if at all possible, come up with some sort of antidote.'

So all we have to do is hope the terrorists wait for a year or two.

'Something you are not aware of, including you Commander, is this morning's developments. Our American cousins have intercepted chatter from the Middle East. Probably Al-Qaeda. The chatter concerns one Usman Fayad.

Luckily for us, they were careless enough to use his name in one of the communications. The intercepted communications were directed, as far as we can tell, to the Algerian terrorist group known as the al-Mulathamun Brigade. We think the man known as Ronaldo is one of theirs.'

The Commander coughed a polite cough. 'Excuse me, Sir Richard,' he said, 'but I thought we were looking at a connection with the Basque separatist group ETA? Ronaldo is Spanish, after all.'

The Commander is not a follower of football, is he? Ronaldo is Portuguese! He's even got a sodding Portuguese shirt on in Brandon's photo! And someone tell him it was just two old codgers who said they thought he looked LIKE Ronaldo. We are not going to arrest THE Ronaldo! Are we..?

While Copeland was being distracted by this thought, Sir Richard had remained stuck in a frown, staring at the Commander.

'Umm, quite so, Commander. Yes... Ronaldo... ETA... Quite... But this new information... um, you know,' said Sir Richard. His entire body gave itself a shake, as if checking he was actually awake and not dreaming, then he returned to addressing the room.

'Popov, Fayad and this Ronaldo were using an old tractor shed near Boston to either make or, more likely, share out Nosoi. As we all know, this Nosoi is stored in liquid form and turns to a deadly gas when heated. In its liquid form it is highly corrosive and Popov and Fayad seem to have got their fingers burnt, as it were. Just a little joke to lighten the proceedings, there.'

That was hilarious, wasn't it? Listen to the silence!

Sir Richard, having waited in vain for the anticipated laughter, continued, 'But there was some sort of accident and some sort of minor explosion: a side effect the Russians seem to have either not known about or just not shared with us. Nitroglycerine is undoubtedly one of the chemicals present in Nosoi, and this has been confirmed by the hospital finding glycerine on what was left of Popov's fingers.'

Ooops! Better check the old todger again, Copeland!

Sir Richard looked grave as he said, 'Without doubt, what we have here is an international terrorist conspiracy. The Chechen terrorists do not have the resources for this sort of operation, but they have got Nosoi, or knowledge of how to make it. In our analysis, they have teamed up with other terror organisations to carry out a series of attacks and release the Nosoi gas in heavily populated areas. London is obviously the first target. These other terror organisations are giving finances, logistics and manpower to make these attacks succeed. We also suspect at least one other organisation is involved and there is undoubtedly a leader of this terror cell.'

Finally, something that makes some sense. Ronaldo would not go and get his Mercedes dirty on a farm if he was the big boss.

Sir Richard turned to the commander and said, 'If you could pass round the files commander.' He addressed the room: 'The file being passed to you is that of the man we believe is the leader. His name is Abdul Karim, formerly known as Prince Abdul Karim, a minor member of the Saudi royal family. As you will see from his file, his country stripped him of that title when he siphoned off a considerable amount of money and fled to the west. The Saudis have been giving us information over the last several months which implicate him as a sponsor of terrorism. More significantly, their information suggests Abdul Karim has been trying to merge several terrorist groups together, including the Chechens. He has been under surveillance since we were first tipped off by the Saudis, but there has been nothing to arrest

150

him on. If we can use Popov to track down Ronaldo, then Ronaldo will lead us to the Nosoi. Once we have Ronaldo, we are sure we can persuade him, with a bit of good old, traditional British seventeenth century torture, into implicating Abdul Karim as the ringleader. Better still, we catch Abdul Karim with the Nosoi in his possession! We will, at last, have enough evidence to take Karim down!' To add dramatic effect, Sir Richard banged the table.

'Here is the plan of action,' Sir Richard went on. 'Inspector Copeland will return to Boston forthwith.'

No golf club lunch? We've already missed the starter! This job is bollocks, Copeland!

Sir Richard gave Copeland a cursory nod. 'Inspector Copeland will act as liaison with the local police and set up surveillance on these Karamazov brothers – they're linked to this somehow and they have been suspected of previous illegal activities, including the sale of firearms. We have a team here going through the papers Copeland got from them and we will work out who else they took to the farm that day. In addition, we are sending a forensic unit to Boston to investigate the farm and Popov's home. An armed response team will be there tomorrow to guard Popov. For the time being he is securely handcuffed to a hospital bed and under heavy sedation.'

Handcuffed to a hospital bed? Do you think you may have left a few minor details out of your report besides the five hundred pounds..?

'That's correct, is it not, Inspector?' asked Sir Richard, looking at Copeland.

Was it correct he was heavily sedated? No. Not anymore according to Dr. Spencer. Was he handcuffed to the bed? No. That was what you had meant to do. You KNEW there was something nagging at you that you had forgotten to do,

Copeland. You forgot to go back and handcuff him to the bed, didn't you? More concerned about getting your golf club lunch, weren't you? And you had better not be going red. And you had better clench your buttocks.

'Inspector?'

'Sorry, Sir Richard,' said Copeland. 'I was just thinking, Sir. He may not be there anymore. Dr. Spencer was getting him moved to The Royal Free, Sir.'

'Yes. We are aware of that. It was in your report,' said Sir Richard. 'We have contacted the Royal and they have a hitch and will not be able to send the specialised ambulance up until tomorrow. The armed response team will be meeting the ambulance at the St. James Hospital and escorting it to the Royal Free. I trust you left the handcuff key with someone responsible at The St. James Hospital in case you are otherwise engaged when Popov is collected? The armed police will be escorting him and we do not want a delay while they are searching for a hacksaw, do we? Ha, ha!'

'Of course, Sir,' lied Copeland.

'Who with? The armed team will want to know who has the key when they get there.'

A name mentioned by Dr. Spencer popped into his head. She had said he had been very helpful. His name was going to be very helpful now.

'With a Junior Administrator, Sir. A Mr. Tom Benson,' said Copeland, hoping he sounded convincing.

You didn't sound very convincing there, did you, Copeland?

Copeland held Sir Richard's gaze until he said, 'Thank you, Inspector Copeland,' and returned his attention to Agent Clinton.

The bag lady leaned over and whispered into Copeland's ear. 'Wriggled clean out of that one, didn't you Lawrence?'

Who the HELL is she?

Sir Richard was still speaking. '...so bearing in mind the current austerity measures we are facing, and bearing in mind the great British public have voted to cut our umbilical cord with our European enemies, ha, ha, I mean our European partners, H.M.'s Government has taken the wise decision to work more closely with our American cousins.' He gestured for Agent Clinton to stand. 'Agent Clinton. Please,' he said.

Work more closely? This sounds ominous.

Agent Clinton stood and Sir Richard sat. She removed her sunglasses slowly, like a magician conjuring a pigeon from a hat, to reveal her wide brown eyes and perfectly manicured slender black eyebrows.

'Thank you, Sir Richard,' she said. 'We have a team from the CDC – that's the Centre for Disease Control, for those of you *Brit cousins* who don't know – hauling their asses over to your little country as I speak. They will be bringing enough biohazard suits for all US personnel. We also wanted a unit of our special forces to join them but your government requested they stay home, so we'll just have to make do with the field agents we have here and the other twenty coming over on the plane. I shall be heading up to Boston with my Alpha team first thing in the morning. We will be searching Popov's apartment as soon as we get there.'

Apartment? Wait 'til she sees it! And she can search all she likes. There's nothing else there. Hang on... biohazard suits for THEIR personnel?

'Most of the CDC team will be going with me to Boston,' Special Agent, very expensively dressed, Clinton announced. 'Some will go to the other hospital where Popov is being taken. If the doctors are right and there is a contagion spread from Popov's skin and infecting the good people of your little Boston village, then we will contain it. Gunny Gregg here will be bringing up a marine detachment from my embassy too. If necessary, we will quarantine the town.'

Humph! Why not just nuke it, just in case?

'The nuclear option is available if we need it,' said Agent Clinton, calmly.

'But not just yet,' Sir Richard interrupted, going slightly red.

'As you say, Sir Richard. Not *yet*,' said Agent Clinton. 'Maybe next week. Besides controlling the spread of this disease, which the Russians did not warn us about, we will be exerting every effort to find Fayad's hand while two CDC doctors will travel to your hamlet of Notting-ham to autopsy the terrorist's body. Our other priority is to track down this terrorist Ronaldo and that means interrogating the owner of Horseshoe Farm and the two old professors. One or all of them may be accomplices. We particularly wish to interrogate this Professor Emily Churchill. She was a professor of sociology and must therefore be a subversive. We are considering relocating all three to another friendly country so they can be interrogated more effectively.'

You know what that means! It means take Professor Emily and Professor Philip somewhere and water-board them until they confess to anything!

'We in the CIA believe this Ronaldo has the Nosoi is in his possession in its liquid form. Popov, whom we have confirmed is definitely not Bulgarian and is undoubtedly not name Popov, probably has some hidden in a shed or garage somewhere in Boston, and that place is what the Snauzer padlock key is for. Fayad may have some hidden somewhere, maybe near the docks where he pretended to be a hobo. We will find it. We are prepared to raid the mosques if necessary.'

What?

'Our analysis suggests they intended to use some heating device to convert it into its toxic gas form where they can do most damage – a subway station, a mall, something like that. All surveillance cameras are being used to locate Ronaldo and watch Abdul Karim. Once heated and the liquid becomes gas hundreds of Londoners will die, and we want to stop them before they use it in the States.'

Isn't the 'special relationship' we have with our cousins across the pond so wonderful?

CIA Chief Special Agent Liza Clinton paused. She tilted her head and slowly, replaced her sunglasses, then leaned on the oak table. 'I shall be running this operation from now on.'

'WHAT!' Copeland heard his own voice shout and found himself suddenly standing. Master Gunnery Sergeant Ross Gregg was also suddenly standing and had quickly positioned his huge body between Copeland and Agent Clinton.

Agent Clinton stood to her full six feet plus heels and folded her arms. She removed the glasses and glowered at Copeland.

'You don't want to work under me, Inspector?' she said.

You were warned, Copeland, but in for a penny, in for a pound.

'No, I don't,' said Copeland and folded his arms too.

'Is it because I'm a woman?'

'No, because...'

'Because I'm black?'

'No, because...'

'Because of my sexual orientation?'

'What?'

'Because I'm a lot younger than you?'

'No! It's because you're a bloody American! An American running a British operation? On British soil? It's wrong!' Copeland blurted.

From behind him, he thought he heard the faint sound of the bag lady giggling behind her hand. He was about to turn and look when DCI Ross spoke for the first time. 'Sit down, Copeland,' he said calmly. 'I did try to prepare you and tell you to keep your cool.'

Copeland hesitated, then sat down, but forcefully to show his ire. To show real British ire, he kept his arms folded.

*Americans running your investigation? What's the world coming to? And she's not THAT much younger than you anyway – twenty years is not **that** much! By the way, what's 'ire'?*

Sir Richard had placed his hand on Agent Clinton's arm. 'Our countries are allies, Mr. Copeland,' he said, oozing an English let's-all-have-a-cup-of-tea calm. 'The interests of the UK and the USA are one and the same. Our Government, at the very highest level, have sanctioned CIA control. Now, Mr. Copeland, are you willing to accept the decision of H.M.'s Government, or not?'

Copeland was tempted to say what he thought, but noticed Sir Richard had used his civilian title, Mr., and not Inspector. It was a pretty blatant indication of his options, so said, 'Of course, Sir Richard. My sincerest apologies, Ma'am. I will carry out your CIA orders to the letter.'

Cowardly weasel, Copeland. Just because he was going to sack you! You should quit anyway!

Agent Clinton replaced her sunglasses. 'Snivelling apology accepted,' she said. 'Gunny, you can return to your seat.'

Master Gunnery Sergeant Brett Gregg sat down, at attention, as was his want.

'I think we are finished here,' said Agent Clinton to Sir Richard.

Come on Copeland! You had questions that needed answers and now you're going to keep your mouth shut because you've already upset your new CIA boss and been slapped down by that snob Sir Richard. Look, they're leaving. And the Commander is going with them. No, don't stand up and show them respect! If you don't get your concerns out now, then when will you? What's the worst... see, too late, you weasel, they've gone!

'Right, gentlemen,' said the little bag lady, who had not stood. 'Now they've gone, gather round and we can start the real meeting and you can tell me why this doesn't make sense.'

Copeland looked down at her. 'Who the hell *are* you?' he said.

She smiled up at him. 'Oh, Lawrence, you should know, but these days I think people refer to me as Mrs. Pickford.'

Sergeant Brandon turned a ghostly white and Copeland thought he actually heard DCI Ross's jaw drop.

'Ronaldo' makes a phone call.

'Fatima? Is it done? Have you got rid of the old couple?

'Why not? You collected everything you needed hours ago.

'And for how long was the satnav taking you down country lanes?

'OK, great. So where are you now?

'Well don't just sit outside their house! Get in there and get the job done.

'Yes, I know I just phoned you.

'Fine, I'll hang up and let you get on with it. But make it quick.

'Yes, I remember you have the family round and want to get back. Salad preparation and all that...

'You're probably right, Fatima. They may well already be wondering where the salad is, but it's not my fault your satnav is crap, is it?

'No, Fatima, I'm not blaming you.

'No, really, I'm not blaming you. I'm blaming your satnav. But Fatima...

'Yes, I did give you their post code, but it's hardly my fault is it?

'It was definitely the right postcode, Fatima. Now you need to get on with the job.

'Oh, don't start whining about the dog again.

'Look, if you feel that strongly then put the dog in your boot.

'Then don't! I don't care. Just get the job done, Fatima. The quicker you get the job done and take care of them, the quicker you get home.

'Yes, I will hang up. I've been trying to hang up for the last ten minutes.

'Yes, fine, I was exaggerating. I know we haven't really been on the phone for ten minutes.

'Yes, I suppose I do tend to exaggerate quite often.

'There's no need for name calling, Fatima... Fatima... hello... Fatima?

D.S. Danny Hesterman. Sunday 28 th August

A Sunday morning seven-a-side friendly football match had taken up Danny Hesterman's morning. His nine year old son was the star player for his team. He was the only player not to score an own goal in their eight goals to one drubbing. Young Davie Hesterman was the goalkeeper and needed some consoling for twenty minutes, and only regaining his smile after two doughnuts.

Returning home, Mr. Hesterman discovered Mrs. Hesterman had devised a plan. If he was going out of town on what should be his day off, they could all come and go for a nice countryside walk. Davie and Daisy could do with some good, clean countryside air. When he had protested, saying he was conducting official police business and had to interview the owner of Horseshoe Farm properly and thoroughly, Mrs Hesterman had given him 'the stare' and said she and the kids could be dropped off at the plant nursery and he could pick them up after – the cafe there had great ice-cream and the kids would love it. Danny relented, knowing once 'the stare' came into play there was no use arguing. She had perfected it over the last ten years on the children who passed through her primary school class. It was withering.

Having a light lunch then getting the kids ready took no longer than usual and they were ready after a mere two hours. From their side of town the Sunday traffic was not a problem and they had reached Ashburton before Daisy went into her repetitive 'Are we there yet?' Danny dropped them off at the nursery, dreading Mrs. Hesterman might see 'A nice big plant' to clutter another room and he would spend the evening vacuuming soil out of the car.

Hesterman knocked on the farmhouse door. A tanned man holding a sandwich opened it. Hesterman showed him his warrant card and introduced himself.

'Detective Sergeant Danny Hesterman,' he said.

'So what's this about?' asked the farmer and bit into his sandwich.

'It's about your old shed, Mr..?' said Danny, expecting an instant reply. He didn't get one. The farmer chewed his sandwich, but Danny noticed the chewing had slowed and the farmer had shuffled across to stand in the middle of the doorway, as if subconsciously barring Danny's way. Experience had taught him to notice these things. This man did not want him inside his house.

'It's Mr. Brown,' said Mr. Brown after he had eventually swallowed. 'What about the old shed?'

'May I come in?' said Danny.

'Do you have a warrant?'

'A warrant? I'm afraid not, Mr. Brown. I just came out here to ask if you knew anything about why your shed has blown up. Seen anyone suspicious hanging around?'

While he was speaking, Danny had casually leaned his shoulder against the hinged side of the door frame and hoped Mr. Brown would not guess he was trying to look into the house.

Mr. Brown took another bite and shuffled across, blocking most of Danny's view into the interior. He chewed laboriously. Danny waited.

'No one suspicious. The shed has blown up, you say?' said Mr. Brown.

'Yes, I'm afraid so. Doors blown twenty, thirty metres maybe. A colleague and I went up there to have a look after an explosion had been reported by the professors living in the end house. I'm afraid your shed won't be much use to you from now on.'

'You went up and had a look? You went over my fields?'

'Yes we did, Mr. Brown. The police do have a duty to investigate such things, you know.'

'So you went onto my property and examined my shed, did you, Detective Sergeant? You didn't come and ask if you could trespass on my land and you never showed me a search warrant, did you?'

Danny quickly considered how to play this. 'I'm sorry you seem to have formed a negative opinion of the police, Mr. Brown. If you wish to put in a formal complaint you can always come down to the station.'

'I might just do that. What was your name again?' said Mr. Brown, waving a finger in Danny's face.

'It's Hesterman, Detective Sergeant Hesterman,' said Danny. 'But just one more thing, Sir. Why do you think your shed blew up?'

Mr. Brown stepped forward and Danny had to retreat a step, but did so at an angle that allowed him to see better into the hall.

'Probably old fertiliser I left there ages ago. Now get off my property, Sergeant Hesterman. See, I remember your name now!' said Mr. Brown, stepping off the door-step.

Even better, thought Danny as he got a better view inside. 'Very well, Sir. I'll be on my way. Sorry to disturb you,' said Danny and went back through the farmyard to his car, wondering why a farmer would have an open envelope full of money – a lot of money – lying on a telephone table in his hallway. When he got back in his car he could see Farmer Brown was still outside the farmhouse, watching him.

On his way back to collect his family, Danny decided to stop off and tell Professor Emily and Professor Philip they had been right about an explosion and the matter was under investigation. When Danny knocked on their door there was no reply and he could not hear the dog barking. Both of their cars were parked beside the house so he knocked again. There was no answer and he surmised they must have gone for a walk with the dog. He decided he would telephone them some other time.

Danny went back to his car, turned the car around and left. Exactly as Fatima had done two hours previously.

'Ronaldo'.

'Hello? Fatima? Is that you?

'No, your name does not come up when you phone. It's a precaution.

'A precaution in case anyone we don't want to gets their hands on this phone. We don't want *them* having everyone's names and numbers, do we?

'You know – them them.

'Them! The Powers That Be, the government, the police, the CIA, the Martians, the Scottish Tourist Board, the Department of Agriculture... Them!

'No, Fatima, the Martians are not really after us. (sigh) I hope you're phoning to say the job is done.

'Good. Any problems?

'Good. And the dog?

'See, I knew you could handle it.

'Well, I'm glad the job went well and the old folks won't be a problem anymore and I'm sorry your mother is refusing to talk to you.

'No, you may NOT tell her what you have been doing.

'She may well be a true believer in our cause, but everything we do now has to stay secret or we could all end up... I think they call it compromised.

'No, not the Martians them, Fatima. The other them.

'How should I know what you should tell your mother? Just tell her it was work. She'll have to live with that.

'I suppose you can tell her after we've used the stuff, Fatima. Once the world has seen what it can do, then you can tell her your part in it if you think you can trust her.

'I do understand. I can see how today has caused you family problems.

'Very well. The next time I speak with Scorpion, I will ask him if you can have a bonus payment for this one.

'Scorpion, Fatima. That's our leader's code name, remember?

'Yes, Fatima, that Scorpion. The next time I talk to him I will ask for a big bonus payment to make up for your inconvenience.

'Yes, Fatima, and extra for the diesel you used because your satnav got you lost.

'OK, you get back to your garden then and enjoy the rest of the barbecue.

'Hey, Fatima, before you go. Does my name come up on your phone when I phone you?

'Ah, I see. My first name and my last name. Now, that's not really such a good idea, Fatima. Could you delete my names in case they get their hands on your phone?

'Who are they? They work for them, Fatima. You know, the them we just talked about.

'Yes, the not the Martians them.

'Yes, you can wipe my name off your phone and still know who's calling you, Fatima, because it is the special phone I gave you to be used only for calls between you and me.

'No, having Snapchat on it is definitely not a good idea, Fatima.

'No, don't bother trying to do anything with it. Throw it in a river or something. Just get a new one, but make sure it's a burner phone.

'No, Fatima, it's just a name for these no-contract phones. It won't catch fire. Remember to put my number in it before you throw the old one away. And, Fatima, just *my* number. No-one else's.

'Yes, that's right. So you can reach me at the secret base.

'No, I'm not there now, I'm at home.

'Ok, Fatima. Goodbye. See you soon.

The man 'they' called Ronaldo looked at his phone. The screen went black. The man 'they' call Ronaldo spoke to the dead screen.

'Fatima, you may be brilliant at what you do, but for everything else you're off with the faeries. Once this is over and the world has been turned upside down, I think we may have to terminate you.'

Mrs. Pickford. 1982 to Present.

A man in a pin stripe suit walked down Bond Street. He carried an umbrella. On the umbrella handle was a small button which, when pressed, caused an inch long needle to project from the umbrella tip. Lethal poison was propelled through the needle.

The assassin spotted his target. It had been easy. The target travelled the same route every day. The assassin walked faster than the shoppers and office workers around him, but only slightly faster so he did not arouse any suspicion. He walked round a woman carrying two large shopping bags full of new clothes, he manoeuvred round a man with a briefcase, side-stepped two young women with spiky hair, around a small, frail woman with her crooked back bent over her walking stick. He was getting close to his target and his thumb started moving towards the release button.

The assassin's eyes blurred. His legs wobbled. He dropped the umbrella weapon. His lungs constricted and he clutched at his throat, struggling for breath. He staggered and fell to his knees. He saw a small, frail woman standing a few feet away and pointing to a small needle protruding from the end of her walking stick. The last thing he ever saw was her smile before she walked away.

Plush carpet covered the corridor of the eighteenth floor of the Crowne Hotel, Belgrade. A woman in a mink coat waited patiently for the elevator. A man, far taller than she, stood beside her. He wore the uniform of a high officer. He had the insignia of a colonel and had medals on his chest which he had awarded to himself for ethnic cleansing.

He looked down at the small woman beside him. The numbers above the elevator doors flashed, telling them the lift was on its way down. The woman dropped one of her gloves and bent to pick it up. The colonel looked down at her as she dropped to one knee, the elevator pinged to announce its arrival and the doors opened. He looked down at the woman and wondered what she was doing as he stepped towards the elevator before looking to see where he was going. His own momentum and the push the small woman gave him as she sprung forward, like a sprinter from the blocks, was enough to take him through the elevator doors and down the shaft. He fell twenty floors into the basement car park before he stopped.

Bad manners and not letting ladies go first, added to his countless war crimes and a little tinkering with the elevator, had been the death of him.

The Columbian drug lord had taken over the penthouse. The floor below was occupied by his armed bodyguards. Access was impossible. He did not leave the hotel. His contacts came to him. His food and his drinks, including his eight varieties of bottled water, were all tasted first. No hotel staff were allowed beyond the bodyguards' floor, including cleaners and room service. Too high for a sniper, too well guarded for an assault, too suspicious to let anyone onto the penthouse level, and bomb sweeps methodically carried out on everything made him untouchable.

Getting a job in the kitchens was not hard for a small, frail woman willing to accept a few dollars a day, and it was easy for her to smear the inside of the wine glasses with an invisible, tasteless liquid before they were sent up to the penthouse. After three days of agony in hospital, the drug lord and his top lieutenants died a painful death. The woman was back in the London office by then.

A civil servant about to sell encryption codes for cruise missile guidance systems accidentally electrocuted himself, though everyone was surprised he was stupid enough to have an electric heater perched on the side of his bath. A Swiss banker, who was laundering terrorist money, was shot through the head while out hunting, though the autopsy revealed the bullet from his brain was not from any of his fellow hunters' rifles. A South African arms dealer suddenly got depressed and committed suicide by throwing himself from a bridge and in front of a train, though that train only travelled that remote location once a week and he had seemingly been quite patient before he jumped.

The countless mysterious deaths were exceeded by the number of prominent figures suddenly finding their reputation trashed in the press, or their mountainous fortunes unaccountably disappearing. Organisations found their investors dissolving, or shares inexplicably plummeting or, of late, their computer systems compromised and leaking sensitive information. Ships sank, factories burned, diamond mines exploded: the list was endless, as were the locations.

Such actions over decades had resulted in the Special Actions Division of Her Majesty's Security Services growing from a minor, subservient Division into a dominant force.

The operatives of the Special Action Division disliked their S.A.D. acronym and began calling themselves Pickfords. They were, after all, in the removal business. The small difference was that one Pickfords was in the furniture removal business and this Pickfords was in the people removal business. And just as the Head of MI6 was called 'C', the head of Pickfords became known as Mr. Pickford, or, as now, Mrs. Pickford.

Even within the security services, the existence of Pickfords was no more than a rumour to most, and that rumour told of a Division which did the jobs the other services could not or would not do. Rumours also told of Pickfords prospering throughout the Cold War and taking on a powerful life of its own, emerging as the most secret and most potent of the Services. It broke the umbilical cord with the Joint Intelligence Committee and only attended meetings when it chose to. Some said they could do as they pleased because they created fear, while others said they achieved their autonomy by blackmail. Most said they were allowed to work above and outside the law because sometimes that was what was needed and the Government and the civil servants, including the most powerful civil servants like the Chair of the Joint Intelligence Committee, all wanted plausible deniability and actually chose not to know.

Pickfords was accountable to no one and received information from everyone. Only Pickfords itself chose when it would intervene, and when it would not. It had its own budget flowing in from several government departments, but other rumours said Pickfords had grown its own investments and assets, and its wealth now rivalled a small country, but without the overheads.

It had its own premises, but no one knew where. It was said that MI5 had tried to locate the Pickfords headquarters in the early 1980s, but gave up the task when MI5 HQ itself inexplicably went into lockdown and a note had appeared on the desk of the MI5 Chief with the words: 'STOP IT! Kind Regards, Mr. Pickford.' It was then the other security services realised Pickfords operatives were embedded in their services too, and though these men and women were loyal to their service, they were more loyal to Pickfords. This went some way to explain why some MI5 and MI6 operatives sometimes, without warning, resigned. They were just transferring. It was the same story in certain specialist military units too, and in the mid 1990s the Special Boat Service had found themselves unaccountably understaffed. Given Pickfords range of activities, specialists must have been recruited from other walks of life too, including computing and finance.

Pickfords had an unofficial motto. They had corrupted Einstein's quote describing his lack of understanding of quantum mechanics when he called it 'spooky action at a distance'. Their motto was: We do spooky action at any distance.

And when the three remaining SO15 officers in the conference room had recovered from their shock and pulled chairs close to the current Mrs. Pickford, she said: 'Whatever you may have heard about Pickfords, let me assure you we are completely committed to our oath of upholding the democracy and sovereignty of the United Kingdom.'

Copeland looked at her and said: 'Now I've got it! You're Beryl!' and they gave each other a hug.

Beth Spencer. Sunday, August 28 th.

The half marathon had not gone well for Beth and she arrived home feeling disappointed she had been so far outside her personal best. She could have blamed the unseasonal high heat and humidity, but she was more tempted to blame the way her work had kept her so busy during the last few days, and had taken her away from her normal training schedule. She resisted the idea that getting nearer forty than thirty may be having an effect.

She had finally finished seething at her performance and the lack of post race facilities when she parked her car on the drive of her semi-detached on the outskirts of Lincoln and checked her phone. Simon had not rung or texted since she had cried off on their dinner engagement the previous evening. When he did not go with her to apathetically cheer her on, he always texted the morning of a run to apathetically wish her good luck, but her phone showed no activity. Should she care? At the moment, she cared more about having a shower and getting changed.

She got out of the car and went to get her sports bag out of the boot. Strange. It looked like there was someone hiding in a car parked on the other side of her road. She could see a shoulder sticking up above the side window. She watched for a moment. The shoulder did not move. She took her bag from the boot and slammed it shut, her eyes fixed on the parked car.

A head shot up and furtively looked around, saw her, and ducked down again.

'Pssst,' hissed a voice from behind her. She turned round to see her neighbour beckoning her over. She dropped her sports bag and went to the fence.

'Beth! Beth!' said the neighbourly Mrs. Pratt, who knew all the comings and goings in the road. She came to the fence.

'Hello, Mrs. Pratt. Anything wrong?' said Beth, warmly, because she knew Mrs. Pratt was a busybody but had a heart of gold.

'Beth, I am doing my duty as a member of the community watch scheme – I am most definitely not a nosy neighbour – and I have to warn you there has been a strange man in that car opposite your house all morning. I think he might be a burglar,' said Mrs. Pratt, eyes wide and finger wagging.

'I think I know him. He's not a burglar,' said Beth.

Mrs Pratt's eyes widened. 'He's a stalker! Can't have beautiful young lady doctors like you being stalked by a rapist! I'll phone the police!'

'No. It's OK, Mrs. Pratt. He's not a stalker. At least, I don't think he's a stalker. I'll go over and speak to him. You go back inside. Don't worry. I still do my kickboxing once a week. Thank you, though.'

Mrs Pratt had a troubled look on her face. 'I'll just watch from inside. My phone is in the bay window, ready for me to dial 999 if I see anything suspicious,' she said and shuffled in her slippers back into her house.

Beth would have rolled up her sleeves but she was still wearing her running vest. She marched across the road and looked into the parked car. There was the back of a familiar semi-bald head. She rapped on the window. Tom Benson stopped hiding his face and looked up. He shooed her away. She knocked again. He shooed again.

'Open the pod bay door, Tom!' she shouted, sure a reference to a classic would get him.

Staying prone across the front seats, he wound down the window.

How old is this car? she thought.

'Get into your house!' hissed Tom Benson.

'You can come in if you want,' said Beth, sure that Tom was too sincere, as well as too small, to be a genuine stalker. Her black belt skills gave her some extra confidence.

'Not yet,' said Tom, moving up a few decibels with his whisper. 'I have to make sure you're not being followed.'

He wound the window shut and threw his face back down onto the passenger seat.

Beth thought for a moment. She realised she had no thoughts appropriate for this situation.

'Er, OK, Tom, I'm going in and having a shower. You, er, keep watch here for a while and ring the bell when you're ready,' she said and started to turn. She stopped and slapped her thigh. She knew that wouldn't do. She tapped the window again and spoke just loudly enough for him to hear. 'We're still a team, right? Just like... Mork and Mindy.' Without lifting his face from the seat, Benson gave her the thumbs up.

Smiling, she crossed the road, waved to the neighbourly Mrs Pratt, scooped up her bag, went into her house and was in her shower two minutes later.

When she turned the shower off, she could hear the doorbell. It chimed repeatedly. Someone had their finger held on it. Fearing Benson would bolt before she could get downstairs to the door, Beth gave her short hair one rub, gave her body one quick towel wipe, threw on a white tee shirt, hitched up her jeans and ran downstairs.

The small, balding, spectacled round face of Tom Benson was looking down the street. His finger was still on the door bell. He was wearing a green short sleeve shirt and green combat trousers. He had his lunch in an opaque plastic container under one arm.

'Tom!' said Beth.

Startled, he jumped back and his finger finally disconnected from the door bell.

'Good, it's you. My camouflage clothes are useless in front of your white door,' he said as he pushed past her.

Beth watched him rush down her hall and towards her kitchen. 'Who else were you expecting to open the door of my house?'

'Quick! Close the door!' shouted Tom, disappearing into the kitchen.

Beth closed the door and followed him down her hallway. 'This is not turning out to be the quiet Sunday afternoon I expected,' she said to herself.

Tom had placed his lunch box on her breakfast bar and was looking inside her toaster when she entered the kitchen. He looked intense. 'Beth! Dr. Spencer! Have you bought anything new in the last few days? Been given any gifts by strangers? Who are Mork and Mindy?' Tom fired off the questions while he searched under the bread bin and inside the coffee maker.

'Er... Tom... What? It's an old TV show. My dad used to have a box set,' she said, then brought herself back to the present. 'What exactly are you doing, Tom?'

'Searching for bugs. They may be listening to everything we're saying.'

'Tom. Just stop. Just stop searching my kitchen and tell me what you're doing here – besides searching my kitchen, that is,' she said, sitting on one of the stools at the breakfast bar and realising the back of her jeans was wet. She still needed to dry herself properly.

Tom Benson finally turned round and said, 'When I finished work I... oh... oh... *oh gosh!'*

For a moment she was puzzled, then she saw where Tom's eyes were looking. She definitely needed to dry herself properly. Throwing on a white tee shirt over a wet body had consequences.

'Tom, please raise your eyes so you are looking at my face and not my... er, chest,' she said as calmly as she could.

'Now, Tom!' she snapped.

He raised his eyes. They started sinking down again. 'I think it's better if I just turn round,' said Tom, turning round.

'OK. Just give me a moment to change. Have some juice out of the fridge. Glasses are in the cupboard above the microwave,' she said, swivelling off the stool and going upstairs.

In a loose blue blouse she returned to the kitchen to find Tom Benson seated at the breakfast bar holding his plastic lunch box between both hands, staring at it.

'I don't mind if you want to eat your lunch,' she said, sitting alongside him.

'This is not my lunch,' he said. 'It's Usman Fayad's hand.'

There was a long, long silence. It was followed by a longer one.

He turned and looked at her. 'Don't worry. I was careful. The box is from the pathology lab. It's hermetically sealed – totally airtight. And I haven't touched it. I had gloves and a mask and I took some of those long tongs things in case I found it.' He turned back and stared at the white box.

'And did you see what sort of state it was in?' she asked

He worked in a hospital. He had picked up lots of medical terminology.

'It was yukky,' he said. 'But something happened that's much, much worse.'

There was a long, long silence.

'OK, Tom, tell me what happened,' Beth eventually said.

He did not stop staring at the box. 'I was wrong,' he said. 'First, I thought this was the start of the zombie apocalypse. Then I thought it was aliens testing us. Then I thought it was a government experiment. I briefly considered a secret Masonic sect. But now I know... It's the Mafia!'

She gave him a while to sit in silence. She put her hand on his arm. 'Come on, Tom. We're a team, remember? Holmes and Watson. Han Solo and Chewbacca. Mork and Mindy. Just tell me what happened. What's got you so scared?'

'I need a drink,' he said. 'Something stronger than orange juice.'

Beth never drank, but found a cheap bottle of brandy she sometimes used for cooking and half filled a tumbler. He took a huge swig and gulped it down. He shuddered.

Then he told her.

Tom Benson, Saturday August 27 th. (The day before!) *(Like a flashback, but without the wavy bits first.)*

By 6 p.m. Tom Benson had finished all the work he intended to do for the day and sat staring at his blank computer screen. He thought about phoning Beth and asking her out to dinner. He had never asked anyone out to dinner before and rehearsed it in his head: 'Hi Beth, want to talk about dissolving hands over dinner?' He thought it didn't sound quite right. Besides, he knew Beth was way out of his league. In fact, he was probably not even in a league. The biggest compliment he had ever got was 'gnome face', and that was from his mother. He gave up thinking about Beth, but knew he needed to do something. After everything he had learned today he could not just go home, eat takeaway and watch Netflix. He really wanted to share his news with his accomplices at the Online Conspiracies Forum, but knew it was more than his job was worth to break patient confidentiality about Popov and his symptoms, and there was not much to say about Usman Fayad other than he had been found dead without his hand...

The idea started as a mild simmer, bubbled for a while, and eventually came to the boil. Benson thumped the side of his fist on the desk, winced, shook the pain from his hand and left the office with a determined stride. He had never done a determined stride in his life and he began to like his new, beardless self.

He went to the empty pathology department, took the bunch of keys from his pocket and helped himself to everything he needed. He threw the blue surgical gloves, the face mask and the white lab coat onto the back seat of his rusty VW Golf. He put the plastic box and the tongs on the passenger seat. Within twenty minutes he had driven to the other side of the town and was on St. Paul's Road: the only road in and out of the docks. He parked in front of a warehouse opposite the end of the small park where Fayad's body had been found. There were no other vehicles in sight. Who worked on bank holiday Saturday evening? He could hear youthful shouts from the park behind the trees and decided to leave the white coat in the car. It was still too warm for a jacket, so he stuffed the gloves into one trouser pocket and the mask into the other. He picked up the box and tongs, locked his car and began walking down the road towards the docks.

To his left was the park. He passed the pedestrian park entrance with a small sign naming the park as St. Paul's Park, and could see a group of youths playing football on the park grass beyond. After the entrance, a shoulder high iron fence bordered the side of the park. On the other side of the road, to his right, he passed a similar fence that ineffectively guarded a group of small engineering factories housed in corrugated iron sheds. Opposite the gates leading into to the factories was the park's play area with a slide, roundabout, and climbing frames. A handful of children were screaming down the slide and two chatting fathers watched them from a bench. Passing further along the side of the park fence, he passed a blue, tubular metal, covered seat. The fence ended, providing a gap for vehicles to enter the park and Benson went through it to go to the covered bench. He knelt down and examined the grass around it. He soon spotted a circle of blood-stained grass. This was where Fayad had been found.

He stood up and looked around. Where had Fayad come from? He considered the rest of the park and the factories, but dismissed them. If Fayad had been sleeping rough he would have had some possessions – at least a coat – and they would have been found by now if they were on the factories' premises, and the park was too open, too exposed to sleep in.

He went back to the road and resumed his walk towards the docks. After taking a few paces, he noticed a red stain in the road. If he had not been looking for it, he would not have seen it. It was small and worn by lorry wheels passing over it. Ten paces further on he found another, then another. Fayad had come this way, bleeding from his amputated hand.

The trail led Benson to the entrance to the docks. The fence was higher here, perhaps eight feet, and the razor wire topped gate was closed and locked. There was a security guard in the hut just inside the entrance, and, as Benson watched, another security guard with a dog emerged from behind a stack of timber just beyond the fence. Security and a dog ruled out

Fayad sleeping inside the docks area itself, but that was where the blood trail seemed to lead.

Benson turned and began retracing his steps. He stopped by the last blood stain in the road, turned and looked back at the port's gates.

To his left was the port's empty lorry park, with a large warehouse beyond it. In front of its entrance was a blue sign with directions to different wharfs. The sign was in front of a solid wooden fence with two trees behind it. Benson walked over and saw a small car park between the wooden fence and the port fence. The wooden fence stood at the corner of the car park, stretching from the lorry park fence, behind the blue direction sign, and turning a right angle before finishing a few metres along the car park.

He went over to look behind the fence, thinking it could have been a good home for Fayad, sheltered by a fence and two tall trees, and perhaps there was a corner next to the lorry park fence which could be made unseen enough for a vagrants home? Benson walked round the end of the fence and saw a parked car, but nothing else. He looked around. The car park was empty. Why would someone park here, as if hiding their car behind the fence when the whole car park was empty? Was the car abandoned? Was Fayad sleeping in this abandoned car? Benson went over to the car and looked inside. There was nothing unusual.

He heard a dog bark, close. Someone shouted: 'Get away from my car!'

He turned to see the security guard with the dog on the other side of the port fence, halfway down the car park. Benson was about to wave to the security guard but thought better of it. Waving long stainless steel tongs in the air might look a little suspicious.

He deduced the car had been parked there because it was probably the best place for shade, and on a day like today it was a good idea to keep the car as cool as possible. No one liked having to wait for a scorching steering wheel to cool down before driving home.

Walking back round the solid fence, he faced an old car park on the other side of the port access road. Only concrete bollards and a small red post box separated it from the road. This car park's tarmac was buckled by underground roots and weeds were growing through the cracks. At the far end there was a patch of grass and a few trees. Benson walked over the cracked concrete and saw low, brick buildings under the trees. As he approached he realised there must have been houses here once and these two structures were outhouses where people went before everyone expected an indoor lavatory.

He went to the nearest. The brick walls remained, but the roof had gone along with the door. He stepped over some tree roots and looked inside. Coke cans and a couple of condoms were on the floor, but nothing else. He walked round a bush and stepped over the remnants of an old brick wall and looked in the other outhouse.

Benson had been so intent on his search he had almost forgotten what he was searching for, so when he saw the severed hand lying inside the old outhouse he vomited. Throwing the box and the tongs to one side he turned and vomited again. He staggered to a nearby tree to lean on and vomited a third time. He gasped to regain his breath, his arms outstretched against the tree and his head down. He wretched a few more times, but nothing came out. He forced himself to take long, deep breaths and felt his stomach gradually settle. He saw vomit on his shoe and turned his foot and tried to wipe it off on a clump of long grass.

He took a final deep breath and pulled himself up straight. He took the gloves and mask from his pockets, and pulled out his handkerchief. He used the handkerchief to wipe the vomit from his mouth and clean his glasses, and instantly regretted doing it in that order. He tied on the mask, pulled on the gloves and picked up the tongs and box, keeping his eyes down. He braced himself and looked into the abandoned outhouse. There was the hand, on the brick floor near the entrance. The skin was flaking and muscles were exposed, but there were no signs that it had started to decompose in the heat and there were no flies on it. Lying close to the hand was a bloody kitchen knife. The brick floor was stained with dried blood. Against the far wall there was a pile of Fayad's belongings, including a coat and a few soup cans, but Benson paid them little attention. He removed the lid from the box and used the tongs with both hands to lift the hand and lower it into the box. He picked up the knife with the tongs, put it in the box beside the hand, dropped the tongs in the box with his discoveries and put the lid back on. He pressed the lid's edges all the way round to make sure it was airtight.

He removed the mask and put it back in his empty pocket. Wait... Where was his phone? He looked around, pulled back clumps of grass, checked around the tree where he had leant to vomit. His phone was not there. Where else could it have fallen out? He remembered he had bent over to look in the car behind the fence. It must have fallen out then.

He unsuccessfully checked around him one more time before picking up the box, stepping over his vomit, walking across the cracked car park, crossing the road and going back behind the wooden fence to search for his phone. The security guard in the gate hut had gone and the one with the dog was nowhere in sight and he supposed they were doing their rounds before the night shift came.

He put the box down next to the front tyre and began searching round the car. He was on his stomach looking underneath when he heard a car approaching, turning, stopping. He didn't really want to go back round the fence and abandon the search for his phone so he stood up to look over the fence, but found he wasn't tall enough. There was a small, round knot hole where the wood had come out, and he bent down to look through.

A dark green car of indistinguishable make had pulled into the cracked concrete car park opposite. Two men, one shorter than the other got out of the front seats. They were wearing long dark raincoats and dark fedora hats. The taller of the two opened the car boot and the shorter one reached in and lifted things out. Benson could not see what the things were, but there was something shiny. They shut the boot, opened the rear doors and hauled two other men out. These two were wearing vests, one of which was covered with blood, and Benson could just make out swirling tattoos down their muscular arms, which seemed to be tied behind their backs. The two raincoat men pushed the two big tattooed men across the car park and into the trees in the far corner, exactly where Benson had emerged a few minutes before, leaving his fresh vomit behind.

Benson kept watching, even though the four men had disappeared into the trees and gone behind the nearest out-house. His back was starting to ache and he was just considering resuming his search when he heard a loud bang. Benson instinctively jumped back. His shoulder bounced off the car door and there was a second bang before he regained his balance.

He went back to the hole in the fence, dropped to one knee, and watched. The two men in the raincoats and hats emerged from the trees. Alone. They went back to their car, stood beside the bonnet and spoke to each other. Benson could not hear them, but saw the shorter man get into the passenger seat and the taller one walk directly towards him. He pulled his eye away from the fence and began urinating down his leg. His heart seemed to have relocated itself into his ears and he put his hands on his ears to try to deaden the noise. His eyes were shut tight and he was on his backside with his back pressed against the fence. His thighs were wet and the wetness had spread to his buttocks. He had the consoling thought that with his eyes closed and his heart pounding in his ears, he would know nothing about it when the man came round the fence and put a bullet in his head. This consoling thought provoked another deluge of urine.

He opened one eye and slowly turned his head to look towards the end of the fence. There was no one there. He lowered his hands from his ears, thankful his heart had subsided into a mere steel drum. He edged himself round and back onto a wet knee to look through the knot hole. The raincoat man was standing a few yards away, in the middle of the road, but had his back to the fence and was looking down the road past the park.

A dog barked and Benson saw the raincoat man walk quickly back to his car. He got into the driver's seat, but the car did not pull away for a few moments. When it did, the tyres spun and threw up dust as it reversed at top speed out of the car park, then swung round and, without stopping, sped off down St. Paul's Road.

Benson sat down again. He was past caring how wet his trousers were. His shirt was almost as wet with perspiration and his hair would have been sticking to his face if he had any for it to stick. He put his hands on his knees. They were shaking, so were his knees. He pulled his knees up to his chin and wrapped his arms around his shins and gripped, foetus like, until the shaking stopped. He told himself he had been in scarier situations than this and reminded himself of that huge spider in his bath, and being in the lift when, for a moment, he thought it had broken down, and, worst of all, the terror he had felt when he ate a yoghurt that was a day beyond its 'eat by' date.

After a few minutes recuperating, he swung onto his hands and knees and crawled on all fours to the back of the parked car. He had one more glance under the car then peered round the boot to see if a security guard was anywhere in sight. It was all clear. He crouched and, keeping as low as he could, made his way to the edge of the fence. He stopped, turned round and went back for the box.

Once he was round the fence he stood and broke into a half jog back to his car. He got as far as the end of park before he forced himself to turn round and head back to the derelict outhouses. As he crossed the cracking car park he lost his nerve and turned again to head back to his car, then stopped, braced himself with a deep breath, turned yet again and went into the trees. He placed the box down beside the first old outhouse and went over the remnants of the wall to the other. He went up to a side wall and stood with his back flattened against it, then edged gradually sideways to the opening. He stopped at the corner, inhaled deeply, held it, and bobbed his head round the corner.

This one flash was all he needed to know he had been right. He had glimpsed the two bodies lying on the floor, exactly where Fayad's hand had been. He edged round the corner as far as where the door had once been. The side of his leg hit something. He looked down to see his leg pressed against a dead man's leg. He sidled back a step, mustered his courage and looked into the outhouse.

The two bodies were lying so one was partially across the other. They were lying in a pool of their own blood and each had a hole in the back of the head. His plan to check their pulses seemed pointless. They had both fallen forwards and Benson could see their hands had been bound behind them with plastic cable ties, pulled tight enough to cut into their skin. He squatted down, reached and lifted the head of the one on top and, as he had suspected he would, he recognised him.

Benson took two careful steps back, turned, walked as fast as he could, grabbed the box and ran back to his car. He put the box in his boot where, luckily, he had a plastic supermarket bag, which he put on his car seat to stop it getting stained from the personal liquid on his trousers.

Within fifteen minutes he was home and fifteen minutes after that he was showered, changed and back in his car. When he released the handbrake to pull away, he saw his phone where he had left it in the glove shelf under the steering wheel.

'Ronaldo', Sunday 28 th. August.

'Mr. Brown? The farmer, Mr Brown? You're not supposed to call this number unless it's an emergency.

'Oh, I see. And what did the police want?

'And you have been well compensated for the shed, Mr Brown.

'Who reported the explosion?'

Damn, thought the man they called Ronaldo. The old couple had already reported it before we took care of them. We should have acted more quickly.

'Yes, Mr. Brown. I am still here.

'What do I want you to do about it? There's not much you can do.

'I see. You're right. They may indeed come back with a search warrant. There's nothing for them to find.

'No, I don't think you need to leave the country, Mr. Brown.

'Yes, they may well arrest you. Just tell them the truth. They can't charge you with anything.

'Yes, if you tell them that you might be in trouble. But you don't really *know* that, do you, Mr. Brown. That's just what you think – just your theory.

'It may or may not be the truth, Mr. Brown. You just tell them the facts and let them find their own truth.

'And how much more do you want to just stick to the facts, Mr. Brown?'

Ronaldo considered. The old Professors had already been 'disappeared'. Another disappearance, such as Mr. Brown's, might arouse too much attention. As long as only the overstretched local police were involved, everything would be alright. Another disappearance like the old professors might draw the attention of more than just the local police. Then they could be in trouble.

'Yes, Mr. Brown, I am thinking it over. It does seem to be rather a lot of money.

'Very well, Mr. Brown, I agree to your terms. As long as you give me your word you will divulge nothing but the facts and you will not, I repeat NOT, share any of your theories.

'Very well, then we are agreed. Another envelope will be put through your door before the end of the week.

'Yes, Mr. Brown, the police may be back before then, but you will have to trust me on this. I honour my debts, Mr. Brown, and we have an agreement, do we not?

'Good. Remember, just stick to the facts, Mr. Brown. Goodbye.'

Beth Spencer and Tom Benson. Sunday, August 28 th.

Tom had finished his story and was pointing to his empty glass. She gave him half as much as before.

'So who were they? The dead people? Hang on! Where did you sleep last night?' she said.

'In my car. I couldn't go to a hotel. These people have people everywhere. They could track my credit card. I haven't got enough cash and couldn't risk using my bank card to get some from an ATM,' he said, emptied his glass in one go and reached for the brandy bottle.

Beth snatched it out of the way. 'You've had enough. Just a few questions then you're getting in the shower and I'm looking to see if Simon has left some of his clothes here. They'll be far too big, but will do while we get yours washed.'

'Is Simon your boyfriend?' asked Tom, looking embarrassed to have asked.

'Yes. No. Was. I don't know. We've been off and on for years – ever since he came to Cambridge to do his PhD. We were on yesterday but I think we are off today. I moved back here a couple of months ago. Again. Let's just say we're having a break. Probably,' she said without stopping for the niceties of punctuation.

'I see,' said Tom. 'Thanks for making that clear.'

'Now, come on, Tom, before you stink the place out. Who were they? The two dead guys?'

'I've seen them before. Their photos anyway. They've been in the local paper. They were arrested for something... people trafficking, worker exploitation, something like that, but they got off. The newspaper called them 'The Boston Mafia' and the story about them said they were Russian and implied they had links to the Russian Mafia. We can search online.'

'So why come here? Why not go to the police?'

He looked at her as if she was crazy for not seeing the obvious. 'Who the hell would kidnap and execute two members of the Russian Mafia? There's only one organisation which could do that and get away with it. The two guys in the raincoats and hats were Pickfords!'

'Pickfords? The people who move your stuff when you move house?'

'This Pickfords is a super secret branch of UK spooks – spies to you. They do all the illegal stuff like assassinations.'

'They work for the Government?'

'That's one theory. A better theory is they work for themselves. Maybe both. Maybe the Government works on the idea that if you want to keep a secret then you must also hide it from yourself.' His index finger was up in quotation mode again.

'Hang on George Orwell!' she said, guessing the quote. 'How do you know this if they are so super secret?'

'Tics,' he said, touching a finger to the side of his nose. 'You know... tics.' He winked at her.

She frowned. 'Tics,' she said. 'Tics? Little bugs that feed off blood? Live in mattresses?'

Tom looked shocked. 'Hadn't thought of that. Maybe we should change our name... We could become...'

She interrupted. 'So who or what are *your* tics?' she asked and could not believe what she was saying.

'Tics is what we call our group. We have a forum on the dark web where we solve conspiracies together. We've proven aliens live here and look just like us. We've got the evidence to show the Americans have already gone to other planets using alien technology from Roswell, which is strange considering they faked the moon landings. And we know the Egyptians didn't actually *build* the pyramids – they just moved the desert away. Kennedy was...'

'Stop! Stop! Stop! Just tell me – why tics!'

'Truth Investigation Council. So we're called Tics for short,' he said and she thought he looked prouder than she had seen him before. 'We investigate until we get to the truth. The truth is out there, you know!'

'OK. Enough,' she said. 'You're getting in the shower now – ah, yes, you are! You're not having another brandy until you do. We can talk again later. I suppose you haven't eaten all day and I've been living on bananas and energy bars. I know it's early but I know a decent Indian that will deliver. You get what I order. No meat – or fish! Throw your clothes out the door and I'll put them in the machine. I'll sort something out for you to wear and leave them by the door. You'll find a towel in the cupboard in the corner of the bathroom. Go!'

He opened his mouth. She pointed. He went.

'Straight ahead at the top of the stairs,' she shouted.

'Whatever you do, don't phone Copeland,' he shouted back. 'He's the one who sent Pickfords to kill those guys.'

After his shower, Benson had to make do with one of Beth's tee shirts and a pair of her yellow lycra cycling shorts. The tee shirt fitted him like a marquee and the cycling shorts were, well, snug.

D.I. Copeland. Sunday, August 28 th.

When they had finished their obscenely long hug, Beryl, a.k.a. Mrs. Pickford, explained their relationship to DCI Ross and Sergeant Brandon. Larry and Beryl became best friends on the first day of their degree course. They were studying the same subject (though they refused to say what) and had found they were in the same hall of residence, though in separate, single sex wings. They had spent days together going to lectures, drinking coffee, having lunch, but mainly walking around the campus talking. They had spent evenings together eating their hall's evening meals and afterwards together in the bar. A group of mutual friends grew around them. For some reason, they never ran out of conversation and laughed at everything together. After the first year, they had shared a house with some of their friends for the next year and a half, until Beryl had moved out to live with her boyfriend. When her relationship did not work out, she started sharing a house with Copeland and some other friends again. At some point, each of them knew the other better than they knew themselves. Then he had met his (ex) wife and, after seven years of a totally platonic relationship (they both stressed), they had grown apart and eventually reverted to shorter and shorter messages in Christmas cards.

She stroked his hair and said, 'The stomach's grown, but nice to see the hair is all still there, Lawrence, even if it has turned grey.'

'It's silver!' he said, grinning.

'I knew you would say that. You always were a vain bastard!' she said and they both laughed and hugged again.

'And you look great,' he said.

'You didn't even recognise me!' she said.

'Just thrown off. I thought you worked for a bank. That's the last thing you told me about yourself in a Christmas card, what, ten years ago?' said Copeland.

'No. I told you I worked *at* a bank, not for a bank,' she said and raised her eyebrows.

Sergeant Brandon could not contain himself any longer and blurted, 'Pickfords HQ is in a bank?'

She looked at him and put her hand on his knee. 'Detective Sergeant Brandon,' she said, 'if I answered that I would have to kill you. Probably with the poisoned needle in this ring on the finger I now have on your leg.'

Brandon looked down at her hand and her ring. He shuffled back in his chair. He looked back in her eyes. He swallowed hard. 'Really?' he said.

She squeezed his leg and he jumped. 'No, just winding you up,' she said, but her face had no humour as her eyes narrowed and she added, 'Or am I?'

She removed her hand from his leg and clapped her hands. 'Right, Coppers, let's get down to business. And from now on I'm Mrs. Pickford again, even to you Lawrence! So, Lawrence, you were moderately intelligent once. At least intelligent enough not to do your own essays and copy mine instead – and don't go on about how unfair it was that I got an A and you got a D when it was the same essay – just tell me what you think. Ask the questions!'

'Right, *Mrs Pickford,*' said Larry Copeland, wishing he had written his questions down. 'I think there's something not right about all this and I have lots of questions. Let's start with Popov. Let's assume he is a Chechen terrorist. So there he is in Chechnya, and even if he's older than his fake passport says, he's still pretty young when the war breaks out with Russia in '94, and is not that old when the second war breaks out in '99, but somehow he gets this powerful, lethal

189

chemical weapon the Russians have called Nosoi. He travels with it, or the knowhow of how to make it, all the way through Turkey and on to Bulgaria. He stays there long enough to learn the language – not an easy language to learn. And Popov doesn't seem to be a fast learner considering he's managed to learn almost no English in the few months he's been here. Why not come straight here instead of learning Bulgarian first? It doesn't take that long to get a fake passport. Anyway, he gets here, still with the Nosoi or the instructions to make it, and ends up living in a squalid bedsit and working for two fake Russians. But they tell us he won't work weekends, so we think he's meeting up with his terrorist friends somewhere and cooking up plans and cooking up Nosoi. Why is he working at all if this is all so well financed? Why does he refuse to go to the farm if that's where he goes anyway to brew the Nosoi with this Ronaldo? Then to cap it all, this ruthless international terrorist takes himself off to the A & E when he spills some Nosoi on his hand?'

'So, Lawrence, what do you conclude?' asked Mrs Pickford.

'Hmmm...' said Copeland. 'He's not a terrorist. He really is a migrant worker. His passport is fake, but he speaks Bulgarian... hmmm... Got it! He's a Serb! The Serbs who live by the Bulgarian border speak Bulgarian and it would be easy for him to slip over the border and pass himself off as Bulgarian with an accent.'

'Or,' said DCI Ross, 'he's a Chechen terrorist who learned Bulgarian from a Bulgarian parent, or something. And he really does go off at weekends to make Nosoi with his terrorist accomplices.'

'Both are possible, though one explanation seems more plausible than the other,' said Mrs. Beryl Pickford.

'And I think Popov had another job on the side that he did at weekends,' said Copeland, 'that's why he didn't like working for the Karamazov brothers at weekends!'

'Any evidence for that, Lawrence?' asked Mrs Pickford.

Come on Copeland, tell her about the five hundred pounds you found in his room, said his inner voice, turning into his conscience.

'No evidence. Just a hunch at the moment,' shrugged Copeland, but saw Mrs. Pickford was scrutinising him closely.

'If you say so,' she said. 'Carry on.'

'So Popov and Fayad end up working in the soon to explode tractor shed a week yesterday and they get something on their hands. Their hands start to dissolve, or necrotise as the doctors keep calling it. Popov takes himself to hospital. A couple of days later, Fayad panics and cuts his hand off, or gets someone to cut it off for him. Maybe it is liquid Nosoi and they were making it with Ronaldo in the old tractor shed, or, more likely, making it *for* Ronaldo. Trouble is, the equipment left in the tractor shed looked like some pretty basic farm type stuff to me.'

'We'll know more after forensics do some tests,' said Ross.

Copeland continued. 'So Ronaldo is seen by old Professor Philip the morning Popov and Fayad go to help at the farm and he stays there after all the workers have gone and blows up the old shed? To destroy evidence?'

Ross cut in again, saying, 'And we know Fayad is a terrorist. We were just told so. They picked up his name in the terrorists chatter they intercepted.'

'Yes, they did,' said Copeland. 'In our experience, Chief, how many times have terrorists used the real name of one of their own during an ongoing attack? Especially when it's an organisation like Al-Qaeda!'

D.C.I. Ross thought. 'Can't think of it ever happening before. Not ever,' he said.

Copeland clapped his hands together. 'Right! Never! Then the Russians tell Western governments all about Nosoi. Sure, they gave us a heads up on Chechen terrorists heading our way a few months ago, but said nothing about Nosoi or chemical weapons or poison gas then, did they? They didn't say anything about Chechen links with Afghans or Algerians or an Arab ex-prince, did they? Then Popov goes to the hospital and they are falling over themselves to tell us about Nosoi. Two of them, one of them being Colonel Vasily Goraya, no less, even goes up to Boston looking for him and plug me for information.'

A momentary pause followed.

Copeland let it sink in long enough before adding, 'Now everyone thinks this Prince Abdul Karim is the mastermind bringing all these groups – which usually hate each other, by the way – they all get together in a farm shed to make Nosoi. In a farm shed? Karim is supposed to be loaded and he uses a farm shed? I'm looking forward to reading *his* file!'

'But...,' said Ross, beginning to hesitate in his role as devil's advocate, 'but... the information from the Saudis has been telling us and the CIA that Karim has been shepherding together different terror groups.'

'Yes, indeed they have,' nodded Copeland. 'I'm sure he is not exactly one of their favourite sons after he spirited away a pile of their money, so what ulterior motive might they possibly have for seeing him arrested and sent back to Saudi? Or better still *removed* by a Pickford agent?'

He looked at Beryl, a.k.a. Mrs. Pickford. 'That's why you're here, isn't it, Beryl? You Pickfords have had a request to eliminate this Abdul Karim, but you are not so sure about him really having a terrorist connection, are you?'

'So far so good, Lawrence,' said Mrs. Pickford. 'There are lots more questions, but there is one big one you are holding back on.'

Copeland looked at the two other SO15 officers sitting in their intimate circle. He had to trust them. The main question on his mind was where he was going to get a good lunch now it was too late for the golf club? But he chose an alternative.

'Who is the mole in SO15? We must have someone here working for the Russians. How else could they know I was in Boston investigating Popov? No way could they hack into GCHQ!' he said.

Mrs. Pickford said: 'That's the wrong question, Lawrence, but while we are on the subject... I really would prefer not to use the poison ring.' The cool air blowing through the ceiling vents was audible in the silence. Mrs. Pickford looked up at the vents.

'It was me!' wailed Sergeant Brandon, cracking under the stress.

DCI Ross was on his feet. 'You! Traitor! You're working for the Russians!' he screamed.

Brandon bent over, and with his head on his knees, put his hands on the back of his neck, as if protecting himself from the exploding bomb Ross had become.

'No, I'm not working for the Russians,' murmured Brandon on the edge of tears. 'You told me to inform GCHQ that we had sent Copeland to investigate Popov as a possible Chechen terrorist. I got chatting to Holly at the coffee machine... I forgot to tell GCHQ. I remembered later and sent the message from home.'

'Oh my God,' said Copeland, slapping his hand onto his forehead.

Ross started jabbing a finger into Brandon's shoulder. 'You're an idiot, Sergeant! Anyone could have intercepted that! You are suspended and will be under house arrest until we investigate this breach,' he said.

Mrs. Pickford clasped Ross's poking finger. 'Please sit down, Detective Chief Inspector. We're not finished yet. Lawrence, do go on with your questions,' she said.

Ross stared at her hand around his finger. He looked at her ring. He began to sit and she released the finger.

'So,' said Copeland, 'if the Russians intercepted Brandon's message, why did they send a senior SVR agent up to Boston? They had told us Chechen terrorists might be coming and we were investigating one. Why were they so interested? Maybe Popov is a big fish and they wanted to whisk him back to Russia to interrogate him themselves, but they could have done that through official channels and still got their way. And if he is a big fish, then we come back to the question of why he took himself to the hospital. Does he know how to make Nosoi and the Russians wanted to get to him before we got the formula out of him? Logically, that must be it.'

Mrs Pickford placed her hands on his cheeks. 'That's it, Lawrence. That's the logical answer. Popov is a Chechen terrorist and has the blueprints for making Nosoi. Even though you have just convinced us Popov is probably not a terrorist – that is the logical answer. Well done. Now... tell me what your police officer instincts tell you,' she said affectionately.

She placed his hands on top of his and looked deeply into his brown eyes.

'This all leads back to Popov and if he is just an everyday migrant worker, then... then... It's all about the Russians!' he said. 'Everything they have ever done is cloaked in deceit and lies. They have been telling tall stories.'

She kept the deep eye contact with him and said, 'I can run with that. But the big question is *why*? What are the Russians, and our Saudi friends, up to? I think our answers are on that farm. Get back up to Boston and take Sergeant Brandon with you. Everyone deserves a second chance and he needs to make up for his mistake.'

She took her hands from Copeland's. She twisted the ring on her finger and placed her hand on Ross's thigh. 'If that's alright with you, DCI Ross?' she said sweetly.

Ross sighed heavily. 'If you say so, Mrs Pickford,' he said.

'Good,' she said, and turning to Copeland, 'Get up there this evening, Lawrence. You will have most of the day tomorrow before the Americans arrive. I arranged a few road works and detours down some very narrow lanes for them when I found out they were getting involved.'

She stood up, but was not much taller when standing. 'I have to go now,' she said, 'and it may be a while before I see you again, Detective Inspector Lawrence Copeland. Look after yourself and do some exercise occasionally.' She kissed him on the cheek and left.

Go on, Copeland... you have a little cry...

Beth Spencer and Tom Benson. Sunday, 28 th. August.

Tom Benson sat in an armchair. Beth had her legs up on her sofa. Fayad's hand was in the fridge. None of the three had spoken since Tom had come downstairs.

'Did you give me this tee shirt on purpose?' asked Tom, eventually.

'What?' said Beth, stirring.

'This tee shirt,' he said. 'It has fish on it with tails made of vegetables. There's a cod with a broccoli tail, a trout with a celery tail, a... don't know what that is with green beans for a tail... Did you give me this tee shirt on purpose?'

'I get fed up of going to restaurants and saying I'm a vegetarian and they ask me if I eat fish. A fish is not a vegetable. I wear it when I go back, if I ever do. It's one of my favourites, so maybe I did choose it on purpose. And the shorts suit you too. You have very nice legs. Very, er, unhairy.'

He smiled. 'Thank you. I think,' he said.

'I'm phoning to see where this takeaway is,' she said. She made the call.

'Great. They are short staffed and say it will be another hour. I couldn't be bothered to lose my temper. Now, Tom, I don't normally drink, but I'm going to get a bottle of wine. This has not been a normal week and this is definitely not a normal day, so I am making it an exception.'

'OK. I'd give you some money, but, you know...' he said.

'No problem. You have enough on your mind. Listen, I was thinking. If you are right about this Pickfords and Copeland, then it might be a good idea not to use my computer. They may be monitoring it. I am a terrorist's doctor, apparently. If we go online looking up these dead Karamazov guys, or even go onto the dark web and contact your forum buddies, we may have visitors before we know it. They would want to know what I'm up to, at the very least. Better safe than sorry.'

He nodded. 'You're right,' he said, 'they could be monitoring your phone too.'

'Hmmm... right. Ok, I won't be long. Help yourself to tea if you want, but I don't have any sugar and you will have to put up with soya milk,' she said and went to the hall to put her shoes on and grab her credit card. 'And, by the way,' she shouted, 'I phoned the ward to see if the ambulance from The Royal Free had picked Popov up. I spoke to that stupid nurse Zora and she had to go and check – she said they were two nurses down and there were no admin staff there to arrange agency nurses, so you might be in trouble. But at least she checked for me and said Popov had been collected. So that's one piece of good news at least, at least the whole country might not get infected by Popov Disease floating about in dust if we're lucky. See you in a while!'

He heard the door shut. He was stunned by what Beth had just said. He just could not believe it. To no one in particular, he said, 'Soya milk? Doesn't she know soya is all genetically modified and will cause her grandchildren to have two heads?'

When she returned she found Tom had laid the table. The food had arrived and Tom had placed the cardboard topped foil containers on place mats along one side of her dining table. She had bought a bottle of red and a bottle of white, both with screw tops because she was not sure if she actually owned a corkscrew. She had also bought a bottle of whiskey for later.

They toasted with the cheap Chardonnay, opened the food containers and spooned contents out as the sun began to set.

Revitalised by half a plate of food and halfway through a second glass of chilled white wine, she was ready to change the subject from where they were brought up and what their parents did. He found out she had six A levels before going to Cambridge to do medicine. She found out he had scraped into Oxford Brookes and studied English literature and philosophy. He had found out she had almost perfect recall. She had found out he kept a little book of quotes. She had asked him his age and she hoped he did not see her look of surprise when he said he was thirty two, or her equal look of surprise when he had told her that he had grown the beard to make himself look younger.

'So, Tom, let's say what we are thinking,' she said.

He smiled at her, hopefully.

'Not that. I mean about what has happened,' she said.

'Oh, that. Right,' he said. 'I was thinking when I was in the shower.'

'Yes, Tom?'

'ACE would be a better name than Tics. Anti Conspiracy Executive – ACE! What do you think?'

Beth could not decide if he was stupid or resilient or if her two glasses of wine was already too much. She tried to remember the last time she had drunk alcohol. The memories were a bit vague, though she thought she may have ended up doing something she would have regretted if she could have remembered what it was she actually did.

She came back to the present to answer Benson. 'Yes. Calling yourselves ACE sounds very, very nice, Tom. But I meant what happened about the murders...'

'Yes, ah! Right! The murders. Well, I did have a lot of time to think while I was outside your house hiding in my car and here's what I think...' he put a forkful of pilau rice in his mouth , chewed nowhere near enough, and swallowed. 'Our man Popov got mixed up with these Russian Mafia guys. They were running guns, then something bigger came along, some sort of chemical weapon. Copeland was on this weapon's trail and...'

'It's called Nosoi,' she said.

'Nosoi? Like the demons of pestilence Pandora released from the box?' he said, his fork frozen in mid air.

She poured herself more wine. 'Yes. That's what Copeland told me. He said Popov might have come into contact with some sort of chemical weapon called Nosoi. Have you heard of it?'

He looked thoughtful. 'No. And that's strange in itself. The Tics – the ACES – know about every dark secret like that.

Who has what chemical weapons and stuff like that – we could have told them Sadam had got rid of his WMDs through his Stargate to hide them on the other side of the galaxy. No matter how crazy it is, we track every little rumour and every little whisper, and the word Nosoi has never been mentioned once, and somebody always says or hears something.'

'OK' said Beth, 'let's assume this Nosoi stuff is really secret or really new and these Karamazov brothers, with their weirdly coincidental name, somehow got hold of some of it. What then?'

'I think they did and they were trying to sell it. Popov and Fayad were working for them. Maybe they were part of their Russian Mafia gang,' said Tom.

'I've met Popov and he doesn't strike me as the Mafia type. And Fayad was living the life of a vagrant, so he was not making arms sales type money, was he?'

'You have a point,' said Tom, rubbing his recently beardless chin. 'So maybe they were just hired help. Just migrants being exploited? Maybe. Anyway, they accidentally got some of this stuff on their hands. Or, the Mafia brothers used them as guinea pigs, or test subjects to show a buyer what the stuff could do. Yes. That makes sense. Guinea pigs! They may have not even known they were exposed to it.'

Beth agreed. 'And Copeland and the security service heard about it and tracked the Karamazov's down. Copeland calls in the removals company – the Pickfords – and they come and remove the Karamazov's! You're right! The men in the raincoats and hats must have been Pickford agents sent to assassinate the Karamazovs!'

'It took me two hours to work that out,' said Tom, dejectedly.

'So...' said Beth excitedly and taking a swig of wine, 'the Pickfords got the Karamazov's to show them where they kept the stuff and they took them to where Fayad cut his hand off. That's where they were hiding the Nosoi!' She gulped more wine.

'I hadn't got that far,' muttered Tom.

'So, when you were collecting the hand – I hope this doesn't put you off your sag aloo – did you see any containers that the Nosoi might be in?'

'I didn't really look,' said Tom, putting his cutlery down, opening the bottle of red and filling his glass to the brim. 'And before you say that we have to...'

'We have to go back to check, Tom!' she held her glass up and they toasted by each drinking half a glass. She declared, 'To Mork and Mindy!' She swigged again. 'To Holmes and Watshon!'

'I think you might have had enough to drink,' observed Tom. 'I don't think you are used to it.' He moved his own, full glass, further away from him.

'Nonshenshe!' Beth exclaimed, feeling very thirsty and finishing off her glass.

'We can't go back there, Beth. The place might be crawling with police. And if it isn't and we are seen, then we will end up as suspects.' He watched her pour another half glass, tip the bottle upside down and when no more came out she grabbed the red and poured that on top of the half glass of white.

'We have to go back, Tom! We have a moral... a moral ... a moral thingy!' she said with a forceful nod of her head resulting in her swaying on her chair.

'You have a moral duty to stop what happened to Popov spreading, Beth. Remember? Popov's Disease you were calling it. Like you said, if his skin is infectious then it could travel in the dust to anywhere and kill thousands!'

'That's it!' shouted Beth, taking another swig of her white and red mix. 'Moral duty!'

'We have to do something with the hand,' reasoned Tom. 'We need to get it looked at. The Royal Free can study Popov, but time might be running out. Come on, Beth! Think! What can we do to save the world?'

Her brow furrowed. 'Cambridge!' she said, seriously. 'We take the hand to Cambridge! A toast to Cambridge!' She toasted, alone.

'No more wine, Beth. Why Cambridge?'

'Did my pathology at Cambridge. Know some people in lab there. Private company. Not nice people. Use animals sometimes. Good at what they do, though. Jonathan very, very good, very nice... Very... athletic... Used him sometimes... to help us. Big micro-soaps... mico-scopes. Lots of whirry machine thingies. Didn't know that did you? Ahh – haaa!' She held her finger up, as Tom did when he thought of a quote. 'How were you to know? You're only a little fellow in a wide world after all!'

'Thanks for that quote Beth. But I am not a hobbit and you would make a very drunk Gandalf.'

Beth leaned across the table and put her face so close to his their noses touched. She said, 'Let's go to bed, Hobbit!'

DS Hesterman. Sunday 28 th August.

Danny's walk with his family was cut short by a phone call from his boss, Detective Inspector Bell, telling him all leave was cancelled and everyone was being called in. They had a double homicide to investigate.

Mrs. Hesterman had protested the unfairness of Danny being called in on Bank Holiday Sunday afternoon, but relented when she heard it was a double homicide. One homicide was rare in a town of less than seventy thousand and two at the same time was unheard of.

When Danny got to St. Paul's Road there was a police cordon and a uniformed officer had to lift yellow tape above his head to let Danny's car pass. He parked just beyond the cordon and walked down to a small car park with weeds growing through cracking tarmac to be met by Inspector Bell.

'You took your time getting here, Sergeant!' snapped D.I. Bell.

'My apologies, Sir. As I said when you called, I was out having a walk with the wife and kids.'

'OK, forget it. So, we sent a uniform down here earlier. The security guards had reported what might have been shots. They heard them yesterday evening and said they had thought it over and thought they had better give us a call. Can you believe it?'

'Probably had something better to do last night, Sir, and didn't want their evening spent making statements,' said Danny. 'Who's been killed?'

'It's the brothers Karamazov. It looks like they were brought here with their hands bound and then both shot at close range through the back of the skull.'

'The Karamazov's?' said Danny. 'Who would want them dead?' He stopped and thought about what he had said. 'Well, probably lots of people wanted them dead. But this sounds like a professional hit.'

D.I. Bell nodded. 'Looks like they were beaten up first as well. But go and have a look. Fresh eyes might spot something I missed. Go around the big tree, round the first old lavvy and over the wall. They are at the entrance to the second old lavvy. Watch where you tread, though. You'll see.'

Danny went to see for himself. He had seen one or two gruesome things in his time, and knew it was always best to expect to see the worst. He stepped over dried vomit and did not have to spend long surveying the crime scene before he ordered all the other officers to get back to the car park, even the plastic gloved crime scene investigator.

When he followed them back to the car park, D.I. Bell was walking towards him.

'Did you order the CSI from the scene, Sergeant Hesterman?' he said.

'Yes, Sir, but let me explain. Remember Copeland briefing you and one of the names that came up was Usman Fayad? The park over there was where he was found. There is some stuff in there that looks like it might be where he was sleeping. There's a lot of stuff a vagrant might have, Sir, but there is also a very new stainless steel flask.'

'Yes, Sergeant, I did look for myself, you know!' snapped D.I. Bell.

Hesterman whispered, 'Fayad, Sir, the Nosoi, Sir, and dead bodies, Sir.'

The dots joined in Bell's head and he whispered back, 'Oh, I see! You're right sergeant. We had best inform SO15 and leave the crime scene for them.'

'Sir, the Karamazov's were tough guys and it would take someone a bit special to beat them up and drag them here. I think I know who did this.'

'We already have a suspect, Sergeant. He was spotted by the security guards and they gave a pretty good description. Undoubtedly a professional hit man. We spoke to some kids playing football in the park and they were here yesterday too. They saw a man with the same description running down the road and get into his car. I got that art student from the college to come down to talk to the security guards and sketch the suspect. I have his sketch here.'

Hesterman looked at the sketch presented to him. In one corner it said '5 ft. 2' and the sketch was of a balding man wearing large glasses.

D.I. Copeland, Sunday August 28 th.

Copeland had dumped Brandon as soon as they left the Met building, saying, 'You're not coming with me, Sergeant. Beryl only said that you were going with me to get you out of trouble. Go home and take tomorrow off, then go back into the office on Tuesday and keep an eye on things from there. You, me and the D.C.I. are the only three people in SO15 who has any clue what's really going on.'

Copeland was glad Brandon did not ask him what actually was going on. All Copeland knew was that he thought he knew what was *not* going on. Sergeant Brandon had protested briefly, but had slunk away home and left Copeland to go back to Boston alone.

He travelled back to Leyton to pack. London was quiet for a Sunday afternoon. Bank holiday Sunday meant half of London was queuing on the road to Brighton, half was queuing on roads into the countryside, half was swarming into London parks, and half could not be bothered to go further than their gardens. London was very overcrowded these days, with double the number of people which could reasonably fit into it.

Copeland went first class and hoped he was right to believe the CIA would be paying his bills from now on. He had never been first class before. He had expected waiters in white coats and red bow ties, but was disappointed to find it was just like standard class, but with nicer seats and no children. He reconsidered. No children? That alone made the extortionate extra cost worthwhile. And he could move about, unlike his journey back to London the day before. He had eaten pre-packed sandwiches on his way from Sir Richard's meeting and went in search of the dining car. Cary Grant and Margaret Lockwood would have never put up with a train without a dining car and when he found only the buffet car he vowed to never watch any film with a train in it ever again: they all lied. He had to eat pre-pack sandwiches again. At least they served minute bottles of whiskey. He bought three.

He finished the sandwiches and poured the second whiskey into a plastic cup (in first class!). He slipped on his reading glasses and opened the file on Abdul Karim.

After the 'Arab Spring' had died down, Karim had fled from Saudi Arabia to a very large bank account in London and arrived in the UK on October 10 th. 2012. The Saudis had made weak diplomatic protests but there was no evidence that Karim had, in fact, stolen any money from them and had committed no crimes, so extradition was not granted.

And the U.K. Government like rich people to spend their money in London, Copeland thought.

Although most of Karim's dealings were through offshore holding companies and although nothing was absolutely certain, he had seemingly used his wealth to buy small cutting edge companies – coating for microchips to keep them cooler, carbon fibre technology, biogenetics, next generation solar panels and a company trying to make a revolutionary new battery, among others. He had also bought, under his own name, a stake in Leyton Orient F.C.

Good man! There's hope for the O's yet! I really hope this guy is not a terrorist! Maybe we could afford to buy someone who can actually score...

There were photos of Karim before he left Saudi, wearing traditional Arab attire, and ones from after he arrived in London. Most were showing him being a multi-millionaire playboy, but one showed him meeting with Mohammed al-Zahari, the leader of Ansar al-Sharia in Libya. It was dated just weeks before he had arrived in London: September 4 th. 2012.

That's the week before Ansar al-Sharia militants attacked the American mission in Benghazi. This does not look good, Copeland. Better put that new goalkeeper on hold too...

The next five pages of the file were transcripts of messages over the last six months from the Saudis, all warning the UK, The US, France and Germany among others, of Karim's intention to carry out an attack.

Interesting Russia is not on the list of targets. Did someone omit them from the transcript or did the Saudis not inform the Russians? Chechen terrorists are involved and they're not attacking Russians? Really?

The transcripts of the Saudi messages dating from the last two months warned that Karim was assembling a team to carry out an attack.

So he must have been under the surveillance of M.I.5. I would know if it had been SO15.

Copeland turned the page and found an M.I.5 surveillance log of Karim's activities over the last six months.

This is a hell of a short list for six month worth of surveillance!

Before the list of dates, time and activities was a note to inform the reader that Karim had become almost a recluse and currently rarely came out of his Hertfordshire estate or his

Knightsbridge apartment. He had lived exclusively at the Knightsbridge apartment for the last six weeks. The only other places he had visited in that time were Harrods (twice) and Kew Gardens (once). He had received few visitors – his business lawyer, his accountant, his P.R. consultant and his stylist.

So he gave up his playboy lifestyle? Why?

There were a few more pages of photographs of Karim. One was of him driving himself from his estate and others were of him entering or leaving his estate or his apartment. Two showed him shopping at Harrods and one was of him admiring a huge plant at Kew.

And he had no social life for six months? He's even more boring than you, Copeland, and no one can be that boring. Unless...

Since the Saudis last warning, a phone tap had been put in place. This proved as exciting as Karim's current social life and consisted of conversations about stocks, possible new acquisitions and... now this was interesting...

Yes! We're getting a new striker! Come on the Orient!

The file's appendix had photographs and biographies of Karim's known associates and his staff, the latter of which consisted of a maid, a chef, and a personal valet, all of whom he had taken with him to his Knightsbridge apartment, and a chauffeur and a gardener he had left in Hertfordshire. A full background check had been made on all of them and they all checked out.

There was a postscript from the Director of M.I.5 complaining they did not have the manpower or resources for proper surveillance on Karim's staff or associates.

You can bet the CIA will find the resources soon enough.

Copeland closed the file and finished the third mini whiskey. Besides the warning from a country who believed he had stolen from them, there was nothing against Karim except the photograph of him in Libya. Copeland had to admit that was pretty strong evidence, showing Abdul Karim had some dubious links. What was more interesting to Copeland was why Karim had abruptly ended his playboy lifestyle at about the same time as the Saudis were sending their first warnings.

The steady rhythm of the train soothed Copeland. If it was M.I.5 running this he would quite happily have let it go, but it wasn't. It was the Americans, and he did have some pride left. Not much, but some.

He removed his glasses and had started to fall asleep when a truth hit him. He had not checked *it* since his shower this morning. He rushed from his seat to the end of the carriage. An elderly gentleman frowned at his undignified haste. He banged the lavatory door shut, unzipped and checked. *Oh, bugger!* He used the lavatory and checked again. The bottle green circle and swirling yellow lines were still there. On *it!* The train swayed, but he swayed more. The images of Popov's crumbling arm shot through his head. He tucked and zipped. He retched over the sink and a trickle of sour whiskey came out.

Better give Dr. Spencer a call, Copeland.

He took his phone from his pocket. He had turned it off for the meeting with Sir Richard and had forgotten to turn it on again. He waited for the logo to spin to a finish and the accompanying tinkling music to come to its end. It seemed to take forever. He dialled Spencer's number. It rang but there was no answer. It went to voice mail. He left a message and started to put the phone back in his pocket, stopped and rang again. Answer phone again. He put his phone away and rinsed his face. He looked at his hands. They had touched *it – his wodyacallit!* He examined his fingertips. Good. Nothing.

*Well, Copeland... Nothing **yet**! But you shouldn't worry about your fingers... it's already got you **down there**!*

He walked back to his seat in a daze. His phone rang. Spencer! It had to be!

'I say, old chap! No phone use in the carriage, you know,' said the elderly gentleman.

Ever the one to scoff at rules, Copeland took his phone out. The display said 'Hesterman'.

Shit! It's not her!

'Shit! It's not her!' said Copeland, agreeing with his inner voice.

'I say! Really! This is first class you know!' protested the elderly gentleman.

Copeland answered his phone. 'What the bloody hell do you want, Hesterman?' He didn't say it quietly.

The elderly man rose angrily from his seat and retorted, 'I say! Uncouth pleb! I shall have you ejected from this train! One is fetching the guard!' He shook his fist at Copeland and stormed out of the carriage. The two other passengers applauded him.

Copeland relented and walked back to the toilet.

'Yes, Danny. Sorry about that. I know you wouldn't be phoning me unless it was really important. I've just, er, well, I'm on the train back to Boston and just, well, er, never mind. Why have you called? What is it?'

Danny Hesterman told him. He ended the call. The Karamazov's dead? Why? And their bodies found where Fayad dossed? And a new stainless steel flask at the scene? Possibly a flask full of liquid Nosoi? And a professional hit! The Karamazovs had been executed by a short, balding man with glasses! Copeland hoped the local TV news broadcast of the artist's impression of the murderer would get some responses from the public.

Bugger all that Copeland! Go and check yourself downstairs again!

'Sod off, you!' muttered Copeland. 'I'm going to solve this case before that Nosoi stuff dissolves me!'

Colonel Vasily Goraya, SVR, former KGB, Order of Lenin, Order of the Red Star, and also known as The Kamchatka Killer, etc. and Captain Nikolay Ivchenko (no citations).

Arriving back at the Russian Embassy, Vasily and Nikolay hung up their coats and hats and changed into their uniforms. These days, Vasily hated wearing his. He was getting too old to walk round with the weight of so many medals.

They met with Viktor Mosovoi and, after they had saluted and he had allowed them to sit, they had given him an account of their activities. He approved, but only after they had explained why they had to kill the Karamazov's from Hackney. Then he had poured them vodka and they had toasted success together.

After they had left the room and were walking down the high vaulted corridor Nikolay said, 'I don't like him.'

Vasily said, 'Be careful, Nikolay Ivchenko!'

'What we are doing will help him, but not the people of Russia,' said Nikolay.

'You are talking like a Bolshevik, my young friend!' laughed Vasily. 'They will say you are a counter revolutionary!'

'It's true, though, Colonel,' protested Nikolay. 'And we have made alliances with...'

'It may be true, Nikolay, and our alliances may be... unusual, but at the moment what is good for Comrade

Mosovoi is also good for Russia,' said Vasily. 'Now, enough!'

'Ronaldo'.

'Scorpion? What's wrong?

'Oh, no! You think they might be watching you and tapping your home phone?

'Is this one safe?

'Good, but...

'That's what I was going to say. I'll let Fatima know.

'Yes, she took care of the old couple. But Farmer Brown phoned and they had already spoken to the police.

'No, I'm sure the local constabulary has enough on its hands without this. There should be no... repercussions.

'Don't worry about the farmer. He wants more money or he will share his theories with the police if they come back. He will get his money and a little something else. We need to make sure.

'No, I can take care of everything. You should lay low until we've finished the tests and then I will contact you on the new phone.

'Thank you, Sir. I too hope I am rewarded in heaven for my work.'

Copeland!

He checked back into the hotel and collected his room key, ignoring the manager's whinging about how the two bloody raincoat gay perverts who had been in the room next to him had left without paying their bill and how their credit card seemed to be blocked or something and how they seemed to speak the Queen's English so nicely too and how he was glad to see him back and would he like dinner because he could order now and the chef who was an excellent Romanian chef not like the other Romanians infesting the town would cook him what he liked before he went home no problem and the waitress would be happy to stay to serve him because he gave such good tips didn't he? and would he like a table by the window overlooking the river and...

Tell him to shut up or you will get your gun out of your case and shoot him in his balls!

Copeland dryly said, 'I'm going for a shower first but I would like anything with a lot of red meat and no vegetables except potatoes – lots of potatoes – a bottle of red, no two bottles of your best red! and a dessert with a lot of pastry and double cream and a double single malt for a starter.'

You didn't ask if the waitress could do extra cream!

'I thought you were my conscience?' thought Copeland back.

Who said?

'Right you are, Sir,' said the manager. 'I'll speak to the waitress.'

'Did you just talk?' thought Copeland.

Me? Never!

'And I'm sure the chef will be able to oblige you,' called the manager.

See? I would NEVER ask the chef to 'oblige' you!

Copeland ignored everything; got to his room; tore off his clothes; got in the shower.

As soon as the water hit his 'nether regions' the Nosoi disintegrating 'concern' washed off. He bent over (with some difficulty) and lifted something from the mesh covering the plug hole.

A circle of green with bold yellow lettering said 'M&S'. It was a sticker from his new underwear.

Next time you examine yourself, Copeland, I suggest you keep your glasses on!

Monday, August 29 th.

Dr. Elizabeth Spencer and Mr. Thomas Benson.

Beth opened her eyes. She lifted her head. A little pixie with a large hammer hit the inside of her skull.

'Ow!' she groaned and let her head fall back down.

She lay motionless, trying to remember. She had been drinking. A lot. There was something about going to Boston and a murder. No, two murders. Then something about a hand and Cambridge. Then something about a hobbit.

Beth shot up and fell off her sofa.

'What the..?' she groaned on her hands and knees. She pulled herself up and sat on the sofa, head in hands. Tom was in the armchair, just starting to rouse beneath a blanket.

'Morning,' he said, opening his eyes and reaching for his spectacles.

'What happened?' she said. 'I feel terrible.'

Tom sat up and let the blanket fall to his waist. 'You mean before or after you called me a hobbit?' he said, tartly.

'I sort of remember something about a hobbit. Did I call you a hobbit? Sorry, Tom. Why did I call you a hob...' She sat upright. 'Tom! Oh, my! Did we..?'

He let her suffer for a while, then said, 'You dragged me to the bottom of the stairs. Very cave-woman. You didn't make it any further. I couldn't get you upstairs so I dragged you in here, bundled you onto the sofa and found some blankets for us both. I figured it would be okay if I stayed.'

'Then we didn't...' she said, and realised she was still wearing the same blue blouse.

'And even if you had dragged me up the stairs, we wouldn't have. You were in no state to know what you were doing,' said Tom.

Beth didn't know what to say, but knew she was blushing. She smiled at him. 'Your hair looks better than mine does first thing in the morning,' she said.

They were up and about before they realised how early it was. At breakfast, Beth had excused herself for the previous evening and muttered something about her not drinking because she got tipsy easily and when she got tipsy she got 'frisky'. Benson thought she had not seemed 'full of energy' when she had collapsed at the bottom of the stairs, but had nodded understandingly.

They packed water, snacks and a severed hand into the car and were on the road before seven. Beth had told Tom she didn't trust his car to make it further than the end of the road and had insisted she was sober enough to drive, but she had to wait because he insisted on moving his car round a corner into a side road in case it was seen.

She had remembered it was Bank Holiday Monday and had phoned someone name Jonathan. Tom was surprised she had the number of someone she had known several years ago, and even more surprised when he agreed to meet her at the lab with some of his assistants. Tom soon worked out that this Jonathan and Beth had been more then work acquaintances.

There seemed to be a lot of road works and difficult detours all around Cambridge, and the journey took longer than they had expected, but after passing Cambridge International Airport they headed east and were soon waiting outside high electronic gates while they opened after Beth had announced their arrival on the intercom.

Beth parked alongside four other cars in front of a white, single storey building the size of an aircraft hangar with the name A & R Biotech in green lettering across the front. A tall, slim, blond haired man came out to meet them. He and Beth kissed cheeks affectionately.

'You don't know what this means to me, Jonathan,' said Beth, still holding his arms. 'I really appreciate it. If there's any way I can ever repay you...'

'I'm still married, unfortunately,' said Jonathan and they both laughed, though Beth's lacked gusto.

Tom had got the box from the back seat and remained serious.

'It's in the box. This is Tom, by the way,' said Beth.

Jonathan scanned Tom's mostly bald head, large glasses, green shirt and combat trousers. He raised an eyebrow and turned back to Beth. 'Let's go in and see if my team can solve the mystery of the melting men,' he said and led them inside.

Following Jonathan down a bright corridor with labs, offices and meeting rooms on either side, they could not help noticing the gap between the resources here and the little pathology department back in the hospital. When they followed him into a lab near the rear of the building, they were even more impressed. There were two electron microscopes and another microscope Beth had never seen before. Jonathan's three assistants were putting on the most modern biohazard suits she had ever seen, and beyond them was a fourth assistant who was already in a suit and in a 'clean' room.

'You can put the box down over there,' said Jonathan, gesturing dismissively to Benson. 'As you can see Beth, things have come on since you were last here. We have been doing pretty well out of the new genetics revolution, stem cell research and immunology, plus a few other sidelines. There are only four microscopes like that in the whole country and these biohazard suits are the best there is. Even we only have a dozen or so. After you told me about some of the properties of this disease, I thought we had better use them. They are acid and corrosive resistant too. We'll get the box into the clean room and start work immediately. You both understand, of course, that anything we find will be the intellectual property of my company, so I'd like you to follow me to my office where you can sign the legal paperwork to that effect.'

'Jonathan?' said Beth, open mouthed.

'It's Ok,' said Tom, gripping her forearm. 'We need this to get done.'

They went with Jonathan and signed, then Jonathan said how he wished Beth could stay and help but she was not insured to work at the lab and if anything went wrong... well, she knew how it was. He showed them out, telling them he would be in touch. He closed and locked the door as soon as they were through it.

As soon as the car doors were closed, Beth fumed, 'The bastard! I thought he agreed to do this out of a duty to prevent a catastrophic disease or because we used to be close. He just saw an opportunity to exploit something rare and make money. And he threw me out! The bastard!'

Tom put his hand on her shoulder and smiled. 'I agreed to sign so easily because I think he might have a few legal problems if he pursues anything. For one thing, they need to find something completely different to the pathology lab back at The St. James. And technically, the hand belongs to the coroner's office as part of the autopsy. It's stolen property. Anyway...' and his finger pointed up into its quote mode as he said, 'The safety of the people shall be the highest law!'

Beth was calming down and said, 'I suppose quoting Cicero does seem appropriate when facing a lethal pandemic. I hope Cicero is right – that we can control our destiny and everything we do is not fate. Now, I suppose all we can do is exercise our free will and choose to go home and wait.'

'Hangovers do put you in a cheery mood don't they?' said Tom, sarcastically. 'I suppose waiting is all we can do for now, but let's see if there are any traffic reports on local radio. We could try to avoid all those road works.'

They listened to the radio and drove for about five minutes before Beth did an emergency stop and looked wide-eyes at Benson.

Detective Inspector Lawrence Copeland.

Copeland awoke to the sound of banging on his door. His evening meal had turned into a celebration of M & S stickers and his head felt heavy. He vaguely remembered being annoyed with himself for not wearing his reading glasses when he had checked himself. The door banging continued.

'Inspector Copeland, it's me,' shouted the voice of Danny Hesterman.

'Go away, Danny. I need a lie-in,' the voice of Copeland shouted back from under a duvet.

Hesterman put his face close to the door. 'It's nine thirty. We have the killer's name!' he shouted.

Copeland shot out of bed and grabbed a bath robe. What! he thought. I'd better get a move on. Breakfast finishes at ten!

He opened the door. 'Wait for me downstairs, Danny. I'll be ten minutes. Order me a Full English so it's there when I come down,' he said.

'Don't you want to know who it is?' asked Hesterman. 'It wasn't Vasily like I thought it might be, it was...'

'It can wait,' said Copeland.

'He was working at the hospital. Probably a cover while he planned his murders. His name is Thomas Benson,' shouted Hesterman through Copeland's closed the door.

Copeland rubbed his face, trying to wake himself up. Where had he heard that name before?

Hesterman waited while Copeland ate his breakfast, waited while Copeland went back to his room to use his 'own' bathroom, and waited while Copeland sat on the terrace, looking relieved about something or other, and smoked his cigarette. At least it gave them more than enough time to fill each other in about how they had spent their commandeered Sunday off. Copeland wondered if he should be telling Hesterman everything. He had been told to liaise with the local police, so he did. He had been very interested to hear about Hesterman's meeting with the uncooperative Farmer Brown, and made him his top priority after first securing Popov to his hospital bed. He had a few hours before the CIA rolled into town.

They decided they both needed to go to the St. James Hospital: Copeland to handcuff Popov to the bed before the armed assault team got there; Hesterman to question staff about the hit-man Thomas Benson, who was not at his home and who had not turned up for work yesterday or today, despite being specifically told he had to by the Senior Administrator, nor had Benson phoned in sick. When Hesterman told Copeland, 'This Benson was posing as a minor administrator – the sort of job anyone could get', Copeland knew where he had heard the name before. Dr. Spencer had said this Benson had been very helpful with anything to do with Popov. Now he could see why.

Why?

Popov had worked for the Brothers Karamazov.

So?

Well, there's a link there!

And?

An angry Copeland slammed the car door shut and went into the hospital with Hesterman. A helicopter went overhead.

As they separated to go their different ways at the hospital entrance, Hesterman finally challenged Copeland about the five hundred pounds. Copeland told him not to worry, he had it in his pocket and he would hand it in before the end of the day. Half of that was true.

Copeland pressed the green button outside Popov's ward. No one pressed the release for him to go in. He looked through the glass panels in the door. He could not see any nurses. He could not see anyone. He pressed again. He could hear it buzz inside when he pressed but still could see no movement.

Maybe they've all died with Popov Disease?

He buzzed again. Finally a young nurse came. He showed his warrant card and she let him into the ward.

'Sorry, mate. Short staffed. Again!' moaned Student Nurse Zora Smith.

'I'm here to see Jakab Popov,' said Copeland.

Student Nurse Zora Smith said, 'He's gone. Ambulance picked 'im up yesterday.'

'No, nurse. There was a change of plans. The ambulance is coming today,' Copeland informed her as he started walking to Popov's room.

He got there, looked through the window and said, 'He's gone!' He rounded on the nurse. 'Where the hell is he? Has he been taken for tests or something? Tell me!'

'Don't you get all ratty with me mate!' retaliated Nurse Zora. 'My family has had loads o' dealin's with the fuzz and I know you can't talk to me like that. You're infringing my 'uman rights you are, talkin' to me like that!'

Copeland wagged a finger in her face. 'If you don't answer me, Nurse, then I will place you under arrest for obstruction,' said Copeland.

'No need to get 'eavy! I told you the ambulance took 'im. That Doc Spencer told us a special ambulance was comin' and it did. Must have been when we was takin' the medicines trolley round yesterday lunchtime.'

'And did you see the ambulance men or women?' asked Copeland, starting to worry.

'Nah, mate. We wuz busy like, what with bein' short staffed and all,' said Nurse Zora, smiling. 'Now, I gotta get back to work. That dragon Jones 'as me on a final warning. 'Ave a nice day!'

Copeland was beginning to doubt he would have a nice day. The small wooden cabinet in Popov's room was open and it was empty. Popov had got up, got dressed and walked out.

The ward door buzzed. Absentmindedly, he turned to see who it was and saw Special Agent Liza Clinton and behind her Gunnery Sergeant Brett Gregg. Copeland experienced an out of body experience and watched as he walked to the door, pressed the button and let them in.

The CIA agent was wearing clothes identical to the ones she had worn at the meeting, except she also had a side-arm in a holster fixed to her hip. The marine had his full combat uniform on and was carrying a side-arm. Their sunglasses appeared to be even more reflective in fluorescent lights.

'Where's Popov, Inspector Copeland?' she immediately asked.

'I didn't expect you here so soon, Agent Clinton,' Copeland evaded.

'Your limey roads are crap, Copeland. Diversions! Road works! Crap! I got a couple of choppers from the embassy to air lift me and some of the boys. We're setting up camp in the field across the road. Now, where is he?'

'He's gone,' said Copeland, innocently.

'As I suspected,' nodded agent Clinton. 'He's been freed.'

'Ma'am?' said Copeland.

'Screw that sexist ma'am shit, Copeland. Call me Sir. And don't tell me you haven't worked it out yet? Holy crap, no wonder you guys need the CIA!' If she had a sense of humour she may have laughed.

'Sorry, Ma... Sir. Worked what out?'

'How the hell did you make it to inspector, Inspector. Think! Who did you give Popov's handcuffs key to? What did he do to those two Russian business men, the Carrymatsoffs? Where is he now?'

Copeland frowned. 'You mean Tom Benson?'

Special Agent Clinton turned and spoke to the marine. 'Gunny Gregg! Give this man a cigar! Just a small one to match the size of his brain!'

Beneath his sunglasses Gunny Gregg smiled a mocking smile.

She turned back to Copeland and jerked her thumb over her shoulder in the direction of the corridor door. 'Go and take some statements with your policeman buddy, Copeland. Then go and search the Carrymatsoffs place. That's an order!'

He walked round her to leave. If she wanted to believe Tom Benson had released Popov from the non-existent handcuffs, then who was he to argue? Benson was already wanted for a double murder, being accused of aiding the escape of a hospital patient slash terrorist was unlikely to add much to his burden.

'Hey, Inspector,' she shouted loudly as he was about to walk through the door and almost three yards away. 'My people tried to book us in at a Regency Hyatt, but this crappy little town doesn't seem to have one and the hotel you're staying at is full. My men can sleep in tents in the field, but I like a proper bed. You know this town. Where's a good place to stay?'

Copeland thought for a moment. Dare he? What the hell! He smiled at her and said, 'Actually, Agent Clinton, Sir, I do know of an excellent place. It has a wonderfully friendly host and food of the highest quality. I'm sure it will have a suitable suite available. The place is called The Happy Jack.'

'Good. Sounds like a quaint place,' said Agent Clinton. 'Now run along, Inspector.'

Dr. Beth Spencer and Mr. Thomas Benson.

Beth had not long driven away from Jonathan's lab when the traffic report came on the radio and the local news followed. She braked so sharply, the car behind had to swerve round them, and the driver made a very rude gesture. Beth switched off the engine.

Beth and Tom looked at each other.

'They think I did it! The news said the police thought it was some sort of gangland hit. I'm a hit man!' Tom was squeezing his face between his hands.

'Stay calm, Tom. You were seen by the security guards and the police have put two and two together and got five. We can sort this out,' Beth reassured him.

'But they gave a full description *and* my name! How did they get my name?' Tom started panting.

Beth shook him. 'Breathe, Tom,' she said. 'Deeply and slowly or you're going to hyperventilate. They must have put your picture on last night's local TV news and someone who recognised you phoned in. We can clear all this up. I think we should phone Copeland.'

'What? No!'

'Breathe or I will have to slap you! Listen! He tried to phone me a few times last night after I had... you know... fallen asleep. He must have heard about the killings and he already knew you were helping me. He must have some information. We can tell him what happened. He can help. What have we got to lose?'

He panted faster. She slapped him. He screamed, 'What have we got to lose? Only our lives if he sends the Pickfords after us too! I'm getting in the back and keeping my head down!'

She drove to the first lay-by they came to and phoned Copeland.

'Dr. Spencer. What a pleasant surprise,' said Copeland.

'This is not a social call, Inspector. Why did you keep phoning me yesterday evening?' said Beth.

'Oh, nothing. It was just a medical question, but it's all cleared up now,' said Copeland.

Part of Copeland was not so sure. *At least you **hope** it is, Copeland!*

On the other end of the phone, Beth lowered her voice. 'Where are you inspector? Are you alone?'

'I'm actually outside the St. James Hospital. If you must know, I'm all on my own having a smoke in the shade of some trees at the edge of the car park. I'm watching the CIA and US marines unload two military transport helicopters. Would you believe they had them at their embassy? Are they expecting London to turn into Saigon?'

'The CIA and the US marines are at the hospital?' said Beth, thinking she had misunderstood something.

'They are over the road from the hospital. Setting up tents and command posts ready for their Center for Disease Control team to arrive,' said Copeland, amused by the American entertainment while he enjoyed his cigarette. 'Hold on a minute... it's going to get noisy. The helicopters are taking off.'

Beth heard them loud and clear on her phone. Inspired into action, Tom finally clambered into the back seat to hide.

She waited for the noise to become distant. 'So, why are the Americans there, Inspector?' she asked, trying to sound nonchalant.

'They have taken over this whole terrorism operation. They want Popov and that Tom Benson, and the CDC is here to prevent a disease outbreak,' said Copeland. 'Doctor? I thought I heard another voice then. Is someone with you?'

'No, no-one, Inspector,' said Beth, furiously waving at Tom in the back seat to shut up. 'I hate to tell you this, but I think you had better tell the Americans that an ambulance from the Royal Free picked Popov up yesterday.'

'Did I just hear a voice saying "ask about me", Doctor?' asked Copeland.

'Did you? I'm outside. Must have been someone walking past,' she said, showing Tom her fist.

'Oh, right,' said Copeland. 'So, the ambulance from the Royal couldn't make it yesterday. As I said, the CIA are running the show now. They're looking for the little guy. The CIA think...'

Tom was banging his head into the back seat, repeating the letters C...I... A each time his head struck.

'I can hear someone repeating CIA, CIA, over and over,' said Copeland.

Beth could not contain herself any longer. 'We need your help, Copeland!' she said, pleading.

What Copeland heard was 'We need your help, Copeland! **Nooooooo!**'

'Dr. Spencer. Who is there with you?' asked Copeland, lighting another cigarette.

Beth could hear her pulse in her ears. It beat three times before she said, 'Tom Benson.'

'Not surprised,' said Copeland, unsurprised. 'He's not at home and hasn't been there for a couple of days. He hasn't used his bank cards or his phone. He had to be with someone he knew, and the local police have worked out he doesn't have any friends.'

Tom leapt up and shouted into the phone, 'Yes I do. They're all online!' Beth pushed him back into the rear. She could hear Copeland laughing.

'So, has he got you tied up with a gun at your head? He is a contract killer, you know,' Copeland teased.

'He saw it happen, Copeland!' Beth blurted.

Copeland inhaled and exhaled. He watched the Americans trying to erect a tent and thought they might do better if they took their sunglasses off so they could see what they were doing. 'Put him on, please, Dr. Spencer,'

Copeland heard Beth trying to get Tom Benson to talk to him. He heard Benson say something about a lawyer before he talked to the cops and he wasn't talking to the man who sent the killers, no matter what.

'Doctor!' shouted Copeland so Benson heard.

'He won't talk to you. He thinks the two men he saw in the dark raincoats and hats were agents from something called Pickfords and they were sent by you,' said Beth.

This was a lot in one sentence for Copeland to take in, especially when all he thought he was doing was having a quiet smoke while being entertained by Americans.

'He actually saw them?' said Copeland. 'And how the hell does he know about Pickfords?'

'Conspiracy nut. It wasn't you, was it?' asked Beth.

Copeland heard Benson shout something about not being a nut but being a tic.

'What? No. Sounds like Russian Secret Service... Tell him I believe him and I promise not to arrest him. Listen, on second thoughts, don't say anything else on the phone. I'll meet you,' said Copeland.

'We're on our way back to my house,' said Beth.

'No. Not there. The CIA will have figured out you are someone he might go to. Sooner or later they will be at your house. We need somewhere else.'

'OK... there's a retail park between Cambridge City and Cambridge Airport. There's a Starbucks...'

'Yes. Good. Wait there. If you see anyone in raincoats – run! If you see anyone in a black suit and wearing reflective sunglasses – run! Sergeant Hesterman is going to loan me his unmarked vehicle and I'm on my way.'

Copeland! Have you ever heard the phrase 'when you're in a hole, stop digging'?

Copeland actually *ran* to find Hesterman. He dragged him away from interviewing a pretty young secretary and ordered him to leave the hospital with him, ordered him to hand over the car keys, ordered him to go and get a uniformed officer and a marked car, and ordered him to go and arrest Farmer Brown. Hesterman had taken everything else in his stride, but arresting the farmer? Copeland told Hesterman to think of something to arrest him for, because if he did not get the farmer into police custody before the CIA got him, then... And while he was up there, arrest the two professors too; on conspiracy to waste police time or something; conspiracy was always a good one – hard to disprove!

Jakab Popov. Sunday, August 28 th. (Another flashback...)

When he left the hospital, feeling much better, Jakab Popov had not realised his front door key was not in his pocket. He gave his last ten pound note to the taxi driver with his left hand and kept the other, less photogenic one in his jeans. Once he had lifted the wooden gate over the broken slabs and was at the bottom of the steps leading up to his door, he removed his disintegrating hand and reached in his pocket with his healthy hand, groping for his key.

He had a vague memory of someone being in his room – not a doctor or nurse, but a man wearing a tie. Jakab Popov remembered harder. The man had been looking in the little cabinet where all his things were. He had left the money but had taken his key. He had been a clever thief, knowing the nurses would see the money had not gone, but not realise the thief had stolen his door key.

Jakab tried to think what advice his mother would give him in a situation like this. He always listened to his mother. He never listened to his father. There was no point, his father did not speak Bulgarian like Jakab and his mother. When he was younger, Jakab had sometimes wondered how his parents had ever got married, since they only knew a handful of words in each other's language. Now he was older he thought that was probably precisely why they had got married.

What would she say? She would say, 'You stupid boy, Jakab! You left that nice hospital and the free food and the pretty nurse with ring through her nose and plenty of fat to see her through harsh winter and now you stand here with no money and no food! Stupid boy, Jakab!'

That's what she would say, and that's why he had left Serbia and gone to seek his fortune where the streets were paved with gold in the European Union and had come to this country called Brexit. But there would be no gold if he did not work, and once his arm was not getting worse any more after it had been put in the magic liquid in the baby bath, Jakab had decided it was time to leave. That doctor was very good and had cured him, hadn't she?

'Stupid boy! How can you work? Your hand has crumbled away like rotten wood and half of your arm is like the rats have feasted on it! Stupid boy!' said his mother's soothing voice.

Where could he go? He could break his bed-sit door down, but the thief would have taken everything. Maybe not the money he had hidden under the carpet? Maybe not that. Maybe not his padlock key either. He climbed the steps and rammed his shoulder into his door. The door did not move, but the steps did. He tried again, with more force this time. One of the last bolts holding the metal steps to the wall started to come loose and Jakab almost lost his balance.

'Stupid boy, Jakab! Now you kill yourself when steps fall from wall! Stupid boy!'

Jakab half-heartedly pushed the door with his good hand. Perhaps he could get in through a window? Two floors up and climbing with one hand? He knew it would be impossible. He could not get in. He could not get his money and he could not get the padlock key.

Jakab sat on the steps and thought for a long time.

The only place left for Jakab to go was to the people who had helped him before. He forced his dead hand back into his pocket, went down the swaying steps, through the wooden gate and walked. He walked until he was across the river. He passed a sorry-looking black dog with a drooping jaw. He eventually found the place on the industrial estate he had visited a few times before. Only twenty four hours before, a dark green car of indistinguishable make had gone through the gates which Jakab Popov was now approaching.

Detective Inspector Copeland. Monday, August 29 th.

The speed limit was exceeded for most of his journey and when Copeland got to the Starbucks he was only just in time. He knew he should have played safe before he left the hospital, but he had decided to risk it. He rushed up to the counter and barged in front of an innocent middle aged woman ordering a skinny cappuccino and dithering about the vital decision of whether to have a chocolate sprinkle on top.

Copeland spoke with the volume of desperation to a girl with a green apron and a vacant look. 'Where's the men's?' he said.

He emerged from a cubicle a few minutes later and his face glowed a contentment only known by over sixties with an empty bladder. He was also happy not to find anything resembling M&S stickers, but washed his hands twice, just in case.

He walked into the coffee shop and saw Beth Spencer at a table by the window. She began to wave, but he frowned and shook his head. He toured the whole lounge before returning to sit opposite her.

'Where is he?' he said as he sat opposite her and leaned across the table.

'Close,' said Beth. 'What was all that about?'

'You might be being followed. I might have been followed. Just checking around. Looking for suspicious characters, alternative exits, possible weapons, all that sort of thing,' he said in a hushed voice.

'Did you learn to do that sort of thing in your training?' she asked, impressed.

'I was trained before they had invented coffee shops,' he said. 'I learned all that sort of thing watching Jason Bourne films. So, where is he? He's not here.'

'You walked past him twice, Inspector. Perhaps it's time to watch those movies again.' She smiled, affectionately. She could not help but like this aging Inspector and, as she watched him frantically looking around to try to spot Benson, she realised he was as much in uncharted waters as she was.

She tapped his hand. 'Do you remember what you told me when I first met you? Just before you went into Popov's room and I asked you what you were *really* doing at the hospital?' she said and waited for him to nod. She thought he looked a little sad. 'You were telling me the truth weren't you? You really thought this was a dead-end case and you had been shipped off here to encourage you to quit?'

Copeland suddenly wished his estranged daughter was growing up to be someone like Dr. Spencer. He nodded. 'Yes, it was the truth. I wish, now, it had remained the truth. But here we are. What's your first name again, Dr. Spencer?'

'Elizabeth, but you can call me Beth,' she said, and they shook hands across the table.

'And I'm Larry,' he said. 'So where is he?'

'Two tables behind you, reading a book. The one drinking tea in a coffee shop.'

Copeland hauled himself round and looked at someone two tables away drinking tea and reading a book. He was wearing a floppy yellow sun hat, a bright orange short sleeve shirt adorned with bizarre red surfboards, and purple trousers. Without his glasses on, he was squinting at a copy of The da Vinci Code.

Beth said, 'He wanted to look inconspicuous so we got him some new clothes from TK Maxx.' She gestured him over to their table. 'He said the brighter the clothes, the less chance of someone noticing *him*. He's right so far, no-one looks at his face!'

Tom looked around furtively before sliding round the intervening table to sit next to Beth. 'Hello, Inspector,' he said, then instantly thrust the book towards Beth. 'This is nonsense,' he said. 'No-one could ever believe this sort of stuff!'

'But, Tom, I thought you loved conspiracy stuff!' she said.

Tom Benson turned to Copeland and said, 'Despite what Dr. Spencer may have told you Copeland, I am not a conspiracy nut. I am a Tic!'

Copeland was about to ask but thought better of it and said, 'Under the circumstances, you can call me Larry.'

Tom shook his hand. 'Beth has convinced me to trust you, but you are yet to prove my trust so I think I'll call you inspector, Inspector.' His finger pointed to the ceiling and, solemnly, he said, 'Tempt not a desperate man!' and nodded his balding head meaningfully.

'Whatever,' said Copeland. 'You can tell me your story. But first, let me tell you some of mine'

On his drive to Cambridge, Copeland had decided he needed their trust more than he needed to stick to the letter of The Official Secrets Act and told them how there was a theory that Popov was part of an international terrorist network led by Abdul Karim and a very nasty gas called Nosoi was about to wipe out thousands. Then he told them his theory about some sort of Russian plot.

Tom Benson exhaled dramatically and said, 'The international terrorist theory sounds much more plausible.'

And Tom Benson told Copeland his story and Copeland was glad Beth Spencer went to fetch coffees and, more especially, cakes while he did.

Jakab Popov, Monday August 29 th.

Jakab had been happy to find the caravan door open when he had arrived the previous day but wondered why Alexei and Ivan had left it unlocked. He had gone in and after waiting in vain for a few hours had made himself at home. There was a chemical toilet and plenty to eat and drink. He had found some blankets and had slept on a couch in the corner. It was quiet and dark, not like the hospital where lights were on all night and night-staff kept shouting down the ward. Jakab had learned English words like 'bed pan' and was hoping to find out what they meant.

He had woken and was pleased to see his arm and hand had not got any worse. If anything, they looked a little better. He cooked himself fried eggs on a little stove in the corner of the caravan, and later ate a tin of tuna followed by a tin of peaches for his dinner. In between he sat on the couch and waited. When he got bored he went over to the chair by the table and waited there. Once or twice he had got very bored and opened the drawers of a filing cabinet, but his mother's voice had told him he should not snoop in other people's things and had shut them again.

He waited until it started getting dark, then he went outside. He looked about and wandered up and down the scrap yard and looked inside the minibuses and looked inside the old washing machines and the old cookers. When it got dark he closed the gates and wrapped the metal chain around them before going back into the little caravan and waiting. Alexei and Ivan Karamazov did not return and he fell asleep.

Copeland, Spencer and Benson. Monday, 29 th. August.

While Tom was telling his story of how he had found the hand and seen the brothers Karamazov murdered and how he had slept in his car and how Beth had taken him in (and not about the Hobbit part) and how they had taken the hand to Jonathan's company lab and how they had heard he was a fugitive on the radio, Copeland's phone had pinged with several texts.

When Tom had finished and Beth had added she hoped Jonathan's lab would come up with some preliminary results soon, Copeland took his phone out and read his messages. They waited.

'Right,' he said, putting the phone back in his pocket. 'A few things to report. Easy ones first. The ambulance and armed escort which were on their way to get Popov were turned round and sent back to London.'

'Why?' said Beth and Tom together. 'He needs to be properly isolated!' added Beth.

'Ah, yes. I didn't quite get round to mentioning it before on the phone, did I? It looks like he walked out sometime around noon yesterday. Not sure how to tell you this, Tom, but they think you helped him.'

'But I was outside Beth's!' protested Tom. 'Hang on... they think... now they think I'm a hit man helping terrorists?'

People were looking. 'Tom! Shhh!' said Beth.

'Police Officer,' said Copeland, smiling at everyone and flashing his warrant card. 'We're just brainstorming a case. No need to worry, folks.'

'It's called a thought shower now,' said Beth.

I know you like her, Copeland. But what is she talking about?

Copeland looked blank, so she said, 'Brainstorming is offensive. It's p.c. to call it a thought shower these days.'

Copeland? What the..?

Tom was across the table whispering now. 'So I'm wanted for a double murder and aiding a suspected terrorist and I've got your guys and the CIA after me? Great!'

'Probably the SVR too – the Russian secret service,' said Copeland, encouragingly.

'I know what they are, Inspector! I am a Tic, you know!' said Tom, collapsing back into his seat and pulling his floppy hat further down over his ears.

What IS a tic? Ask him, Copeland.

Beth had been thinking. 'This is bad,' she said. 'If his skin is still shedding and it carries the infection... And even if the shed skin isn't infectious, the disease is probably infectious by touch. It killed all his skin bacteria and there were no flies on Fayad's amputated hand, remember? This is *really bad*! He has to be found.'

Copeland swallowed hard. 'So his shed skin might be infectious..? Er, good to know... So... Yes! Second piece of news! The full CIA and CTC teams are all in Boston and have nearly finished setting up their camp in the field opposite the hospital. The town will have lots of tourists in black suits and some in yellow suits tomorrow.'

'That's good,' said Beth.

Is she crazy, Copeland? They're Yanks!

'Are you crazy?' said Tom 'They're Yanks!'

There's hope for this boy yet!

'Next piece of news,' said Copeland, 'is that they have finished the autopsy. They are pretty sure Usman Fayad died of a massive heart attack brought on by shock. They think he cut his own hand off, judging by the angle and ineffectiveness of the cuts. There was no sign of anything suspicious on his arm or anywhere else, including internally.'

'Well that's sort of good news,' said Beth. 'Heart failure is common after trauma. I was hoping his death wasn't disease related.'

'And the other piece of news is good and bad. Sergeant Hesterman has got Mr. Brown, the farmer, in custody. He went willingly once Hesterman had told him it was either talk to him or be water-boarded the CIA.'

'Why has he arrested a farmer?' asked Tom.

'Tell you in the car when I take you to a hotel,' said Copeland. He looked at Tom Benson's clothing. 'I suppose it had better be somewhere where they get people coming and going all the time and are used to oddballs dressed for Miami Beach,' he said.

Tom folded his arms and hurumphed.

'But,' went on Copeland, 'there was no sign of the old professors and the neighbours say they haven't seen them since early yesterday, and I don't like the sound of that.'

'Oh, the farm!' shouted Tom. 'Beth told me. It's where they were making that deadly terrorist dirty bomb thing. The lethal Nosoi gas stuff that dissolves people!'

I take it back, Copeland. There is no hope for this boy. But didn't Beryl the Mrs. Pickford say something about going back to...

Copeland noticed a sudden silence, looked around to see everyone staring at them and had to show his warrant card again and reassure the Starbucks patrons they were just thought showering possible scenarios – just a police pastime, really, honest – there wasn't really any lethal, skin dissolving gas – honestly there wasn't. The coffee drinkers closed their open mouths and suddenly seemed to need to get home quickly, and the whole lounge emptied rapidly.

'Listen, Mr. Benson,' Copeland hissed, if I am going to get you out of this mess, then you need to be careful what you say and how loud you say it. And when I drop you at a hotel, stay in your room. Get pizza delivered, drink tap water – just stay out of sight and don't talk to anyone. Clear?'

'Do you have some money I can use, Inspector?' asked Tom casually.

He can't use his cards, Copeland. They will be on to him in minutes. And you can't use yours to pay for his hotel. Or use a local ATM. If they find him and his big mouth, it will lead back to you. So, Copeland, do you have any money you can give him? Is there something you might just have found under a carpet and which you now have in your pocket?

'Bugger it!' groaned Copeland angrily as he slammed the five hundred pounds down on the table.

Special Agent Liza Clinton. 29 th August. Monday.

C.I.A. Special Agent Liza Clinton removed her reflective sunglasses and checked her underlings had completed their tasks. She had made her rounds with Gunny Gregg at her elbow. Marines and CIA agents saluted as she passed. Doctors and scientists from the CDC just looked bemused.

She worried the heels might snap off her Jimmy Choo shoes. The field was hard after so long without rain. Whoever owned the field would show up sooner or later to protest at the rows of tents and marquees which had been erected. She would give them a large cheque from the bank of Uncle Sam, the owner would look at the amount and grin, and the USA would own another piece of England.

She toured in front of a marquee and Gunny Gregg ticked his checklist. Mess hall – check. Latrine – check. Showers – check. Cinema – check. Heavy weapons – check. Testing lab – not quite check.

She turned carefully on her four inch heels and looked down at the six feet two Gunny Gregg. 'That's it, Gunny. Get my chopper ready,' she said. 'I'm going to my hotel.'

Gunny Gregg saluted at attention. 'Yes, Sir Ma'am!' he said, and ran off across the field.

Agent Clinton replaced the sunglasses on her nose and followed at a more leisurely, careful, don't break the Jimmy Choo heels pace.

She took off in the helicopter and returned ten minutes later and, with the same four black suited agents, got into a black, tinted window SUV. She had discovered Boston has less than one helipad.

Four men wearing black suits, white shirts, black ties and the obligatory CIA reflective sunglasses had leaped from the SUV as soon as it stopped. Passers-by had ducked into shop doorways as soon as they saw the holsters under their jackets. One of the agents held a back door of the SUV open for Chief Special Agent Clinton to get out while two of the agents went inside to 'secure the perimeter'.

Agent Clinton was impressed by the unique facade of The Happy Jack. It took a lot for Agent Clinton to be impressed.

Mainly she was impressed by the way such an establishment somehow managed to stay in business. The garish green sign with flaking paint impressed her less than the three suspended lanterns without glass. She approved of the way the English flag was displayed in the window: it was good to honour the flag, just like she saluted the Star Spangled Banner every morning before her hour at the shooting range. She also approved of the three yellow signs in the other window proclaiming CCTV was operated on the premises. Clearly, the owner was both patriotic and keen to keep poor people off his premises. Maybe it would be palatial once inside, she thought, and after all it *was* recommended by Copeland.

She went through the solid wooden door and into the Happy Jack and remembered that Copeland was a limey fool.

She had heard something about this being a Bank Holiday and the Brits all had a day off work – unless they worked in a shop and, for some reason, then seemed to have to work longer hours. Someone had told her it was like Labour Day back home and she had wondered why Brits needed a day to celebrate the achievements of workers when none of them did any work.

The Happy Jack was crowded. Comparatively crowded, at least. The bank holiday had been celebrated by a local worker and many claimants of unemployment benefit since opening time, eight hours previously. They had been in a good mood and only one fight had broken out in the last hour, and everyone was so drunk they even carried on talking when the two strangers in black suits came in because they had looked OK because they had been wearing ties so must be rich and might buy a round for everyone.

When Special Agent Liza Clinton walked in the bar fell silent. She strode like a catwalk model to the bar, confident the local rednecks were all stunned by her Givenchy fitted black leather jacket, her Escada trousers, her Ellie Saab blouse, or her (slightly dusty) Jimmy Choos. It could be her Stuart Phillips hair – he does do it *so* well!

Barman Bill was wiping glasses when she got to the bar. He could not be bothered to look up. He guessed it had gone silent because a beautiful woman had entered the bar and his customers were gawping.

'I have a suite booked here,' said Agent Clinton. 'Please tell your bellhop to get my cases from the car.'

Bill continued wiping the glass. 'The American. Yeah, we have your room ready,' he said.

'And I will require dinner in your dining room. I am in the mood for foie gras. I know it's kinda passé, but I'm just in the mood, you know?' she said.

'Fwar graar?' said Barman Bill, not looking up. 'Is it sort of American gammon? We've got gammon. And mushy peas. A local delicacy, them. You're in room two. Up the stairs past room one.' He pointed to a door beside the dart board, which was above four bald men playing dominoes, who were having trouble holding more than five pieces at once or count the dots after their eighth pints.

Agent Clinton huffed and Jimmy Choo shoed it to the door, a man in black in front of her and one behind.

When they were through the door, one of the pool playing youths said, 'She's gonna have fun tonight! Two blokes!' and everyone in the bar laughed a good, deep male laugh, including the women.

Agent Clinton was back at the bar within two minutes.

'What the hell do you call that shit hole of a room, mister!' she said as she banged her hand on the bar and spray erupted from a bar towel. Her blouse was stained!

Barman Bill stopped wiping the glass and looked at her hand. His face slowly lifted until he was looking at her face.

He said, 'Black...'

She punched him and said: 'I'm Afro-American, you dick-head!'

Detective Inspector Larry Copeland. Monday, August 29 th.

Some physicists believe there are an infinite number of universes, existing beyond our own. And if there are an infinite number of universes then there are an infinite number of us – of every one of us – living in those infinite universes, those multiverses. In one such universe, Detective Inspector Lawrence Copeland had immensely enjoyed his Cumberland sausage and mash with red onion gravy, followed by chocolate cheesecake, and was now sipping a cognac and smoking a cigar on the hotel patio. He was enjoying the warm, late summer evening and watching the street lights twinkle across the river.

Our Universe's Inspector Copeland had the first mouthful of Cumberland sausage interrupted by a fist banging on his table. He looked up to see a lopsided Agent Clinton towering above him. She did not look happy.

'Look at this, Copeland!' she yelled, thrusting her hands out. One hand had a heel-less shoe and the other gripped broken sunglasses. Her hair was tousled, her collar torn, and there was a blood stain on the shoulder of her leather jacket.

'Would you like a drink? I'll get the waitress,' Copeland said, soothingly.

She dropped her broken sunglasses and shoe, leaned over his table and lifted him from his seat with his shirt collar. A not inconsiderable feat of strength given his stomach alone weighed more than most people. She seemed a little unhappy.

'This is because of you! You sent me to that goddam place! You told me it was a hotel! If they hadn't all started fighting each other instead of us, we would have had to use lethal force!'

Copeland was struggling to breathe, but he was more concerned that the bottle of full bodied Rioja had been knocked over when she had hauled him over the table. He dreaded to think which part of his anatomy was currently in the mash with the sausages, but it put him off eating another sausage ever.

'It has rooms...' he gasped.

She hauled him up further so his eyes were inches away from hers. 'I ought to shoot you!'

His brain said: *Stand up to her, Copeland! Be a man!*

Copeland said, 'Please don't shoot me.'

'Maybe I could just get my boys to rough you up,' she said, giving him a shake and a smile.

Over her shoulder he could see four other CIA agents who all looked equally dishevelled and blood stained. All of them had their jackets unbuttoned and shoulder holsters on view. The other diners were a frozen time tableau, with food balancing on forks, wine dripping down blouses, and open mouths.

Copeland heard only one voice in the complete silence.

Come on, Copeland! Tell her to go and fu...

'I'm really sorry you didn't hit it off with the barman Bill and his customers,' said Copeland, wanting to be as apologetic as he could.

Hit it off! Excellent sarcasm, Copeland! One for the Brits, old chap!

With worrying ease, Agent Clinton removed one of her hands and somehow managed to grip his collar with just one hand tighter than she had gripped it with two. Her free hand picked up the onion gravy boat and poured it over the top of his silver hair.

She thrust him back across the table into his chair, picked up her broken sunglasses and Jimmy Chou and hobbled out of the restaurant, followed by her four subservient agents.

Copeland remained motionless in the chair for some time as the gravy drained down his face and the other diners gradually resumed their meals, their conversations inspired with frequent 'And did you see..?' and 'What about the..?' comments.

The waitress stood beside him and timidly asked, 'Would you like anything else, sir?'

He considered the question before answering. 'I'd like a towel and then I'll have the same again, please' he said, getting over his sausage in the sausages analogy.

Tuesday, August 30 th.

Agent Clinton and her team were up at dawn. They showered and queued for breakfast. She had breakfast brought to her in her private tent by Gunny Gregg and ate while considering which of the other black clothes she had brought with her she would wear.

Beth Spencer was up at dawn, pacing and waiting for her mobile phone to ring. She hoped Jonathan would ring with news soon, or ring to say he had left his wife and see if she would like cocktails sometime.

Jakab Popov was up at dawn and wishing he had checked the date on the can of peaches he had consumed the evening before.

Tom Benson was up at dawn because he had not gone to bed. He had spent the night peering outside from the side of a hotel curtain.

The SO15 forensic team was up at dawn and splitting themselves into three groups: one for Jakab Popov's bed sit, one for the farm and one for Usman Fayad's outhouse home. Their main topic of conversation at their hotel breakfast was how the guy in the restaurant had got gravy poured on his head.

Danny Hesterman must have been up at dawn because he was banging on the door of room 105 at The Red Lion Hotel.

'Not again!' groaned Copeland, pulling the duvet over his head.

This was all getting too much thought Copeland as he walked along the side of the river to join Danny at the police station. He could not remember the last time he had worked this hard and even his third cigarette of the day was not giving him enough nicotine to make him feel properly awake. After another quick and somewhat apathetic check down below, he had started his day by having to choose either trousers with gravy on the front, or the old ones with his urine down the leg. He had opted for gravy and another shopping trip later. He hoped it would be a quieter day and he would find the time.

For some reason Mr. Brown the farmer had refused to speak to anyone but Copeland. He suspected Danny had told the farmer SO15 were on the case and it was a case of talking to them or having a long vacation with free water-boarding courtesy of the CIA. Copeland did not suspect that Danny had needed to explain water-boarding was not like surfing. Farmer Brown had soon chosen to talk to them and only them, and Copeland was the only one of *them* in town.

Copeland was trying to pick solidified gravy and mash from his groin when Danny brought Mr. Brown into the interview room from the holding cell. He had been read his rights when arrested but had refused his phone call or any legal representation.

'Right, Brown, tell us everything,' began Copeland, just wanting to get it over and go shopping. Another coffee would be good too. Maybe a pastry.

'I haven't got any theories. No theories. None at all,' said Farmer Brown.

'You know I'm SO15 and this is being treated as a terrorism related investigation, don't you?' Copeland said, sounding exasperated.

'I don't know anything about terrorists. I'm just a farmer. Wheat mostly. A bit of rape for the cooking oil. That's me,' said Brown.

Danny had been enterprising and had downloaded a photograph of Ronaldo onto his phone. Ronaldo was in shirt and tie and eating something. Danny thrust the phone into Farmer Brown's face.

'Do you know this man?' said Danny, threateningly.

Brown jerked his head back. He looked at the photo. He looked at Danny. He looked at Copeland. He looked at the photograph again. He said, 'Don't *you* know? It's Cristiano Ronaldo. Old photo, though. He's got a Manchester United tie on.'

'Don't get clever with us, Brown!' snapped Danny.

'I wasn't. Just saying it's a Man U. tie,' said Brown.

Copeland lowered Danny's arm from in front of Brown's face. 'We know that's Ronaldo, Mr. Brown,' said Copeland, suddenly finding himself the 'good cop'. 'We want to know if you know anyone who looks like Ronaldo.'

Brown thought so hard his brow twitched and his eyes flickered across the ceiling. He finally looked back at Copeland and said, 'No. I don't.'

Danny was on his feet and aggressively leaning across the table. 'The man in the black Mercedes who used your old tractor shed! What about him, eh?' barked Danny.

'Oh, him,' said Brown and went into brow twitching again. 'I suppose he might look a bit like Ronaldo since he went to Greece for a few weeks and if Ronaldo was maybe ten years older and had a bit of grey hair above his ears and was about four or five inches shorter. And if Ronaldo had thin lips. Like, really thin lips. Yeah, I suppose there is a bit of a resemblance now you come to mention it.'

'We think he is an Algerian terrorist. He's involved with a pretty extreme Muslim group,' said Copland as he eased Danny back into his seat.

'No, don't think so,' said Mr. Brown. 'He's Jewish.'

Now it was Copeland's turn to have a furrowed brow. 'Jewish? How do you know that Mr. Brown.'

'His name is Abraham,' said Mr. Brown.

'And did he give you his last name,' asked Copeland, anticipating a major breakthrough.

'Yes,' said Farmer Brown, 'and I remember it because it's the same as the city.'

'And what city would that be, Mr. Brown?'

'Lincoln.'

Copeland took a deep breath and said, 'Please wait here, Mr. Brown, while Sergeant Hesterman and I go for a coffee. Would you like us to bring you anything when we return?'

'Tea two sugars,' said Farmer Brown, smiling with relief now he had been such a big help.

When they returned to the interrogation room, Copeland felt more awake. The adrenalin surge when he heard the name of his suspect, and the way it had turned from excitement to anger, had helped. So had the coffee and the cold water on his face. In contrast, Hesterman was feeling dejected.

'So, Mr. Brown, if we can resume? You say you met this Abraham Lincoln and spoke to him. Indeed, it appears he even discussed his holiday with you. Tell us more,' said Copeland as serenely as he could.

'Well,' said Mr. Brown, pausing to sip his tea. 'He comes to me about a year ago looking to rent out a field or two. Offering big money he was, so I showed him round the farm. He liked the field with the old tractor shed in it and offered to rent that from me. I said yes, of course. Who wouldn't for that kind of money? Then this Abraham chap wants to know where he can hire or buy some farm machinery. So I ask him what he needs and it just so happened he liked what I had to offer and he hired them from me too. Well, he hired the tractor and bought the other stuff.'

Copeland and Hesterman looked at each other.

'And what did he do with the tractor?' asked Copeland.

'He didn't do anything. He paid me to do it. Straightforward stuff really, common-a-garden planting and harvesting. I did that for him with my harvester a couple of weeks ago. Must have fertilised and sprayed it himself, or got someone else to do it.'

'What about the farm machines he bought from you, Mr. Brown?'

'Oh, them! Couple of old things I was keeping in the old tractor shed in that field anyway. Just an old press and a filter. Got newer ones with all the money he gave me.'

'And what did you use this press and this filter for, Mr. Brown?'

'Making the Rapeseed oil. You see, what you do is you get the seeds and you...'

'Thank you, Mr. Brown,' said Copeland. 'Please finish your tea. We'll just have a word outside.'

When the door was closed behind them Copeland said, 'What do you think, Danny? Sounds like a pretty straightforward farming operation – planting, harvesting and so on.'

'Must be some sort of cover for what they were really doing in the shed. There must be more to it than making cooking oil,' said Danny.

'He *must* know something else,' said Copeland, and they went back into the room.

'Mr. Brown,' said Copeland. 'Let's see if I've got this straight. This Abraham comes to your farm and hires a field and a shed for a year. You plant some rape for him and you don't see him again until you help him harvest it?'

'That's right. Well off and on. Saw him sometimes when he comes and he sticks a boat load of money through my letter box every now and again, so I guess he was on his way back from the field or something. Told me about his hols. Nice chap.'

'And did you see anyone else going to that field, or, more importantly, go to the shed? Any other machines? Any other people?' asked Copeland.

Mr. Brown thought and said, 'No. Nothing. Then again it is a long way from the farmhouse. I didn't even know the shed had blown up until another envelope appeared with another wad of cash and a little printed note inside saying sorry about the shed.'

'And have you been up there since? To see the shed?'

'I didn't care that much about it. Never used it, but I walked up there after this Sergeant here came to see me. Shed was blown up, or down, alright. Machines inside looked like write-offs. Looks like there was a fire too – the walls are blackened. Seeds probably burnt too. What a waste.'

'Have you seen this Abraham since?'

'No. Spoke to him on the phone though after the Sergeant had called.'

He has his phone number! Yes!

'And what did he say when you phoned him, Mr. Brown?'

'He said if I told you the truth he would give me another two thousand pounds,' bluntly said Mr. Brown.

'He said what?'

'He said I had done nothing wrong and I should tell you the truth. I suppose he's right. All I did was hire him a field, a shed, sell him a few old machines and give him a couple of mornings of my time.'

'Thank you for your time Mr. Brown. We will need to keep hold of your phone, but you may go,' said Copeland. From the corner of his eye he saw Danny's look of astonishment.

Mr. Brown said, 'Don't care about the phone. No one phones me anyway. But what about the CIA carting me off?'

'Quite right, Mr Brown,' said Copeland. We will arrange a car to take you to a hotel somewhere out of town for a few days – at the tax payers expense of course.'

'I'll live with that. Nothing much to do on the farm now the harvest is sorted. You paying for my meals too?'

'Er, yes, I suppose so. But not your drink. You will have to pay for that yourself. Keep the receipts,' said Copeland.

Not the drinks? You hypocrite, Copeland!

'If you wait here, Mr Brown, someone will be along to collect you presently. I understand you packed before you were brought here? Good. Just one more thing, Mr. Brown. You are aware that Abraham Lincoln is the name of an American president, aren't you?'

'Really?' said a surprised Mr. Brown. 'Well, I never knew that. But this Abraham Lincoln had an American accent, though. Maybe it's the same bloke.'

Jakab Popov. Tuesday, 30 th August.

By the time Jakab finished expunging the rancid peaches, the factory alongside the scrap yard was grinding metal into machine parts. Jakab was reminded of the sound the drill had made when the dentist had drilled into his tooth. It had been the one and only time he had been able to afford a filling, and it had been a long time ago. He wished he could have afforded the injection first too.

He had examined his arm. It was no worse. Not much better, but no worse. He was content with that. He knew enough to know he had to try to keep it clean. He washed it under the tap in the sink beside the toilet and he found some white cream under the sink so tried to smear that on where there was something left to smear it on to. He found some cling film in a cupboard next to the little cooker and wrapped it around his arm, just like that nice astronaut doctor lady had.

After looking out of the window for an hour after the grinding factory noise had begun, Jakab decided Alexei and Ivan were not coming back today. He needed fresh clothes and had seen some in some drawers next to the couch where he had slept. He tried to use the shower but it did not work, so he washed his whole body with water from the sink and was annoyed when the water made the cling film peel off and he had to wrap his arm again. All the clothes were too large for him so he kept his jeans on and tucked the blue shirt he had found deep inside his jeans and rolled up the sleeve on his good arm. He was thrilled to find a pair of leather gloves and he tried them on. Big, but good enough to cover his hand and, smiling, he forced his finger bones into the gloves. He also found a red baseball cap which he thought was cool. He put it on and looked through the window again.

He was starting to feel hungry, but his mother had advised him to only drink water when he had a bad stomach, so he followed her advice and did. He started looking through all the drawers and finally got to the filing cabinet. There were lots of metal rimmed, cardboard dividers with little tabs sticking up. Each tab had a name written on it and Jakab started looking for his own name. He found it and looked into the divider. There was nothing there, except for a brown envelope that had slid almost under the next divider. Jakab pulled it out. He tipped the envelope up and two keys fell out. He had found a door key that looked just like the key to his door the thief had taken from the hospital. The other key had the word Snauzer written on it and decided to keep that too in case the thief had found his and stolen it. He put them in his pocket. He was replacing the envelope next to the 'Popov,

Jakab' tab when he saw something in the front of the filing cabinet drawer. He looked outside again before he took it out. He removed the elastic band from the bundle of fifty pound notes and counted them. There were forty.

His mother's voice rang in his ears. 'You take money from these bad people and they will mess you up bad, Jakab,' she was screaming, but he forced the money into his jeans pocket anyway.

Now he had money – lots of money – and his keys. He would get his things from his bed sit and, if the tubby thief had not found it, get what was padlocked safely in the garage.

Beth Spencer, Tuesday, August 30 th.

Beth had wanted to phone Tom all morning, but knew she dare not. She wanted to go and see him, but Copeland had refused to say where he was going to take him. (This was mainly because he had no idea where that was when she had asked.) She had phoned Lincoln Hospital and told them she was taking the day off for personal reasons. When they asked her how the HPT was going she had struggled to remember just when she had been sent to Boston to lead the Health Protection Team – it seemed a lifetime ago. She had said she could not talk about it for reasons of national security and her supervisor had gone very quiet before asking if it was anything to do with that junior administrator from The St. James killing those two entrepreneurs. She had said no and ended the call.

How had two thugs who exploited migrants suddenly become entrepreneurs? she thought. Bloody press!

Her phone was next to her as she went crazy on her exercise bike and the phone stayed next to her on the shelf in the bathroom when she took her shower. Simon was gone, Tom was in trouble, and the man she had once thought was 'the one' was only interested in intellectual property rights and the money they could get him. She hated everything. She found something left over from Easter and dyed her hair red. There was not much dye left, but enough for hair that was just long enough to run her fingers through.

The heat wave was continuing and she paced around the house in shorts and tee shirt. She prepared some food ready for later and put it in her fridge. She paced some more.

Her pacing was interrupted by her door bell. A woman and a man in black suits, black ties and reflective sunglasses were holding up CIA badges and a letter signed by the Home Secretary giving them complete police and intelligence services powers. They lowered their sunglasses and looked her up and down. The CIA man looked her up and down again. So did the CIA woman. They wanted to know about Tom. She said she hardly knew him. They wanted to search her house. She let them but insisted she stay with them, which made the search longer. They eventually left, satisfied, once they had looked her up and down again. She paced again, ate a banana, paced, drank a smoothie, paced.

She almost jumped when her phone finally rang. She grabbed it without looking at the display.

'Jonathan?

'Oh, it's you, Simon.

'Who's Jonathan? Yes, errr... Just a work colleague who's working on a project with me.

'Well, I'm sorry *you've* been too busy to call,' she said and abruptly ended the call.

That was it: the final straw. He had been too busy to call! She changed into jeans and trainers, grabbed a denim jacket and left for Cambridge. Intellectual property rights or not, health and safety insurance or not, she was going to Jonathan's lab.

It was mid-afternoon when she was pressing the gate intercom and being surprised by Jonathan telling her he was glad she had come.

'I was about to give you a call,' Jonathan said as they walked down the corridor to his high tech lab. 'The animal infection trials are still ongoing, but no signs of infection yet. We have found something, though. Actually, we've found a lot.'

She followed him into the outer part of the lab and he sat her in front of a screen. He said, 'These are some high resolution images we've taken.'

'It looks like coagulative necrosis,' she said, looking at the pictures on the screen. 'The inside of the cells has turned gelatinous. It's classic denaturation, just like an egg going from transparent to white when it's boiled. But the pathology lab would have picked that up on the most basic microscope.'

'It's only in cells at the edge of the necrosis. The ones that were about to rupture. I'm guessing the pathology lab only got ruptured or healthy cells. I think we only got these because this hand has been amputated and it sort of caught the process in mid-action.'

'These cells show the classic signs of ischemia causing a lack of oxygen. This only happens when the blood supply is disrupted and usually only in organs like the kidney, not the hand and arm,' said Beth staring at the pictures.

'We found something incredible,' said Jonathan.

Beth waited.

'What, Jonathan? What was incredible?'

'The reason for the oxygen deficiency. The chromosomes in the mitochondria have been changed. They are producing nickel based S.O.D. as well as their own.'

This time Beth was silent.

'Beth? You know what I'm saying?'

'Yes, Jonathan, I do. These cells have been genetically altered to produce a type of superoxide dismutase enzyme no mammals produce. Superoxide dismutase, or SAD, mops up our free oxygen radicals. If this is added to our DNA then our usual SAD and this one combined could wipe out all the oxygen in the cell and we get a type of coagulative necrosis.'

'There's more, Beth. Those changes produce hydrogen peroxide, which is corrosive enough, but there are also genetic changes that produce formic acid – pure formic acid. And we have esters coming from somewhere and they must be coming from the changed mitochondrial DNA too. No wonder these cells are rupturing. The chemicals these DNA changes are producing are a mixture of acid and corrosives and they just dissolve that cell wall and then dissolve through part of the cell wall of an adjacent cell, the altered DNA migrates into the next cell and the process starts again. And like the pathology lab, we found a whole host of lipases too. It's amazing really.'

Beth was silent.

'I'm just thinking how I can explain this to someone who has no science background. Such as, for instance, a police inspector.'

Jonathan was thinking too. 'That won't be easy,' he said.

Beth said, 'How about... It's something that breaks through the cell wall, changes the genetic structure of the cell so it starves itself of oxygen and in the process makes enough corrosives and acid to dissolve the next cell wall when the first cell disintegrates because of the acid and corrosives inside it?'

'And the lipases act as enzymes to speed the whole thing up,' said Jonathan.

'Yes,' said Beth.

'Hells bells!' exclaimed Jonathan. 'Whatever is causing this could wipe out all advanced life on Earth!'

Beth's eyes widened. She cried, 'That's it! Jonathan you're a genius. So am I! I know what *is* causing this.'

'What?' said Jonathan.

'Sorry, Jonathan. Thanks for the research, but it's my intellectual property now. Someone will be in touch to collect the hand. Good luck making money!' And Beth was already out of the seat and running back to her car.

Detective Inspector Larry Copeland, Tuesday, August 30th.

The shopping had gone well and Copeland had two bags full of M&S menswear. He was enjoying a pastry and coffee in a lovely little cafe and removing all the new clothes labels, just in case, when his mid-morning bliss was interrupted.

His phone screen said Ross.

'Morning, Chief,' said Copeland, happily. 'How's things? We have a name for Ronaldo from the farmer. It's Abraham Lincoln. I was about to phone.'

'Special Agent Clinton is filing an official complaint against you,' Ross said, sombrely.

'What? Because I gave her the name of a shit hotel? And she's already had her revenge for that!' complained Copeland.

'No, Inspector,' said Ross, 'because you omitted to tell us that Popov had a Quran, a book written by Osama bin Laden, and a prayer mat in his bedsit, just like Fayad had in his hovel too. And you failed to tell us there was a stainless steel flask in a cupboard behind Popov's frying pan. It exactly matches the one found where Fayad slept. The flasks are being brought back to London for tests and you are going to explain yourself to Agent Clinton before she has you suspended. Get to Popov's place now. And no more theories about the Russian SVR lying to us – that theory is dead in the water now.'

Copeland's mood was entirely ruined. It was so ruined he left the pastry half eaten and strolled back to the hotel to change before sauntering out again. He passed a pawn shop with a colourful window poster saying the shop sold something called Zombie Juice. Zombie juice? He read it more closely. Zombie Juice came in several disgusting fruit flavours for 'your vaping experience'. Copeland had no time for anyone who had to obtain their nicotine from anything that wasn't natural, and to confirm his conviction took out a Marlboro and lit it. He exhaled, regained some composure, coughed with feeling, and phoned Danny to meet him outside Popov's bed sit.

He was soon walking down East Street and wondering why he was wearing a suit when the sun was blazing. He sucked furiously on the cigarette. For some reason the traffic was at a standstill.

How the hell did you miss a prayer mat, a Quran, a bin Laden terrorist manual and a silver flask, Copeland?

Halfway down East Street he could see why traffic had stopped. A black SUV was across the street and two CIA agents were turning pedestrians around. As he approached them at a half jog and sweating, he threw his cigarette into the gutter and began reaching for his warrant card. One of the agents pulled back her black jacket and put her hand on her holstered pistol.

Copeland! She's flicking the safety off!

Copeland's hand had reached down into his jacket inside pocket and was touching his warrant card. The agent's gun was out and the other agent drew his. Their left hands supported their right, with fingers on the triggers. The barrels were pointed at Copeland,

'Down on the floor! Hands behind your head,' shouted the female agent.

Copeland hesitated with one hand half inside his jacket. He withdrew it slowly and started to lower himself to the pavement.

Bloody hell Copeland, this lying down is getting hard work. It'll mess up another new suit as well.

Copland felt a gun pushed into the base of his neck and a hand reach inside his jacket and take out his warrant card. The pressure of the gun barrel eased.

'You can get up, Inspector,' said the female agent. 'It's Inspector Copeland!' she shouted to her colleague as she re-holstered her firearm.

Copeland was having trouble getting up and she had to take his elbow and help him.

He heard the male agent laugh. 'Liza Clinton wasn't exaggerating was she? He does look like he's about to give birth!'

The female agent loosed his elbow and handed him his warrant card back. From behind her sunglasses she said, 'So you're the old guy who didn't search Popov's place properly then gave his handcuff keys to a hit man? Boy, are you in deep doodie! Better mosey on down the street and grovel to the boss before you get shipped to Guantanamo.'

Copeland brushed himself down, dabbed his perspiring forehead with his handkerchief, decided to be British about the whole thing, said, 'Sorry to have troubled you, Agent,' and carried on down East Street.

Outside Fenney's Kitchens, on the corner of Dragon Street and opposite the Happy Jack, Special Agent Liza Clinton was surrounded by milling CDC scientists in yellow suits and six black suit, black tie, reflective sunglasses agents. One agent was pointing to an alley running down the side of the Happy Jack.

She saw Copeland coming. Copeland thought a smile might work.

'You're a bigger idiot than I thought, Copland,' she screamed at him. 'And I thought you were a pretty big goddam idiot to begin with!'

Come on, Copeland! She's just a bully! OK, a very tall, very strong, athletic bully, but just a bully. Tell her what for!

Copeland said, 'I'm sorry, but...'

'Save it, Copeland. We've found the padlock. Draw your weapon and follow me,' she shouted as she ran across the road and down the alley with her six agents, all with pistols drawn.

Copeland sighed. 'Now I'm expected to run as well?'

His default mode of apathy finally won out. He followed at a more leisurely pace and emerged behind the Happy Jack into a narrow road with a few garages down one side and CIA agents down the other, pointing guns at a red metal, up and over garage door. At the end of the access road a group of onlookers were quickly gathering. One of the agents was dispatched to keep them back. Copeland thought he recognised the face of an unshaven man in a red baseball cap.

You know your memory is going, don't you, Copeland?

Matching the face to a name was just coming to him when an agent unlocked the huge padlock and it fell with a metallic clunk onto the concrete.

'Now!' shouted Agent Clinton.

The agent grabbed the base of the garage door and flipped it open. The other agents rushed past him, pointing their guns into all corners of the garage. Someone was nudging Copeland's shoulder. He turned to see Danny standing beside him.

'What the hell is going on?' said a dumfounded Danny.

Copeland had his hands over his ears, anticipating gunfire, but guessed what Danny was asking. 'CIA,' explained Copeland.

He saw the crowd of onlookers had grown, but the man in the red baseball cap was no longer to be seen.

You let Popov get away again, didn't you, Copeland?

Copeland lowered his hands from his ears. He and Danny Hesterman followed the CIA agents into the garage and looked at the rusting body of an eight year old Toyota Avensis.

Special Agent Clinton was waving the barrel of her pistol at the car and glaring at Copeland as if not being able to shoot a terrorist with a whole magazine of armour piercing bullets was all his fault. 'What the hell is this, Copeland?' she demanded.

It was Danny who answered for him. 'It's a taxi,' he said.

Jakab Popov, Tuesday 30 th. August.

Jakab Popov sat on the couch in the Karamazov's musty caravan inspecting his hand and arm. It was no worse, but it was starting to hurt and there were a few black spots beginning to appear. He went to the sink, filled it and put his arm as deep into the water as he could. The cold water made it feel better.

He took the red baseball cap off and placed it on the draining board. He thought about whether he should go back to the hospital. Men with guns were blocking the way to his home and they had found the car. He had nowhere else to go. He could stay there, in Alexei and Ivan's caravan. Perhaps they had gone on a holiday. He had heard of such things. What would they say when they came back and found he had been living in their caravan?

'What do you think they will say, stupid boy?' his mother's exasperated voice cried. 'You think they will be happy you are living in their place? NO!'

The man – the thief at the hospital – he was there with the black suited men and women with guns. He must be their leader. They must be another gang come to take over, or maybe secret police, or maybe both. They were not normal police. They had no uniforms and no big dome hats like the Bobby police. These were The Secret Police wearing sunglasses.

He took his hand from the water and raised it to his nose. It was beginning to smell like an old cabbage. He put it back in the sink. He wanted to go home, back to his mother.

Detective Sergeant Brandon, Tuesday, 30 th August.

Detective Sergeant Brandon had arrived at his desk in SO15 at his normal time and only D.C.I. Ross had given him a long hard stare. He sat at his terminal and read the reports coming in. He learned how the surveillance team on Abdul Karim had been increased and about what had been found at Popov's bed sit and Usman Fayad's outhouse squat.

As he watched his screen a police report came in from Boston, stating a witness had named Ronaldo as Abraham Lincoln, who did look a bit like Ronaldo and had an American accent. Brandon thought the official line of keeping him as 'Ronaldo' made sense. The CIA would probably not really want to hunt down and shoot Abraham Lincoln. The search for the two retired professors who could identify him had proven fruitless.

There were preliminary reports from the forensics teams coming in. They told Brandon the Karamazov brothers had both been killed by a single shot to the back of the head, and there were some samples of dried blood being sent for DNA analysis, along with an awful lot of dried vomit.

The CDC team from America were testing everyone in the hospital who had any contact with Popov, but there were no signs as yet of any spread of the disease, though they did mention one student nurse who had refused to be tested on the grounds it infringed her human rights. For some reason, Special Agent Clinton had ordered part of the CDC team to go and take very painful spinal fluid samples from everyone in a pub called the Happy Jack.

There was another, typically brief report, from Copeland, saying he had been contacted by Tom Benson and Benson had claimed he had seen two men kill the Karamazov's. Copeland had added he believed these two men were Vasily Goraya and Nikolay Ivchenko of the Russian SVR, but gave no reason why he thought Benson was telling the truth or why he thought SVR agents would kill the Karamazov brothers.

What Copeland thought did not seem to matter anymore: Sergeant Brandon also saw an official complaint from Special Agent Clinton claiming Copeland was not competent to act in any capacity because he had missed vital evidence when he had searched Popov's flat and had jeopardised the lives of thousands by entrusting Popov's handcuffs key to an assassin.

Brandon thought things looked bleak for Copeland and even bleaker for Copeland's theory that Popov and Fayad were no more than who they said they were. Besides the radical Islamic teachings book of Osama bin Laden, there were the flasks that were remaining sealed until they could be examined in an airtight lab. There was the toxic Nosoi, right in those flasks, and they had been in Popov's and Fayad's possession. Popov's phone log seemed to be nothing more than a string of taxi fares, and Farmer Brown's phone log had led to a woman who worked in Aldi, so it was clear Ronaldo was using the time honoured terrorist tactic of buying stolen phones and leaving fake numbers to mislead any investigation. Brandon knew that because it was all covered in basic training.

As he watched his screen, Brandon saw a report from a CIA agent come in about the garage. He had just started to read it when his screen went blank. Large words in red flashed three times on the screen: **Urgent GCHQ. Live feed**.

Brandon went into DCI Ross's office without knocking. 'GCHQ live feed,' he said.

Ross scowled at him, but turned his monitor on. Brandon moved behind him and watched over Ross's shoulder, fully expecting to be told to leave.

'Fill me in, Sergeant Brandon,' said Ross as the screen came to life.

'It's a live feed from CCTV in Knightsbridge, Sir,' said Brandon. Surveillance team reported Abdul Karim leaving his apartment and GCHQ were ready to get all the CCTVs in the area on to him. He's going up Hans Crescent towards Brompton Road.'

'There's one of our teams trailing him?'

'A team of three, I believe, Sir,' Brandon informed Ross.

They watched the slim, dark haired, angular featured Abdul Karim walk past the five storey redbrick Colombian Embassy. He was carrying nothing and was walking briskly towards the camera on the outside of the Valentino corner of Harrods.

'Nice pin stripe,' commented Ross. 'Probably cost me a year's salary to get one of those suits.'

'Where's he gone?' asked Brandon.

'Oooh! That's new,' said Ross as a subtitle appeared in a box at the bottom of the screen. 'I heard they were finding a way to link in the radios from surveillance teams into real time CCTV.'

The subtitle said: **Subject has entered Harrods.**

The screen flickered while the GCHQ operator switched to Harrods internal cameras. Karim was moving through the ground floor towards the centre where there was not a camera.

A subtitle said: **Confirmed, Control. Moving in closer.**

The GCHQ operator found a better view and zoomed in on Karim at a counter.

'What's he doing?' asked Brandon.

'Looks like he's treating himself to a large box of Harrods chocolates,' replied Ross.

The camera followed Karim when he moved away from the counter towards the escalator. The camera cut and tried to locate him. He was on the escalator. A woman in a flower patterned dress was close behind him. She appeared to be looking at her watch very closely.

The subtitle said: **I'm on the escalator behind the subject.**

Brandon said, 'The woman in the flowery dress is one of ours. Hey! It's Holly!'

'You're very quick, Sergeant,' said Ross, sarcastically.

The camera cut to one viewing the top of the escalator. Karim was nowhere in sight.

The subtitle said: **He's going straight back down. He might be on to us.**

'Now he's seen you talking into your watch, Holly, I'm sure he is on to us,' commented Ross.

CCTV shots flicked from one to another, caught Karim as he disappeared into a group of shoppers and lost him again.

Got him. Hans Road exit.

The screen flickered again and picked Karim up heading south west on the Brompton Road. He walked briskly almost as far as the London Oratory and went into a cafe. The screen flicked between cameras but went back to the one covering the cafe exit.

I'm across the road from the cafe. Holding position.

Five minutes went by. Then ten.

Order understood. Going in now.

The CCTV showed a tall man wearing a white shirt and grey summer trousers crossing the road and entering the cafe.

Subject is... oh, shit!

Please have a seat. I have ordered you a cappuccino. If you wear shoes like that, you can hardly afford to buy your own coffee in Knightsbridge.

The subtitle box was suddenly removed from the bottom of the screen.

'I think he's made our second man,' said Brandon.

'You think?' said Ross.

The screen showed a flustered surveillance operative emerge from the cafe and say something into his conspicuously bulky gold watch. He clearly got a loud reply because he removed his earpiece and held it away from his ear. Ross and Brandon watched him retrace his steps to the other side of the road, replacing his earpiece as he dodged a cyclist.

Karim emerged from the cafe and, chocolate box under his arm, continued his journey down Brompton Road and into Thurloe Place. He crossed the road, stopped and looked back down the street.

The subtitle said: **He's going bloody miles! I'm knackered.**

Karim must have seen the white shirt of the surveillance man because his pace quickened until he broke into a run and entered a building. The text box eventually reappeared at the bottom of the screen.

He's run into the Victoria and Albert Museum.

The screen flicked from one camera to another. They searched every floor of the museum, but Abdul Karim was nowhere. Ross and Brandon waited, but the cameras kept searching the museum – including the gift shop. Finally, Ross turned the screen off.

'They will let us know if they find him,' said Ross. 'In the meantime, Sergeant, I want you to look at every possible terrorist target in the area. We know it could be Harrods or The Victoria and Albert, but get me a list of every other possible high profile target.'

'It could be the cafe,' suggested Brandon. Ross threw a pencil at him.

Abdul Karim met Fatima under the stairs in the Victoria and Albert Museum. She gave him a new phone, a wide brimmed cream Penmayne designer hat, a light grey Armani jacket and a passionate kiss. He emerged from the museum fifteen minutes later, judging that to have been plenty of time for those following him to panic and be rushing around the upper floors of the museum searching for him. Without looking round he continued to his destination.

Ten minutes later, a woman carrying a large box of chocolates left by the same exit.

Ronaldo (a.k.a. Abraham Lincoln), Tuesday 30 th. August.

The man they called 'Ronaldo' did not recognise the number but guessed who it was and answered his phone anyway.

'Good. I'm glad Fatima got a new phone to you, Sir, er, Scorpion. Now I have your number I shall get a new one too.

'The tests are going very well indeed. It really is more potent than we could have ever hoped. The first rabbit didn't last long, only a few seconds really. We had to make some modifications because the stuff is so powerful...

'No, no. The last test went perfectly. We are well ahead of schedule.

'Yes, I'm sure we can use it. The stuff is...

'What? Fatima has been talking to you again about the name for it? Please tell me...

'But, Sir! That's a terrible name! I told Fatima we would think of a new one. She had no right to...

'Well, er, ok, right, if you like the name, Sir, I suppose...

'Yes, Sir, I realise you are financing this whole thing and if you like the name then we keep the name.

'I understand, Sir. Of course we need a name when we are on the front page of every newspaper, but...

'When? That soon? When I said the end of next week, I meant the end of *next week*...

'Yes, Sir, we'll work round the clock. All the tests will be finished. I'll make sure of it. But we will have to get a flask to London.

'Meet you and Fatima? Do you think she is the best person for the job? I think she might be telling members of her family too much and she could compromise everything, Sir. I think we may have to terminate her.

'Oh, I didn't know you two were... involved. Sorry, Sir.

'Thank you for your forgiveness, Sir. I will get in touch with you with a new phone and make the final arrangements, Prince.

'Ooops, sorry, Scorpion. Of course I'll remember to only call you Scorpion from now on.'

Copeland and Hesterman, Tuesday 30 th August.

Special Agent Clinton had not been interested in the Toyota Avensis with the taxi signs once they had found nothing inside except a mobile phone. She had left the car in the hands of a forensic team and was only interested in getting the phone back to her embassy to be cracked. She was not interested in a lowly police sergeant in the shape of ex scrum half Danny Hesterman trying to explain the significance of the taxi, especially when he pointed out she did not have a search warrant and could not use the phone in evidence. She had made it abundantly clear that Popov would not need a trial where he was going and if the 'two Dicks' did not get lost they would join him there.

Unsure if she was referring to them as detectives or something else, Copeland decided to do what he did best and suggested lunch.

At Danny's request to eat elsewhere they passed the door of the Happy Jack, which was in some sort of CDC lockdown anyway and emitting screams and cries of 'not another big sodding needle', and made for Copeland's hotel. They slung their jackets over their shoulders and sauntered along East Street. Car horns were blasting and angry drivers were being held back by a line of uniform police in front of the black CIA SUV across the street. An irate mayor, wearing his chain of office, was berating the male CIA agent and a uniformed Inspector Bell was trying to calm him down. Hesterman and Copeland slipped by without being noticed.

Leaving the blaring horns behind, Copeland lit a cigarette and they walked in silence to the hotel. They found a table on the patio overlooking the mud of the virtually dry river. Years of smoking had dulled Copeland's nose, but Danny had to hold his nose until he got used to the smell coming from the riverbed.

The waitress soon came and took their order. 'Not many customers today, Inspector C,' she said. 'Some sort of kafuffle in the town and nothing seems to be moving.'

'Yes,' said Copeland. 'A kafuffle seems to be what is going on all right.'

The drinks were brought – lemonade for Danny and a pint of lager for Copeland (because he was determined to cut down on his alcohol and lager wasn't real beer, was it?) – and Copeland asked Danny to explain the taxi in the garage.

'We have been trying to crack down on rogue taxis. It's a problem in just about every town these days. They haven't got a real license but just put fake taxi signs and fake licenses on the vehicles and Joe Public thinks they are OK. They're not – no insurance, no driver vetting, nothing legal at all. We think our local ones were being run by the Karamazov's but every time we've managed to catch one the driver refused to talk.'

'So you think Popov was driving an illegal taxi for the Karamazovs?' said Copeland.

'Yes. He wouldn't need much English. All GPS stuff through the phone. It explains where that five hundred pounds came from. It was his takings for the weekend and he hadn't turned it over to Alexei and Ivan yet. And remember when Alexei Karamazov told us Popov refused to work weekends? Popov probably refused to work during the day because they expected him to be driving his taxi at night.'

'Hmmm,' said Copeland. 'Makes sense. Fits in with my theory too. The Russians would not want us to know Popov was a taxi driver at weekends and not an international terrorist. They were after him to silence him, just like they silenced the Karamazovs.'

The food arrived. Danny was trying a better salad and Copeland was trying to lose weight by only having a salmon and cream cheese bagel with a side order of chips.

'So,' said Copeland with a mouthful of bagel, 'now I know where to find Jakab Popov and Tom Benson.'

Hesterman almost choked on his lettuce. 'What? How do you know?'

'Where else would Popov go? He's at the Karamazovs – probably in their caravan wondering what to do. I saw him watching us get into the garage this morning. And I know where Tom Benson is because I took him to the hotel myself. Let's see them try to suspend me now!'

Danny Hesterman struggled with which question to ask first. 'Saw Popov? Suspended? What hotel?'

Copeland downed half of his lager and smiled. 'Don't look so worried, Danny. What's the worst that can happen?'

Danny thought for a moment and said, 'Er, terrorists could gas half of London? We could be locked up for the rest of our lives? A disease could wipe out this whole town? That's in no particular order of priority of course.'

'Oh, Danny, have a chip and relax. Latest reports are showing there is no disease spreading anywhere. Fayad died of heart failure after he cut his hand off and Popov is well enough to be walking round town. Tom Benson didn't kill anyone, that was our SVR friends Vasily and Nikolay – you remember them? And there is nothing to prove there is any such thing as this Nosoi, except what the Russians are telling us. Ex Prince Abdul Karim was a playboy with lots of money who happened to get his photo taken with one of the wrong sorts of people and everyone thinks he's a terrorist leader because the Saudis say so – and they have it in for him because they think he stole a load of their money.'

Danny chewed and thought. 'What about the explosion on the farm and the missing professors?' he said.

Copeland! Beryl said go to the farm!

Copeland finished off his pint and raised a hand to attract the waitress. He smiled and pointed to his empty glass when she came. Danny phoned dispatch to send a car to the Karamazov's to collect Jakab Popov.

Copeland bit into his bagel wishing he had ordered something more substantial. He sighed before saying, 'The forensics on the exploding shed aren't done yet, Danny, but let's face it, it wasn't much of an explosion and no one seems to be worried much about terrorists having explosives. Well, not these terrorists anyway. And the old professors might have just decided to go away for a few days. They are retired, you know.'

'A romantic break? Those two?' said Danny. 'I can believe your evil Russian empire theory more easily than I can believe those two went for a romantic break. Not together, anyway.'

Patting Danny's hand, Copeland said, 'You're a cynic, Danny. Old people can be in love too, you know.'

Viktor Mosovoi, Tuesday August 30 th.

Colonel Vasily Goraya, SVR, former KGB, Order of Lenin and Order of the Red Star, etc., and Captain Nikolay Ivchenko stood to attention in the middle of the vast, plush office in the Russian embassy. It smelled of expensive carpet and fresh leather and polished wood. The air conditioner in the ceiling whirred above their heads. They looked sideways at each other then back at the short, fat man with the snub nose and frog eyes who had summoned them to his office. They had stood at attention for over ten minutes and watched him stare at the papers on his desk. He had not looked at them once.

Viktor Mosovoi had a volcano building inside him and he wanted to wait for it to erupt before he let its full fury loose onto these two uniformed imbeciles. He felt his pulse thumping in the veins in his neck and decided it was time to let it out before his heart decided to explode. He swept the papers from his desk – no mean feat for a man with short arms and a large desk.

'You told me nothing could go wrong! Now this!' he bellowed.

Vasily tried to speak, 'Mr. Mosovoi, Sir...'

'You! You, Goraya! You told me everything was going better than planned! Only yesterday and the day before and every day last week you told me this! There are people in Kamchatka who remember you, Vasily Goraya! When the President sends you there they will skin you alive! Slowly!'

'But, Sir...'

'Our inside agent tells us Abdul Karim is ready to turn the world on its head and you whine excuses? He knows where he is going to use it but keeps it to himself and tells no one! No one! And you whine excuses? Get out of those stupid uniforms and get back to Boston or to Knightsbridge or somewhere, but do your duty and make this plan work or your balls will be my new paperweights. Yours too Nikolay Ivchenko! Go! Go!'

Vasily and Nikolay saluted, did a one hundred and eighty degree parade ground turn and marched out. Nikolay closed the double door behind them.

Vasily said, 'You're right, Nikolay. I don't like him either.'

'What can we do?' said Nikolay as they walked back to their rooms to change. 'We already moved the timetable up by three months when we found out about Popov. We thought it would take them months yet to synthesise the final liquid. Now our agent inside his group informs us it is ready for use. How could anyone have foreseen that?'

Vasily stopped and put his hand on Nikolay's shoulder. 'The British and the CIA may not stop them in time. We must find out where Karim has it hidden. Find it and destroy it.'

'And kill everyone who knows how to make it!' said Nikolay, enthusiastically.

'Or get the CIA or the British to kill them for us. It would be much neater that way. Oh, Nikolay! Do not look so disappointed. You are a young man with plenty of killings still ahead of you. Now, get changed and meet me in operations. They need to double their efforts and locate that phone trace. Then we are going back to Boston. We need to locate their base and I'm sure they did not move this Nosoi too far!'

Nikolay laughed.

Dr. Beth Spencer, Tuesday 30 th. August.

While Tom got his things together, Beth sat on the hotel bed and tried to phone Simon. She regretted hanging up on him. His phone went straight on to answer phone.

'Hi, Simon. It's Beth. Sorry about hanging up. Please call me as soon as you can. We need to talk,' she said and pressed the red symbol.

Tom was standing with all his worldly goods in a plastic bag. They consisted of the clothes they had bought at the TK Maxx and a few toiletries Copeland had picked up for him on the way to the hotel.

'So... Simon?' Tom asked. 'Did he call?'

'Yes, he did, and I was short with him and now I regret it.'

'Gone off Jonathan then?' asked Tom with half a smirk.

'Huh! Right off,' answered Beth.

'How about hobbits?' smiled Tom. 'Hobbits who like the new look red hair?'

She smiled back. 'I like hobbits just fine. As friends.'

'Oh, right,' he said, shuffling his feet and looking out of the hotel window.

'Good friends,' added Beth.

'Understood, Beth,' said Tom. 'But how did you find me?'

'Easy. It's the closest budget hotel to the Starbucks we met Copeland in. I knew he wouldn't take you far. And I knew your room because I saw you look out of the window when I pulled into the car park – not very clever for a hit man and international terrorist, if you don't mind me saying so, Tom.'

'Proves I'm not, then, I suppose. What's your plan, Beth?'

'I have a plan to get you out of the hotel without anyone recognising you as 'The Boston Shooter' – that's your media name, by the way. I'm taking you back to my house. I think it's safe now the CIA have come and gone. I'll drop you nearby and check with my neighbour, Mrs. Pratt. She'll know if there is anyone suspicious hanging around, and I'll do a couple of walks up and down just to make sure. It'll be dark when we get there, so that should help get you in unnoticed. Then we need Copeland again.'

'Do we really need him? He didn't even get my Romeo and Juliet quote,' complained Tom.

'Yes, we do need him. I think might have figured this whole thing out, but I need to do a little more research and sleep on it and I will tell him and you together tomorrow.'

'I can't wait to hear what the truth of all this... Aha!' said Tom with index finger raised. 'Truth is truth to the end of reckoning.'

Beth laughed. 'I will go Measure for Measure with you Tom, and say: Most strange, but yet most truly, will I speak.'

'You regale me as Shakespeare's fair Isabella, whilst I doth quote Beatty in Fahrenheit 451,' said Tom and they both laughed.

They fist bumped and Beth shouted, 'Mulder and Scully ride again!'

'So let's go,' said Tom.

'I just need to use your bathroom,' said Beth, grabbing the shopping bag she had brought in with her.

Tom sat on the edge of the hotel bed and waited. He stared at the floor in front of the bathroom door, wondering what she had discovered and waiting for her to emerge. When the door opened he was lost in thought.

'What do you think?' she said. 'I've sort of used your idea and I thought distracting people from looking at you might be a good idea to get you out of here.'

Tom saw a pair of white, very high heeled sandals, strapped above her ankles. His eyes went up Beth's legs. He swallowed hard. Eventually, his eyes reached the black leather mini skirt she was wearing, and the studded leather belt level with his eyes. He coughed. He had to force his eyes further up to see her tight white, sleeveless top. The low cut and the lacing up the front meant whoever made it had been economical with the material, leaving barely enough for the imagination. Her make-up had been applied with care for colour: the bright red lipstick made her lips naturally pout, the rouge accentuated her high cheek bones, and the heavy green eye shadow brought out the sultry green of her eyes. She had combed her short red hair with the fringe to one side and left strands of red hair in front of her ears.

'How do I look?' asked Beth, and did a sideways turn, then another so her back was to him.

A point of her red hair touched the nape of her neck and the back of the lace up top did not seem to start much above the studded belt. The clothes, what little there was of them, emphasised her slim, film star curves.

She completed her turn and faced Tom again. She put her hands on her hips and stood with her legs apart.

'Well?' she said.

'Er, you, er, look like a, er, a...'

'A hooker!' she said, pleased and smiling a perfect teeth smile.

'Er, yes,' said Tom, then not wanting to upset her he quickly added, 'A very expensive one, though,' and wished he had stuck to just 'yes'.

'Good,' said Beth. 'This is my plan to get you out of here unnoticed. People won't look at you when I am dressed like this, will they?'

'I think you are probably right there, Beth,' Tom said, feeling very hot.

'I think any women we pass with me dressed like this will be disgusted and any men will see me as some sort of sex object. Disgusting! I mean,' Beth said, 'just look at these heels.' She lifted a foot out towards him. The short skirt moved further up. 'Just look Tom! I mean! What do these heels say? They are better for spurring a horse than for walking in! I could really dig these in if I had a stallion between my legs!'

Tom nodded, desperately wanting to look somewhere else.

She lowered her leg. 'And look at how short this skirt is – it's not even real leather! Who would be seen dead in this? Though, I suppose it does show my legs off well. All that exercise does help one to keep in shape. Do *you* think my legs look good in this skirt Tom?'

Tom found himself totally unable to speak. He nodded, hoping his eyes did not look as big as they felt.

'And this top! I mean! Look!' and ran her fingertips down the inside of her bare cleavage and down to her exposed naval.

Beads of perspiration were forming beneath Tom's nose.

Beth turned round and looked over her shoulder at him. 'But do you think this skirt makes my bum look big from the back? Hey! You can't see anything you shouldn't from the back can you?'

Tom was looking hard to see if anything he shouldn't see could be seen.

'Oh, no!' Beth said, putting her hand over her lips, 'What about if I had to bend over and fasten my shoe, like...'

Tom leaped up from the bed. 'Stop it, Beth!' he said, angrily. 'You're messing with me again just like you did that morning in my office. You didn't fool me then and you're not doing it now.' He was wagging his finger at her.

She turned to face him. She pushed her shoulders back and the front lacing stretched open further. With the heels on, their height difference was distinct and Tom's eyes were exactly level with the most pertinent part of the bodice's lacing. He willed his eyes to look away. He failed.

Beth looked down at him. A short, balding man in large spectacles and boyish, bookworm face, his arms out wide in exasperation, clothed in his green shirt, combat trousers and... oh dear...oh dear, oh dear.

This time it was Beth who was finding it hard to raise her eyes and look him in the face.

Tom said, 'It's no good hanging your head and looking embarrassed, Beth. It was a good idea. I know you're trying to help. I'll put my floppy hat on and we'll just go.'

She said, 'Just stay where you are and let me think.' Her eyes were fixed on his stomach, just below his chest.

'What?' he said, throwing his arms wide again.

'The thing is, Tom... Wow...' she said and took a deep breath and blew it out between pursed red lips. 'The thing is, you may not be very tall but it looks like you are... Yes, well... It might be best if you carry your bag in front of your, er, well, er, I was going to say your... um, yes, your...ummmm... where was I? Bit distracted... You know, to cover up, sort of. But on second thoughts and after closer inspection, maybe you should carry your bag higher up. A lot higher up. Or you will be drawing a lot more attention than me.'

Tom Benson looked at where her eyes were fixed. He looked down towards his chest. He blushed. He grabbed the supermarket carrier and held it in front of him.

Beth thought the carrier bag was just big enough to cover his embarrassment, but only just. She thought the slogan on the bag was ironically appropriate. It said, 'Every little helps.'

Listen, Copeland. This is a waste of time. We need to get back to the farm.

For once, Copeland listened to his better self. He had a nagging feeling there was something there they had missed, or seen but not really seen. Or someone had said something about going to the farm.

'No good sitting here watching the world go by and waiting for them to suspend me,' said Copeland, standing and swaying. 'I've had an idea. Let's go back to the farm and have another look at that shed. I'll drive.'

You've had an idea! Bloody cheek, Copeland!

Hesterman had had plenty of shocks for one day: Copeland had told him about the meeting after the official meeting with the mythical assassin, Mrs. Pickford; all about Abdul Karim; how Tom Benson had been hidden away; where Popov was hiding out; watching Copeland eat a huge slice of chocolate cake with extra cream. These were all shocks enough, but the thought of Copeland driving after three pints and a double brandy followed by a glass of port with the cheese board shocked him most. Now Copeland was drinking a Cointreau and claiming the orange in it was one of his 'five-a-day'.

Hesterman said, 'I'll drive.'

Danny skirted round the town's traffic chaos, but the sun was sinking behind the trees and the forensic team was starting to pack away by the time they got to the demolished shed. Hesterman parked in exactly the same spot and they tried to retrace their steps, dodging the white suited forensics team as they did so.

'We stood here' slurred Copeland, looking at the destroyed shed. It was different. The forensic team had moved the roof and dragged the machines away and broken them up.

'The doors are... not still in the hedge,' said Hesterman, turning to look. 'It's no good, Inspector. It's all different. The forensics team have moved everything.'

It was a stupid idea coming all the way out here, Copeland!

'It was your damn stupid idea to come here again!' snapped Copeland.

Hesterman squared up to him and said, 'It was not my idea! It was yours! You're drunk, Larry! Let's go!'

'Yeah, maybe I had too much for lunchtime. Again,' muttered Copeland. 'Yeah, let's go. But I need to pee first. Maybe over...'

They looked at each other. Copeland knew he had said something important but the alcohol in his brain blocked what it was. It was also impairing his ability to remain vertical.

It's been a bad few days. Don't worry about it, Larry.

Copeland said, 'You called me by my first name again! That's nice!'

Hesterman watched Copeland swaying and said, 'Yes, Larry. I have called you by your first name. You wanted to pee, remember? Maybe if you went over there where you went the other day?'

Hesterman had to steady Copeland past the outline of the burnt shed and past some of the forensics team. He heard one of them say something about it being the same bloke who got attacked with gravy by the tall yank chick. Danny ignored him.

Danny watched Copeland try to get his zip down a couple of times and knew Copeland had the dexterity of a complete inebriate, and Copeland trying to look over his rotund stomach to see where the zip was located was not helping his balance either. Danny Hesterman was a family man and had to think long and hard about how much more help he should, or could, give Copeland. He glanced over his shoulder, hoped no-one was looking, got down on one knee in front of Copeland, held him upright with one hand and unzipped him with the other.

Someone in a white suit shouted, 'Hey! None of that here!' Get a room!' followed by general laughter.

Hesterman prayed Copeland could manage the rest without his help and quickly went behind him. He closed his eyes and only opened them when he heard a splashing sound.

'I had Popov Disease,' muttered Copeland.

Nooooo!. Don't tell...

'I got it on my glove and then went for a pee. Just like this,' slurred Copeland.

Danny Hesterman started to back away. He had heard there was probably no contagion, but even so...

Copeland slurred on, 'So it was on my penis thingy. But it was Marks and Spencer's in the end.'

'That's good,' said Hesterman. 'We should tell the hospital it's all the fault of M and S.'

Copeland laughed and started to turn round, spraying. Danny Hesterman pointed him back in the other direction, keeping a grip on Copeland's shoulders.

One of the forensic team saw him holding Copeland upright and came over to them. 'Need a hand, mate?' he said, and quickly added, 'A hand holding him up, I mean. Not any other sort of hand. Just holding him up. No offence. Live and let live.'

Danny wanted to punch his white hooded head but smiled and said, 'Might need a hand getting him in the car in a minute, but do you know what this black stuff in the hedge is?'

'You've asked the right person there, mate. Done a few cases on farms before I moved to the Met, I did. That's the leftover stuff from when they make the rapeseed oil. Usually made into feed for animals, but 'spose they don't have many animals here so they just chuck it.'

'Oh, right' said Danny. 'Just normal farm stuff then.'

'That's right, mate. Bit different, though. It's usually more sort of grey than black like this stuff. Think it's black like this in the States though.'

Danny felt a growing excitement and the need for extra help to keep the swaying Copeland vertical. 'How come it's darker over there?' he asked.

'Dunno, really. Think they make some sort of genetically modified stuff they call canola oil. Better brand name than 'rape oil' I suppose,' said the forensic man. 'You know... rape... not great on adverts...'

'And do they have a different name for this black stuff over there?' Danny asked, hopefully.

'Let's think... Oh, yes, that's it. They like a friendly name for all sorts of shit over there don't they? They call it canola cake.'

Copeland drooled, 'Mmmm... cake,' sounding too much like Homer Simpson for Danny's liking. Danny ignored him and spoke to the forensic man: 'Canola cake, eh? Thank you. Please get some samples, but get them very, very carefully.' Reminiscent of a piglet, Copeland began to snore. Still holding him up, Danny peered round his arm and said, 'And I think I will need some help back to the car with my sleeping friend now. Any of your lot brave enough to tuck him back and zip him up?'

The forensic man grinned. He shouted to a man about to get in their car. 'Hey, Roger! Get over here. I think you'll enjoy this.'

Evening, Tuesday 30 th August.

Copeland awoke in the back of the unmarked police car. The lights of the police station car park allowed him to see his watch said 10.15. He rubbed his face and heaved himself out of the car. He swayed and had to lean on the roof for a few moments before starting his walk alongside the river back to the hotel. He knew what had done this to him. He had survived Popov disease given him by an M & S sticker only to succumb to oranges in the Cointreau.

The noise from the hotel's patio bar grew as he neared the Red Lion's car park, and aromas of meat and pastries flicked across his nostrils, but he was not tempted by the bar or food and went through the lobby and up to his room.

He sat on his bed and stared at the floor. 'Maybe I deserve to be suspended,' he said to himself, took his clothes off and had a very long shower.

Feeling clean and M and S sticker-free, and wearing only a bath robe, he hung his suit up, emptied the shopping bags and put all his new clothes into drawers. He checked his holster and gun were still on the top of the wardrobe and sat back on the bed with a glass of water.

He finally checked his phone. There were three text messages. One was from Hesterman, one from Ross and one from Dr. Spencer. He read them: Hesterman's said there was to be a dawn raid on the Boston central mosque; Ross's said Copeland's suspension was still going through – sorry Larry; Dr. Spencer's said the case was solved.

Copeland cheered up. One out of three was good enough to inspire him to go and search for a fish and chip shop and investigate whether the bar downstairs had a nice bottle of Merlot to take the taste of the water away.

283

Beth Spencer and Tom Benson.

The plan Beth had come up with to make sure no-one noticed Benson when they exited the hotel worked perfectly. No one noticed him at all. The hotel was deserted.

Beth had intended to slip her jeans and jacket on to cover her skimpy clothes as soon as she got back to the car. Tom had intended to stare out of the passenger window. Beth had intended to keep her eyes on the road. Tom had intended to be dropped off round the corner from her house in case it was under surveillance. Beth had intended to check with the neighbourly Mrs. Pratt to find out if anyone suspicious was about before getting him inside.

None of their intentions happened.

Beth's car stopped abruptly on her drive and she dashed to the door with her keys. He dashed in behind her. She did not need a glass of wine.

Wednesday 31 st. August.
Copeland and Hesterman discover the truth.

The day had started with a surprise for Danny Hesterman. Copeland was up when he got to the hotel.

The dawn raids had been conducted with ruthless American efficiency and the other workers who had been to the farm had been tracked down and put in orange suits with bags on their heads, taken to the field opposite the hospital and airlifted away. The mosque had been raided. Since it had once been a coach house and was, therefore, the size of a coach, it had not taken much time to search and find nothing unusual except some very annoyed worshippers. Liza Clinton had rounded them up anyway, given them each a new suit, told them orange was the new black and absolutely refused to let them make a phone call to close the Karachi Curry Garden for the rest of the year.

On the way to Beth's, Copeland received a message from Ross. Forensics had found nothing in the stainless steel containers found at Popov's or Fayad's. The books and prayer mats were all brand new and had no hair fibres, fingerprints or, well, anything at all. The conclusion of the CIA, and backed by The Commander and Sir Richard, was that the containers were going to be used to collect and transfer The Nosoi to the terrorists targets and the religious items were being saved as special items before they went on their suicide missions but there had clearly been some sort of accident with The Nosoi and they had got the liquid form of it on their hands. The terrorist target, according to the best analysts at the CIA, was Harrods food hall, and the Nosoi gas would wipe out the customers in the upper floors too.

DS Brandon had shaken his head at all this. He had been doing background research on Usman Fayad and found he was a Zoroastrian, and not a Muslim extremist. Nobody seemed to care.

When Hesterman and Copeland got to her average, semi-detached house, a beaming Beth answered the door in tee shirt and shorts and showed them into her average, semi-detached lounge, dominated by a large, colourful painting of a tropical shoreline above the fireplace. She gave them tea and told them Benson would be out of the shower soon.

'Nice tea, Beth,' said Copeland, making himself at home in an armchair and refraining from asking for biscuits. 'I like the new hair. So what have you found?'

Beth sat on her sofa and hooked one leg under her. Hesterman tried to remember he was married and looked out of the window. Benson arrived wearing his camouflage gear and no shoes. He seemed completely indifferent to two police officers being in the room and had a cat-who-got-the-cream smile on his face.

'How are you doing, Benson?' asked Copeland, unsurprised to see him there. Benson answered with a wide grin and shook hands with DS Danny Hesterman.

Danny smiled. 'So you're the guy who beat up the Karamazov brothers then put a bullet in their heads? Well done!' He slapped Benson on the shoulder and knocked him three steps sideways, but Tom laughed and Hesterman joined in.

Beth ran her fingers through her short red hair and said, 'Just one thing, Larry. Have you found any evidence of Canola? It's like rape, but...'

'But it's genetically modified,' interrupted Danny, who had spent some time on the Internet after the last visit to the farm and had glanced and seen Beth run her fingers through her hair before he looked out of the window again with a more determined interest and adding, 'Yes. We saw some at the farm. It looks like some Canola cake was dumped in a hedge.'

'That confirms it,' said Beth. 'They aren't making Nosoi. They're making biodiesel, or something like it. They have found a way to make it all happen inside the seeds themselves.'

Copeland was already lost. 'What do you mean?' he asked, frowning.

'Canola is used for biodiesel, Inspector,' Beth tried to explain. 'The trouble is, it's quite a difficult industrial process. The oil from the plant has to be reacted with ethanol or methanol. But there are some primitive organisms called eukaryotes. Some of these make methane, some use it, and methanosarcina barkeri has an enzyme called superoxide dismutase and archaea have ether based cell walls that...'

'Whooaa!' protested Copeland. 'Lots of big words there. What's an enzyme?'

'They speed things up,' said Beth. 'Like OMP decarboxylase makes things go ten to the seventeen times faster.'

'Is that quick, then?' asked Copeland.

Beth sighed. 'Yes, quick. It can make things happen in about eighteen milliseconds that would otherwise take seventy eight million years.'

'That's a long time,' said Benson, remembering, according to the trailers, Jurassic Park had taken only '35 million years in the making'.

Beth smiled at him. He picked up a cushion and put it on his lap. He smiled back.

Danny Hesterman saw and coughed.

Copeland was looking at his shoes while his brain caught up. 'You're saying this is not poison gas, not Nosoi, but some sort of genetically engineered biodiesel, and something went wrong?'

Beth looked back at Copeland as he raised his head. 'Not necessarily wrong,' she said. 'What happened to Popov was probably because he handled the waste – the Canola cake – with his bare hands. The machines were old, from what you told me, and they probably only half did their job extracting the oil from the seeds and some got on his and Fayad's hands too.'

'So it is dangerous?' asked Danny.

'It shouldn't be,' said Beth. 'My best guess is they had cuts when they handled the half processed canola cake. Otherwise there would probably have been no reaction on the dead skin on the outer layers. The genetically modified canola got straight into their blood and caused a chain reaction of imploding cells. Putting Popov's hand in water with the isopropyl alcohol I added may save his arm. We should have thought of it sooner.'

Copeland had no idea what she was talking about, but noted the words 'best guess' and 'probably'. He looked at Benson, who was looking at Beth. 'Are you alright, Tom? You look uncomfortable. We're not here to arrest you, you know,' he laughed.

Tom Benson fidgeted in his seat and clutched the cushion onto his stomach. 'I'm, er, fine... just really feeling... oh, dear... feeling a bit flushed.'

Beth got up and went into the kitchen.

Danny had been thinking. 'This is illegal. No genetic planting is allowed.'

'Really, Sergeant? Seriously?' said Tom Benson, who had sighed with relief when Beth had left the room. 'Then why is so much of it going on? Even the conspiracy web sites gave up on it five years ago. For example, tomatoes' defences against caterpillars have been engineered into lots of other plants. You just get seeds on the internet. Do you think the Ministry of Agriculture can track every sale? I suppose you think they have special undercover teams that tap phones and put people under surveillance too?'

Danny looked deflated. Copeland looked like he didn't care: he never ate vegetables anyway unless they were chips.

Beth returned with a notepad and her laptop.

'It's all here,' she said. 'This explains how they genetically engineered the rape and at least two different sorts of methanogens and methanotrophs to produce pure biodiesel inside each seed. That's what Popov and Fayad handled when it was half processed and set off a genetic chain reaction destroying their cells, causing a form of coagulative necrosis, but probably not contagious. All the animals at the Cambridge lab are fine.'

'That's good then,' said Copeland, breathing a sigh of relief Popov would not infect half of England and that he could finally stop checking his nether region.

Beth said, 'The thing is, the tests were with cells from Fayad's hand, but that was dead. Popov may still be able to infect others, at least by touch. You have found him haven't you?'

Copeland and Danny looked at each other and realised they had not heard anything since Danny requested a car to be sent to the Karamazov's. They had just assumed... Copeland forced a smile and said, 'He was hiding in the Karamazov's caravan,' which was true.

'Good. He still needs isolation,' said Beth, sounding relieved. She looked at Tom again, bit her top lip and said, 'I really need, er... to go and exercise. Want to come, Tom?'

Copeland had a notepad and a flash drive dropped on his lap and the laptop was given to Hesterman. They had no time to speak before they were alone in the room.

'Oh, right, lots of big words there, alright' said Copeland. 'Shall we pool our resources, Danny, on the coffee table? Gone to exercise? She must have something upstairs she wants to ride on.'

Danny raised his eyebrows.

'You know, like an exercise bike,' Copeland informed him.

After a short choking fit, Danny started by Googling something in Beth's notes called F.A.M.E. – fatty acid methyl esters and noticed it was a process when making biodiesel that could produce formic acid and had glycerine as a by-product, and how the whole transesterification reaction could be made to happen with the lipases enzymes from candida albicans. He had not seen any of these words before and had to look twice before he could spell 'mitochondria'.

Copeland watched Danny for a few minutes, helped him Google superoxide dismutase, then made an important decision he knew could affect both of them. He clicked his fingers and said, 'I'm going to look for biscuits.'

Wednesday 31 st. August. 'Ronaldo' is on his phone.

'Scorpion?

'Yes. That's why I've phoned. The tests are finished already. It really is better than we could have ever hoped.

'No, Sir, there were no more mishaps like with the rabbit...

'Yes, you do indeed keep reminding me they call them the VW Golf over here. Sorry.

'Yes, alright, Sir. Whatever. I'll call it Flame if that's what you have decided.

'Yes, I know it's the FAME process with an extra letter L standing for the lipases. I get it, but I still think it's a crap name.

'You want me to meet you and Fatima on Friday?

'Harrods? Why Harrods?

'Ah! She does like her chocolates. I suppose it's not too far from there. What about the surveillance on you? The Ministry of Agriculture seems to be taking us planting genetically modified crops a bit seriously... Oh, shit!'

Ronaldo whispered, 'I'm in a pub, Sir. Phone reception is poor at the secret base. Two guys in raincoats and fedora hats have just walked in.

'No, Sir, I don't think they're from The Ministry of Agriculture... I'm sure I just saw a gun.'

'Two pints of Guinness, if you please bartender,' said Vasily Goraya, leaning on the bar.

Nikolay Ivchenko was using his phone to get maps of the area and trying to see if there were any disused airfields nearby. They hardly gave the dark haired man sitting in the corner of the lounge bar, and who looked a bit like Ronaldo and was talking on his phone, a second glance.

Copeland and Hesterman try to understand the truth.

Copeland was staring at the scientific information Danny had got up on the screen. He sighed heavily.

'The truth is, and what I find really disturbing, is this,' said Copeland sombrely to Danny Hesterman. 'She hasn't got any biscuits. Been through all her cupboards. What the hell is that thumping noise? What the hell are they doing up there, moving furniture?'

Danny went red. 'Er, aerobics?' he suggested.

Copeland sat down and half heartedly looked at the laptop screen. 'They both look like they've hardly slept all night,' he said. 'Guess they've been working on these notes.'

Danny opened his mouth, closed his mouth, looked at Copeland, shook his head to check he was actually awake, and nodded.

'Now what?' said Copeland tilting his head to listen. 'They must be jumping up and down on one leg now!'

Danny looked at him again.

'Why are you raising an eyebrow at me, Danny?' asked Copeland. 'Do you know something I don't?'

'Well...' said Danny.

'Oh my God!' cried Copeland. 'Sounds like they've started jumping up and down even faster now. Bloody fitness freaks! Let's just have a look at the notes.'

'I think...they...' faltered Danny, '... they are... I think they are good notes. Explains it all.'

Copeland put his glasses on and read through the notes. 'Did you hear that?' he said when he was turning the chemical formulas on page three upside down to see if they made more sense.

'I definitely did not hear anything at all,' Danny said, resolutely.

'There it is again,' said Copeland, stopping to listen. 'It sounds like Beth must have hurt herself. She's a doctor, she'll know what to do. It says here this biodiesel could be cheap to produce and maybe really efficient... Damn! Of course! I understand what they're doing now!'

'Who?' asked Danny, trying hard to focus on Copeland and not any other noises.

'Russia! The Saudis!' said Copeland. 'Oil producers, Danny. If this stuff is half as good as Beth seems to think it is, their economies could collapse almost overnight.'

Danny thought and said, 'And Abdul Karim is bankrolling it, so the Saudis leak his name. And the Russians feed everyone a story about a poison gas so we stop them!'

'I think you've got it, Danny,' said Copeland. 'Oh, dear, maybe Beth hurt herself more than we thought. I can hear her screaming now. Maybe we should go and check.'

Danny Hesterman shook his head. 'I don't think that would be a good idea, Inspector.'

Jakab Popov.

Jakab Popov left the caravan with the roll of fifty pound notes in his pocket. When he heard the siren, he instinctively hid behind a parked van and the police car sped past. It would have been speeding to the scrap yard eighteen hours earlier but, like every other car in town, it had been gridlocked because some Americans had cordoned off all major roads without warning and everything had backed up and ground to a halt. Drivers had abandoned their cars leading to more chaos.

Jakab Popov had decided it was time to go home. His hand and arm seemed to be getting better, but he was still debating whether to go back to the hospital first.

'Stupid boy!' scolded his Mother's voice. 'Your hand smells like a rotting fish. You go to hospital and they keep you there forever and the gangster secret policeman thief he will come.'

Jakab walked towards the train station. He knew all the back streets to the station and decided to circle round by the little mosque. He wondered why the doors had been knocked down and why someone was throwing out used smoke grenades. He made a detour and walked past the lock up where the Karamazov's kept his old taxi. The door was open and inside was completely empty. While he was close, he thought he would have one last look at his old bedsit and stood outside the Happy Jack pub and looked up at the window.

Two youths with tattoos came out to smoke and looked at him. He nodded and touched the peak of his baseball cap with his good hand. They turned their backs on him and lit their cigarettes. A child on a bicycle ran over his foot. He yelped. The two youths turned and laughed.

He heard them talking about something and heard words like, 'Never be able to bloody sit down again! Bloody big needles, those were!' Jakab had no idea what an arse was or how deep a needle could apparently go into something called a buttock.

'They've got it in for us because of that fight with the Yanks,' said one of the youths.

'And all Bill was gonna say was something about how black her sunglasses were,' said the other.

Jakab ignored them because he had no idea what they were saying. He went down the alley and looked at his arm. His mother was right. If he went to the hospital he would be there forever and the sunglasses police would get him. It was time to go home.

Copeland makes a discovery.

'Had a good work-out?' asked Copeland when Tom Benson and Beth Spencer came back in the room over an hour later. 'Not really into exercise myself. Got any biscuits?'

Tom and Beth looked at each other. They looked at Danny Hesterman, who shrugged. 'I think we had a really good work out, Inspector,' smiled Tom.

Beth nodded vigorously. 'Very intense,' she added, looking flushed as if she had, indeed, had a very intense work out.

Copeland nodded knowingly. 'Glad you enjoyed your... what's the right word..? Aerobics.'

Hesterman was blushing again. He thought it was perhaps time for him and Mrs. Hesterman to put the kids to bed early and have an early night doing some aerobics themselves.

'Anyway,' said Copeland, 'looking at this lot, it seems we have a genius who could topple the oil industry and save the planet from global warming at the same time.'

'You understood it?' said Beth, sounding surprised and sitting next to Copeland on the sofa.

Copeland... didn't she have a bra on under her tee shirt before they exercised...

Copeland said, 'I don't understand any of it. But how do you know all this, Beth? I know you took Fayad's hand to that lab and they did loads of tests, but even so...'

Tom Benson said, 'Richard Feynman was wrong for once when he said the imagination of nature is far greater than the imagination of man.'

'Maybe he forgot women,' said Beth, but smiled at Benson.

'Bloody hell! You two can't need *more* exercise!' exclaimed Hesterman, flopping back into the armchair.

'I know about this,' said Beth, ignoring Hesterman and looking at Copeland, 'because my definitely ex-partner,

Simon, works in this field and I used to help him and I have almost total recall. This is one of my ideas.'

Hesterman sat bolt upright. He and Copeland looked at each other.

'Does he look like Ronaldo?' asked Copeland.

Beth laughed. 'Of course not! You told me more than once that you were after someone who looked like Ronaldo.'

She got up and got a framed photo off the mantelpiece. The photo had been turned face down. 'This is Simon and me on holiday in Greece earlier this year,' she said, handing the frame to Copeland and folding her arms.

Copeland passed it to Hesterman. Hesterman tried to look at Simon in the photo and not at Beth in a bikini and said, 'Where's he from, Dr. Spencer? Does he have an American accent?'

'He's Canadian,' said Beth, 'but he looks nothing like Ronaldo, does he?'

'You do know who Ronaldo is?' said Copeland. 'He's a footballer.'

Beth's brow furrowed. 'No,' she said. 'Everyone knows Ronaldo Macedo is an artist. That's one of his above the fireplace.' She pointed at the scene of the tropical shoreline with palm trees in the foreground.

'Have you heard of Cristiano Ronaldo, the footballer?' asked Hesterman, seeing Copeland had gone into shock.

Beth scrunched her nose. 'Don't really like football,' she said.

Simon: AKA Ronaldo.

Simon had found a newspaper on the next table, held it up and opened it as wide as it would go. His phone vibrated in his pocket. It was his old phone, not the new one. He looked at the display. It said Dr. E. Spencer. He had never got round to updating it to just 'Beth'. He tapped 'reject call'. He did not want to discuss the demise of their relationship with Beth and saw no point in taking her calls. He had far more important things on his mind, including two shady looking individuals with shoulder holsters.

He peered round the newspaper to see the two men wearing long dark raincoats waiting for the heads on their Guinness to settle and the glasses to be topped up before they carried their drinks to the table Simon had leaned across and snatched the newspaper from.

The tall one said something Simon guessed was Russian and the shorter one said, 'Best we speak English, Nikolay. We do not want to arouse suspicion.'

Simon thought wearing raincoats in a heat wave would arouse suspicion, and flashing a side arm in a shoulder holster when you turn round with a pint of Guinness in your hand didn't help either.

'Anything on the map, Nikolay?' said the shorter man.

'There are a three abandoned airfields within thirty miles, Colonel Goraya... der'mo! I mean, Vasily,' said Nikolay. 'All are airfields they once used in the war *we* won against the Nazis.'

They're looking for our secret base! thought Simon.

He heard the one called Vasily say, 'Our agent on the inside says it is an abandoned airfield. They have the stuff there to test it. It must be close.'

An agent on the inside! Simon thought, shocked.

His phone vibrated in his pocket. It was the new one. He did not take it out and kept the newspaper held high.

'We will find them by nightfall,' said Vasily. He leaned over the table and whispered, but Simon could still hear him say, 'And then you can put a bullet in their heads, Nikolay.'

'Jolly good show!' said Nikolay and gulped down a celebratory mouthful of beer.

Copeland et al.

Copeland had been sent into the street to smoke. Beth had opened the door and waved him even further away.

Hesterman came out of the house and joined Copeland. 'Good news and bad news. The bad news is Popov was not at the Karamazov's. The good news is they're making some lunch.'

Copeland thought the good news outweighed the bad and smiled, took a long drag of the cigarette and threw it down a drain as he made his way back into the house with Danny struggling to keep up.

In the kitchen, Copeland saw Beth and Tom had prepared vegetarian dips with olives and celery and raw carrot and wholemeal pitta. There was orange juice in a jug.

Copeland looked aghast. 'Come on, Danny,' he said. 'There's a pub at the end of the road.'

Hesterman was more than shocked when Copeland ordered shandy to go with his pie and chips. He was more than more than shocked when Copeland had offered to buy him lunch.

'It's a sort of thank you,' said Copeland. 'I'll be taking Beth's work to the Commander tomorrow to try to get this mess sorted. I may not see you again, Danny.'

'Do you think that's the end of it then?' asked Danny.

'Hopefully, but I doubt it,' said Copeland. 'We know it's all about genetically engineered stuff for fuel, but the big wigs have all got their tails up and are convinced this Nosoi is really some sort of tissue dissolving gas and Abdul Karim is behind it. They've probably already briefed sniper teams. All I can do is take these notes and flash drive from Beth's, hope this ex boyfriend picks up his phone, get you to drive me back to my hotel and go back to London. I've phoned The Chief. He's got me a meeting with the Commander tomorrow. As for Popov, he can't get far without a passport. They'll soon find him.'

By the time their lunch had arrived, Simon was speeding back to the airfield and telling everyone to go home. They had helped him put the containers of Flame, as it was now being called, into the back of his black Mercedes. The four terabyte external hard drive with all their data was in his glove compartment.They all left minutes before the Russians arrived.

By the time Copeland was patting his full stomach, Simon was driving to London, and he began to consider who the traitor working for the Russians was. He knew it could not be any of his team at the airfield or the Russians would have found them immediately. No one back at the London lab had any idea this was going on. It had to be someone who knew there was a secret base but did not know where it was.

Simon pulled into a layby. He took his new phone out and rang Abdul Karim.

'Hello, Scorpion. We have a problem,' said Simon. 'The Russians came to kill us – I have no idea why – and we've abandoned the secret base at the airfield. I have all the stuff in my car. We have a traitor. Someone has been telling the Russians everything. I've no idea who it could be.'

Thursday, 1st. September.
Detective Inspector Lawrence Copeland, S.O.15

DCI Ross had managed to get Copeland five minutes with the Commander. The Commander had called him a lunatic and told him to get out of his office after two.

'Thanks for the tea and chocolate digestives, Chief,' said Copeland, sitting in Ross's office and recalling a pleasant final evening in the hotel and the leaving cake they had presented him, though the staff had looked disappointed he didn't share any of it. He had also enjoyed travelling first class back to London, but had avoided eye contact with the elderly man he had been scolded by on his way to Boston a few days earlier.

'I don't get it,' said Sergeant Brandon from his chair in the corner of DCI Ross's office. 'Why is no one listening? We've even found out the chap we were calling Ronaldo is Dr. Simon Bowyer, PhD., and he's a completely respected biochemist and geneticist.'

Ross and Copeland shook their heads. 'Groupthink,' muttered Ross, seeing Copeland had a mouth full of biscuit. 'They have got something in their heads and all the facts are made to fit their theory. They are convinced Simon Bowyer has sold out and is using the information brought from Chechnya by Popov to make more Nosoi.'

'But there is no such thing as Nosoi,' said an exasperated Brandon. 'It was all a lie.'

'We know that, but everyone else is gearing up for a terror attack on Harrods and the Russians have told everyone they have intelligence it's happening tomorrow,' said Ross. 'The bigwigs' theories all fit like a jigsaw if you bang the pieces in hard enough.'

'Nice biscuits, Chief,' said Copeland.

Sergeant Brandon stood up. 'We have to *do* something,' he said, increasingly exasperated and shaking a fist.

Ross settled back in his chair with a digestive. 'The CIA are everywhere. Special Agent Liza Clinton is on a mission. CCTV is being monitored throughout Knightsbridge. Sniper teams have been briefed. Any ideas, Sergeant?'

Sergeant Brandon opened his mouth to speak and closed it again. Repeating the process failed to provoke any sounds. He sat back down and put his chin in his hands. 'They'll wait for Simon Bowyer to turn up with a flask and as soon as he hands it to Abdul Karim, they'll take them both out.'

'No,' said Copeland, 'I think they'll just kill them where they stand, Sergeant.' He took another biscuit.

Brandon was on his feet again and on a roll. 'We have to stop the meeting. If Beth Spencer can't get her ex on the phone, she'll have to come here in person.'

Ross was shocked. 'That's a good idea, Sergeant Brandon. If she can get to Simon before he meets with Karim, we may yet prevent a bloodbath in Harrods food hall.'

'Be bad for trade,' said Copeland, 'but would make my last day on the force more interesting.'

'Last day, Sir?' Brandon queried, letting his animated arms fall.

Ross answered. 'Larry's suspension is going through. He has no chance after he missed the evidence under the sink in Popov's bedsit.'

'But, Sir,' said Brandon, 'we know the Russian SVR put that there, and they put similar stuff where Usman Fayad was sleeping rough. The books, the prayer mats, the empty flasks... We know they killed the brothers Karamazov so they could not tell anyone the Russians had found Fayad's place and planted...'

'Yes, yes, yes, Sergeant,' said DCI Ross. 'We know that, but Sir Richard and the Commander and the bloody CIA are still on theory A.'

Copeland stood up. 'Right,' he said, meaningfully, 'I'm going for lunch.'

Lunch! Copeland! But we need a plan!

Ross looked as astounded as Copeland's conscience sounded. He said, 'Lunch! Copeland! We need a plan!'

Copeland took another chocolate digestive and smiled. 'I'll phone Beth Spencer to get her to come to London right away. Brandon, you email me everything we know. Chief, sort out some reliable back-up for tomorrow.'

Brandon and Ross looked confused.

'Oh, come on, Chief,' said Copeland. 'Catch up! We need help here. So, Sergeant Brandon, I repeat, email me everything we know. But, go and do it from home, just to make sure.'

'But it'll be intercep...' began Detective Sergeant Brandon. 'Oh, I see.'

Copeland phoned Beth on the way to lunch at the golf club. She sounded as if she had been exercising again. She was definitely out of breath. He heard Benson ask if it was Simon on the phone. He sounded close. He had obviously been exercising too.

Beth had agreed to be in London when she heard the plan to prevent Simon getting a bullet in his head, though she had seemed to consider it for a long time first. Benson had asked who was paying before he had gone to book a suite at the Bulgari Hotel. It was close to the tube and Harrods and he thought Beth would like the pool and it had great room service. He booked the Bulgari Suite because it was good value at only just over six thousand a night. He booked three nights.

Beth did not tell Copeland she would not be travelling alone.

Friday 2 nd. September. Nearly Everyone.

Beth let Copeland into the hotel suite just after 8 a.m. It was his last day as a copper and he was going to make the most of it. The day was already turning out to be better than he had expected as he sat on the four-seater leather sofa and made an exception to eating fruit. Strawberries were okay when there was champagne to go with them. The maple syrup on the pancakes wasn't bad either.

'Nice room, Beth,' commented Copeland, observing the room was bigger than his house. 'Did you need two bathrooms and a separate dining room? Where's the bed?'

Beth smiled. 'And the room service is excellent. We haven't moved since we arrived.'

'That's nice,' said Copeland. He choked on the champagne. Beth slapped him on the back. 'Who's we?' he spluttered.

'Morning,' said the little man with big spectacles and a shiny head as he came into the room.

'What the hell is he doing here?' blurted Copeland.

Beth sat next to Copeland and put a hand on his shoulder. 'I couldn't really leave him on his own, could I?' she said, apologetically. 'And I'm helping him with his new exercise programme.'

Copeland huffed but nodded. 'I suppose hiding out here is as good as anywhere. London is a big place. And the sofa is easily big enough for him to sleep on.'

Beth and Benson gave each other a look. 'Quite,' they said together and laughed like ten year olds.

'You look very professional, Dr. Spencer,' said Copeland when their giggling had died down and he finally noticed she was wearing a black suit similar to the one she had worn the first time they met. 'You'll need an umbrella though, it's pouring down.'

Tom Benson looked strangely confident and not out of place in an orange Hawaiian shirt and yellow Bermuda shorts. He sat cross legged on one of the huge, black leather armchairs and said, 'Why are you wearing an earpiece, Larry?'

'A sergeant name Brandon is monitoring all the feeds and giving me updates, Tom. It seems the Harrods chocolate section is the likely meeting place,' said Copeland. 'The snipers are in place on rooftops everywhere and Special Agent Liza Clinton has about twenty CIA agents secreted around. You can tell who they are because they're all wearing sunglasses.'

'But it's raining,' observed Beth.

It was Copeland's turn to say, 'Quite.'

Jakab Popov. Friday September 2 nd.

Jakab Popov was glad it was finally raining in England just before he left. He was now the Romanian Georghe Fumar. The passport he had found in the filing cabinet in the little caravan proved it. Jakab and Georghe looked vaguely similar and no one ever really looks at the passport photo in Dover, especially EU nationals going *out* of the country. The real Georghe Fumar would not need his passport anyway. Georghe had been lucky enough to work on a certain farm one Saturday a few weeks ago and Georghe was consequently enjoying a holiday in the sunshine in Guantanamo Bay.

Jakab had remembered someone else having a black arm like his. He remembered it well because the other man had said the English doctors had said the flesh was not black but 'gan-green' and they had used something called 'maggots-because-of-the-cuts'. Jakab had found his own maggots and put them on his arm.

By the time he got back to his mother in Serbia, it would all be fine and he could get back to working on the family farm. He thought about all the days he would spend with his father in the fields and almost turned round to go back to Boston.

'Stupid boy, Jakab!' shouted the voice of his mother in his head. 'You bring fifty those pound notes home to your Momma now!'

By the time the ferry got to Calais, the maggots Jakab had put on his arm were all dead. They had dissolved.

Mr. and Mrs. Professor.

Elderly Professor Philip Sawyer and not quite so elderly Professor Emily Churchill had been taken care of by Fatima. Very well taken care of. They could not even remember which one of them had entered the competition and won the holiday in Rome, but had spent the whole time there with each of them claiming the credit. The nice lady had even picked them up from home and taken them to Luton Airport, though they had only just made the plane because the nice lady's satnav did not seem to be particularly good.

The nice lady had even arranged the very best of kennels for Benjy while they were away.

'She was a nice lady, that Fatima,' said Mr. Professor as they got off the plane.

Mrs. Professor was amazed that after forty years of marriage they had finally found something to agree on. 'Yes, Fatima was a very nice lady,' she said.

Simon.

Simon Bowyer, a.k.a. Ronaldo, a.k.a. Abraham Lincoln, a.k.a. ex-Beth Spencer partner, had been thinking and he did not think Fatima was a very nice lady at all since he had concluded she was the spy in their midst, but Prince Karim had turned his phone off and Simon could not warn him. Simon had decided Fatima should definitely be terminated: he would rip up her contract as The Prince's PR agent himself.

Simon parked his Mercedes in the Pavilion Road car park and took the one flask of Flame super-biodiesel from his boot. It was swaddled in a foam casing, but still placed it carefully in his black shoulder bag. He knew this was not the fuel they thought they were making. It was better. One litre could last an average car for over three hundred miles. The first VW Golf test engine had buckled with the strain and they had needed to modify the fuel injection system for the other rabbits. (*Damn! Did it again! Rabbits are called Golfs over here!* he thought.) He had some qualms about how much farmland would be used to plant his new, genetically modified Canola that made the biodiesel inside the seeds, but saving the world from global warming was a far bigger goal, and he knew even the poorest farmers in the third world would be able to plant the new seeds. He had made sure they were drought resistant and never needed fertiliser or spraying. He had dreamed of his Nobel Prize and forgotten it was all Beth Spencer's idea.

He still hated calling it 'Flame'. He thought it made it sound like it was going to set everything on fire. Maybe it was, metaphorically at least. And the awful name had been that traitor Fatima's idea, and she was absolutely not a nice lady at all. Simon still preferred the super biodiesel to be called 'Pangloss' after one of his heroes because, after all, it was going to bring in the start of the best of all possible worlds.

As he walked down Basil Street and approached Harrods, he thought about this and how he wished he had brought a raincoat to protect his best grey suit. He did not notice the six red dots on his back and he was definitely too far away to hear the rooftop marksmen say, 'Target acquired. Shall we neutralise Ronaldo – er, I mean Bowyer – now?'

Beth and Copeland Visit Harrods.

'We've got to go,' said Copeland, touching his earpiece. 'Simon is almost in Harrods and Karim is on the move.' He stuffed the last pancake into his mouth.

Benson said, 'I'll get my new flip-flops and straw hat.'

'What? NO!' shouted Beth. Copeland tried to say the same but a whole pancake in his mouth made exclamations difficult.

'Come on, Beth!' protested Tom. 'We're a team! Butch and Sundance!'

Beth grabbed Tom's shoulders and pushed him down onto the sofa. 'They died! You stay there, Tom,' she said. 'They still think you're an international assassin who helped Popov escape.'

It was an easy mistake to make. Tom looked very international in his orange Hawaiian shirt and yellow Bermuda shorts.

'Beth! Come on!' Copeland barked.

First time you've barked in twenty years, Copeland.

Beth caught Copeland up at the elevator. Copeland said, 'I suppose he had to give you a quote before you left. Was it

Shakespeare again like the one he used in Starbucks? Romeo and Juliet, Act 5, Scene 3, I think it was.'

Beth was surprised. She hadn't expected Copeland to know, so she thought it best not to mention the quote Tom had just used was from Henry V, but she had liked being told she had witchcraft in her lips.

'By the way, Beth, you've somehow smudged your lipstick,' said Copeland. 'Need a hanky?'

The elevator pinged at the ground floor and, as soon as the doors opened, Copeland sprinted out. Copeland's sprint was a slow jog for Beth Spencer.

'Brandon's in my ear. Simon is almost in Harrods and Abdul Karim has just entered Hans Crescent with a woman. They think it's his public relations woman,' he panted after a few steps. 'We're never going to make it!'

They had not put their umbrellas up and ran with them like relay batons into Brompton Road and past Porsche Design, dodging the swarming shoppers.

'Whooaa,' shouted Copeland, slowing to a walk. 'Karim has gone into Claudie Pierlot, whatever that is.'

Beth put her umbrella up but continued to walk briskly. 'Women's stuff. Probably getting his girlfriend something,' she said. 'We can make it.'

Copeland agreed and lit a cigarette. She knocked it out of his mouth, scowled and briskly headed for the store's door. Copeland gazed longingly at his cigarette, disintegrating in a puddle, before following her.

A doorman in a green coat and hat opened the door and they walked into luxury accessories.

'Bit posh in here,' commented Copeland. 'Looks like a senior citizens day out as well. It's crowded. They all have umbrellas too... how... coincidental.'

Prince Abdul Karim was happy. He was with the woman he loved and had just bought her the most expensive handbag in Claudie Pierlot's, He would soon have the flask of liquid in his hands and by tomorrow he would be on the front of every newspaper. Fatima had her arm in his and he felt like the luckiest man alive: once this was all over he would ask her to marry him, though he was not looking forward to meeting her family and he tried to keep his smile fixed when the thought crossed his mind. From what Fatima had told him, her mother would not think him worthy for her daughter, despite being a prince and one of the richest men in London. Another perfect selection of chocolates would smooth the introduction.

Fatima was happy. This was all going according to plan. She even had an expensive new bag she could sell for double the price when she got back to Russia. The CIA would take care of her temporary boyfriend as soon as that idiot Simon handed the flask over. She smiled back at Karim, thinking how the Americans could always be trusted to shoot first and ask questions later, especially when they had been led to believe the targets were holding a lethal terrorist weapon. She could see agents following and flanking as they made their way through the store towards the chocolates. Did Karim really think her mother ate so many chocolates? Still, she and everyone at the embassy enjoyed them with their vodka. As soon as Simon appeared she would slip away and enjoy watching the news to see how two terrorists were shot dead and prevented from committing an atrocity.

Simon was not happy. His best grey suit was soaking wet and he had been accosted in the cosmetics hall by a family. He had refused to give the boy his autograph and had to insist several times that he was not Ronaldo, and didn't his Canadian accent prove it? Unmoved, the boy's father had become aggressive and Simon had closed his eyes and held his shoulder bag in front of him to block the inevitable punch. He opened one eye only when the mother had calmed her husband down and led him away. It was then he noticed there seemed to be a surprising number of people wearing black suits and sunglasses, as well as a surprising number of elderly people with brollies.

Ten minutes later, wandering through the wide corridor of luxury jewellery, he realised Harrods was like a huge maze and thought it was time to find someone and ask for directions.

Special Agent Liza Clinton had been happy. Everything was in place and everyone knew their jobs: as soon as Karim had the flask of Nosoi, their orders were shoot to kill. From her vantage point on the stairs near the corner, she could see over the heads of the crowded shoppers and staff and survey most of the basketball court size hall.

Across the hall was the long speciality tea counter, with golden tins of different teas on shelves up to the ceiling, and beyond those the brown jars of expensive coffees behind the circular coffee counter in the far corner. Besides the entrances to her immediate left and right, another entrance was to the right of the coffee counter, and along the right hand wall was the long, glass chocolate counter. A candy counter stood near the centre of the room, flanked by white, gold edged pillars and surrounded by head-high displays of brightly wrapped gift boxes. Only the pillars and a high golden pagoda display blocked her view.

She was enjoying the moment and the aromas of the chocolate, coffee and tea hanging in the air, then she had seen

Copeland and her mood had been changed by an eruption of anger. She hoped he would get hit in the crossfire, and if he was not, then maybe she would make sure a stray bullet from her gun accidentally hit him between the eyes.

At the chocolate counter, Beth scoured the crowd trying to spot Simon. Behind her, Copeland was hypnotised by the chocolates and his face was being drawn to the glass.

'Can I help you, Sir?' asked an assistant wearing a green blazer and white boater.

Copeland looked up. He knew that face from somewhere.

Not again, Copeland!

'Got it!' said Copeland, pointing at the elderly, grey haired man behind the counter. 'You were on the train! In first class!' Both ways!'

'Sorry, Sir. I think you must be mistaken.'

'But you had a go at me for...' said Copeland before he realised and stopped himself. 'Oh, yes,' he said, winking. 'My mistake.'

Brandon spoke into Copeland's ear piece. Copeland turned to Beth and said, 'Karim is here, Beth, he's...' Copeland stopped talking and his head and eyebrows started to twitch.

Briefly, Beth thought the years of smoking and indulgent living had finally caught up with him and Copeland was having a heart attack. 'Oh' she whispered, 'he's behind me isn't he?'

The elderly man behind the counter said, 'Good day, Prince Karim. Your usual order is ready,' and handed a gift wrapped box to Fatima.

Beyond Copeland, through a momentary gap in the crowd, Beth glimpsed Simon enter the hall through the entrance next to the coffee counter. She was not surprised when his usual lack of navigation skills turned him right instead of left and she lost sight of him as he disappeared into a group of back-pack tourists by the coffee counter.

Special Agent Liza Clinton had spotted her targets and was making her way across the white tile floor, moving to her left towards the tea counter, ready to get behind Simon as he emerged from the coffee smelling huddle. Her hand was reaching inside her Givenchy leather jacket towards her shoulder holster.

A small man wearing an orange Hawaiian shirt and yellow Bermuda shorts and a very nice new pair of flip flops hauled himself onto the top of the coffee counter, stood and waved his straw hat in the air.

The elderly man behind the chocolates counter was totally indignant and used strong language, exclaiming: 'Tut, tut. I say! That chap is improperly dressed.'

From the top of the coffee counter, the thin, diminutive Benson pointed at the CIA agents and shouted, 'Hey! Men in Black! Those are not the droids you seek! I'm an international assassin!'

Beth clasped a hand to her forehead. 'Oh, no!'

Shoppers turned to look and laugh at Tom Benson. Simon turned to look. Liza Clinton and the CIA agents turned to look and did what they usually did when caught by surprise – they took out their guns. A little old lady in a moth eaten cardigan sidled alongside Simon as the security guards surged past to grab the man on top of the counter and shoppers started ducking when they saw the guns in the hands of the men and women in black.

Agent Clinton had started to aim at Simon, but turned to point her gun at Benson. Like the Red Sea before Moses, like wheat before a gale, like shoppers seeing an angry six foot two woman in four inch Jimmy Choo heels with a gun, everyone parted.

Agent Clinton took aim and began to squeeze the trigger. A green jacketed security guard ran to tackle her. She put a fist out and met his skull with her knuckles. For a moment, he looked stunned, then his knees buckled and he toppled over. The shot rang out.

Tom Benson looked down at the bullet hole.

Shoppers screamed and swarmed away from the gunshot.

Tom Benson looked at the bullet hole and could not believe what he saw.

Abdul Karim and Fatima jostled into Beth and Copeland and the crowd swept into them, squashing them against the glass counter.

Over the crowd shouting, 'Gun! Gun!' and the security guards changing direction as neatly as a figure skating walrus to bring the CIA agents to the ground, Tom Benson looked at the bullet hole and wondered how this could happen.

'Tom! Tom!' screamed Beth as the stampede pushed her along the counter.

Tom Benson looked at the bullet hole and got angry. He pointed at Liza Clinton and shouted, 'You just shot my new hat!' She pointed her gun at him again. He said, 'Oh, shit!' and dived behind the counter.

A tubby elderly man in a tweed jacket jostled into Liza Clinton just as she fired her second shot.

'Oh, NO!' shouted Copeland when he saw where the shot had gone, just before he was overwhelmed by the stampeding shoppers.

'Where the hell's Tom gone? Did she hit him?' cried Beth, looking at the forlorn face of Copeland as it was pressed against the glass by two women who made even Copeland look slim. He disappeared under the scrum. Beth found one of his legs, dragged him out and pulled him through an access gap. Copeland found himself on his knees behind the counter.

Beth grabbed Copeland's face between her hands. 'Did you see? Did she shoot Tom?'

Copeland was shaking his head. 'It was awful,' he muttered.

Beth slapped him. 'Get a grip, Inspector! Was Tom shot?'

'The glass,' said Copeland. 'She hit the glass. And there were cakes on it... ruined... what the hell did you slap me for?'

Liza Clinton was looking around from the vantage point of her four inch heeled Jimmy Choo Romy 100 Light Mocha and Black Speckled Glitter Dégradé Pointy Toe Pumps (Italian made). Screaming shoppers surged in every direction, but she spotted the open-mouthed statue that was Simon. She turned her gun back on him. As Agent Clinton aimed, the small bag lady hooked her brolly handle round Simon's ankle and tugged. Simon fell on his backside, looking stunned but gripping his shoulder bag to his chest.

Behind the counter, Beth knelt and peered through the trays of chocolates. 'What the hell is going on? Lots of the old folks are battering the people in sunglasses with their brollies,' she screamed. 'Larry! Put that chocolate down!'

'Hmmm, nice,' chewed Copeland, sitting with a tray on his lap.

Other shoppers joined them in the sanctuary. Copeland tried to share his chocolates but the other patrons seemed to be more interested in curling up into balls with their hands shielding their heads, which Copeland thought strange since no more shots had been heard above the sounds of the screaming shoppers. Beth risked a glance over a tray of white chocolates to see a security guard, aided by an elderly gentleman with a brolly, pounding the sunglasses of a CIA agent, and two other senior citizens sitting on another as a third pensioner jabbed a tranquiliser needle into the agent's leg. Unfortunately, Beth did not see Liza Clinton, who, having run out of other targets, was aiming at the back of Copeland's head.

Beth sat down on the floor next to Copeland. 'It's bedlam out there,' she said.

Copeland wanted to make his own, informed decision so turned, knelt and leaned forward to inspect the chocolates up-close. Liza Clinton's bullet singed the top of his silver hair.

Copeland looked over his shoulder at Beth. 'Bloody hell! She's nuts!' shouted Copeland. 'There's glass all over the marzipans now. We'll have to have the truffles.'

Beth was face down on the floor and desperately trying to pull Copeland down with her.

The food hall suddenly quietened and Beth risked kneeling up beside Copeland for another look. DCI Ross, in uniform, had entered with a riot squad. Special Agent Liza Clinton was being handcuffed. All the senior citizens with umbrellas quickly disappeared. Simon, Karim and Fatima were nowhere in sight. Ross was looking around and spotted the back of Copeland's silver hair. He walked round the counter.

'Allo, allo, allo! What's all this then?' he said. 'I hope you're paying for those yourself, Larry, so don't bother with the receipt.' Smiling, he held out a hand and helped Copeland to his feet.

Copeland groaned, 'Umph! Getting up gets harder!' but managed to keep the tray of chocolates in his free hand.

'Where's Tom Benson?' asked Beth.

'No idea where anyone is,' said Ross. 'I only know no-one was shot.'

'That's nice,' said Copeland. 'Want a truffle? They've got cognac in them.'

Beth and Larry in the Street.

DCI Ross stayed to clear up the mess while Beth and Copeland went in search of Tom and Simon.

'Inspector Copeland,' Beth said, 'I'm not sure you are meant to take a whole tray of truffles out of the store.'

They emerged on the Valentino corner and looked down Hans Crescent, Basil Street and the pedestrianized area. There was no sign of Tom or Simon or Karim. A woman with dark hair carrying a box of chocolates was texting and walked straight into Copeland.

'Sorry,' said Copeland. The woman stared at him and walked on.

I recognised her from somewhere, Copeland. Haven't we seen her in Tesco Express?

'That's her!' cried Beth. 'The woman who was with Abdul Karim!'

Fatima disappeared into a throng of shoppers.

'I thought I recognised her from somewhere,' nodded Copeland.

Beth punched his shoulder. 'You only saw her five minutes ago!' She thumped his shoulder again. Tears were in her eyes. 'Where is he? Where is he?' she repeated, hitting Copeland's shoulder harder each time she said it.

Copeland held her arm.

Well done, Copeland. Hold her arm. She knows how to punch!

'Beth, calm down. We'll find Simon, don't worry,' said Copeland. Her other fist hit his jaw and gave him a clue he had not said the right thing.

A large black limousine pulled up in front of them. The opaque dark window slid down as Beth pulled her fist back again.

A small round face with no hair and colossal spectacles appeared. Beth ran over and kissed it.

Copeland... I thought she was... you know... Simon... the one with Ronaldo's face and physique. How come she's..?

'Oh, shut up,' said Copeland.

Tom Benson broke the kiss. 'Edward Lewis and Vivian Ward!' said Tom with a grin, opening the door and pulling Beth into the car.

Copeland could see the female half the connection but struggled to see Tom Benson as Richard Gere, but at least there was a limo there for the happy ending.

Epilogue.

Everyone in the Rivea dining room of the Bulgari Hotel assumed Tom Benson and Mrs. Pickford must be eccentric multi-millionaires. Who else would eat at a top Knightsbridge hotel dressed for the beach or looking like a bag lady? Copeland got more stares than they did because of the chocolate on his trousers. It was just below the waist, where he had sat in a tray that had been knocked from the shelf. It was brown chocolate.

'At least the stain is at the back for once,' he said quietly to himself as they were shown to a round mahogany table under the sweeping, circular staircase, suspecting it was permanently reserved for Mrs. Pickford.

'So, Beryl,' he said out loud after the waiter had taken their order. 'You intercepted Sergeant Brandon's email to me as I hoped you would. So now you know what all this was about.'

Tom Benson had asked the same question ten times already. 'Are you *really* Mrs. Pickford?'

'Yes!' hissed Beryl and Copeland.

'Please keep my identity secret, Mr. Benson,' said Beryl Pickford, taking out her phone.

'Or I'll just disappear one day!' laughed Tom.

'Yes,' said Beryl, glancing up from scrawling through her texts and staring at him.

Tom went quiet, but he did notice Beth had been quietly finishing her second glass of wine and he smiled, expectantly. He had worked out the other meaning of the word 'frisky'.

'Simon is safe,' said Beryl. 'I got him out just before the CIA got to him. He's confirmed two of the men at the farm cut their hands. He's accepted thirty million and a nice house on a Caribbean island in exchange for his car and its contents.

We would have gone up to fifty million, silly boy. I hope you aren't too fond of him, Dr. Spencer.'

'Who?' said Beth. 'Oh, Thimon? Not so much for the last five yearth. He thought he wath too clever by halfs and couldn't take hith drinkth neetha.'

'And Karim,' said Beryl, 'is laying low and we are moving his assets to a different identity.'

Copeland stroked his chin. 'And they agreed to all this?' he asked, reflecting that without Karim there would be no new striker for Leyton Orient this year and how the season could get grim.

Beryl, the Mrs. Pickford, put her hand on top of Copeland's as she said, 'They had a choice, of course, Lawrence.'

Tom could not contain himself. 'Take the money or be bumped off, eh?' he joked.

'Quite,' said Mrs. Pickford. 'Now keep your voice down, the head of French Intelligence is just over there.'

The first course arrived. Beth was not impressed that Tom Benson had chosen octopus and took his plate away from him. He thought it best not to protest that octopus was not a fish, but called the waiter over and changed his main course from steak.

'We always wondered about Karim being involved in terrorism,' said Beryl. 'He had a reputation as a reformer who believed in democracy. Poor, naive boy. Whatever will these young people believe in next? We now know the photo of him in Libya was taken because he had gone to persuade them to follow a peaceful course. Just bad timing, really. We've also tracked down those two retired professors. Simon and Karim had got them convinced they had won a holiday of a lifetime. Simon has already told us Fatima took them to the airport. She's a Russian SVR agent, by the way. Her real name is Major Ludmilla Lopotin – she specialises in acting stupid.'

'That's how the Russians knew what to feed us, and they've got away with it,' said Copeland, ruefully.

Tom Benson raised a finger and said, 'Always forgive your enemies – nothing annoys them so much.'

'Oscar Wilde quotes notwithstanding,' said Mrs. Pickford, 'Fatima should be back in the Russian Embassy by now. My agent behind the counter gave her some special chocolates and with any luck she'll soon be sharing them with Vasily Goraya and that awful oligarch chap, Viktor Mosovoi. They will have some awful stomach pains tomorrow and no stomach to have pains in at all within forty eight hours.'

Tom Benson again drew on his knowledge from working in the NHS. He said, 'Yuk!'

'As for Liza Clinton,' went on Beryl Pickford, 'she'll be sent home after this.'

'She'll never work again, especially when her namesake becomes President.' observed Copeland.

'You never know,' said Beryl with a distant look.

Copeland thought he might put a bet on the other guy. He said, 'You know, Beryl, I guessed he was one of yours behind the chocolate counter – as were quite a few of the shoppers.'

'Reinforcements came out of retirement,' explained Beryl. 'But without Mr. Benson's distraction it could have got very ugly. You were very brave Mr. Benson.'

Benson held himself up to his full five feet two and puffed out his bony chest.

Beth raised a finger, looked at it as if she had never seen it before, took a deep breath, concentrated and said, 'Weeds are flowers too once you get to know them!'

'Thanks for that, Beth,' said Tom Benson, but smiled anyway.

Copeland mentally ran through botanists to identify Beth's quote: Charles Darwin? Carl Linnaus? Marie Stopes? He plumped for the oldest one he could think of and said, 'Was that Su Song, Tom?'

'No,' said Tom Benson. 'It was the greatest philosopher ever: Winnie-the-Pooh.'

Beth had gone back to enjoying her third glass of wine and working out how long the elevator would take to get to their suite on the tenth floor and whether they could get some 'aerobics' in and make it back before the main course arrived, or maybe before the coffee, or maybe for supper. 'Hangs on!' she said, loudly. 'What's happenings to the Nosoi? Ooops, too loud. Shhh!' She continued in a whisper loud enough for the next table to hear. 'Wine! Never drink it. Bad! But I mean all the stuff they maded? And all the formulash and wothnot?'

Beryl, the Mrs. Pickford, looked at each one of them. 'If this gets out... well, just don't let it. Even on the Tics dark web conspiracy site, Mr. Benson.'

Benson and Copeland swallowed hard. Beth swallowed her fourth glass of Chablis.

'The Pickfords have a lot of financial interests,' said Beryl Mrs. Pickford. 'Including oil. It is not in our best interest to have the oil market, er, shall we say, under stress. They were meeting in Harrods and then taking their so-called Flame biodiesel to Imperial College. Once the science boffins there had seen what it could do then the cat would have been out of the bag, so to speak.'

After seeing what it had done to Popov, it occurred to Tom that the Pickfords also had a potential genetic bio-weapon too. He bit his lip and pretended to be looking for a waiter.

Copeland put his cutlery down and stared at Mrs. Pickford. 'You've changed, Beryl. You are compromising principles for money. You never would have.'

Beryl placed a hand on Copeland's. 'Only until we get rid of all our oil stocks, Lawrence,' she smiled, 'but glad to see you still have a sense of morality. Do you want a job with us?'

'What? You're serious?'

'Just background checks, surveillance, that sort of thing – nothing, er, distasteful. We have a partner for you. We've got his kids into a good school and his wife a new job with a promotion, and we've got them a nice place by The Tate.'

Beth slid her hand on top of Tom's, slurring, 'Hello, my little hobbit with the big...'

Beryl's eyes widened. Copeland's fork hovered. The people on the next table listened.

'...heart,' finished Beth.

The people on the next table seemed disappointed and began their own conversation again.

'My partner will be Danny Hesterman, won't it?' asked Copeland. Beryl nodded.

Copeland thought about working with Danny as a Pickford Agent. He removed the healthy looking pine nuts from his stone bass carpaccio starter. He watched Beth and Tom rush towards the elevators after they blurted something about it being exercise time. He smiled at Beryl and said, 'Good. Danny owes me a lunch.'

Beryl looked hard at Copeland, put a hand softly on his and said, 'Lawrence, you need to do some exercise too.'

Copeland raised an eyebrow.

Footnote: Two weeks later.

Jakab Popov happily threw both his arms around his mother's neck. The next day she had an unusual rash.

Author's note.

I came across an article involving genetically engineered canola for biodiesel, which gave me the initial idea for this book, in the summer of 2016. When I started researching further I could not have suspected that processes like the one Dr. Bowyer achieved in the novel have been attempted for at least the last ten years.

Ronaldo Macedo really is an artist.

Leyton Orient were relegated at the end of the 2016-2017 season.

Printed in Great Britain
by Amazon